# MAISEY YATES

## Wild Ride
### Cowboy

HQN™

Recycling programs
for this product may
not exist in your area.

ISBN-13: 978-0-373-80364-4

Wild Ride Cowboy

Copyright © 2017 by Maisey Yates

This edition published by arrangement with Harlequin Books S.A.

For questions and comments about the quality of this book,
please contact us at CustomerService@Harlequin.com.

® and TM are trademarks of Harlequin Enterprises Limited or its
corporate affiliates. Trademarks indicated with ® are registered in the
United States Patent and Trademark Office, the Canadian Intellectual
Property Office and in other countries.

www.HQNBooks.com

**Printed in U.S.A.**

**In Copper Ridge, Oregon, lasting love
with a cowboy is only a happily-ever-after away.
Don't miss any of Maisey Yates's
Copper Ridge tales, available now!**

### From HQN Books

### From Harlequin Desire

### Look for more Copper Ridge

For more books by Maisey Yates,
visit www.maiseyyates.com.

# Wild Ride
## Cowboy

# The Donnellys

## A COPPER RIDGE FAMILY TREE

Finn (half brother)

& Lane Jensen

Cain (half brother)

& Alison Davis

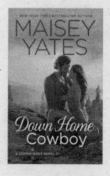

AVAILABLE
APRIL 18, 2017

AVAILABLE
JUNE 27, 2017

Alex (brother)

& Clara Campbell

Liam (brother)

& Sabrina Leighton

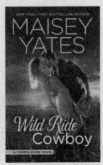

AVAILABLE
AUGUST 29, 2017

AVAILABLE
OCTOBER 31, 2017

# CHAPTER ONE

HE WAS PERFECT in every way.

Clara Campbell didn't even bother to hide the look of longing she knew was currently etched on her face. Asher was facing away from her anyway, working on making a cappuccino behind the bar—for her—so he wouldn't notice if she spent a little while admiring the elegant way he moved while he steamed the milk.

Okay, maybe most people wouldn't be applying words like *elegant* to the process of steaming milk. But in her mind, Asher could do no wrong, and everything he did was poetry. Including his work as a barista at Copper Ridge's newest artisan coffeehouse, Stim. Which was little more than a hole in the wall in the building down near the sea that used to house Rona's diner.

The diner had closed a few months back and had since been bought, gutted and remodeled to fit several new businesses that were geared toward the influx of tourists that had been passing through Copper Ridge, Oregon, in increasing numbers over the past few years.

It was perfect for Clara since Stim sat along the coastal highway, right at the turnoff she took to head inland to Grassroots Winery, where she was working part-time—and it gave her an excuse to see Asher every morning.

Too bad she didn't like coffee.

But sacrifices had to be made for love.

And she did love him. Well, as much as you could love a guy you hadn't so much as gone on a date with.

She'd met Asher at an open-house event the winery had hosted as something of a relaunch of the brand, when Lindy, the owner, had officially gained full ownership after her divorce.

He'd walked into the converted barn, where Clara was serving drinks, and it had been like a light shone down on him. Even in the crowd of people he stood out to her.

From there she'd found out where he worked and developed a fake coffee habit. Which made her sound a little like a weirdo as things stood now, but would be a charming story to tell later if things worked out.

"Here's your cappuccino, Clara." Asher turned and passed the coffee across the counter. There was no lid on the white paper travel cup yet, which gave her a moment to admire the heart he'd traced into the foam. Okay, it was kind of a fern. But like…a heart-shaped fern. And either way it made her own heart skip a few beats.

"Thank you," she said, doing her best not to blush when she looked directly at him in all of his man-bunned glory.

He was lean and rangy, wearing a T-shirt for a band she'd never heard of and would probably hate if she did. But she liked the look of the shirt, so she didn't really care about the band. Plus, it was nice to listen to him talk about music and how every popular song had the same three chords. Sure, afterward she got into her truck and put on the popular country music station, but he was passionate. She liked that.

Even if her tastes were regrettably mainstream.

She loitered at the edge of the counter for a moment. She was running early for work. She'd built in extra time for this stop, so she could afford to linger a little.

He lifted his brows, his dark eyes questioning. She would answer any question he wanted. "Did you need anything else?"

*You.*

"No."

"Okay." Then he turned around and began cleaning up the drink station. She let out a long, slow sigh. She really didn't have a reason to linger.

Slowly, very slowly, she added one sugar packet to her coffee. Then another one. Then a third. All while watching Asher. She wasn't going to drink the coffee so it didn't really matter what it tasted like. And since she wasn't going to drink it, she wasn't going to stir the design away either.

Reluctantly, she covered the coffee with a white to-go lid then turned to walk out the door. She didn't make it very far, though, because she ran right into a brick wall.

Well, it wasn't really a brick wall. It just felt like one. Large, hard and uncompromising. But breathing. Which brick walls definitely didn't do.

"Clara Campbell. Fancy meeting you here."

Clara blinked and stared up into Alex Donnelly's forest-green eyes and felt a strange response that seemed to originate in her stomach and travel upward to her chest, where it twisted, hard and sharp.

After looking at Asher, his understated physique and much softer brown gaze, the sight of Alex was jarring. Too intense. Too masculine. Too a lot of things.

His dark hair wasn't military short anymore. It was long enough to hang into his face. He pushed it back off his forehead and again, something twisted, low and deep inside of her.

And then it wasn't only his features that seemed too sharp. It was seeing him at all. She had been studiously avoiding him ever since he had moved back to Copper Ridge. If ever she'd caught a glimpse of him out of the corner of her eye, she'd gone the other way.

The last time she'd seen him up close had been at Jason's funeral.

Pain washed through her, canceling out all of the good Asher feelings from only a moment before.

No wonder she'd had such a strong, immediate response to the sight of Alex. The man was dragging a bunch of her baggage in with him. Another thing she liked about Asher. He was separate from her life. From her pain.

Alex was all wound up in it.

"Hi, Alex," she said, clutching her coffee cup tight, the warmth bleeding through to her palms. Which she was grateful for at the moment since her stomach had gone ice-cold at the sight of him.

"I've been meaning to stop by," he said.

"That's really okay," she said, and she meant it. More than okay. Jason's death meant that she was alone. Both of her parents were already gone. They'd had children later in life, and when her mother had gotten sick, her father had done everything he could to make his wife comfortable as her health declined. She'd died when Clara was twelve. And there had been no amount of preparation that could soften the blow. No amount of expectedness that could have made it feel less like a giant, ugly hand had reached into their life and wrenched the beauty out of it, leaving nothing but a dark abyss.

Their father had thrown himself into work. Into the ranch and into drinking. He'd tried to be there for his kids, but it had been too hard for him to look at them sometimes. And Clara could understand. It had been hard to look at him too. Hard to look at him and see the grief, stark and horrible on his face.

And then he'd died of a heart attack when Clara was seventeen, the stress of caregiving and loss too much for his body.

And now Jason.

A black sense of humor honed out of necessity—since a good portion of her life had been very dark indeed, and she'd had to find ways to laugh—forced her to wonder if she should look out for stray lightning bolts.

Whatever the reason—hex, divine intervention or plain bad luck—the Campbell family hadn't been very long-lived.

So now Clara was alone. And really, she wanted to get to the business of being alone. She did not want to deal with Alex's dutiful presence. Because that's all it would be. He and Jason had been in the military together, they'd been friends and brothers in arms.

She had a suspicion Alex had even been there

when her brother was killed. So of course the guy felt some sense of… Something. A desire to make sure she was okay. The need to check on her and the ranch, and whatever else.

But she didn't need that. She didn't need anybody coming into her life and carrying a portion of the weight for a limited time. She wanted to get on with that permanent, hard stretch that was the rest of her life.

She didn't want a false sense of ease. That would only make it all the harder when she was alone again.

"It's not okay, actually. We have some things we need to discuss."

Clara looked down at the top of her coffee cup and wished that she hadn't put the lid on, so she could make a show out of studying the milk-froth fern. "Oh. Do we?"

"Yes."

She looked at the clock on the wall and regrettably she had time.

Time she had built in so she could make conversation with Asher if he'd been in the mood to make conversation. Not so she could hassle with Alex and the myriad emotions just looking at him made her feel.

"Well, I'm on my way to work," she said, edging around his masculine frame and backing toward the door.

"You have a job other than working at the ranch?"

She should have known the big, muscly soldier wouldn't take hints well. "Yes," she said. She didn't elaborate.

"Where at?"

She made an impatient sound she didn't even try to cover up. "Grassroots Winery."

"I haven't been out there yet. Maybe I should check it out."

Rather than answering, Clara lifted her cup to her lips and absently took a drink. She grimaced, barely stopping herself from spitting out the hot liquid. It was still bitter, with a kind of sickly sweet flavor running over the top of it. Compliments of that extra sugar she had dumped into the cup to linger over Asher a little longer.

She really, *really* didn't like coffee.

Alex treated her to a strange look.

"It's strong," she said, gesturing with the cup. "Just the way I like it."

"Glad to hear that."

"Well—" she waved her fingers "—bye." She continued walking past him, heading out the door.

Much to her chagrin, he followed.

She paused, turning slightly in the gravel parking lot. "You didn't get your coffee."

"I actually wasn't there for coffee. I don't like places like that."

"Why not?"

"You can only get one size. What the hell is up with that? I don't need some hipster giving me prescriptive coffee. I don't need to be told the way they think coffee must be served to be better. I need it the way I want it."

He stopped walking, crossing his arms over his broad chest. He was wearing a plain, tan-colored T-shirt and a pair of dark jeans. Somehow, even out of uniform, he still looked like he was in one.

"Why did you stop in then?"

"I saw your truck outside."

She frowned. "You acted surprised to see me."

"No," he said, "I believe what I said was 'Fancy meeting you here.'"

She rolled her eyes. "Well, you knew how I would take it." A strange sense of disquiet stole over her, a feeling of creeping tension.

"I tried to call your cell phone," he said.

She blinked. "How did you get my number?"

"It was on some paperwork I got from the attorney's office. It looked like something we both should have had copies of."

Right. Paperwork that was probably sitting unopened in a pile on her table. To go nicely with the messages from the lawyer she'd been avoiding. He'd tried to talk to her at the funeral too. But she hadn't been able to handle it. Because then they'd be talking about her brother's estate. Which was what your possessions turned into when you were dead.

An *Estate*.

She'd had to discuss her mother's. Then her father's. She'd had the feeling she'd crawl out of her skin talking to anyone about her brother's. It was stupid, and she knew it. Ignoring bills didn't mean they didn't need to be paid. Ignoring a lawyer wouldn't make Jason not dead.

But once she talked to him, it would all feel final. And she couldn't handle that. She was barely keeping her head above water. She was dependent on her routine. These quiet mornings where she got coffee she didn't want to drink from a man whose whole being made her feel...happy. If only for a few moments. Then she would go and work at the winery showroom until closing time, enjoying being surrounded by people. Then she'd head home. Home to her empty house, where she would do any chores that needed doing before she fell into bed, passed out, didn't dream—if she was lucky—and repeated the whole thing the next day.

Maybe it was denial. But she deserved a little denial.

Alex was interrupting her carefully orchestrated coping mechanism. She didn't like it. "You took my phone number from a piece of paper?"

"I told you, I need to talk to you about a few things. I assumed you knew some of this—I thought an effort had been made to contact you."

Her cheeks got hot, and she went prickly all over. Efforts probably had been made, but she just hadn't been able to cope. Which made her feel small and humiliated. She hated it.

Alex continued. "Your brother had a will."

She didn't want to do this. Not here. Not now. She couldn't talk about Jason. She couldn't talk about his will. She couldn't deal with this. "I have to go to work," she said.

She was going to deal with all of this—Alex, Jason's will—someday. But not today. She just didn't want to do it today.

"What time do you get off?"

"Six. But I'm going to be really tired and I…"

"Why is your phone turned off, Clara?"

She blinked hard, and yet, no matter how much she wanted him to disappear, no amount of blinking accomplished it. "It's not a big deal. I don't use my phone." She wasn't paying her bills. That was the truth. There was some money, it wasn't like she was destitute. But there was something about dealing with the mail right now that felt overwhelming. Envelope after envelope, cards, condolences, bills addressed to Jason like he wasn't dead. Like he could come back and open them.

He couldn't. He couldn't do anything.

"I've been busy," she said. "I forgot to pay the bill. That's all."

She wasn't going to admit her mail gave her anxiety. What kind of twit had mail anxiety?

Well. She did.

"And if I come to your house at six tonight are you going to be there? Or am I going to have to stalk you at your favorite coffee place again?"

She frowned. "Come to think of it, it's a little bit weird that you were able to find me here."

"Not really. I saw you here yesterday when I drove into town. I took an educated guess this morning and decided I would stop in. It's pretty lazy stalking, all in all."

"Lazy stalking isn't really less disturbing than energetic stalking."

"You can avoid all future stalking if we could just talk now," he said, his expression suddenly turning serious.

"No," she said, the denial coming out quickly.

She really couldn't deal with this now. She couldn't deal with discussing Jason in the past tense. Couldn't deal with talking about his will in a parking lot. Couldn't face looking at all the things her brother had left behind, his worldly possessions, which no longer belonged to him because he wasn't part of the world anymore.

Hell, she couldn't open a damn phone bill. She wasn't going to do any of the rest of this.

"Then we'll talk later. If I have to camp out in your yard, we'll talk later."

Then he turned and walked back toward his truck, leaving her standing there with her cappuccino.

She took another sip. "Dammit!"

She forced herself to swallow it, rather than spitting it out into the gravel, on the off chance Asher was watching.

She had to get to work now, she couldn't worry about Alex. Whatever he had to say to her, she would take care of it then. Her life had already been rocked beyond recognition in the past couple of months. There was nothing Alex Donnelly could say that would bring it crumbling down now.

VERY FEW PEOPLE would call Alex Donnelly a coward. He had dodged gunfire, survived a rain of mortar shells—more than once—and worn full tactical gear in arid heat that could practically bake a loaf of bread, or a man's brains for that matter.

But he had been a little bit of a coward when he'd allowed Clara Campbell to put off their conversation about her deceased brother's will.

The fact of the matter was he had been a coward for the past couple of months that he'd been back in Copper Ridge, and had avoided having the conversation with her at all. He'd had his excuses, that was for sure.

Some of them were actually valid. Like the time

he'd put into investigating the legality of what her brother had asked him to do. And then the time spent going over the letter Jason had left. The one that clarified just why he wanted things this way and made it impossible to deny him.

Still, Alex had waited to talk to Clara, even after that.

At first, it had been out of deference to her grief. And after that, because he was trying to get his feet underneath him at the Laughing Irish ranch, which he worked at with his brothers.

Frankly, after losing his best friend and his grandfather, he'd had enough to deal with without adding Clara to the mix. But it couldn't be avoided anymore. And when he had discovered her cell phone was turned off, he'd felt guilty for avoiding it as long as he had.

Clara must be hurting for money. Enough that she had taken a job at Grassroots Winery, and was letting bills go unpaid.

He'd expected her to call if things were that bad. Hell, he'd expected her to call period. But the way she'd acted at the coffee shop, it didn't seem like she'd spoken to anyone about the details of Jason's will.

Now that he thought about it, if she had, she probably would have come at him hissing and spitting.

She might still. But she was late.

Alex pushed his cowboy hat back on his head and looked at the scenery around him. The ranch was small, and so was the ranch house. Rustic. From his position on the front porch—which was squeaking beneath his cowboy boots—he couldn't see the highway.

Couldn't see anything but the pine trees that grew

thick and strong around the property, standing tall like sentries, there to protect the ranch and all who lived there.

"Well, you're doing a pretty piss poor job," he commented.

Because damned if the Campbells hadn't been through enough. But he was here to make things easier. He knew—was one hundred percent certain—that Clara wouldn't see it that way initially. But this was what Jason had wanted, and he knew that Jason had nothing but his sister's best interests in mind when he'd made out his will.

Alex owed it to his friend to see his last wishes carried out. No question about it.

He took a deep breath, putting his hands on his narrow hips as he turned a half circle to take in more of the property. The driveway needed to be graveled. It was slick and muddy right now, even though it had been a few days since it had rained.

There was a truck and a tractor that Alex would lay odds didn't run, parked off in the weeds, looking like metal corpses left to rust into the earth.

The place needed a lot of work. It was too much for him to do by himself, let alone one woman. One grieving woman who was having to work part-time on top of doing the general ranch work.

He figured at this point the place wasn't really functional. But he was forming some ideas on how to get it working again. On how to make sure Clara hadn't just been saddled with a millstone.

Or, more accurately, that he hadn't been.

The center of the sky was dimming to a purplish blue, the edges around the trees a kind of dusty pink by the time Clara's truck pulled up the long driveway into the house. She stopped, turning off the engine, staying in the vehicle. She was looking at him like she was shocked to see him, even though he had told her he would be there.

He shoved his hands in his pockets, leaning against the support for the porch, not moving until Clara got out of the truck.

She was such a petite little thing. And she had definitely lost weight since he'd seen her a few weeks ago. He couldn't imagine her taking on a place like this, and suddenly he felt like the biggest ass on the planet. That he had stayed away because she was going to be angry, when she had clearly been here working her knuckles to the bone.

Jason had been clear on what he wanted. The fact that Alex had screwed it up so far seemed just about right, as far as things went.

"Big wine-tasting day?" he asked.

Clara frowned. "No. Why?"

"You're home late."

She raised a brow, then walked around to the back of the truck and pulled out a bag of groceries. "I had to stop and get stuff for dinner."

"Good. You *do* eat."

She frowned. "What does that mean?"

"You're too skinny." He felt like a dick for saying it, but it was true. She was on the sadness diet, something he was a little too familiar with. But he'd learned not to give in to that in the military. Learned to eat even when his ears were ringing from an explosion, or the heat was so intense the idea of eating something hot was next to torture. Or when you'd just seen a body, bent and twisted under rubble.

Because food wasn't about enjoyment. It was about survival.

A lot like life in general.

Clara Campbell needed help surviving. That was clear to him.

Clara scowled even deeper as she walked toward him. "Great. Thanks, Alex. Just what every woman wants to hear."

"Actually, in my experience, a lot of women would like to hear that." He snagged the paper grocery bag out of her arms as she tried to walk past him. "SpaghettiOs? What the hell is this?"

"I call it dinner."

"Sure, for a four-year-old."

"I'm sorry they don't live up to your five-star military rations. But I like them."

She reached out and grabbed hold of the bag, trying to take it out of his arms.

"Stop it," he said. "You've been working all day. I'm going to carry your groceries."

She bristled. "You're insulting my groceries. I feel like you don't deserve to carry them."

He snorted, then turned away from her, jerking the bag easily from her hold. "Open the door for me."

"I thought military men were good at taking orders," she said. "All you seem to do is give them."

"Yeah, well I'm not in the army now, baby." He smiled, and he knew it would infuriate her. "Open the damn door."

Her face turned a very particular shade of scarlet but she did comply, pulling out her keys and undoing the lock, then pushing the door open. He walked over the threshold, and a board squeaked beneath his feet. He made a mental note to fix that.

"The dining room is just through there, set the bag on the table." She walked in behind him. "See? I can give orders too."

"While eating SpaghettiOs." He set the bag on the table she'd indicated, then took a look around the room. It was sparse—the floor, walls and ceiling all made with rustic wood paneling. There was a red rug on the floor with a geometric design that provided the only bit of color to the room, other than a big, cheery yellow cabinet that was shoved in the back of the kitchen, packed full to the brim with white plates. It seemed a little incongruous with the rest of the place. And at odds with the rickety dining table and its mismatched chairs.

He had never been to Jason's house before. They had met when they were in high school, and consequently, had spent their time hanging out away from the watchful eyes of parents and guardians. After that, they'd wound up serving together in the military.

The place was…well, *cozy* was a nice word for it. *Eclectic badger den* possibly less nice but more accurate.

"I'm hungry," Clara said, fishing one of the cans out of the bag. "Don't taint my SpaghettiOs with your judgment."

"Wouldn't dream of it."

He watched as she moved around the efficient little kitchen, making small economical movements, getting out a blue-and-white speckled tin bowl and a little pan, then opening the SpaghettiOs and dumping them in it. She put the pan on the front burner, turning it to high, then whirled around to face him.

"Okay. What are we talking about?"

"Do you want to wait until you've eaten your dinner?"

"No." She turned around and opened the fridge, pulling out a can of Coke before popping it open and taking a long drink. She didn't offer him one, he noticed.

"I was contacted by your family lawyer shortly after Jason's death."

Clara crossed her arms, her lips going tight. "Okay, why did he call you?"

"Why didn't he call *you*, Clara? I expected you would have talked to him."

She bit her lip. "Well. He did. But we didn't *talk*." Alex stared her down and her cheeks turned increasingly red as she shifted her weight from foot to foot. "I've been busy," she added defensively.

"Well, if you hadn't been too busy for the lawyer, he might have talked to you about the fact your brother's will concerns me."

"Excuse me?" This was the part he had been avoiding. The thing he had not been looking forward to. Because his friend had left him with property, had left him with his earthly possessions and a letter explaining his feelings, which ultimately were only that: the feelings of a dead man. Alex had to try to fill in blanks he wasn't sure could be filled. He'd tried to reason it all out to decide if he could justify defying Jason's wishes. He hadn't been able to. So here he was.

"He left me in charge of the estate," he continued. "The ranch, everything on it, everything in it, the house—until things are stable or until one year has passed."

Clara didn't move. The only indication she was reacting to his words at all was that her face had gone completely waxen.

"Do you understand what I'm saying, Clara? I have a stake in this house now. And in this ranch. Your brother left me in charge."

## CHAPTER TWO

"CLARA?"

Clara knew she was supposed to respond. She was supposed to say something. Yell, maybe. Or cry? Something. Alex was standing there telling her he was now linked—legally—to this place that she had poured her whole self into.

She'd grown up here. All twenty-one years of her life. Jason had joined the army when she was just eight years old, coming back intermittently when her parents hadn't been able to care for her. But since she'd turned eighteen it had all been on her.

There had been no college. No dates. There had been this ranch. It was hers. And now he was just... taking that?

She didn't scream, though. Instead, she just stood there, numbness spreading from her mouth to the rest of her face. She was way too familiar with this feeling. With the moment the earth fell away and the world shifted. With innocuous moments rolling over and becoming something significant.

With her life changing completely between one breath and the next.

That was the worst part about this moment. Not that it was singular in its awfulness, but that it wasn't.

Of course there was more. Of course there would

be no putting her head down and simply getting over this. Moving on to the next thing. Getting used to her new, incredibly crappy normal.

Alex had just redefined normal. Again.

Asshole.

That little internal invective seemed to wake up something inside of her and her gaze snapped to his. "He left everything to *you*?"

"Yes."

"Why?" She was shaking now, a strange, deep trembling that started at the center of her chest and began to work its way out her limbs. "Why would he leave everything to you? I'm the one who's been living here. I'm the one who's been taking care of this place while he was deployed."

"He wanted to make sure you were taken care of," Alex said, his tone maddeningly flat.

"Then he shouldn't have died!" The words exploded from her, and it didn't matter if they were fair or not. It was how she felt. And Jason was dead anyway, so he couldn't hear them. Couldn't get a sense for how upset she was that he had died.

"But he did," Alex said, his bluntness offensive to her wounded heart. "And he made it pretty clear to me what was supposed to happen if he did."

"I am a grown woman, why did he think he needed to send you here? I've been here without him all this time." She didn't feel like a grown woman right now. She felt like the floor was shifting under her feet and she didn't have the strength to stay standing.

"You're not a grown woman to him, Clara," Alex said, slipping up and talking about Jason as if he still thought anything. As if he might be about to walk in the door from a long fishing trip. "The way he talked about you…you were his kid sister. He worried about you constantly, and he worried especially about what would happen to you if he couldn't come home to you."

Clara's eyes felt scratchy with the effort of holding back all the emotion that was swamping her.

Jason had been her hero. He'd taught her to ride a horse. He'd taught her to fish—which she'd hated, but she would go with him anyway. Every weekend he was home, he would pack a picnic with the sandwiches he knew she liked and they would drive to the river.

He'd park his truck on the side of the road and they'd hike down the sandy trail together and sit on the rocks for hours. Talking while they sat there mostly not landing any fish.

And when she'd complain, Jason had always said, "This is why they call it fishing, not catching."

The image of her brother standing out by the river with that carefree grin on his face felt like a stab to the chest.

Alex shifted, rapping his knuckles on her table. "He wrote me a letter."

"What are you talking about? He wrote you a letter that was like… Open in case of my eventual death?"

"Something like that."

"Wow."

She didn't know what else to say. Somehow, the fact that there was a letter almost made it worse. Of course, Jason had known that his death was a possibility. Every soldier knew that. But Clara had never allowed herself to think about it.

Somehow, it was less disturbing to imagine he hadn't really given it much consideration. Envisioning him sitting down and writing a letter about what Alex should do if he died… It… It enraged her. Even if it was unfair. The fact that he had thought it through that deeply, but had still been in the military, had still put himself in that kind of danger…

He had fully imagined a future in which he might be gone and she might need help. Where she would be left alone and he might have to assign somebody the responsibility of taking care of her.

He had known he could die. Known enough to prepare for it. It made her furious. Absolutely furious.

"He loved you, Clara," Alex said, his soft, apologetic tone worse than the arrogant tone he had used when commenting on her dinner.

"If he loved me so much, he shouldn't have re-enlisted in the military after our father died," she said, finally giving voice to the small, useless, mean thoughts she'd been having ever since she'd gotten the news of his death. "If he loved me so much, he would have stayed here. He would be here helping me with the ranch. Rather than sending a surrogate in his place. Did you all love the military so much that you couldn't stay away? Is it better than this ranch, this town?"

"He *believed* in the military," Alex said, his voice rough. "He believed in the ideal of serving something bigger than himself. No matter whether it was perfect or not, he believed in doing something. He died for that belief, and he knew that was the risk."

He had died across the world, away from her. He had left her alone. Had truly left her without any family at all. And whatever ideals Alex spoke about, she couldn't share them.

Somewhere beneath the grief and anger, she was proud of her brother. Of his service. Of his selflessness.

But mostly… She just wished that he had applied that selflessness to her. If he was going to sacrifice his life, why couldn't he have done it in Copper Ridge, near the only family he had left?

Then she wouldn't be alone.

Those thoughts swirled around in her head, caused tension to mount in her chest, a hard little ball of anger and meanness that she couldn't quite shake. Didn't really want to.

"What exactly do you think you're going to do with the ranch that I can't do?" She crossed her arms and cocked her hip to the side, treating him to her hardest and meanest stare.

"What exactly have you done with it?" He looked around. "As near as I can tell, you have a bunch of old, rusted-out equipment that isn't going to do you any good."

"I've been living here and I've been running this place ever since Jason reenlisted. And yeah, maybe I haven't managed to keep up on everything. But I've been shifting my focus. We did beef for a long time, but an operation this size… It isn't sustainable. Especially not with so much local competition. The beef thing… That was my dad's. And Jason kept it up from a distance. But a couple of years ago we decided to sell."

"Great. What do you do now?"

"We invested the money back into the house. And also in bees."

"Bees?"

She sighed. "Yes. The goal was to start producing our own honey. It's something that I could easily handle on my own. I don't need to hire workers to help with that, and I can also maintain a job away from the ranch while the hive is getting established. For the first year, you can't actually take their honey, you know."

Alex rocked back on his heels. "No. I don't know that. Because I don't know anything about bees."

"Bees are fascinating creatures, Alex," she said.

Alex just stared at her. Her eyes clashed with his, and her stomach lurched unexpectedly. She looked away from him, counting the mugs on the shelf behind him.

"Bees," he repeated finally.

"Yes."

"What else?" he asked.

"What do you mean what else? What do you expect me to do?"

"Your brother was pretty clear in the instructions he left. He wanted the ranch to be an asset to you, not a liability. He wanted me to help you out until this place is solvent. Or until it's sold."

Those words made her heart slam against her breastbone, made abject terror race down her spine, flooding her veins with a spiky kind of horror. "I don't want to sell," she said, the words sure and certain.

The house was small, and it was definitely in rough shape in some ways. But this house contained the story of her entire life. This was the only place that had memories of her family all together. And, yes, there were memories of losing those family members here too. But she'd gotten pretty good at living with those.

This house contained every feeling she'd ever experienced. Good and bad. Her mother had scrubbed this place until it was spotless. Until she had been too ill to clean anymore. Her father had worked the land until his body gave out on him.

Jason had joined the military to help support the place financially, and then when their father had died he had come back and worked until Clara had been old enough to handle herself and keep the house on her own. Even then, all his money had gone right back into this place.

The Campbells were dead, by and large. This ranch, this land, was all that was left.

She would be damned if she walked away from it. She had already given up a lot to be here. And she owed it to her family to keep the ranch going. So that the legacy could live on, even if the rest of them didn't.

"If you don't want to sell, then what do you want?"

"I could... I can keep working at Grassroots. It's not hard. And I've been managing. There's a small garden here and it produces well. I basically have all the resources to get a good farmers' market booth together. In between the two things, I should be able to make it all work."

"And what about having a life? Working a farm, doing a booth at markets, working at a winery... When do you expect to take a breath, Clara?"

"I don't want to take a breath, Alex," she said, the words harder, more brittle and honest than she intended them to be. "Because breathing hurts."

Silence fell between them, no sound beyond the persistent ticking of the kitchen clock. The one that Clara never looked at, that was never right. It had just always been there, so she had never moved it.

"Then that's what I'm here for," he said, his voice rough. "To help out until it quits hurting."

Something about those words made her want to strike out at him. Made her want to push him away. Mostly because she didn't know how to do this. Didn't know how to be taken care of. Not that her father hadn't been there for her—not that Jason hadn't been. But always, always, they'd had their own grief, equal to her own. This was different. Not that Alex wasn't sorry his friend was dead, but Jason wasn't his brother. The grief was hers. And Alex was offering to take care of her until it passed.

Alex was giving her permission to collapse.

She wasn't going to take it. She couldn't.

"What do you propose?" she asked, gritting her teeth and doing her best to recover from that little moment of honesty.

"Clara, you're not handling this. You as much as admitted that you're not paying your bills. You don't want to sell, but if you don't pay for stuff, you're going to get it taken from you. And whatever you feel about being busy right now… It would be for the best if we can get the ranch to the point where it's self-sustaining. I know that you're going to get some money from the military, and until then I'm willing to put my own money into this place."

Suddenly she felt drained. Felt defeated. Because while part of her wanted to stand here all evening and wage war with Alex, the fact of the matter was she'd already lost.

She let out a long, slow breath, then walked back to the stove, dumping the contents of her pan into a small bowl. "I'm going to eat," she said. "Do you want to join me?"

"No thanks. I don't order off the kids' menu anymore."

She shoved a bite of canned pasta into her mouth. "Your loss."

"I'll take a Coke."

"Go right ahead," she said, talking around her bite. "You probably have dominion over the Coke too."

"The fridge, maybe. The contents, probably not."

"Help yourself, anyway," she said, tugging her bowl toward her and hunching over it ferally.

He took a soda out of the fridge and popped the top on it, and for some reason, she watched as he brought the can to his lips, watched as his Adam's apple bobbed up and down while he took a long swallow of the beverage.

She looked back into her bowl of SpaghettiOs. "So what's your brilliant plan for fixing my life? What are you going to invest in? I mean, this is your ranch now. I guess you can make it whatever you want. Buy a bunch of big-ass cows."

"Like you said, there's a lot of competition for beef. And frankly, this operation just isn't big enough to play in that arena. But I do have an idea. And it kind of goes with your…bees."

She let out an exasperated sigh. "What?"

"Bison. There's a market for lean beef, organic stuff. We can get away with having a smaller scale operation. We would need to get better fencing, but most everything that you used for the cattle would work. And frankly, the farmers' market idea is a good one."

"Are you suggesting I sell honey, tomatoes and bison?"

"Yes. That's exactly what I'm suggesting. I have the money to invest in this. I want to do it. And I think it's the best thing for you."

Clara bristled. "You think it's the best thing for me. Based on speaking to me all of five times in my entire life? Based on the fact that you knew my brother? You don't know what I want, Alex."

"Okay. What do you want?"

His green eyes were intense on hers, and she didn't know what to do with that. Didn't know how to answer the question, mostly because she hadn't expected him to pose it.

She had the fleeting image of Asher. Of him living in this little house with her. Enjoying a simple existence. Keeping bees, making honey. He could make artisan coffee and maybe they could have goats. She could make room in her garden for kale. She didn't like tomatoes either, and she grew those.

She wasn't going to tell Alex any of that.

"I'm not really sure," she said. "I would settle for not being further traumatized by life at this point."

Those eyes softened a little. "Unfortunately, none of us gets that guarantee."

"I've noticed."

"Think about it."

She shoved another bite of food into her mouth.

"What's the point in me thinking about it, Alex? You own this place. Your word is law."

"It was never my goal to come in here and take over everything."

She snorted. "That is completely not true. Of course it was your goal. That's why you're here. To claim ownership. To take control."

"Maybe it is. Why would that be a problem for you? You can continue to do what you're doing. I'm just going to help get things more established, that's all."

"Excuse me for not exactly buying into this idea that you're being a philanthropist here on my ranch. This benefits you financially. Or, it will."

Alex's jaw tightened, his face so still it had the look of granite. "I don't need your money, Clara. But you need my help. And whether or not you believe it, I'm here because Jason asked me to be. Because I fought alongside him and that means something to me, Clara. Whether you can understand it or not, it does."

She swallowed hard, feeling unsettled, feeling uncertain. First off, she didn't know why she cared that he was here. Except that he was so large, broad and confrontational. Except that he made it feel so real that Jason was gone. Really gone. He knew things she didn't know about her brother's final moments, she was certain. She was also certain she didn't want to know them. At least, not now.

But if Alex wanted to pour his money into the ranch, if he wanted to add another stream of revenue, there was nothing really to fight about.

She closed her eyes for a moment and had the oddest sensation that she was adrift on a river she didn't want to be on. Drifting toward God knew where. On a raft she had never consented to get onto in the first place.

No control. None at all. But then, what else was new?

"Fine. Get your bison. Fix stuff. Whatever you need to do to feel like you've seen to Jason's final wishes." The word *final* stuck in her throat, snagged on a notch of emotion, making it feel as if she couldn't breathe.

"I will." He stood, gripping the brim of his hat and tipping it forward slightly. "I'll be at the ranch bright and early tomorrow morning."

"And I'll be at work."

His lips twitched. "But first, getting coffee again? Since you like it so much."

Her face heated, and she fought against the blush she knew was intensifying. She was not a thirteen-year-old girl with a crush. She resented him for making her feel like one.

"Yes," she responded. "Getting coffee again. My favorite."

He lifted a brow but said nothing. "I'm sure I'll see you tomorrow at some point."

She nodded, and then Alex turned and walked out.

For some reason, as soon as the door closed behind him, a tear rolled down Clara's cheek. And then another one. Maybe having Alex here should have felt like the answer to something. A wake-up call at the very least. That somebody had come in and seen just how unprepared she was to deal with all of this.

To move into a life that had to function without Jason in it. Forever.

And whether or not he intended to be, Alex Donnelly was a symbol of that.

## CHAPTER THREE

ALEX WAS IN a mean mood by the time he got back home. It was late, and he was starving, and he was still replaying the scene with Clara over in his mind. He really should have gone to see her sooner. He had noticed the stacks of mail sitting on the counter. Had noticed the general state of disrepair of the place.

But he had a plan now, one that had been affirmed when he'd gotten there and spoken to her.

Bees.

Of all the hipster bullshit.

"Where have you been?"

Alex's older half brother Cain was walking toward the main house, probably heading down from the little converted barn he lived in with his fiancée, Alison, and his teen daughter, Violet.

"Busy," Alex responded.

"Well, considering you didn't just follow that up with sexual innuendo, I'm going to go ahead and guess that you were actually taking care of that property you've been needing to see to."

"Not that it's your business, but yes." There was no reason for him to be short with Cain. But since his older brother was an extreme hard-ass and didn't seem to care, Alex didn't see a reason not to be.

"Good," Cain said. "About time for you to man up."

"Thanks. Next time I need your opinion on my masculinity, I'll ask. Right after I finish polishing my dog tags and disassembling my AR."

"We could save time and you could just whip it out and measure, Alex. I'm not threatened by that."

"What are we measuring?" Finn, Alex's other older half brother, chose that moment to walk out the front door.

"What do you think?" Alex asked.

"Wow. Okay. I think I'll pass on this brotherly bonding experience," Finn responded, clearly picking up on the tone of the conversation without further hints.

"You weren't invited," Alex said cheerfully. "And I'm starving."

"You're in luck. Lane cooked."

Finn's fiancée usually did cook. She owned the specialty food mercantile on the main street in town, and had a passion for not only spreading good food around, but for elevating the eating experience of the Donnelly brothers—or at least trying to.

If she had seen what Clara was eating tonight, she probably would have force-fed her some kind of specialty cheese.

Alex walked up the steps with Cain behind him. Then the three of them filed into the house. Whatever Lane was cooking, Alex could smell it already. Something warm and comforting. Something that smelled like home. Not Alex's childhood home, but the way he had imagined other people's homes had smelled.

Or maybe, it smelled like this home. This was the longest he'd been in one place for a long damn time.

It was strange just how easy it had been to get used to it. Living here with so many people. When he walked into the kitchen, Liam was there already, the only brother he'd been raised with. He was sitting at the counter, making conversation with their niece, Violet. Or rather, he had a feeling Liam was doing his best to harass Violet, since she was looking mildly perturbed and more than a little amused.

Cain's fiancée, Alison, was busy cooking with Lane, both women wearing aprons as they dashed around the kitchen. It was like Alex had fallen into some kind of manic 1950s dream.

Violet, who was sixteen and more than a little surly, grabbed a potato chip out of the bowl that was sitting on the island and crunched it noisily.

"This is bad for feminism," she announced, talking around a mouthful of chip.

"How so, Violet?" Lane asked, turning and putting one hand on her hip.

"Cooking for the men," she returned.

"Maybe if we were doing it out of obligation, but Lane and I like to cook," Alison said. "In fact, our chosen careers center around food."

"Mmm," Violet made a musing sound.

"I cook," Lane said, lifting a brow, "your uncle Finn does the dishes, which I don't like to do, and it works for everyone. But most importantly…"

"We choose to do it," Alison finished.

"I choose to sit and eat potato chips," Violet said, clearly also choosing to remain unmoved on her position. And unmoved in general.

"I'll help," Liam offered, standing up and slapping the countertop.

"You absolutely will not," Lane said, turning around and pointing her spatula at him. "I haven't forgotten the great over-salting incident that happened last time you *helped*."

"I'll help by sitting here," he said, grabbing a chip out of the bowl.

"Smells good," Alex said, shoving his hands in his pockets.

"Thanks," Lane returned.

"Where have you been?" This time, it was Liam who asked the question.

"It's really touching how concerned you all are about my whereabouts," Alex responded.

"I wasn't concerned, jackass. I was mad because you got out of doing your evening chores."

"Wow, Liam. Maybe you should tell me about your childhood." Alex leaned in and stole a chip. "You seem to have some issues."

"You were there for my childhood. That's possibly *why* I have issues."

Alex snorted. "I'm pretty sure our dad is the reason we both have issues."

Finn snorted. "I think he's the reason we all have issues."

Their father had done one thing well—made children he wasn't particularly interested in raising. Cain and Finn had different mothers, with Cain being raised in Texas and Finn in Washington. Though Finn had come to live on the Laughing Irish ranch with their grandfather when he was only sixteen.

Liam and Alex had grown up with their mother

in a different part of Washington than Finn, and had spent sporadic summers in Copper Ridge.

Until recently, the half brothers had all spent a limited amount of time together. Though, truth be told Alex and Liam hadn't spent all that much time together either, since Liam had left home at eighteen.

As soon as he could, Liam had gone off to school. And he didn't return home. Two years later, Alex had enlisted in the military, and he'd done the same—left it all behind.

Liam had gotten a scholarship that had paid his way through, and as far as Alex knew, was the only one of them to get any kind of higher education. Liam didn't talk about it much though. He never had. And whatever work he had gotten into afterward, he wasn't doing it now.

Damn. They really were dysfunctional.

"So, what were you doing?" Liam asked, clearly not content to let the subject drop.

"I had to go and handle that property I'm responsible for," he said, "like I told you guys a month or so ago."

"What's the situation with that?" Finn was the one who posed that question, and Alex wasn't particularly surprised. His brother would need to know how it would impact the work that was happening around the ranch. They were all part owners of the Laughing Irish now, but Finn had bled for this place since he was a teenager.

They all loved it in their own way, but nobody loved it like Finn. That was another thing Alex paused to marvel at for a moment. The fact that they were all getting along as well as they were. Claiming their part of the inheritance, rather than taking a payoff. Finn had been less than amused when they'd first showed up, but gradually it had all started to work, and he'd come to see them as more of an asset than a burden.

Mostly.

"I'm going to be doing some work on it," he said. "For up to a year, I have decision-making power on the place and then it will pass to Clara's possession. Right now, it's part of Jason's estate, and I'm the executor. And if I end up dropping the ball here, I swear I'll hire somebody to pick up the slack. And I'll pay for it out of my own pocket. But this is something that I have to do."

"I'm not sure I know this story," Alison said, opening the oven and taking out a pie.

"It's not a feel-good one," Alex said. "An army buddy of mine was killed in action about six months ago. He left me his ranch."

Alison's eyes went wide. She set the pie down on a trivet on the counter. "Really? I'm so sorry."

"Yes. His sister isn't very happy about it, but he did it to help her."

"You're talking about Jason Campbell and his sister Clara," Alison said, "aren't you?"

"Did you know them?"

Alison shook her head. "Not Clara. I kind of knew Jason in school. Not well. But I saw him there, and around town over the years. I was sad to hear about his death. I met Clara when I started doing some work with Grassroots Winery."

Alex cleared his throat. "Jason kind of…left her to me. She doesn't have anyone."

"And you're supposed to drop everything and help

her?" That question came from Liam, his voice surprisingly hard. "You have your own life. Didn't your friend consider that?"

"As he was considering his death at the time, I suppose he figured I could take the inconvenience. You know, since I'm above ground." Clara was mad at Jason for his decision. His brothers clearly thought it was crazy too. It made Alex feel defensive of his friend. The fact that Jason was willing to do anything—even inconvenience Alex—to protect his sister, to make sure that she was taken care of, was a mark of what made him such a good man as far as Alex was concerned.

He and his brothers had been self-sufficient from the beginning. There had been no alternative. They also hadn't been raised to be close. He and Liam were close enough, but it wasn't that same caregiver relationship Jason had had to Clara. He had been ten years older, and they'd lost both of their parents. He'd felt responsible for her in a way Alex had never felt responsible for anyone.

"Sorry," Liam said. "You're supposed to hire someone to cover for you here? Why not just hire someone to work at the Campbell Ranch?"

"It's not just about working on the ranch," Alex said. "Clara isn't functioning on her own. She's not paying her bills. And I think Jason was afraid that might happen. He wanted to make sure she had… Another older brother around to look after her."

Something inside of him—deep inside of him—rebelled at the thought of being Clara's older brother. It didn't sit right.

She was just so damn pretty. That was a fact, and

one he'd never been blind to. Of course, there was
a difference between realizing a woman was pretty
and wanting to actually touch that beauty. Clara was
off limits. She always had been. But now more than
ever before.

He thought of her extreme, ridiculous and unin-
tentional double entendre earlier. About him getting
too close to her hive.

Yeah, she was beautiful. Blond hair, full, pink lips.
Skin that looked so soft any man could be forgiven
for thinking about brushing his fingertips against it.

But that… That crazy bee thing. And the fact that
she seemed to think it wasn't completely transparent she had a crush as deep as the Pacific Ocean on
that ridiculous barista in that equally ridiculous coffee shop, all spoke of not only their decade-wide age
gap, but the gap they had in life experience.

He shook his head, banished any thoughts of her
skin or her lips from his mind, and focused on the
brother thing. Or, if not brother, then at least the fact
that he had been entrusted with protecting her.

There were any number of women with soft skin
in Copper Ridge—he assumed—and if he was starting to think in that way, he was going to have to find
one of them.

He had really enjoyed harassing Cain and Finn
about their celibacy before they'd found their respective fiancées, and implying that he himself was getting a lot of play. But the truth of the matter was all
he'd done was a little flirting over at Ace's bar.

He enjoyed that. Spending a few hours blowing
smoke and telling tall tales. Having a group of women

look at him like he was interesting, funny and not…
Well, what he was.

He preferred the joke, every time. Because the fact
of the matter was when he was alone, there wasn't
much to joke about. There were just endless images
of the kind of carnage he had witnessed during war.
The darkness serving as a reminder for what it was
like to hunker down for hours in a bunker and wait
out threatened attacks.

To watch your best friend bleed out in front of you.
A guy who had someone depending on him.

Unlike Alex.

Well, now he did. Now Clara was his responsibility. And dammit all, he was going to take care of
her. He didn't have time to sit around and feel sorry
for himself. Didn't have the luxury of feeling like it
had been the wrong man's blood that soaked into the
desert sand that day.

Jason was gone. Alex was here.

End of story.

"Whatever you need to do," Cain said. "Do it. We
can cover it here. Unless Liam can't pull his weight."

Liam shot their older brother a look. "Maybe some
of us like having a life off the ranch."

"You don't have one, though. No matter how much
you try to make me believe it. Anyway, some of us
like our lives right here on the ranch. Don't ask me
to feel bad about that, because I don't."

"Glad to have your support, Cain," Alex said, cutting off the bickering between the two of them. "Of
course, I was going to do it either way."

"I figured as much," his brother said. "I also

thought that this was a great way to come out looking benevolent."

Finn laughed. "Yeah. That's what they say about you, Cain. That you're extremely benevolent."

"As dictators go, he's not that bad," Violet offered as she jumped down from the stool and grabbed a handful of chips before wandering out of the room, looking at her cell phone.

Alison made a squeaking sound. "I don't mind taking orders from him," she added, the words coming out quickly. "That was difficult to hold back, but I was not going to say it in front of his daughter."

Cain grinned, and Alex wanted to punch him. He imagined this was exactly what Cain had felt like for the past few months while he and Liam gave him endless hell over his lack of success with women. Now he was smug. And Alex and Liam were celibate.

"You could also not say it in front of his brothers," Alex said.

"You're adults," Alison remarked. "You can deal."

"Some of us have already dealt with enough trauma," he returned. "I'm a soldier. I fought for this country. I've been through enough without being exposed to insinuations about my oldest brother's sex life."

He didn't actually care. But he did like a joke. Especially one that worked to make his past less serious somehow. That made him feel like maybe it wasn't that big of a deal. Like maybe it was a movie or something that happened to somebody else.

"Thank you for your service," Alison said drily. "But it does not exclude you from being treated like I would treat any of my brothers."

He couldn't even be irritated at her. Because he knew that Alison had had a difficult life. He also knew that she didn't have any siblings at all. Family. That's what they were. That's what they were becoming anyway. More seamlessly than he had imagined was possible.

"Okay," Lane said, turning away from the stove. "Everybody quit bickering. It's dinnertime."

CLARA FOUND HERSELF dragging at work the next day. She'd had a near impossible time sleeping, and that was making it difficult for her to keep a smile pasted on her face in the tasting room. Summer was drawing to a close, the wind whipping down from the mountains taking on a sharp edge that spoke of the coming fall.

But that didn't mean tourism in Copper Ridge had abated any. The weather was mild on the coast when the rest of the state was dry and hot or buried beneath snow, which made it ideal pretty much all year round. Though, once it got into October, the fog would start to linger longer and longer, stretching into the afternoon then rolling back in as the sun went down. That would last all through the winter, though there were still people who came to visit during those months.

Especially those who found the low, gray sky atmospheric. Or who just liked getting away from other people.

Even inland, at the winery, it was much cooler than it was down in the southernmost part of the state, and people had migrated upward en masse to escape the last gasps of summer heat.

The sky was bright and blue today, and customers

were out in force. Locals who had a day off, coming in to order a flight of wine and a tray of cheese, mixing in with the tourists.

The large, converted barn was full today, the tall tables made from wine barrels all taken up.

And Clara was doing a pretty poor job serving everyone, and she knew it. She slunk behind the counter, hoping she could extricate herself from customer service, that Sabrina or Olivia might take a hint and leave any kind of straightening up to Clara while they handled the guests.

She could only hope that Lindy, the owner of Grassroots, didn't come in. Lindy had been extraordinarily gracious to Clara, both in offering her the job, and in training her. Lindy had gone through a nasty divorce a year or so ago and she was very sensitive to the fact that Clara was grieving a loss. Much more so than most bosses would be. Much more so than any boss had to be.

But it had been six months. And a sleepless night wasn't the best excuse for shoddy work. Not only that, it wasn't fair. Wasn't fair to her coworkers. And it certainly wasn't fair to Lindy.

Clara sighed and put her head down, then squatted behind the counter, hunting for a bar towel so that she could wipe down surfaces and look busy.

"Are you okay?"

Clara looked up and saw Sabrina leaning over the countertop, staring down at her. She and Sabrina had forged a pretty strong work friendship in the months since Clara had started at Grassroots. She had a feeling it could be more than just a work friendship if

Clara ever took Sabrina up on her offers to go out after work.

She should, really.

Sabrina Leighton was Lindy's sister-in-law. And Clara had never really felt comfortable prying into the particulars of all of that. Or asking why Sabrina and Beatrix—Lindy's ex's sisters—still hung around the winery instead of siding with their brother. She was curious. But if she asked, then Sabrina would have the right to ask how Clara was doing. To want real details. And Clara...didn't want to get into real details.

"I'm fine," she said, lying.

"You seem distracted."

Darn Sabrina. Couldn't she be more tunnel-visioned like their other coworker, Olivia?

"I didn't sleep well last night," she said, going with honesty. "Actually, I think I'm kind of an ogre today. Would you mind handling the customers? I'll do any and all grunt work."

Sabrina smiled. "That's fine."

She was too nice. It made Clara feel like a jerk.

"Thank you." She retrieved a towel and stood up.

"Is anything going on... Or..."

Clara sighed. "It's complicated. And I'm sure you have things to do."

It wasn't really complicated. And she didn't have a reason not to tell Sabrina about the situation with Alex.

"Everybody seems settled right now. Tell me about complicated."

"It's not interesting."

"Is it a guy?"

"Well, yes." If Sabrina were an antennaed creature, said antennae would've been pointing straight upward. "Not in *that* way," Clara added, her cheeks starting to feel hot.

"In what way?"

"I've been avoiding dealing with Jason's lawyer," she said, keeping her voice quiet.

"I understand that," Sabrina said. "I get it. Legal stuff is terrible and my only experience with it is as an observer. Lindy and Damien's divorce was just… so toxic. And the fight over the winery and whether or not the prenup meant Lindy got it… My parents were horrible to her. Damien was horrible. I never want to talk to a lawyer again. Anyway… This isn't about our drama. It's just to say I understand why that must be completely overwhelming on top of everything else."

"Except it turned out the lawyer was calling me for good reason. My brother didn't leave the ranch to me."

Sabrina's eyes widened. "What?"

"Apparently, he left it to Alex Donnelly. Well, I mean, not for…forever. But he's in control of it for a year, before it passes to me."

She had entertained the idea of contesting it…for about a minute. She could hardly manage to open her mail. And anyway, it was only for a year. A year of Alex. But there was an end point. She could handle anything for a year.

Sabrina's entire demeanor changed. Her usually cheerful mouth went flat, her blue eyes turning cool. "Alex Donnelly?"

"Yes," she said. "Is that…significant in some way?"

For some reason, she imagined Sabrina and Alex

together. *Together*, together. It made her throat feel tight.

"I'm not a fan of the Donnelly brothers," Sabrina said, her tone stiff. "I don't know Alex that well. I just can't imagine him being less of an asshole than Liam."

Her lips looked pale all of a sudden, her expression strained.

"Well. I'm kind of stuck with this one. Unfortunately."

Clara had a feeling there was a lot more to the story about Liam Donnelly. And she also had a feeling it absolutely was in *that* way. Clara didn't have any heartbreak like that in her past. She'd experienced too much heartache in the form of death, loss and grief. Putting herself out there romantically hadn't seemed worth the effort.

Until Asher. He was…well, it was difficult to explain, even to herself. But he was just so fascinating. So unlike her. So unlike everything in her life. He felt like hope. Like the possibility of something new.

She didn't like to think that Asher could end up replicating in her the strange heartbreak-induced facial expression that things with Liam had clearly provoked in Sabrina.

Clara had been through enough.

She needed something good. She deserved something good.

"Alex isn't going to come up here, is he?" Sabrina asked. "I mean, the Donnellys aren't going to start hanging out here?"

"He's not my guardian," she said. "It's not like we're close or anything. Or like he's taking care of me. Although, I think that is maybe what Jason was thinking."

Her stomach clenched tight. It was so easy to feel mad at Jason, but the anger made her feel guilty too. And she knew that regardless of how she felt about him going back into the military after their father died, no matter how much she wanted to second-guess all of it, she couldn't demand answers of a dead man. But why couldn't he simply have stayed with her? Why had he felt compelled to test fate like that? If he didn't care about himself, the least he could have done was care enough about her.

Then again, she supposed whatever this was with Alex…it *was* Jason caring in his way. Through somebody else. By not being here. By sending a check. In this case, he was sending a friend.

She gritted her teeth. She wasn't being fair. She knew that. She was just in the anger stage of grieving, wrapped somewhere around denial. Angry denial.

"I mean, of course if they come up here it's fine," Sabrina said, forcing a smile. The color returned to her cheeks, to her lips, and she seemed to be grappling now with feeling embarrassed. "I'm sorry. It's really stupid. The whole thing about me not liking the Donnellys. It was a long time ago. A lot has changed."

"Is there a meeting I don't know about?"

Olivia Logan had walked across the dining room, and was now standing behind Sabrina looking, well, smooth and implacable and impossible to read.

It was difficult to say whether Olivia liked them or not. She wasn't unkind at all, she was just extremely focused. On work, on her boyfriend. And there was a kind of natural aloofness to her demeanor.

But then, her ancestors were quite literally the founders of Logan County, the namesakes. It was entirely possible she perceived Olivia as being slightly uppity for that reason alone.

"No," Sabrina said. "We were just talking about family stuff."

Olivia's mouth tightened into a firm line. "Oh."

"Do you need help?" Sabrina asked.

"Oh, with all the guests? Actually, no. Everything is handled." Olivia was a funny, efficient creature. She was nice enough, but sometimes seemed like she didn't quite understand how to make light conversation. She was intense and goal-oriented, which made her good at every job she set out to do. But made her not so great with small talk.

Not that Clara was an expert in it.

"Do you guys want to hang out tonight?" Sabrina looked so hopeful. And it made Clara feel slightly guilty.

Olivia looked surprised. "Me?"

"Yes. All three of us."

"I can't," Clara said, feeling like a jerk. Because she actually could. And she maybe even should. "I mean, Alex is at the ranch. He has been all day. And I need to see what he's thinking about doing. But once I get settled… Once *everything* is a little bit more settled I think maybe I can go out sometime."

Sabrina turned her focus to Olivia, slightly less hopeful-looking now, but clearly still eager.

"I'm closing tonight," Olivia said. "It will be really late by the time I get out of here. So I shouldn't."

Grassroots Winery was nestled in the trees, between the communities of Copper Ridge and Gold Valley, where Olivia lived.

"I understand," Sabrina said, sounding slightly deflated.

"Well, Bennett dropped me off this morning and he's getting me tonight too. I don't want to put him out," Olivia added.

Bennett was Olivia's boyfriend. Clara had only seen them together a few times but she couldn't really see them as a couple. He seemed protective of her, caring even, but in a lot of ways, more like a brother. A strange observation for someone with as little experience as Clara had, but she figured if even she got a strange vibe, something had to be off.

"Sorry," Clara said, truly meaning it.

Sabrina lifted a shoulder. "That's okay. Some other time."

When the shift ended and Clara got in her car to leave, she was still thinking about Sabrina. About the offer of friendship that Clara hadn't taken. But it felt too hard right now. Like it would intrude too much on the little bubble she'd created for herself.

Grief, she realized, was such an isolating thing.

It was just that Clara had been relishing the isolation. Accepting the social parts in small doses. In the interactions with Asher that she chose, with the job she had taken at Grassroots. The little chats that she had with Sabrina while she was working.

She wasn't craving mass amounts of human interaction. And the potential problem with that was on the other side, she wouldn't have a lot of connections when she was ready for them again. She wondered how long it would take her to get to that place.

Clara sighed and successfully spaced out most of the half hour drive along the tree-lined highway back to the ranch. Alex's truck was in the driveway, and the sight of it made Clara's heart slam against her chest. He really was here. And she really was going to have to deal with him.

She put her car in Park and killed the engine, getting out and shutting the door with gusto, hoping her completely unsubtle arrival would draw him out of hiding.

But when she saw Alex striding across the property, the very idea that he might have been hiding seemed ludicrous.

He walked out of the barn, his white hat tipped low over his face, his torso bare. He was wearing work gloves and low-slung jeans, a pair of cowboy boots. Positively nothing else.

She couldn't look away. She was utterly transfixed.

His chest was deep and broad, well-defined with hair slightly darker than what was on his head sprinkled across it, thinning out and tapering down to a line that disappeared between the waistband of those very, very low pants. Very low.

He lifted his hand and pulled one of the work gloves off, the muscles on his torso and forearms shifting with the movement. Then he tugged off the other glove, and she could only watch the sure, strong movements of his fingers, the way his biceps jumped as he lifted his arm, then lowered it.

His ab muscles moved with each step he took, but as incredible as they were, she found herself completely taken in by another set of muscles. A line that cut in hard at his hip bone. She had never been big on science, but she had a feeling that even if she had paid attention in anatomy class she wouldn't have known the name of that muscle, because every single one of her brain cells had been wiped out by the sight of it.

Alex was…well, she had always known that Alex was good-looking, but it had been kind of abstract in her mind. Because while she had always known he was handsome, he was also very much not the kind of man she was drawn to.

He was too hard. Too masculine. And she would have said she was definitely not the kind of woman who was into overly muscled physiques and body hair.

Apparently, part of her appreciated those things. At least, as an objective observer and admirer of… beautiful things. Though, thinking of him as beautiful in any context just seemed wrong.

Alex wasn't beautiful. He was too hard to be beautiful.

"You're back," he said.

His voice sounded so casual and normal, and she realized it was because he hadn't just experienced an entire internal episode that had caused him to question fundamental things about himself.

"Yeah. I had an earlier shift today. Are you…are you working a bachelorette party, or…"

"It's hot," he said, looking down at his own bare chest, which prompted her to follow his line of sight.

Good God.

There was sweat rolling down between his pectoral muscles—see, that she remembered—and it should have looked gross or unclean in some way, and instead she found it fascinating. Vital. Alive.

That made her shiver.

She wrenched her gaze away from his body, and forced herself to look at his green eyes. She found that didn't help at all. Her mouth felt like it had been stuffed full of cotton. Her head did too, actually.

"I can honestly say I've never decided to work shirtless just because it was hot," she said, immediately regretting the words, because there really was no point in continuing to talk about his state of undress. Talking about it only drew attention to the fact that she was aware of it.

She did not want to be aware of it.

She took a step back.

He lifted a shoulder and she forced herself to keep her eyes locked with his. To not look down and see exactly what that motion had caused the musculature on his chest and stomach to do in response.

Her fingertips tingled and she wiggled them.

He didn't say anything, he was just looking at her. She wasn't sure what he wanted her to do. What he wanted her to say. She supposed it didn't matter either way. Because since when had she cared about his expectations or whether or not she met them? She didn't.

"What exactly did you do today?"

His lips tipped upward into a lopsided smile. "Is that the game? Are we pretending that you're the ranch owner and I'm the lowly ranch hand?" He shoved his hands in his pockets and yet again, it was a study in self-control to keep her eyes on his face. "Because I do like to play games sometimes, honey. As long as you understand who's really in charge here."

She forgot about his bare chest. "You're an ass."

"Maybe, but I'm a hard-working one. One who's going to help fix your situation here. Come with me."

And just like that, she found herself trailing behind him, any illusion of home-court advantage lost as she stared at the broad expanse of his back while they walked to the barn.

His back was nearly as problematic as his chest. It filled her vision, and she found herself pondering the exact nature of what a nice-looking back was. She had never really considered it before.

She didn't allow herself to look below his belt line. Because she was a lady. A lady who had looked at Asher's butt this morning. It was her preferred butt. Alex's was not. And she wasn't going to test the theory by looking. She didn't need to.

Not that casual perusal of the male form equated to feelings.

It was just that she wasn't the kind of person who engaged in that kind of casual perusal. She liked Asher. Had actual, deep feelings for him, harbored hopes about a future. It didn't matter how good-looking another guy was.

Asher, seeing him every morning, getting her daily coffee—which she summarily dumped out—from him had provided a kind of light in a long dark tunnel.

Alex's bare chest could not compete with that.

Alex paused at the barn door. "After you."

"Now you're being chivalrous?"

He shrugged again, then went ahead and walked into the barn in front of her. She scowled, but followed after him.

And then she stopped dead. There were coils of fence rolled up and stacked six deep against the back wall. A pile of lumber lay on its side on the ground, fenceposts, she assumed.

And there was a tractor sitting in the middle of the barn that had been pulled apart.

"What exactly are you doing with the tractor?" she asked.

"Making sure it's fixed."

"You're going to fix it? Do you know what you're doing?"

"Kind of. I have a little bit of experience doing emergency fixes on heavy equipment. Plus I called Anna McCormack for a consult. She said she could order a couple of parts for us at a lower rate, and gave me some instructions over the phone."

"Doesn't she want to do it so she can get paid?"

"She was happy enough to help me out. I explained the situation to her."

Right. So Clara was on the receiving end of pity tractor help. Well, wasn't that what all of this was? Pity help?

"Great," she said, knowing she didn't actually sound like she thought it was great.

"And the fencing is for the bison."

"Right. I forgot you were actually doing that. Bison."

"Unless you're planning on running this place the way your father did, then I think you're right and beef is completely pointless. But if you want to go the direction of that more organic, specialized stuff…"

"Right. I get it."

"You only have to put up with me for a limited time, Clara, and the sooner we get things sorted out, the sooner I can get out of your hair. I've actually done research on this," he said, the expression on his face sincere and not at all pitying. She wasn't sure what to do with that. "And I mean, I went over a lot of options. Sheep. Llamas."

"Llamas?"

"I discounted that pretty quick. They're mean as far as I can tell."

"Don't they spit?"

"That is what I hear," he said.

"I could do without spitting livestock, to be honest. Apart from everything else, I don't need an animal hocking a loogie on me while I'm trying to take care of it."

"Fortunately for you, bison don't spit. I think they're the best option for this area, and for your property in particular. But they need damn sturdy fences."

"Apparently," she said, surveying the equipment.

"I saw your beehives, or whatever those are. I didn't want to get close, you know, in case I became a target."

"I have a suit," she said. "A bee suit."

He arched a brow. "Like a bee costume?"

"No," she responded primly. "The kind you put on that keeps them from stinging you."

"Less interesting than what I was imagining." His smile was wicked, and she wondered exactly what he had been imagining. Probably nothing. Probably he was messing with her. Or maybe it was still just the fact that he wasn't wearing a shirt.

"Less interesting, maybe," she said, still not quite sure what he meant by that, "but effective."

"Well, sometime you'll have to show me. The bee suit. And the bees."

"Sure," she responded.

He reached over toward a peg on the wall and took

his T-shirt off it. It was gray and faded, and when he pulled it over his head, she was powerless against the urge to watch the way the motion affected his muscles. The way they shifted. The way they bunched. Rippled.

The material of the T-shirt was thin, and it clung to his body, and for some reason, it didn't seem any less obscene than his near nudity had. She swallowed, and it was hot and prickly.

"Dinner should be ready," he said.

She blinked. "Dinner?"

"Yeah, I put something in the Crock-Pot."

"I have a Crock-Pot?" She wrinkled her nose.

"Actually, I don't know if you have a Crock-Pot. My future sister-in-law sent one. To be clear, I didn't cook, I just followed her instructions." He smiled, sure and easy. She didn't feel sure or easy. She felt clumsy, awkward. She couldn't figure out why.

"Thanks," she mumbled, following him out of the barn and back up the well-worn footpath that led to the house.

She didn't really know what to expect when they got to the front porch. If he would stop at the door or assume he was joining her for dinner.

When he opened the door and held it for her, she assumed he would be taking his leave. But then he came inside behind her, his heavy footsteps making that first floorboard squeak. It made her feel conscious of how long it had been since she'd spent any meaningful time in the house with someone else. That second squeak upon entry.

It made her feel unaccountably lonely. Sad.

She didn't know why a squeaky floorboard had the power to do that.

Alex walked across the kitchen and opened a few cabinets, his movements confident even though he clearly didn't know where anything was. His gestures were broad, firm. When he took the bowls out of the cabinet and set them down on the counter, he didn't do it tentatively.

It was funny because she had watched Asher make her drink this morning and yet again she had thought of his movements as elegant. There was nothing elegant about Alex's movements. They were like the rest of him. Rough, masculine. Somehow lethal-looking.

She had imagined that when Asher put his hands on her skin, if he ever touched her hand, he would apply that same fine elegance to his actions. If Alex ever touched her, with all that hard-packed muscle, and those work-roughened hands, he might break her.

*Why are you comparing them?*

A good question. Probably because she had such limited interaction with men. And these particular two men were as opposite as they came.

Anyway, Alex didn't fare well in the comparison. And she ignored the strange tightness in her lungs that accompanied that thought.

She didn't *want* to be broken. She was broken enough.

He opened the Crock-Pot, and ladled a couple big scoops of stew into one of the bowls. "Come get it," he said, pushing the bowl away from him slightly, before picking up the second one to serve himself.

Her throat tightened. Almost closed completely.

She opened the silverware drawer and took out a spoon, then retrieved the bowl. "Thank you."

"Sure."

He got his own spoon, then took two cans of Coke out of the fridge, sliding one over to her before he popped the top on his own and took a seat.

That was two times he had served her first. It shouldn't matter.

But she noticed.

She pressed her spoon down into the thick stew and tilted it sideways, grimacing when she unveiled an onion. She carefully shunted it off to the side and scooped a chunk of meat onto her spoon.

"I'm thinking it'll probably take about two weeks to get the facility prepared to bring in animals," Alex said, taking what appeared to be a very reckless bite of stew as far as she was concerned.

"Two weeks? That's it?"

"Should be about that long."

"That's not much time for me to prepare for big stinky animals to be on my property," she said, flicking another onion off to the side before she took another bite.

"Well, there are already *stinging* animals on your property, so why not?"

She shrugged, then took another bite of stew, grimacing when she bit into a carrot that clearly had a hidden onion welded to the back of it. She looked around and cursed the lack of napkin.

She decided she wasn't going to try to muscle past it out of politeness. It wasn't like Alex himself made the stew.

Clara stood and took two quick strides to the sink,

leaning in deep before she spit the carrot and onion down the drain. She turned the sink on, then the disposal and tried to ignore the fact that she knew Alex was watching her.

She straightened, brushing her hair out of her face. "I don't like onions."

She walked stiffly back to her seat and sat down, making a point to be a little more careful with the dissection of the stew from that point on.

"And you don't like coffee," he noted.

She furrowed her brow. "I like coffee."

"You don't."

Clara narrowed her eyes. "You don't know my life."

"You don't like coffee, you don't like onions. You *do* like SpaghettiOs and apparently prefer Coke to beer."

"Beer is gross," she countered.

"Right, but SpaghettiOs are fine dining." He shook his head. "Okay. You don't like beer. What else don't you like?"

"The list of what I like is shorter and takes less time," she said.

"Okay. What *do* you like? Because if I'm going to bring you food sometimes, it would be nice if you didn't have to tiptoe through your dinner like it was full of land mines."

She sniffed. "Nobody said you had to bring me food. But if you must know, I like pasta as long as there are no onions. Or excess greens."

"Hamburgers?"

She nodded. "Without lettuce."

"What are your thoughts on kale?"

She frowned. "What are your thoughts on evil?"

"Chard?"

"Satan's preferred salad fixing."

"Do you like any kind of lettuce?"

She scowled. Then she realized that she was doing a very good impression of a cranky child. But, oh well, she didn't like feeling she had to give an account of the things she enjoyed eating. No one had cared if she ate her vegetables for a long damn time.

"A salad with iceberg lettuce is fine," she explained. "As long as it has cheese. And a lot of dressing. Good dressing, though. And not blue cheese."

"I think I'm getting the picture. Pretty sure I can work with these instructions."

"Pizza is good," she said.

"Obviously. But pizza without beer?" She stared back at him blankly and he sighed heavily. "I'm going to have to stock my own, aren't I?"

"Alternately, you could let me handle feeding myself, which I have done pretty successfully for the past ten years."

"I think you and I might have different definitions of the word *successful*."

She rolled her eyes and took an ostentatious sip of her Coke. "I didn't ask for your definition of anything."

"I'm going to get you eating less canned pasta."

She squinted at him. "You'll have to pry it from my cold dead hands."

A smile shifted his handsome features, the expression as affecting as it was infuriating. "Lasagna?"

She narrowed her eyes. "Acceptable."

"As long as there are no onions."

"Obviously."

"Save your canned food for an emergency. I'll bring dinner tomorrow too."

She rolled her eyes but continued eating in silence, putting her focus on making sure she didn't get an undesirable bite again.

"What time do you get off tomorrow?" he asked.

The question jarred her focus away from her stew. "I'm off tomorrow. I'll be here all day."

"Okay. Then I'll come in the morning, and maybe you can show me around the ranch. Show me the bee suit."

She sighed grumpily. "I have a feeling the bee suit is only going to underwhelm you at this point."

He lifted a shoulder, pushing himself into a standing position and bringing his Coke can to his lips. He knocked it back, finishing off the drink. "I think I can deal with it. See you tomorrow?"

"Yeah. Okay. Tomorrow."

She stayed sitting at the table while Alex walked out the door. And she tried to ignore the inexplicable feeling of pressure in her chest.

It was nice to have somebody take care of her like this. But it wasn't something she intended to get used to.

If there was one thing that life had taught her at this point, it was that people didn't stay forever. And the increased attention you got after you lost someone didn't last.

Heck, there was a stipulation in the will that made it clear it wouldn't last.

She swallowed around the prickly feeling in her throat, then picked up her bowl of stew. She wrinkled her nose and dumped the remaining contents back into the Crock-Pot. Then she took a can of Spaghet-tiOs out of one of the cabinets and set about fixing herself some dinner.

## CHAPTER FOUR

WHEN ALEX PULLED UP to Clara's farmhouse—*his* farmhouse, technically—the next morning, he did not expect to see Clara standing on the front porch.

But there she was, blond hair fashioned into a long braid that was slung over her shoulder, a blue speckled mug in her hand. She was wearing a flannel shirt and a pair of jeans that he thought might be too tight for doing effective outdoor work in. But they did a damn fine job of showing off her long, shapely legs.

Who knew that Clara Campbell had the kind of thighs a man wanted to lick? Get his face between. Get his body between.

*You can stop that right now. She's Jason's sister, not some woman you want to pick up at a bar.*

That thought shamed him, because the real issue was he was too used to thinking of women as a collection of beautiful body parts he might want to touch. Not that he didn't care about the woman herself, he did. It was just that he didn't have relationships.

Which meant that the shape of a woman's thighs and the size of her breasts became essentially the sum total of his requirements. It made it too easy to look at a body first, and think about who she was second.

Which was why he had thought of Clara's thighs

that way. Not because he was attracted to her specifically. Because he was attracted to women.

He had seen Clara a handful of times when she'd been a kid, but not much since. And that meant it was difficult to reconcile the woman he was dealing with in the present with the child he remembered from the past.

The woman she was now…

He found her way too attractive, and that was just wrong.

He gritted his teeth and put the truck in Park, killing the engine and getting out. He might have slammed the door shut with a bit more force than was strictly necessary. It rattled the whole truck, and he hoped it would rattle some damn sense into his brain.

"Good morning," he said, finding that smile of his easily.

Never let them see you sweat. Not when they were pointing a gun at your face. Not when they were saying you should've never been born. Never.

It was something Liam had always told him. In fact, it was the last thing his older brother had told him before he'd left home at eighteen.

*Keep your smile, Alex. Even if it's just to say screw 'em. Keep your smile.*

She made a huffing sound. "Is it?"

He looked around, looked up at the unseasonably clear sky, the brilliant green of the pine trees that closed in around them, then he took a deep breath. "The sun is shining and we're still standing. Constitutes a good morning as far as I'm concerned."

"Well, seeing as it's my day off, my requirements

for a good morning centered around a cozy blanket and a soft mattress."

He was suddenly overtaken by the strangest, strongest desire. To see her sleep. Her face neutral, peaceful even. That pale blond hair spread over her face, her dark lashes fanned out over her cheeks.

He strode toward her, reached out and took the travel mug out of her hand. "For me?"

Before she could answer, he took a long sip of the hot beverage. Then he grimaced. "What the hell is that?" he asked as the sickly sweet, borderline syrupy concoction slid down his throat.

It was her turn to grin. "Hot chocolate."

"That's not hot chocolate. That's a cup of hot sugar."

"It's four packets and a handful of marshmallows."

He handed the mug back to her. "That's disgusting, Clara."

She sniffed and treated him to a very haughty look. "I assume you were hoping for coffee? Because I think *that's* disgusting."

He snapped his fingers. "I knew it."

She rolled her eyes. "Fine."

"You like hipster boy. You don't like coffee."

Without deigning to answer, she stomped down the steps, heading toward the path to the barn. "Are we going to stand around talking about boys or are we going to go work? I've already braided my hair, Alex, so I don't need your help there."

He chuckled and followed her, forcing himself to find amusement in the determined set of her shoulders, and to keep his eyes off her ass.

He collected all of his tools, then opened the barn up. While Clara waited, he went back and got his truck, bringing it in so he could load it up with fencing supplies.

The whole time Clara watched, mute.

"You want to help me with this fencing?"

He knew she wouldn't say anything about being a lady and not doing heavy lifting. Because if there was one thing he had figured out about Clara in the short time he'd been here, it was that she had that same stubborn streak her brother had.

Though, there weren't really any other similarities between them. Jason had been bold, brash. Quick with a joke, and quick to run toward danger if he thought someone was in need of help. Alex had liked the guy on sight.

Jason had had it rough, there was no doubt about that. By the time Alex had met him, his mother had been sick for most of his life. They'd both enlisted in the military at eighteen. And when they were twenty-two Jason's mother had passed away.

When Jason's father died, he'd left the military for a year, returning home to take care of his sister. But once Clara had reached age, he'd enlisted again. Ultimately, Alex and Jason had found themselves on the same base over in Afghanistan. At first, he had imagined it would be a good thing to be out there with his buddy. A guy who had his back.

Of course, now he would give a hell of a lot to make sure that Jason was never there. Or to take his place if it were possible.

Jason had more than had his back. Jason had been a friend, a brother Alex had never deserved.

On summers spent in Copper Ridge Jason had been the one to bring him into a group of friends. To treat him like he belonged. His own father hadn't had an interest in him. A group of strangers actually wanting to spend time with him had been healing in a way he hadn't known he needed.

And it had been because of Jason.

He stopped thinking about his friend then. About the differences between him and his sister. Jason with his dark hair and gray eyes, and Clara with her pale beauty and sparkling baby blues.

He had to focus on the present. Focus on this fence.

"I suppose I could help," Clara said, looking stubborn.

"Better get some work gloves. You don't want to tear up your hands."

She rolled her eyes. "I do know how to do basic ranch work, Alex. I grew up here." She walked to a wooden box that was up against the wall and opened it, taking out a pair of leather gloves and smacking them against the edge of the box. "I do not need to put my hand in there and grab a spider," she muttered, smacking them a few more times.

Then she put them on, curling her fingers as if to signal her readiness.

"No spider?" he asked.

"Am I fetal and weeping on the floor and threatening to amputate my own hand?"

"Doesn't look like it."

She lifted an eyebrow. "Then no."

"Excellent," he said.

He walked over to one end of coiled-up fence length and picked it up. She grabbed the other. Granted, she wasn't contributing a whole lot, but there was something he enjoyed about goading her into helping out. They lifted the fencing into the back of the truck, then repeated the process with the next roll of metal. When they finished with the fencing, they began to move the posts. They worked in silence, and there was something oddly companionable about it.

He looked up, and noticed that some pale wisps of hair had escaped the braid, falling into her face. As they worked, she would stop and shake her head sometimes, trying to flick the hair out of her eyes. But she never stopped. Never stopped working. Never asked for a break. Not even to fix her hair.

Clara was soft in a great many ways, and she was hurting. That much was obvious. But she was also tough. Determined and stubborn. A whole host of big, deep things were contained in that petite, compact frame.

"Okay, that's enough for now," he said, when they had the bed of the truck mostly full. "We can drive out and get the lay of the place. Start replacing some of the fencing. Should go pretty quick since we don't have to dig new post holes."

"Right," she echoed. Still wearing the leather work gloves, she opened the passenger-side door of the truck and got in. She grabbed hold of the handle just above the window, as if she were bracing herself for a bumpy ride. And right then she looked like some kind of ranching wet dream. Pretty and soft, but ready to work with those gloves and that very practical flannel top.

He nearly grabbed a wire cutter to cut his thumb— anything to redirect that line of thinking.

He got into the truck and started it, hoping she wouldn't notice his momentary distraction. His moment of lecherousness.

She didn't, and the fact that she didn't was a testament to just how messed up it was that he would think of her in any way other than as Jason's little sister.

"So…do you have some kind of rancher fantasy or something?" she asked after they'd been driving along the dirt road for a few moments.

Judging by the way he'd been reacting to her, he apparently did have some kind of rancher fantasy, but presumably not the kind she was asking about.

"No," he responded. "But I made my life about the military. About brotherhood. That's what Jason and I had. Brotherhood. You don't leave a fallen brother, Clara. You don't." He kept his mind purposefully blank when he spoke the words, because he didn't want to relive that moment. Didn't want to see it in his mind. "And when he's gone, when you can't help him anymore, you do what you can for those he left behind. It's the right thing to do."

He heard her swallow, looked over and saw a tear slide down her cheek.

"I really do miss him," she said, her voice soft.

"Me too," Alex said. "He was the first friend I made here during the summers I spent with my grandpa. Do you remember that red Jeep of his?"

"Yes," she said.

"We used to stand up in the back while he drove."

"That was stupid," she said.

"Yeah. We were stupid. We were sixteen." Invincible. Damn. Why hadn't Jason been invincible?

"It's funny," Clara said. "I would go so long without seeing him while he was on deployment. And I was kind of used to that. He joined the military so long ago, when I was so young. And when our parents… Well, he came back for a while. And that was nice, but I'm used to doing things on my own, and when he left again, I just got accustomed to it all over again. But knowing he won't come back is different. It feels different. It's so final. Sometimes I try to pretend he's just on a really long deployment." She took a deep, choking breath. "That he's just still out there riding around in a Jeep, looking badass."

He didn't know how to do this. He didn't know how to be there for someone. But he was the only one who was here for Clara. The only one who was left. So that meant he had to step up.

He looked out the windshield, eyes fixed on the dirt road. "The good news is," he said, speaking slowly, "that he's doing something better than that right now, I'm sure. Because trust me, a guy like that gets ushered right into the good part of heaven."

Clara laughed, the sound shaky. "You think so?"

He wanted to think so.

"Oh yeah," Alex said. "God probably showed him where all the good fishing holes are. And he's not driving around some barren desert breathing in dust and hoping today is not the day you get mortared. No. He's not worried about that anymore."

Alex fought to keep his throat from closing up, to keep a wall of emotion from crushing him beneath its weight. "I think the only thing he'd worry about is you," he continued, his voice rough. "But I'm aiming to make sure he doesn't have to."

Silence settled in the cab of the tuck. Then Clara cleared her throat. "You think he's fishing up there, huh?"

"You know he is. And he doesn't have to lie about how big the fish is anymore. They're all monsters." The ridiculous image made him smile. And he felt gratified when he looked over and saw that Clara was smiling too.

They got out of the truck at the old pasture where the cows had been once upon a time. The fence had certainly seen better days, and even if it were in great shape, it wasn't going to be enough for bison. They needed good, strong materials, and the older one was sagging and falling over. So that meant refencing the entire pasture.

But he was happy enough with that. It gave him a goal. Gave him something to work toward. Something to give Clara. Something to give back to Jason.

He gritted his teeth. He owed the man more than he could ever repay.

And he sure as hell didn't deserve any of it.

When they got out of the truck, he tossed Clara a pair of wire cutters. "Okay, what we're going to do is go down the fence and basically cut. Should be quick enough. We'll get to the posts afterward."

Clara nodded, and they set to work silently. She was a fast worker, and she was a hard worker, and as he'd observed earlier, she didn't seem to want to show the need to stop as long as he was still going strong.

So they worked until his shoulders ached, until he was hungry enough that he couldn't keep going.

"Hey, Clara," he called. She was several links down the fence, working her way in his direction. "Why don't you open up the truck? I have a cool chest in the back. We can tailgate."

"What do you have in there?" She wrinkled her nose as she peered toward the cool chest, looking skeptical and vaguely mouseish.

"I brought sandwich fixings. Nothing is on the sandwich as of yet. You can choose."

"What kind of meat?"

"Well, I brought roast beef since I noticed when you ate the stew you seemed to like beef."

She frowned. "I don't like it cold."

He looked at her and tried to figure out if she was kidding. Judging by her expression, she wasn't. "I also brought turkey."

She smiled at that. "Well, I do like turkey lunch-meat."

He stared at her. "You don't make any sense, do you know that?"

She scowled at him, her pale face streaked with dirt, her cheeks bright pink. Her nose was a little sunburned, the upturned tip as pink as her cheeks. And then his gaze dropped to her lips. They were soft, full. At least, they looked like they would be soft. But he wondered if they'd stay soft if he leaned in to kiss them. Or if she'd firm them right up and try to bite him.

He would deserve the bite. Hell, he deserved it just

for thinking about her like that. But the knowledge didn't stop him from thinking it. Also, the idea of her biting him when he pressed his lips to hers didn't cool him off like it should. No, his body found that every bit as intriguing as the idea of a kiss.

They made their way back to the truck and Clara hoisted herself up on the tailgate, opening the cool chest and rifling through the contents. She happily retrieved a Coke, popping the top while she continued to forage for sandwich toppings. She pulled out the bread, then grabbed the turkey. She took out the bottle of mustard and some pickles and nothing else. He found himself grimacing as he watched her assemble the sandwich and take her first bite. But then a smile spread over her face, and he couldn't even judge her for her choice of lunch because he just felt accomplished at the fact that he'd given her something she actually wanted.

After that, he set out to make his own sandwich—with roast beef, since Clara had used all the turkey, which had originally been for him, dammit—and cheese, lettuce, tomatoes and mayonnaise.

Clara narrowed her eyes and looked at him, where he was standing. "Your sandwich looks gross," she informed him.

"So does yours," he said, walking over to the truck and lifting himself up next to her on the tailgate. He pulled a beer out of the chest and popped the top on the edge of the truck bed, and the two of them ate in relative silence, staring out at the work they had done for the day. At the discarded fencing, broad expanse of land and all the work they had ahead of them.

Clara popped the last bite of sandwich in her mouth

and brushed crumbs off her lap. Then she lifted her hand, shading her eyes, and looked out toward the horizon. Up at the mountains.

"I can't tell you how long it's been since I've been this deep into the property," she said. "I've kind of gotten into my routine. Going to Grassroots, doing the small garden, checking on the bees. It keeps me close to the house."

"Yeah?"

"I think it feels too lonely. I mean, realizing how big this place is, and I'm here all by myself. It just feels sad."

"You're not alone anymore," he said.

*At least not for now.* But he left that part unsaid. Still, judging by the way she breathed in deep, by the way her shoulders sagged slightly, he could tell she had heard it somehow anyway. That she felt it.

He looked over at her, gazed at her profile, at the way her lips curved down, at that fine blond hair catching in the breeze.

As if sensing his perusal, she looked over at him. The breeze kicked up just then, and he caught her scent. Irish Spring and skin, nothing extraordinarily feminine. Just her.

His stomach tightened, and he found himself fighting the urge to reach out and touch her face, to see if her skin was as soft as he thought it might be.

Instead, he lifted his beer bottle to his lips and took a long, slow drag on it.

Clara looked away sharply, and he wondered if she had somehow sensed his thoughts again.

"We better get back to work," she said, hopping down off the truck.

He nodded, setting the bottle down. "All right, boss, whatever you say." And he smiled that easy smile because it was better than honesty at that moment.

As far as he was concerned, it was better than honesty almost always.

## CHAPTER FIVE

CLARA QUESTIONED HERSELF as she walked into The Grind early the next morning. It was Asher's day off, apparently, and he had not been in Stim when she had driven by that morning, so she had left and gone to Cassie's coffeeshop because she liked their hot chocolate better.

Stim had some kind of bitter, extra dark chocolate, and that was not what she wanted. Frankly, she didn't like anything on their menu. None of it was sweet. And as Alex had pointed out the day they had run into each other there—or rather, the day he had *orchestrated* the two of them to run into each other there—everything only came in one size.

The Grind was busy. It was a place people liked to sit and hang out at, as opposed to Stim, which seemed to attract people who were there to get something to go. There were only a couple of tables in that shop, and they didn't have the variety of baked goods that The Grind had.

Of course, really, she should be back home in bed. It was just that she had woken up early after barely sleeping the night before, and she had known Alex would be coming by the ranch soon, and she hadn't wanted to be there when he arrived.

It was silly, but spending the day with him yesterday had left her feeling emotionally wrung out.

They had talked about Jason, and while that was probably a good thing, it was also hard.

There was something about being around Alex that made her skin feel like it was too tight, made her scalp feel prickly and sensitive. It was the emotional thing, it had to be.

It couldn't be anything else. All she had done was toss and turn until the sky had turned gray this morning.

It was cloudy now, and she had a feeling the time on their sunny weather had run out. It'd been an abnormally warm streak, with blessedly clear skies.

But of course the clouds always rolled back in.

She waited patiently in line until it was her turn, and then ordered an extra-sweet hot chocolate with whipped cream and candy cane pieces from the girl behind the counter.

She also got a brownie.

She figured if people could justify eating doughnuts for breakfast, a brownie should be fine.

She took her treats back to one of the bistro tables and sat, pulling out her phone—which still didn't have service, but could hook up to Wi-Fi and had games that were functional—and started playing a puzzle game.

She was in a blissful state of sugar-fueled zoning out when the chair across from her moved. She looked up and her eyes clashed with Alex, who was standing there holding a to-go cup.

"What are you doing here?" she asked, realizing belatedly that it wasn't the friendliest of greetings.

"Getting coffee," he said, "since you apparently don't have any."

"Oh."

She was still being very unfriendly, but she was not ready for this. She was not ready for him.

"I was on my way to your place," he said, "and I stopped in here because I realized I needed another hit."

She scrunched her face up into an expression of faux concern. "Are you stalking me lazily again?"

"No. Just stalking caffeine." He took a seat across from her without asking for her permission.

She could only marvel at how badly her avoiding-Alex plan was going.

He looked at her cup, which had whipped cream still covering the top of the drink, little candy pieces nestled upon it. "Do I want to know what that is?"

She frowned. "A cup of diabetes, and it's no one's business but mine."

He shrugged. "Suit yourself. I need harder stuff."

"Chocolate has caffeine, you know."

"Right. I prefer not to screw around with mine."

She lifted her cup to her lips and took a sip, and he did the same.

She couldn't help but watch the way his lips touched the rim, the way he held the cup in his hand. Which really was rather large. And masculine.

She returned her own cup to her lips and took a swallow that was much too large, scalding her throat.

She put the hot chocolate down, pulling a face.

"I didn't think you worked today," he said.

"I don't," she responded tartly.

"Then what are you doing out? I thought you were all about sleeping in and blankets and stuff."

"I couldn't sleep last night, if you must know," she said, opting for honesty, though God knew why.

"Why?"

He made her want to throw her hot chocolate in his face. He was just so…persistent. He was caring, in a way that he could never sustain. She didn't want to get used to having someone around again only to have to deal with them leaving. There was no point to it. And she was just…exhausted. Tired of that kind of thing.

"I was thinking about Jason," she said finally.

"Sorry."

"You don't need to be sorry. You didn't kill him."

Neither of them said anything after that. They just sat there, sipping their respective drinks.

Alex made her more aware of her surroundings, hyperaware, and when the door opened again, her head whipped around to look. Sabrina walked through, and stopped when she saw them.

"Hi, Clara," she said, her voice stiffer than usual.

"Good morning," Clara said.

"Just grabbing coffee on the way to work," Sabrina continued. She was shifting her gaze between Clara and Alex with an odd expression on her face, and Clara wanted desperately to tell her that whatever she was thinking, it wasn't that.

"Us too," Clara said, then winced because she'd made it sound like they'd gone to coffee together, or that they were a unit functioning as one. An *us*. "I mean, I was here. Alex happened to be here too. Separate from me."

"Okay," Sabrina responded, her expression growing still more skeptical.

Clara knew she was already verging on protesting too much, but as Sabrina walked toward the counter to get her coffee, Clara had to fight with herself to keep from laying on more excuses and justifications.

"Now she's thinking weird things about us," Clara said.

"Weird things, huh?" Alex asked. "What kind of weird things?"

"You *know*," she said, not bothering to hide her exasperation.

The door opened again and Clara turned to see who it was this time.

Her heart jumped into her throat.

She reached across the table, yanking Alex's cup of coffee from his hand, then shoving her mug of hot chocolate into the blank space in front of him as she lifted his cup to her lips and took a sip. She did her best to control her face as she glanced to where Asher had just come through the door.

He was looking straight ahead at the chalkboard menu above the counter, his expression serious.

"Hi," she said, her voice sounding high and stupid.

She wanted to bite off her tongue. What had she been thinking trying to get Asher's attention? She was with Alex and he was going to think she was *with* Alex. And then Alex was going to mock her mercilessly later. And she had surrendered her hot chocolate.

Asher turned toward them, confusion and surprise on his handsome face.

Alex, for his part, seemed to be frozen between

what looked to be a state of amusement. He looked from her to Asher, then back to her.

Clara wanted to punch him.

"Are you cheating on Stim, Clara?" Asher asked, treating her to a warm smile as he shoved his hands in the pockets of his skinny jeans.

She had determined she wasn't going to compare him to Alex, but it was difficult when they were in such close proximity to each other. Alex was broad, big. He was wearing a battered old jacket, a blue Henley with the top two buttons undone, and his white cowboy hat, now sitting on the table because he'd removed it when he'd sat down. Asher was shorter, his frame more slight. He had his hair back, and was wearing a leather bomber-style jacket that looked new, along with a sweater and a scarf. His jeans looked distressed, but artfully so.

Looking at Asher made something in her chest ache. He was just…everything she wasn't. And part of her thought that if she was just able to be with him, to be near him, he could give her some of what she lacked.

He was polished, put together, and she was sitting there in a flannel drinking a hot chocolate.

Well, at least now she didn't look like she was drinking a hot chocolate.

"I could ask you the same question," she countered playfully, tucking a strand of hair behind her ear and tilting her head to the side. "Are *you* cheating on Stim?"

"Checking out the competition," he said, smiling. "Actually, I like a variety of roasts. What Cassie has here is pretty good. It's nice to change it up."

"Oh yeah, me too. I'm all about the um…variety. In roasts." Clara lifted the coffee again, but she didn't actually take a drink this time.

Asher's gaze slid to Alex, and so did Clara's.

"This is my brother's friend," she said, the words coming out quickly. "My brother who died."

Asher flinched, and she realized she'd done a pretty ham-fisted job of introducing that topic. "Oh, sorry. I didn't know."

"It's okay." She hadn't gone out of her way to talk to Asher about Jason. In fact, she had kind of done what she could to avoid bringing it up with him. It made him even more of a safe space. More of a vacation from the rest of her life.

"It's just… He's helping me out with some things. My brother left him some stuff."

"Okay," he said, nodding. She couldn't tell if he was relieved, or if he was wondering why she was bothering to give him so many details. She wished she knew something about men—*anything* about men.

"Well, I'm meeting some friends for a hike in a bit, so I've got to grab my coffee and get moving. It was good to see you."

"You too," she said, watching him as he walked to the counter. Then she let out a long breath she didn't know she had been holding and set the coffee down. "Stupid small towns."

"Well, that was quite the display," Alex said, sounding decidedly amused now.

"Shut up," she responded.

"So you have to pretend to like coffee all the time for this guy. Not just so you can go in and buy coffee

from him, but so he doesn't know you're basically a
hummingbird who exists on sugared nectar."

"I am not a hummingbird," she groused.

"You probably have the heart rate of one, considering how much junk you consume on a given day."

"Bite me," she said.

Alex only stared at her, his green eyes sharpening
slightly. And she felt it. In her chest. Like something
inside of her had turned over.

She breathed in deep, trying to dispel the tension.
It didn't work.

"He seems…like he's from Portland," Alex said.

She had a feeling that wasn't a compliment.

"He *is*," she said. "He moved out here to help start
the coffee shop. He likes the slower pace. And how
authentic everyone is here."

"I see." Alex rubbed his hand across his chin, the
sound of his palm moving over his whiskers like
sandpaper on wood. "So, you know a lot about him.
But he apparently didn't know you had a brother that
died. And he thinks you like coffee. Does he also
think you like kale salads?"

She picked a candy piece off her cocoa. "Kale has
never come up in conversation."

Alex looked over to where Asher was standing,
now ordering his coffee. It looked like a long, involved ordering process. There were hand gestures.

"Really?" Alex looked incredulous. "He seems like
the kind of guy who brings up kale on the second or
third conversation."

She tapped the side of her mug. "We did talk about
quinoa once."

"That's hilarious."

"He says it's problematic because of the way that it's sourced." She had been relieved because quinoa was on her "never try" food list.

"And you want to date him?" Alex asked, his eyebrows raised. "You want to go out with this guy, invite him in after, make out with him on your couch?"

Clara felt her face getting warm. "I don't... I *like* him. Yes, he's into some different things than I am. But that's actually good. It's interesting. I haven't... I've never done anything, Alex. I live here. I've always lived here. I've always had the ranch. And knowing Asher has taught me new things."

"Let me guess...he's part of your honey initiative."

She let out an exasperated growl. "We *might* have had a conversation about the issues with the bee population and why producing your own local honey is an asset."

Alex shook his head. "Well, isn't that something. The girl who can't swallow an onion got bees because some hipster coffee shop guy told her to. And she also does her best to choke down black coffee in his presence. I mean, I guess you can't fight that kind of attraction. If you're willing to do those things for him..."

She didn't like that he was making fun of her. That he was taking this incredibly private thing that she had never experienced before and making light of it. She also didn't like the fact that she couldn't quite connect his words with the reality of the situation. *Attraction. Making out on her couch.*

Of course she was attracted to Asher. She had just checked out his butt the other day.

But for some reason, reminding herself of that just reminded her of seeing Alex's bare chest.

"Yeah, so what?" She did her best to keep her face steady, to keep her expression smooth, even though she had a feeling her cheeks were rosy. "I want to get into his pants."

"I don't know, honey, those pants are pretty tight. I think getting into them would be a challenge."

She made a scoffing sound. "You're horrible."

He stood up. "Maybe." He swallowed down the rest of the coffee. "I'm going to go work now. I'll see you at the ranch. Give you some time to talk to your boyfriend."

"Are you in high school, or what?"

"Are *you*? Because if not, why are you waiting for him to make a move? If you really want him, you should ask him out. Life is short, right?"

And then Alex walked out, leaving her at the table by herself.

Asher chose that moment to turn around, and he noticed that Alex was gone. His expression shifted slightly, and he walked back over to the table. "So, he's just your brother's friend?"

"Yeah," she said quickly.

"Okay," Asher said. "Well, I'll see you around."

He started to walk toward the door and Clara bit her lip, warring with indecision. Then she figured, *screw it.* "Wait," she said. "Are you...do you...do you want to hang out sometime? I mean, you said you did. But can we pick a tangible time to do that?"

Asher assessed her slowly. "Sure," he said. "What did you have in mind?"

"Well...there's a farm-to-table dinner event happening at Grassroots Winery. I thought maybe you would want to go."

They were serving absolutely nothing at that dinner that Clara could force down her throat, and she had no idea what she was doing.

"Yeah, that sounds good. When is it?"

"Next Sunday night. If you're free. It's at seven."

"Sure," he said. "Sounds good. Want to meet in the parking lot at Stim?"

That was a little disappointing. She wanted him to pick her up. So that later, he could drive her home. And then maybe there would be couch making out.

But if meeting in a parking lot worked for him, she wasn't going to complain about the details.

"Perfect," she said.

"Great. See you."

Part of her wanted to demand that he write it down in front of her so she knew he wouldn't forget, but she had already made the first move, so she wasn't going to be a crazy person.

"See you," she said.

She finished drinking her hot chocolate slowly, until she could no longer justify avoiding real life, and the ranch.

As she walked to her truck, she kept her mind firmly fixed on The Grind and the conversation she'd had with Asher. The fact she had a date with Asher.

That felt…like it had to have happened to someone other than her. And considering how her life often went, it was nice to feel not so much like herself. Even if it was just for a little while.

## CHAPTER SIX

CLARA SEEMED TO be avoiding him, so when she appeared in the barn around four o'clock, Alex was surprised.

What had been going through her mind when he had run into her this morning in the coffeehouse, he couldn't say. Except that she had not been overly excited to see him. Or maybe that was an understatement. She may well have been actively avoiding him.

And then that skinny-jean-wearing idiot had come in. Alex didn't like that guy. In his estimation, if a man wanted a woman, he should do something about it.

This guy, skulking around town with his scarves and ferrety face, clearly wasn't man enough to do that. Or he didn't want Clara. In which case, she didn't need to be wasting her time on him.

Obviously, Clara didn't feel the same, since she seemed to be glowing when she walked into the barn, the smile on her face one of immense satisfaction.

"Did you get into those skinny jeans?" he asked, knowing he was being a little mean, but not feeling all that guilty when her cheeks turned pink.

"I got a date," she said. "So thanks for suggesting I make that happen."

"Anytime. But you know he should have been the one to do it."

"Come on. You can't have it both ways. Like you said, I'm not in high school. So why should I wait around?"

"Well, it's a valid point."

"Of course you think so. You made it."

"I can't help it if I'm brilliant."

Clara rolled her eyes. "I didn't really come out here to thank or congratulate you. I just thought you might want to see the bees and get some honey so that you can take it home and give some to Lane. You were talking about seeing if she wanted to sell any in her store. I thought you might want to sample it."

"Do you have a spare bee suit? Because I don't want to end up looking like an extra in a horror movie."

She laughed. "Yes. I do."

She walked over to the storage closet there in the barn and threw open the doors. She rummaged around for a moment before surfacing with two generic-looking white shirts and masks.

"Even with one of these on I'm probably going to end up looking like the extra in a horror movie," he commented, taking a mask and shirt from her hand.

She gave him some gloves next, and the two of them outfitted themselves over the top of their clothes.

"Nothing on the bottom?" he asked.

"No. Just make sure you tuck your pant legs into your boots."

He bent down, grumbling while he complied. "I don't want to get stung in the junk."

Clara made a strange, choking sound. "Well, nobody does."

"Okay. Lead the way."

Clara did, taking them out of the barn and walking down a narrow path that led farther away from the house.

He could hear the buzzing before he saw the hives. There were five of them, little rectangular wooden structures spread out in a clearing, lilac bushes all around. And bees. Thousands and thousands of bees. Swirling lazily between the purple flowers and the wooden structures.

"Okay," he said. "This is a horror movie."

"Don't say that about my bees," she said, forging ahead. "They aren't a horror."

"I disagree. Pretty much any animal in mass quantity has the potential to be horrifying."

She made a scoffing sound and moved toward one of the hives. "Hummingbirds? Which are on my mind as you recently compared me to one."

"Thousands of hummingbirds descending upon you. The sound of their wings would be deafening. They would suck the nectar…from your body."

She jerked her head sharply, and he assumed that she had rolled her eyes. He couldn't see very well through the netting he was wearing over his face, and he certainly couldn't see through to hers.

She bent down and picked up a metal canister with a spout that looked something like a mini watering can. Then she grabbed what looked like a handful of wooden shavings and stuffed them down into the bottom of that metal can. That done, she pulled a matchbook out of her pocket, lit the match and threw it inside. Smoke started to pour out of the spout, and she stuck a lid over the top of it and walked over to the hive.

"They don't like the smoke," she said simply, taking one of the slats off the top of the hive. It was covered with angry-looking insects, and Clara waved the smoker around in front of it, causing most of the bees to dissipate.

"You look like you've been doing this for a while."

"About two years," she said. "At first, I did find them worrisome. But you get used to them. They get used to you. They're kind of cute."

"Doesn't like coffee. Thinks bees are cute. That's a concerning list of attributes, Clara."

"Whatever. Asher doesn't think so. Clearly." She grabbed a brush and dislodged a few stray bees that were clinging to the honeycomb that was built on the wooden frame she was holding. She set the honeycomb in a plastic bin beside the hive and put a lid over the top of it. Then she retrieved another wooden slat and repeated the same action.

"He doesn't know that you hate coffee."

"I'll tell him someday."

"That sounds like a good depressing art-house movie," Alex said. "One depicting the bleakness of suburbia. One day, twenty years into their marriage, the wife confesses that she's always hated coffee. The husband doesn't know who she is anymore. Starts sleeping with an eighteen-year-old."

She shook her head. "I hardly think my not liking coffee will trigger a midlife crisis."

"But somehow it's a big enough deal that you're keeping it a secret."

She made a funny, indignant squeaking noise. "Because if he knows I don't like coffee then I won't have a reason to go see him other than the fact that I'm hung up on him, and that's embarrassing and humiliating."

"Now you've asked him out. If it goes well, it won't matter if he knows you like him. You'll want him to know you like him."

She put the second slab of bee-free honeycomb into her bin and closed the lid again before picking it up. "This is enough for tonight," she said.

"What do you do with it now?"

"Decap it and then put it in the strainer. I'll show you."

"Let me take that for you," he said, reaching out and taking the bin from her hands.

She looked up at him, but her expression was inscrutable through the layers of netting. "Thank you."

The two of them started to head back toward the barn. "I think I owe you an apology," he said.

"For which thing?"

"For which...wow." He snorted. "Am I that offensive?"

She shrugged. "You're just *you*, I guess."

"Ouch. I take it that was not meant in a complimentary fashion."

"It wasn't really meant in an insulting one either."

"I don't believe that. But, regardless, I owe you an apology about the bees."

"A bee-specific apology. Well, that is a new one."

"You really know what you're doing here. It's impressive."

She pulled the headgear off and shook her blond

hair out, and this time he could most definitely read the *screw you* in her blue eyes. "Well, thank you, Alex. I wasn't exactly looking for your approval. I know that I'm doing a good job with this. I hadn't quite gotten to the point where I was ready to turn it into a product I could sell, but I'm definitely getting there. And I knew that I could. The thing about the bees is that they're relatively low maintenance. And that fits into my schedule. I planned all of this, Alex. Because I'm used to having to take care of myself."

He felt like an ass now. But then, that was nothing new. "I'm sorry I accused you of doing it just because of that guy."

"Asher. His name is Asher."

"Okay." But he wasn't going to say his name.

"You can take the headgear off now."

He realized then that he was still wearing the net. He pulled it off and then proceeded to remove the rest of the protective gear while Clara did the same.

He did his best not to watch as she pushed the bulky suit off, revealing the shape of her slim figure beneath. But it was hard not to.

She took the suit from him, and went back into the storage closet, rummaging around for a moment before returning with a big metal canister-looking thing and a large white bucket.

She propped the canister up on the wooden storage bin, then placed the bucket underneath the spigot.

"So now I just need to get my roller," she said, grabbing it out of the white bucket, "and then we decap the honeycomb here. Just getting the wax off. You can cut it off if you want to save it, but I haven't gotten to the point where I'm doing anything with it."

"No beeswax candles?"

She smirked. "Someday. When I'm the perfect hipster farm wife." She sounded casual, but her cheeks turned pink again.

She really did have a thing for that guy. The appeal escaped Alex. Not that he was into men anyway, but if he were, it would not be a guy like that. Hipster guys had no practical application as far as he was concerned. Though he supposed they did make coffee. Even if it was pretentious coffee.

Silently, Clara set to work on the honeycomb, pressing the spiked roller over the top of it from all directions until the heavy wax coating was diminished. Then she put the entire wooden frame in the canister and set to work on the other one.

She repeated the process with the second frame, then put a lid over the canister. "And now the extracting. Which is the fun part."

She plugged it into an outlet in the wall and it started to churn, wobbling slightly as it worked.

"Is it spinning?" he asked.

"Yes. And it will strain all the honey out. Make sure there aren't any chunks."

He watched as a stream of golden honey started to run out of the spigot and into the white bucket. He looked over at Clara, whose face was positively brilliant with joy.

This was hers. Something she had cultivated for herself. A way she had come up with to make the ranch work for her, without help. She'd had no help for all this time. That was just starting to sink in.

She was alone. And he'd come in and pretty well made light of all that she'd built for herself.

"You're amazing, Clara. Do you know that?"

Her head whipped around, one pale brow raised. She looked at him like he was a giant, talking spider. "I'm sorry, what? Did you get stung by a bee? Is your airway swelling? Has it cut off the oxygen to your brain?"

"No," he said, laughing. "I just think that you deserve more credit than I gave you in the beginning. I kind of burst in, determined to fix this, and it turns out it wasn't really broken."

"Well," she said softly, letting out a long, slow breath, "it's not like I was functioning perfectly."

"Are we ever supposed to function perfectly? Because if so, I'm failing there too."

"How?" she asked, her eyes glued to the honey. "I really want to know. I want you to list your failings so that I can feel better about myself."

"Well," he said, leaning against the barn wall, kicking his feet out and crossing his arms over his chest, "first of all, I showed up at the Laughing Irish ranch to collect my inheritance after my grandfather died, which made my older brother Finn mad, because of course he's spent his entire life working that ranch, and now suddenly we all own an equal share. But of course, I didn't tell him. About this. About the fact that I was going to be responsible for your ranch. No. I just worked my way into carrying a quarter of the weight and then abandoned them so I could do a bison start-up here."

"Overachieving at ranching endeavors is hardly failing, Alex. If you want to make me feel better about myself, you're going to have to try harder than that.

Could you possibly be a little more of an ineffectual loser?"

She looked comically hopeful, and then she stuck her finger into the bucket of honey and pulled it out slowly, thick, golden liquid running down the digit. Then she slipped her finger into her mouth, drawing it out on a long glide. And he could do nothing but watch. Inappropriately. As her lips wrapped around her finger, and her tongue slid along the length of the bare skin.

And he couldn't help but imagine her doing the same to him. If he stuck his finger in the bucket of honey and offered it up to her, pressed it up against those lips. Inevitably, his mind went even further and started to imagine other things she could put into her mouth.

He bit down on the inside of his cheek. Hard. It was ridiculous. Fighting any kind of attraction for his friend's younger sister. For Clara. Clara, who was ten years younger than he was. Clara, who was vulnerable, fragile, and definitely in need of protection and support.

She did not need him to fantasize about touching her soft skin. She needed him to touch her even less.

Alex had never had a girlfriend in his life. He hooked up. He made sure everyone got what they wanted. Then he said goodbye.

He was only good for a night.

And Clara Campbell needed a hell of a lot more than a night.

If she wanted a more convincing picture of what a dick he was, he could tell her what he had just been thinking. That would convince her. It would also ruin everything. Just another trauma he was basically responsible for in her life. He would skip it.

"I think it's done," she said, eyeballing the extractor. "I'm just going to take it out to the hive and let them do the cleanup for us."

"I'll do it."

"Without suiting up?" she asked.

"No."

She laughed. "I'll be right back."

She picked up the extractor and walked out of the barn, leaving the partially full bucket of honey behind.

He watched her leave, and this time, he didn't bother to prevent himself from checking out her behind. As soon as she closed the door behind her, he let his head fall back against the wall with a hard thunk. He deserved the pain that resulted.

He wasn't ready to admit that he wanted her. Not her specifically. She was a woman. And she was beautiful. Plus, he was hard up. He'd been back in Copper Ridge for nearly four months and in that time hadn't come across anyone he wanted to hook up with. It was a symptom of a much bigger issue. And he knew it. The truth of the matter was he hadn't met anyone he wanted to be with since Jason had died. Since he'd watched Jason die. For him.

Since he'd watched as his best friend flung his body in front of his and the rain of bullets that would've certainly hit Alex were all absorbed by Jason.

White light flashed before his eyes and he closed them, gritting his teeth against the pain. It was like he could feel the impact of the gunfire all over again. Like he could hear it. Ringing in his ears.

"Alex?"

He straightened, opening his eyes and looking over at Clara. He felt the impact of her down to his gut. Like another explosion. Only this one was different. This one felt good.

And he realized something he hadn't let himself fully admit before this moment. He hadn't truly wanted a woman in more than six months. Clara was the first one. And he didn't *want* to want her.

But maybe it didn't matter anyway, because she wanted someone else. Thank God for that. Because he was going to let that other guy have her. And he was going to stay the hell away.

But for a moment, he was going to let himself stand there and want her. Because it felt good. It felt damn good. Even though it was wrong.

"Are you okay?" she asked, looking confused.

Of course she was confused. He made no sense. None of this made sense.

"I'm fine. Just had an early morning."

"Are you ready for dinner? I am." She reached down and grabbed the white bucket, and he immediately took it from her hands.

"Sounds good," he responded.

"We can have bread and honey with whatever you brought."

He smiled. "That sounds extra good."

It was strange, Clara being friendly to him. Them having a truce. Actually inviting him to dinner instead of scowling at him like she was waiting for him to go away.

The entire walk back to the house, all he could think of was that he had neglected to tell her his biggest failing of all.

That the real reason he was here helping her, protecting her, lusting after her, was because he was alive thanks to her brother's sacrifice.

His biggest failing was being alive when his best friend was dead.

## CHAPTER SEVEN

ALEX HAD BROUGHT spaghetti for dinner, and much to Clara's delight, it was one hundred percent nitpicky taste bud approved. There was also a loaf of soft white bread provided by Alex's other soon-to-be sister-in-law, Alison, who owned the town bakery. He had, of course, provided fresh Laughing Irish butter, and now they had honey too.

The spaghetti was long since eaten and the two of them were both gratuitously continuing to devour the bread, mostly as a vehicle for the butter and honey.

"We need to leave some for Lane," Clara said, eyeing how much they had eaten.

"We had a vat of it—that should be easy enough."

"I don't know, when we're out of bread I'm thinking I might escalate to just sticking my face in the bucket."

"It is pretty good," he said.

"Did you know that eating local honey can help with your seasonal allergies?"

Alex laughed, and it created a kind of strange space in her chest that seemed to exist just to hold whatever feeling his laughter conjured up inside of her. She didn't know what it was. Only that it felt weighted, heavy. Maybe because she knew no matter how quick Alex was with a smile, they shared a common pain.

That they both knew how difficult life could be. That they knew the cost of things.

But he smiled anyway. And he laughed.

This time she had made him laugh, and that—she was discovering—held its own kind of satisfaction.

Even if he was laughing at her entirely sincere bee trivia.

"I didn't know that, no," he said.

"Well, now you do. Honey is beneficial," she said, sliding her chair closer to the cutting board that had the bread on it, taking another big spoonful of honey and drizzling it over the top of her selected slice.

"I'm enjoying it, which means I already considered it beneficial."

"I don't think that's how that works."

"Of course it is," he said, dipping the spoon back into the bowl and lifting it straight to his lips, taking an unashamed spoonful of the honey all on its own. "'Good for you' is a complicated concept, Clara. A series of checks and balances. Sure, there's good for you in terms of vitamins and minerals and all of that. But does it make you feel good? Does it make you happy? Those are important questions to ask too. If the answer is no, then I always wonder why people are working so hard to prolong a miserable life. I mean, in the grand scheme of things, I think it's better to have a few less years with cake, than a few more with kale, right?"

"Is that what you do? You just do what feels good?" She watched as he stuck his thumb into his mouth and sucked off some honey that clung to his skin. She realized that over the course of the past few days she had watched his mouth quite a bit. And that she'd catalogued those moments.

His mouth on her hot chocolate cup yesterday. His mouth on his coffee this morning. His mouth right now.

"I've done a hell of a lot that feels like garbage. I believed in the ideal behind serving in the army. It gave me something to be. Something bigger than myself. And growing up like Liam and I did, I liked that. I like feeling like I mattered. Like I was doing things. Fixing things.

"But within all of that is a lot of hardship. It's service, plain and simple. It requires you to do a hell of a lot you don't want to do, and see a lot you wish you could go back to not even being able to imagine. But you don't. You don't forget. You don't just go back to how it was before. There is no going back. So yeah, in the pockets in between that, I've made it a point to indulge in things that made me feel good. Because I'm far too familiar with the alternative."

So was she, even if it wasn't in the same way. She was familiar with loss. With normal, everyday moments being twisted and turned, becoming defining moments when you least expected them to. Days that had started out sunny turning into the darkest of nightmares.

She took the spoon out of his hand and dipped it into the honey bowl, then popped it into her mouth, sliding it back out again slowly. And then something else hit her. Because yes, she had shared a cup with Alex—twice now—but in those cases she had not pressed her lips to the exact same place his had been.

Right now, her mouth was following the exact same path as his just had.

That hollow feeling in her chest spread downward to her stomach, and then down lower still. The spoon suddenly felt warmer in her mouth, as though she could still feel the heat he'd left behind.

She removed it quickly then.

"Live fast. Die young," she choked out.

"Eat honey. Hell, yeah."

She laughed, pressing her hand to her forehead and resting her elbow on the table, the giggles escaping somewhat helplessly. "It's not funny," she said, wiping a tear from her cheek. "I know too many people who died too young for it to be funny. To even pretend."

She wondered then if the tear had been from the laughter, or from something else.

"That's the thing," he said. "We know. We know that we aren't guaranteed a long ride. So it's best to make it a fun ride, right?"

She nodded slowly, and looked down at the bread in front of her. She wasn't sure she resembled that mindset at all. She didn't live any kind of blissfully, blindingly fun existence. Mostly, she just had *an* existence.

She had small pleasures, sure. Little things. Quiet things. Nothing resembling loud and reckless.

But hey, she had asked Asher on a date. That was something, right? It was new, at least. Something she hadn't done before.

"Yeah," she said, her voice sounding rough. She lifted up the bread and took a bite, chewing slowly as she set it back down on the plate in front of her.

Alex leaned forward in his chair, his hand extended, and he brushed his thumb across the corner of her lip. It felt like getting punched in the stomach, except it wasn't painful, just impactful. And hot somehow. As if all the heat from his skin had magnified, intensified, beneath hers, traveling down through her limbs, pooling in her stomach. Lower.

And then he drew his hand back and pressed his thumb to his own lips, sticking his tongue out and sliding it along the edge of it.

"You had a little honey," he said, "just there on your mouth."

She was shaking. But she was pretty sure it was only happening on the inside. Where she felt like she was about to experience an eruption of some kind.

She had never felt anything quite like this. Anticipation of…something. Hot and cold. A little bit sick to her stomach. Unsettled. Anxious for something she couldn't put a name to.

"Thank you," she said finally, because she had to say something, didn't she? Otherwise it would look weird. He would know how weird it was. How weird she felt.

That she could still feel his touch against her skin.

"No problem," he responded.

He stood suddenly, pushing his chair back almost violently. "I should go. I've got work to do at my own place tomorrow. So I won't see you."

"Okay," she said, feeling slightly numb.

"Okay. I'll pick up Lane's dishes later."

"Wait! Don't forget her honey." Clara scrambled up from her seat and lurched toward the cupboard, taking out a small mason jar and bringing it back over to the table. She efficiently spooned honey into the jar, picking up the bowl and tipping it, pouring the rest in before screwing a lid in place and extending her hand to offer it to Alex.

He reached out and took it, his fingertips brushing against hers as he did. Rough. His hands were rough. Probably from all the hard work he did. On the ranch. In the military before that. She wondered if Asher's hands were rough. But then, she didn't know why they would be. Unless he had a secret woodworking hobby when he wasn't making coffee.

It wasn't like she needed a man's hands to be rough.

Those words caught in her brain and began to swirl around in a circle. Need. Man.

What exactly did she think she needed from a man anyway?

She didn't have any specific images to go with that. She only had a feeling. A hot, hollowed-out feeling that made her skin feel too tight.

She didn't need anything. She had gone out of her way to not need anybody for a very long time. It wasn't about need. It was like Alex had just said. What was the point of living a long life if it wasn't a good life? If you didn't enjoy it.

No. There wasn't anything like need on the table here.

Except it was the word that kept echoing in her brain as that touch of Alex's fingertips to hers reverberated through her entire body.

*Need. Need. Need.*

She swallowed hard, that sensation that lingered, remained and was spreading.

"When will I see you again?" she asked. "That

came out a little more dramatically than I meant." She grimaced. "I just meant...when will you come back?"

"Day after tomorrow. I'll check in. Did you want me to come by tomorrow night for dinner? Or...did you need help with anything else? I can take some of your mail home and sort through it."

She looked at the stack of envelopes on the counter. "No. I can do it. Thank you."

He nodded once. "Of course. Whatever you need, Clara. Whatever you need from me, you know I'm going to be here to give it to you."

There was that word again. *Need.* Spoken right from those lips, those lips that she was so utterly captivated by. In his voice, that voice that seemed to echo around inside her body. In his eyes...green like the trees and so serious she couldn't help but take everything he said straight to heart.

She opened her mouth to tell him she didn't *need* anything. But those words wouldn't come out. Because right now those words felt like a lie. "Thank you, Alex. I'll remember that."

And then he nodded once and turned and walked out of the house, the honey jar clutched in his large hand.

His *rough* hand.

She turned away from the door, determined not to keep watch over his going. Not to keep looking like a sad puppy watching her owner leave the house.

She started to put the pasta away, started to gather up the bread and wrap it in some Saran Wrap so she could store it. And she wondered. She wondered if more than just his fingers had calluses. If his palms were rough, as well. And what that might feel like against her hand. Against her skin.

Against her bare back…

She gasped, tore a chunk off the loaf of bread and stuffed it into her mouth, as though the distraction of eating might do something to turn the tide of her thoughts.

She pressed her palms flat against the counter and lowered her head, looking to the side, seeing that big old pile of mail. It made her throat feel tight. Filled her with a sense of dread. She didn't make any sense. There was something so desperately wrong with her. So incredibly off. That she couldn't open her mail. That Alex was making her feel dizzy and off balance.

Like she had questions about things only he could answer. Like what rough hands might feel like against soft, naked skin. His hands. Her skin.

She lifted her hands, pressed balled-up fists to her eyes, took a moment to catch her breath.

That thinking was just crazy. And it had nothing to do with what she wanted out of life. Life was short. They had just been talking about that. And she knew what she wanted to do with hers. Wanted to fashion this ranch into something that could be hers. That could be hers and maybe even Asher's. Yes, she knew that harboring fantasies of marrying the guy was a little bit nuts when they'd never even been on a date.

But it wasn't like she thought too deeply about that. It wasn't actually about the future. It was about now. Because going into the coffee shop and seeing him every morning was a bright spot. Because it made life feel normal, and a little bit warmer. It made her feel not so alone.

It also kept her from *needing*.

And to a degree, it kept her from reality. Alex kept bringing up the fact that Asher didn't know she hated coffee.

Was her excuse for keeping that from him really what she kept telling herself? Really what she kept telling Alex? Or was it an extension of that fantasy situation? The one where she didn't have to deal with the life she had and got to spin herself stories about the life she maybe could have had.

About the kind of food she might have enjoyed if she hadn't grown up on canned goods because of a sick mother and an inept father who didn't know how to do anything beyond use a can opener. Because she had then been left with a brother who had to work constantly to keep them afloat, and who wasn't any better at cooking than their old man had been.

Because all she'd ever known were rough, practical men, and something about Asher seemed different, and that felt… Well, sometimes it felt like eating a spoonful of straight honey. Good.

And maybe it didn't have a place in her life, but part of her wanted it anyway. Part of her wanted him to fit. Wanted to make herself fit. So she could have a different life than one marred by hardship and tragedy.

Alex's rough hands, easy smile and dirty mouth didn't have a place in that.

He was too much a part of all of this. Too much a part of Jason and the ranch and a life she already knew about. Sadness. Loneliness.

She took a deep breath. She didn't even know why she was thinking of him in these terms. Yes, there was something when he touched her. Something that felt a lot like temptation. The kind of temptation she had never felt before, wanted before, faced before.

But she didn't especially understand what she was supposed to do with that, or why her brain was taking it seriously at all. Why she kept trying to compare and contrast Alex—as if she wanted remotely the same thing with Alex as she did with Asher. She didn't. She couldn't. She wouldn't.

She scrubbed her eyes, trying to alleviate the stinging sensation behind her lids.

Today had been a good day. It really had been. She had shown Alex the bees and he had maybe even understood a little about what she was doing here, about her ability to take care of herself.

About the fact that she didn't need him.

And if he didn't believe it, maybe it would just serve as a reminder to herself.

It would have to.

## CHAPTER EIGHT

"So, EXPLAIN TO ME again exactly what you're doing on the Campbell ranch?"

Alex had been expecting the question from his half brother Finn, but he hadn't expected Liam to care what was going on at all. Mostly because ranching wasn't really Liam's forte, in spite of the fact that he had thrown himself fully into the Laughing Irish operation a few months back, like the rest of them had.

Alex had the feeling Liam was just here because he didn't know what the hell else to do with himself. Not because he had any particular love for the spread. Or for the work.

But now that they were in the barn, the milking machines hooked up to the cows, Liam seemed chatty about all things rural.

"Well, I just placed a large order of bison," Alex said.

"Bison?" Liam asked. "What the hell?"

Alex turned to look at his older brother—his older brother who hadn't been taller than him in quite some time. They weren't all that far apart in age, but for years, Liam had been bigger, stronger. And then Alex had caught up. Caught up, but never exceeded. The two of them were both over six feet now, and could look each other right in the eye. And of the two of them, Alex had more experience with an AK.

"It's a logical solution to Clara's cash flow issues," he explained.

"I thought there was a payout from the military when a family member was killed."

Alex lifted a brow. "Did you look into that when I enlisted?"

"Hell no." Liam shook his head emphatically. "I bet Mom did, though."

Ouch. And damn. And probably true.

The mention of their mother killed the conversation for a moment. He and Liam didn't have a lot in common. Not really. But they did have their terrible upbringing to bond them.

Though, in truth, it hadn't really done much to bring them closer. In fact, it had done a pretty damn good job of driving them apart. Because both of them had left home the minute it was possible, and hadn't looked back. Still, they'd seen each other off and on over the years, even if they hadn't exactly been each other's confidants. And they gravitated toward doing things together now they were back in each other's lives. Still, that was drinking and talking smack. It wasn't really heart-to-heart stuff.

"Yeah," Alex said finally. "It's probably kind of a drag for her that I came back in one piece. I would've been worth more in a box."

"To her maybe," Liam said. "Not to me."

His brother rocked back on his heels and stared over at the cows, pretending to be engrossed in the milking. Which Alex knew he definitely was not.

"Wow." Alex cleared his throat. "That was border-line sensitive bullshit, man."

"Don't get used to it." Liam grabbed hold of a rake and started clearing away stray bits of hay and cow crap. "So. Is that all that's happening with Clara? Bison? Because she's hot."

Alex scowled at the mention of his charge. "She's twenty-one," he said, as if that should put his thirty-three-year-old brother off the scent immediately.

Liam looked unabashed. "So? Doesn't bother me any. She's my type."

"You talk a good game, Liam, but we both know you aren't getting laid. We both know that the only time your head turns is when Sabrina Leighton walks by."

Sabrina Leighton was a topic that was off-limits, and Alex damn well knew it. Even if Liam had never said so, all the Donnellys knew it. They'd witnessed a few extremely awkward encounters between the two of them over the past few months, and though Liam had never admitted it, it was clear something had happened at some point.

Alex knew he was being an asshole. But it was stress relieving. Stress relieving in a way that milking cows could never be.

"Old news," Liam said.

"And yet, that old news seems to be the only news you want to read."

"She's hot too," Liam said, his expression blank, shuttered. But then, that was typical of his brother. "I'm not neutral to her."

"And let me guess, you hit that before." Alex hated himself in that moment. He was such a dick.

Liam's expression turned to stone. It was rare that he saw his brother angry. He wasn't effusive in his attempts at seeming normal like Alex was, but he had never given off quite the same angry vibe that Cain, their oldest brother, did. But in this moment, he was positively radiating with murderous intent.

"I never touched her," he said, his voice hard. "And you don't get to talk about her like that. You don't know anything about it, or about me."

"I don't know anything about you because you've never told me anything," Alex said.

Because Liam had been distant since he'd left home at eighteen. And he seemed to like it that way.

*Keep smiling.*

That was the only advice he'd ever gotten from Liam. Even after their dad left.

"Right. But you talk about your life, so clearly I should get on that sharing and caring stuff."

Alex shrugged. "My friend got shot to death. I inherited the responsibility of his ranch, albeit temporarily. I'm ordering bison. Good talk."

Liam shook his head. "Are all brothers this dysfunctional, you think? I mean, do all men have this much trouble communicating with each other?" The question caught Alex off-guard, since Liam had seemed opposed to any deep bonding only a moment earlier.

"I don't know a lot about your life from when you left home, Liam. Did you get a philosophy degree I wasn't aware of?"

"No. Just wondering."

"Clara is a nice girl," Alex said finally. He looked over at the gauge on the milking machine and pre-

tended to check it. "And she's alone. I think that
sucks. I want her to feel less alone. And I owe her
brother. Believe me when I say that."

"What happened?"

Alex was on the verge of telling him. He could. If
anyone would get it, the whole story and how Alex felt
about Jason's death, he imagined it would be Liam.
Because Liam's roots had grown out of the same poison soil as Alex's. His half brothers were his blood,
there was no question about that. But they had grown
up separately. They had grown up in different circumstances.

Liam knew. He knew exactly where Alex had
come from. He knew exactly why Alex was the way
he was. And Alex knew the same about him.

But Jason's death, and the circumstances surrounding it, didn't feel like something he was prepared to
share. In large part because he felt like when he finally did talk about it, Clara was probably the first
person he should tell.

It wasn't his tragedy. That was the thing. Regardless of how he felt about it, he was the one who was
alive.

"Not something I feel like talking about."

Liam nodded once. He didn't press. Not because he
was sensitive, Alex imagined, but because he didn't
want Alex treading on his own sacred ground.

"Okay," Liam said. "Is the Campbell ranch going
to become your new project?"

"What do you mean? I already told you, I'm com-
mitted to helping Clara out, just like her brother asked
me to."

"I mean are you going to abandon the Laughing Irish and make the Campbell spread your focus?"

Alex took a deep breath, looked out the open doors of the barn at the mountains and the thin band of gold that lined their edges as the sun began to rise.

"Of course not," he said. "This is ours. The only damn thing our family name ever gave us. I'm not going to abandon it. Ever."

He hadn't stayed in one place too long since he'd been a kid. By design.

"Good. You should stay here. You deserve it," Liam said. "Our bastard father certainly never gave us anything."

A whole backlog of words got bottled up in Alex's throat. He had a lot to say about what their father had given them. About what having him in their lives had done. To them. To their mother. But then, maybe their mother would have been the same, no matter what.

But the fact that James Donnelly's favorite pastime was having children and the fact that Mira Donnelly had given birth to two of them had made her feel like she had a claim on that man. And that Liam and Alex were her ultimate trump card.

That was all they were. Pawns in the games their parents played.

"Well, now we're the ones with this place," Alex said. "An apology from our grandfather for raising such an asshole of a son?"

Liam's mouth tipped upward into a smile. "I'd like to think so."

"Why are you here, Liam?"

There was a long pause. "I might ask you the same question."

"Because I'm done with the military. Because I watched my friend die." He looked up and met his brother's gaze. "And I can't do that again. Because I wanted to do something real. Save the world. And now I'm questioning whether or not I accomplished anything at all. But here…at least here you can see the results of your work. Helping Clara, well, it feels like something. I'm a man who doesn't feel like he has a hell of a lot."

Liam nodded. "I've spent a lot of years making a lot of money, Alex," he said slowly. "That felt good for a while. It felt like progress. It felt like it mattered. But then I just kind of came to the end of it. I can't even describe it. I set out to make something of myself, and somewhere along the way I forgot why I was doing it." He shook his head, laughing. "And then I realized there wasn't a reason at all. There wasn't anyone who gave a damn. Not even me."

"So you came here?"

"I figured it was as good a time as any to try and find a damn to give."

"Have you found it yet?"

"I found maybe half a damn. I figure eventually I'll find the rest."

Alex looked at Liam. Really looked at him. He had deep grooves bracketing his mouth, new lines by his green eyes. His brother looked tired. Older. And for the first time, Alex thought maybe Liam was the one who'd had it hardest the past few years. Yeah, Alex had lived through war. And that wasn't a small thing. But for a while, at least he'd felt like he mattered. He'd felt like what he was doing mattered. And there were plenty of people who reinforced that feeling. Who thanked him for his service. He was a veteran, part of something bigger than himself. A band of brothers and sisters, servants of their country.

Liam had…well, he had to wonder if Liam had just felt alone all this time.

"Well, we can always go shovel some cow shit and see if you can find the other half buried under there somewhere."

Liam laughed. "Sounds good. Well, not good, but…at this point, I guess it sounds like life."

Alex nodded. "I guess it is."

Right about now, this life seemed like a pretty good thing.

# CHAPTER NINE

SHE HAD NARROWED it down to three outfits. Which she thought, with a week's notice, was pretty good.

Clara growled and stared at her bed. There was option one, a pair of skinny jeans and a soft-looking gray shirt, which she thought might send the message she wasn't trying too hard. And then there was a white maxi dress, which she was a little afraid made her look like she was applying for the position of *bride*. Finally, at the end of the row was a yellow sundress that was adorable and bright, but Clara had concerns about being chilly if the wind whipped up.

It was sunny outside currently, but the forecast had promised rain would roll in eventually in the evening, and typically when rain was promised on the Oregon coast, rain eventuated. Oftentimes, even when rain wasn't called for, it eventuated. Basically, one always had to be prepared for rain.

She started to pace, feeling more than a little worked up. She was meeting Asher in the parking lot of Stim in just over an hour. She had put each outfit on approximately ten times over the course of the week. She had put them on at least three times today.

Clara looked over at her phone, which was sitting on the bed, the screen dark. It wasn't back in service yet. But her landline was. And she did have Sabrina's number in it.

She felt a little guilty about calling Sabrina to ask for advice when it wasn't like she confided in Sabrina about much of anything. And she hadn't taken her up on her offer to go and hang out after work yet.

Maybe this would be the olive branch. Apparently, date panic spurred you out of isolation faster than just about anything else.

Clara picked up the cell phone and opened her address book, scrolling until she found Sabrina's number. Then she grabbed the landline and dialed.

Sabrina answered on the second ring.

"Hello?"

"Sabrina? It's Clara."

"Clara! What number is this?"

"My home number. My cell phone isn't…working. I just had a question to ask you. I know it's random. But I have a date tonight and I can't choose what to wear."

"Your cell phone isn't working?"

She winced. "No."

"Darn. If it were, I'd have had you send me mirror selfies."

Well that would have been convenient. "Sorry."

"No. Don't apologize. Where are you going?"

"Actually, we're going to the dinner at Grassroots tonight."

There was a small pause. "Do you actually…like anything on the menu?"

Clara's face heated. "Not really. But he wanted to go out, and that is definitely the kind of thing he's into, so I figured I should aim for an activity he'll enjoy. Sadly, kale salad is kind of in his wheelhouse."

There was another pause. "Really? I didn't peg Alex for being a kale guy."

Clara's heart slammed against her breastbone. "Alex? Who said anything about Alex? I have a date with Asher. Asher Martin, the barista at Stim."

"Oh." Sabrina sounded legitimately surprised. "I just thought… I mean, after I saw you with Alex the other morning…"

"I knew you saw that. But I promise, there's nothing happening with Alex and me. I mean, not like that. He's…he's kind of old."

Sabrina snorted. "Um. He is not."

"He's my…well, he was my brother's age."

"He's still hot," Sabrina pointed out. "All the Donnellys are. Sadly. But had you been going out with Alex I would have issued you a pretty stern warning." Clara heard Sabrina let out a long, slow sigh on the other end of the phone. "I know Alex isn't his brother. But you have to figure that two guys who grew up together probably have quite a bit in common."

"And Liam hurt you," Clara said, pushing a little further than she normally would have.

"Yes," Sabrina said. "I promise I'm not usually such a psycho about it. But, with him being back in town, and the town itself being so small…it's been a little challenging. Just… I would hate for you to make any assumptions and end up getting hurt. That's all."

"Alex isn't like that," Clara said. She wasn't sure why she should feel defensive of Alex. Except, he had never done anything to her. He was here, trying to help her take care of the ranch, trying to do what

Jason had asked of him. She didn't know Liam at all, but she was sure that Alex didn't deserve to be tarred with the same brush as his brother. Particularly not over something that had happened years ago.

"Not that it matters," Sabrina said. "Because you have a date with Asher?"

"No. It doesn't matter to me. Except that Alex is kind of…a friend. He's been helping me, and I appreciate it."

"Well, that's good. Now, what are your clothing choices?"

Clara took a breath. "Okay. I have a white maxi dress…"

"Too bridal. He won't be able to handle it."

Clara laughed. "That was my concern. Then I have jeans and a T-shirt, which I thought maybe said I wasn't trying very hard."

"Sure. And that is pretty good logic. But are you trying?"

"I am trying *so* hard," Clara said. "I want him to like me *so much*."

"Option three?"

"A short yellow dress. Maybe with boots."

"Short dress. Go for it. I think that'll send the right message."

Clara picked up the fluttery, yellow item of clothing. "Yes. Except, I'm afraid that it might be too cold for the dress. And, if I wear it in spite of the cold, it looks like I'm trying to show off my legs."

"Well…are you trying to show off your legs?"

Clara made an exasperated sound. "Can you stop being so logical, please?"

"There is nothing wrong with showing a little leg, Clara. No matter the weather."

"Fine. I'll wear the yellow dress."

She held it up in front of her, and turned and looked in the mirror. Anticipation tightened her chest.

"It's sexy," she said finally. Helplessly.

"Isn't that a good thing?"

"I don't know. I don't think of myself as sexy. I've never tried to be sexy." That was potentially a little more revealing than she had intended it to be. But she had called Sabrina with date panic, so she was unloading all of the date panic.

"There's nothing wrong with being sexy," Sabrina said. "Not that I have a lot of experience with that either. But, honestly, at least one of us should be going out and having a good time."

"Thanks," Clara said, feeling increasingly nervous. "Okay. I have to go. I have to…get sexy, I guess."

She got off the phone and turned her efforts toward getting dressed, getting her hair in order—not that it ever did anything. It just kind of hung there, limp and pale—and doing some basic makeup.

She grabbed a denim jacket—something that would look all right with the dress in case it got chilly—and took one last look in the mirror before she headed out of her bedroom and toward the living area.

She took her purse off the peg and walked out onto the porch, just as Alex's truck pulled into the driveway. Her heart tripped and fell, all the way down into her stomach, seeming to hit every rib on the way down.

She had not intended for Alex to see her in this

dress. He got out of the truck and slammed the door, then just stopped.

He looked at her, his eyes flickering for a moment, his jaw tight. She stood there, frozen. Like a deer caught in the headlights.

Or just a woman, caught by Alex's intense stare.

"Where you headed?" he asked.

"I have a date," she responded, trying her best to keep her face blank.

Alex's dark brows locked together. "He's not picking you up?"

"No. I'm meeting him."

Alex huffed out a laugh, crossing his arms over his broad chest. Saying nothing.

Clara scowled. "What, Alex? If you have a comment, go ahead and make it."

"When I go on a date, I pick a woman up," he said. "That's all."

"Great. Well, that's not what we are doing. Sadly, I didn't ask for your help coordinating the date. So I'm going to go. What are you doing here, anyway? It's Sunday night."

He lifted a shoulder. "When I go on a date, I pick the woman up, and when I commit to taking care of a ranch, I commit to taking care of it, no matter what day of the week it is."

"Good to know."

He looked her up and down, his expression disapproving, a muscle in his cheek jumping. "You're going to get cold."

Just like that, she released her hold on her denim jacket, dropping it into the chair on the porch. "No, I won't. I'm going to be fine."

She walked toward her car, taking long steps, not caring that her dress was flaring up well past her knees.

A large, warm hand wrapped around her upper arm, stopping her in her tracks. His whole hand was rough. She had wondered. And now she knew.

She turned toward him, her eyes clashing with his. Right now, they didn't make her think of the evergreen trees that covered the mountains around them. No. Those were cool, stately. Right now, his gaze was anything but cool. It burned. Burned straight through her.

"What?" she asked, her voice coming out much thinner, much huskier than she had intended it to.

"Have fun," he said, releasing his hold on her.

"I will. I'm going to have the most fun. The most fun ever." She jerked open her car door and got inside, and she didn't question the way her heart hammered in her throat, or the fact that her hands were shaking.

It was just excitement. It was just because of Asher. That was all.

KALE TASTED LIKE dirt and sadness.

And the dinner was beautiful. It really was. There was one long table set up in one of the old barns at Grassroots, gorgeous rustic centerpieces, candles and Christmas lights making the entire place glow.

Asher, for his part, looked handsome, with his man bun and black, slim-cut pants, paired with a blazer.

None of it helped her choke down the kale salad. Or the beets that were served with some kind of stringy microgreen and aerated goat cheese that tasted like a barnyard. The dinner was fish and she had nearly died trying to choke it down.

Maybe that was an overstatement.

But the real tragedy was dessert.

The only thing on offer to drink was coffee and tea—neither of which she liked, so she had ended up with just hot water, leaving her tea bag discreetly to the side—and the dessert itself, the one thing that she had thought would be safe, was, well, it wasn't dessert.

Because in absolutely no world was dessert a no-sugar-added blanched pear with whipped goat cheese and basil.

"This is so nice," said the woman sitting next to Clara.

That was her other gripe with the evening. They were sitting with strangers. At one long table. She didn't want to make conversation with strangers. She had wanted the chance to make conversation with Asher. But apparently, Asher was super friendly and thought nothing of bringing said total strangers into their loop.

"It is," Asher agreed. "I really don't like sweet desserts."

Clara blinked. "What other…kind of dessert…is there?"

Asher laughed, as though what she had said was the funniest thing he'd ever heard. She would give him that, he did seem interested in what she had to say. It was just that over the course of the evening she had rarely known what to say. Fortunately, Asher and their dinner companions didn't suffer from that. They talked, Clara hid her food. In a napkin, in a potted plant. Wherever.

"There's this kind of dessert," he said, smiling that dazzling smile of his. Honestly, he must use whitening strips or something.

"It's definitely…original," she said, pushing at the squishy pear with the back of her spoon.

Honestly, they might as well have just called it a plate of *disappointment* with a scoop of *hell no* and a garnish of *why God why*.

He was watching her intently now, looking at her mouth. The way that she had been watching Alex's mouth the past few times she had seen him.

She frowned. She didn't want to think about Alex. She definitely didn't want to think about the way he had acted at the house just before she had left for her date. Or the way she had felt when he had curved his fingers around her arm, left that impression of his hand behind.

The woman next to her, and her date, started to make conversation with Asher about types of pears and the importance of eating local and organic food.

Well, in fairness, Clara imagined that they were talking to her too, it was just that she had absolutely nothing to contribute to that conversation.

But, while Asher was distracted, she took a large scoop out of the side of the pear and lowered her spoon, then flicked the bite across the barn and into a small, potted tree.

Her lips twitched, and she felt somewhat satisfied with her successful slam dunk of unwanted food.

She smiled vaguely and nodded through the rest of the dinner, and when everyone around her was finished, Asher looked at her half demolished pear and frowned.

"Didn't you like it?" he asked.

"It was great. But I'm just so full." That was a lie. It was a filthy lie. She was so hungry she thought she was going to die.

She would possibly give her right arm for some Chef Boyardee. Or a steak. Just a simple steak with salt and pepper. And it could be local or organic or whatever, as long as it was beef.

"Cool," he said.

She had no idea how to respond to that.

They had driven over to Grassroots together from Stim, which meant they were going to have to go back down together too. And for some reason, she felt uncomfortable with that now. Felt awkward. Maybe because it was the end of the date and that had potential expectation to it.

As they walked out of the barn and headed toward his car, she realized she wasn't sure how she felt about those expectations.

The air felt heavy, the scent of salt and brine coming in off the water suddenly stronger. And then a fat raindrop landed on her bare shoulder and she shivered. That made her think of Alex too. Stupid Alex.

He was the reason she didn't have a jacket. Because he had goaded her.

She got into Asher's car, and looked at his profile. And she realized that she didn't want to kiss him. Not even a little bit. She didn't want to make out with him on her couch.

And that felt like Alex's fault too.

Because he made her skin feel hot, and she felt

compelled to look at his mouth. Because she had questions about his mouth. Like how it would feel pressed against hers.

Suddenly, she wanted to cry. This was just stupid. It was so stupid. She was on a date with the man of her dreams. The man who had been the man of her dreams for the past four months.

Seeing him, talking to him, had been the one bright spot in this hideous haze of grief. And she finally had a date with him. She should be happy. It should make her happy. She should want to kiss Asher. She should want to sleep with Asher.

She didn't. She didn't want any of that.

She swallowed hard, trying to keep from crying there in the car.

Asher plugged his phone in, and then messed with the screen until music started playing over the speakers. It didn't sound like singing. It sounded like whining. Like howling. Which in all honesty fit. Because she felt like howling too.

"Have you ever heard The Fox Tales?"

She assumed that was who they were listening to now. "No," she said.

"Yeah, I'm not surprised," he responded. "They're kind of an obscure band out of Eugene. I got really into them after I saw them open for Far from Ashes."

She put her hand to her forehead and rubbed it slowly. "Cool."

She wondered if that was why he had said that same word earlier. Because there had been absolutely nothing else to say. She didn't know how to talk to him, and she had no idea how to fix that. It had been fine, making small talk with him when she got her coffee at Stim. And she managed to talk to Alex just fine.

*Alex.*

Why did she keep thinking about Alex?

They were mostly quiet on the drive down to the coffeehouse, and when they pulled into the parking lot, Clara scrambled out comically quickly. But she just couldn't face a long, awkward moment where there were questions about whether or not they would kiss each other.

When she looked back down into the car, she could see that Asher was somewhat surprised by that. He looked…well, he looked almost amused. But he didn't say anything.

"Thank you," she said. "For dinner."

"Did you enjoy it?"

"It was fantastic."

"Great. Maybe we can do it again next time they have one of those dinners? Or I could always take us over to Eugene. Actually, the band I was just talking about is playing there again soon, and they have some great farm-to-table restaurants there."

She had acted weird, and she had declined to kiss him, and now, he was escalating the kind of date they might go on. One that included a road trip a couple hours away.

A date that sounded almost literally like her worst nightmare.

"Yeah. Maybe when I come in for coffee…"

"Sure," he said, keeping his tone casual. "That sounds awesome."

She tried to force a smile, then waved before turning and walking to her car. The rain was falling in earnest now, hitting her bare shoulders and rolling down her arms, making her shiver. She got into the car, pressing her hand against her forehead and pushing raindrops from her eyes.

She sat there for a moment, letting the heater warm up, watching as Asher drove away.

She hadn't kissed him. She had been difficult, almost impossible to make conversation with. And he wanted to go out with her again.

She pressed her head against the steering wheel. "He likes you, you idiot."

He really did. He liked her back. At least, he liked the idea of who she was, based on what she had shown him. And she…she didn't feel anything. She kept thinking about Alex. And his stupid lips. His green eyes. His big, rough hands. His particular brand of rampant masculinity that should absolutely not be her type at all.

Alex wasn't a fantasy. He wasn't an escape. He was too real for that. Too big, too hard…too Alex.

Rage began to bubble up in her chest, and as she put the car in Drive, she gritted her teeth, trying to hold back the growl that was building inside of her. This was his fault. All of it. She had been fine before he had come. And if Alex weren't around then things with Asher would have been amazing. She wouldn't have had Alex in the back of her head goading her about Asher not knowing she didn't like coffee. She wouldn't have visions of him, superimposed over the man right in front of her. The man who was actually on a date with her.

The man who had gone out with her because he

wanted to, and not the man who was around just because her brother had told him to be.

Shaking, she drove back to the house, praying that when she got there, Alex would be gone. Because all she wanted to do was strip off her damp dress, climb into a hot shower and wash all of this disappointment off. To start again. To go and get a coffee from Asher tomorrow morning and make plans with him to go to that ridiculous concert.

When she pulled into the driveway, she saw Alex's truck was still there. She cursed. Loudly.

Then she found herself getting out of the car, nearly stumbling as she walked down the now muddy path toward the barn. The light was on, so she thought there was a pretty good chance he was in there. He wasn't. But the back door was open, so she walked through the structure and continued on through.

"Alex?" She shouted his name, not caring if she was subtle. Not caring about much of anything. She had no idea what she was going to say. She just knew that she felt like she was going to explode. She was so angry, and he had to answer for it. He had ruined her date. Absolutely ruined it. And she was not going to let him get away with that.

The field behind the barn was more or less barren, and the light was getting dimmer and dimmer, the sun sinking behind the mountains, a sliver of rose gold casting dramatic reflections on the overcast sky.

The rain was falling hard and fast, and her yellow dress was clinging to her skin, the raindrops running down her legs and into her boots. Her hair was soaked, hanging lank and stringy down her back.

And she was shivering. She could really use that denim jacket.

That made her mad at Alex all over again.

And then he came walking into view. His white cowboy hat on his head, his denim shirt clinging to his broad chest, the top few buttons open, showing a wedge of muscular body, water sluicing down and disappearing beneath the fabric.

"I have a bone to pick with you, Alex Donnelly," she said, walking toward him.

He looked at her, his expression no less stormy than the weather around them. "Oh, do you?" He sounded tense. Out of patience with her. And for the life of her she couldn't figure out why he would be irritated with her.

"Yes. I do."

"Did you have a good time on your date?" he asked, his words hard.

"No," she said, the words vibrating through her. "No, I didn't. And that's why I'm mad at you."

"You're mad at me because you had a terrible date with a man you have nothing in common with? You're out of touch with reality, Clara."

"I am not. I like him. It doesn't make any sense that the date would be so... I was bored, Alex. Bored, and I didn't even want him to kiss me. And he would have kissed me. He would have. I would have gotten my first kiss tonight." Alex jerked slightly when she said those words, a flash of surprise in his eyes. "Except I didn't want it."

"Clara," he said, his voice sounding like a warning.

She wasn't going to take his warning. He could take it. And he could shove it.

"You ruined it. You've ruined this. You were in my head the entire time, and it isn't fair."

"Do you want to know why the date was terrible? It's because you don't actually like him. And he doesn't like you. You don't know him, and you've never given him a chance to even find out if he might want to know you. All he wants is locally sourced kale-based bullshit. And you," he said, taking a step toward her, reaching up and pulling off his hat as he did, "you have the palate of a five-year-old."

"Yeah, so what? You make fun of me for having the palate of a five-year-old. It's not like you accept me for who I am."

"But you'll tell me to fuck off. With him, you drink coffee you hate and go to some fancy dinner that serves nothing you eat, when what you really want is a hamburger. With him, I imagine you listen to music that sounds like coyotes being beaten to death by a classical guitar, even though we both know you like Luke Bryan. You don't do anything you like with him, you can't eat anything you like with him, you're not even a person that you like with him. How can you possibly be surprised that you didn't have fun with him?"

"I wanted to!" She was screaming at him now, right up in his face. "I wanted to enjoy that stupid dinner. And I wish I liked kale. I want to like it. I probably would have if I didn't grow up eating canned food. I want to be normal. I want to be like other people my age. People like him. I wanted to go on a date and get a kiss. Maybe more. But you know what? I didn't want the stupid kale. And that dessert…it was an abomination. It was my one and only hope, and they served fruit and cheese. That isn't dessert. And I was surrounded by people who acted like that was somehow preferable to a piece of cake. I know what I should want. I should want kale. But I just want the cake, Alex."

Suddenly, she felt exhausted. She felt sad. She felt defeated.

"This was supposed to be my moment to eat honey with the spoon," she said, not even entirely sure what she was trying to say anymore. "But it wasn't."

Alex took another step toward her, his green eyes glittering, the raindrops rolling down his face. And then he reached out, curving his arm around her waist, his hand, big and warm on her lower back. And he was looking at her, really looking at her, like he could see inside of her.

Like he could see that she had fantasies about his mouth that she hadn't even allowed herself to fully comprehend. Like he could see that her breasts were aching and her nipples were tight. Like he could tell that she ached between her thighs in a way that was entirely foreign to her.

"Honey is for beginners," he said, his voice rough. "If you want the cake, Clara, have the cake."

"I don't… I can't…" She didn't know what she was trying to say, and more than that, she didn't know quite what she wanted to do. But then, she didn't have to.

Because then, Alex closed the distance between them and captured her lips with his.

## CHAPTER TEN

INSANITY. THAT'S WHAT IT was. At least, that's what he should think it was. But the moment his lips touched Clara's, he lost the ability to care about sane, crazy, right or wrong.

Her skin was slick with rain, and hot with *her*—so perfect and alive—and he didn't much care if it was crazy.

The entire time she had been on that damn date, he had been burning rage off like a man possessed. He had pounded nails, chopped wood and ripped fence posts out of the ground with his bare hands. And when a sliver had driven itself deep in his palm he had been glad. Because at least that had forced his mind clean for a moment. Blank.

Had given him a few moments' peace instead of the mental torment that came with imagining Clara out with that douche bag.

Captain No Dick and his too-tight pants.

He should be glad for her. Glad that she was out on a date with him. Because he was exactly what she needed. Probably. Close to her age. The kind of guy who didn't take things too seriously. In a good way. The kind of guy she could have some fun with.

Except that had forced him to think about the kind of fun a guy like that would want to have. And how there was no damn way he was worthy of a woman like Clara.

Not that Alex was either. And he shouldn't be thinking about her in those terms. But every time he imagined Asher putting his hands on her, putting his lips on her, Alex couldn't help but imagine himself beating the hell out of the guy, then pulling Clara into his arms.

And now he had done it. Well, he hadn't had to beat up her date, but he had pulled her into his arms. And now he was kissing her, exactly like he had forced himself to never fantasize about.

Oh, he had started to. Had wanted to. Had felt that hard, tight knot in his gut demanding that he turn that vague arousal into a full-fledged fantasy. But he hadn't allowed himself to do it. No. He had embraced denial. He had embraced good behavior.

Screw that.

Now he was kissing her. Deep and hard, and exactly the wrong way to kiss a woman who'd just confessed that she had never been kissed before.

She'd never been kissed before. That reality roared through him like a triumph and that should make him feel ashamed. But he didn't. He couldn't.

Rain was pounding against the back of his neck, rolling down his shirt collar, soaking him clear through to the bone, but he barely felt it. He was on fire inside, so if the rain did anything, it just kept him from turning to ash right where he stood.

Maybe the kiss had started out as an attempt to show her something. To teach her a lesson about attraction. To show her that no amount of pretending to like kale and coffee would ever replace real, raw desire.

But the moment their lips touched that had burned away. And it became about him. About what he wanted. About what he had barely allowed himself to admit he wanted.

Except, no matter how firm he'd been with himself when it came to not forming the words in his mind, he'd always known it would be like this if he touched her.

He'd known if they kissed, it would teach her more about desire than a lecture ever could. He'd known—deep down—that if he ever took her in his arms, he would make sure he erased Asher's name from her brain.

Because this thing between them was powerful. Had been from that day in the parking lot at Stim. He was pretty damn sure there had been something there when he saw her at the funeral. But then both of them had been consumed by grief, and it had manifested itself in the form of a dull, hard ache that had bloomed in his chest and spread outward. The deep desire to make sure she was taken care of, to give her something, to help her in some way.

The truth was, the ferocity of that feeling had shocked him. As had the feeling of being unequal to the task. And maybe that was why he had avoided Clara for so many months since coming back to town.

Or maybe it was this. Maybe it had always been this.

He parted from her for a moment, taking in the sight of all her beauty.

That tiny, yellow dress of hers was clinging to her

curves now, sticking to her skin thanks to the rain. The material was nearly transparent and he could see her tight, hard nipples through the fabric. He dropped his hat, not caring if it fell in a puddle, and wrapped both arms around her waist, drawing her hard up against his chest as he kissed her again.

He angled his head, forcing her lips apart as he stroked his tongue against hers. She gasped, small firm breasts pressed against him, making him so hard he was sure he was about to bust through the front of his jeans.

She didn't know how to kiss.

That fact didn't discourage him. Not in the least.

It should. Dammit all, it should. But if it wasn't him teaching her, if it wasn't him holding her in his arms, it would be Asher.

And there was no way in hell, Earth or heaven he was going to let some other man teach her how to do this. No. This moment was his. He didn't deserve it. But he was going to take it.

She lifted her hand, tentative fingertips pressing against his jaw, sliding from just beneath his ear down to his chin. Soft. Inexpert. Nearly enough to make him come then and there. He forced himself to get a grip on his control.

She angled her head then, and her tongue darted out, slipping into his mouth, sliding down against his lower lip, around the perimeter. He shivered, shook, like he was the damn virgin.

A virgin. Dammit all, Clara was a virgin. His best friend's younger sister. His dead best friend's younger sister, who'd been put in his care. Forget foxes. He was a tiger in the henhouse, and he was ready to devour her whole.

She was holding on to his face with both her hands now, clinging to him as though he might escape her, her lips savoring his, her whole body pressed against the length of his own. She had thrown herself into this, into their kiss, and there could be no question about whether or not she wanted it. Clara Campbell might try to eat kale for Asher, but she hadn't even been able to eat a sliver of cooked onion for him. He doubted she would submit herself to a kiss in the rain if it was anything less than what she wanted.

She didn't know better. She didn't know from desire. Didn't know from attraction, from need. Didn't know where this was headed.

He did. His cock was hard, and he was so close to the edge, one more shift of her hips against his might send him straight over. If it had been any other woman, he would have had that wet dress pushed up over her hips by now. Would have freed himself from his jeans and thrust deep inside of her.

But then, if it had been any other woman, they wouldn't be here. He wouldn't be this close to losing it. Wouldn't be so mindless with need that foreplay, finesse and basic precautions didn't seem all that important.

She pushed her hands into his hair, tangling her fingers deep in it, clutching his head tight. Her teeth scraped against his bottom lip and he groaned, barely able to keep himself together. He tightened his hold on her. He reversed their positions, pressing her up against the side of the barn.

He rocked his hips forward, letting her feel just

what she had done to him. Letting her feel just how hard he was. She gasped, wrenching her mouth from his, letting her head fall back against the roughhewn wood.

"Alex," she said, breathless, panting, her blue eyes clouded with desire.

Rain rolled down her face, like tears she hadn't yet shed. Tears the earth seemed to know she would. For him. For this. Because she was inexperienced, and she was young, and no matter what he might tell her, no matter what he might tell himself, there was no way it could end without them.

And that did it. That brought him crashing back to reality.

Lungs burning, he stepped away from her, cursing that moment of sanity with his every ragged breath.

"Alex…" He couldn't tell what the use of his name meant there. If it was a question, if it was a command. But it didn't matter. Clara wasn't going to dictate this thing between them. She couldn't.

He was supposed to protect her. More than that, if she knew…

She would be disgusted that she'd ever touched him.

"Do you want to do that with him?" His voice was rough, hard, and he hated himself a little bit. But then, what else was new?

"I… I don't understand."

"Your date. Do you want him to grab you, do you want his tongue in your mouth? Do you want him to grind his hard cock up against you? Is that what you want?"

Her eyes widened, the way her hair was, slicked

back and soaking wet, her skin washed clean by the rain, combining to make her look as young and innocent as she was. "No."

It was a simple answer. A quick one. And his body gloried in it.

His brain knew he shouldn't. But more masculine parts of him gave a big *hell yeah*.

"That's why your date sucked. Because if you're going to pretend to like food you hate, and to care about music you think is awful, you better really want to have his hands on you. If you don't…it just isn't worth it."

He turned away from her, bent down and picked up his hat from a puddle of water, shaking it out.

"I want you to put your hands on me."

Her words were soft, and they nearly blended in with the sound of the falling rain, but they hit him like a bullet between the shoulder blades.

He turned back to face her. "You don't know what you want."

"Yes I do. I want…what we were just doing."

He shook his head. "No, baby."

"Don't try that with me, Alex. You kissed me like that to teach me a lesson, and we both know it. You've been dismissive of Asher and the way that I felt about him from the beginning. So great, you were right. I wasn't that into him. I was into the idea of him. And I…my heart would really like it if I could be into the reality. Because I love the idea of him. I love the idea of the relationship we could have. But…that's not this, is it? That's not desire. It's not attraction. And I do have to have that. You can't just have good intentions and fantasies of keeping bees together."

He should feel like he'd won something, since she'd apparently now processed the lesson he'd wanted to teach her. But now he was questioning himself. His motives. Everything.

And he couldn't do more than this. It would be wrong, whether she understood it or not.

"Well, you're not going to get beekeeping with me, Clara. This? This is all I've got. I can give you down and dirty, no question. But you need to wait until you find the guy who can give you both."

Alex knew when the time came, he would sure as hell hate that guy too. But it didn't matter. Because what could he offer her? Sex while he fixed up the ranch. And hell, his body liked the idea of that. But everything inside of him, everything that made him a good man, a good soldier, a good brother in arms knew he couldn't do it.

Jason had asked him for one thing. He had asked him to take care of his little sister. And he sure as hell hadn't meant by screwing her senseless.

"What if I don't want both? I've never felt like this before. I didn't know I could. And I need… Alex, I need something. I just feel so alone all the time. And cold. And this felt…hot."

He firmed his jaw, gritted his teeth. This was as good a time as any. He had to do it. For both of them. "Clara, I saw Jason die."

She jerked back, as though he had struck her. She wiped at water running down her face, then wrapped her arms around her midsection, like she was trying to hold herself together. "I had a feeling you did."

"There's more to it than that. Jason died taking a bullet for me. He saved me. I'm standing here because he's dead. Standing on this ground because he's underneath it."

The color drained from her face, from her lips, and she shivered. Seeming cold for the first time.

"Think about how you feel about that trade and let me know if you still want this."

He turned away from her again. She wouldn't want anything more. Not after that. Hell, he would be lucky if she wanted to speak to him. She had been angry at Jason already. For dying on her. But it was more than that. He had sacrificed himself.

And he knew—with all of himself—that Clara was wishing at the moment she could make it so Alex traded places with Jason. So that Alex was the one in the casket.

And that was fine by him. Because it was nothing he hadn't thought himself, even wished for.

He walked away from her without looking back and told himself it was for the best.

ON NUMB FEET Clara stumbled into the house. She was freezing cold, and her lips were still tingling, still swollen from Alex's kiss.

*Alex.*

Her head was aching, a dull, pounding sensation.

She had been told the story of how Jason had died, in very vague terms, as though people were trying to spare her. She'd known that his actions had prevented people from dying. But nobody had said that he had literally thrown himself in front of a bullet to save Alex.

Clara covered her mouth with one hand, then the other, bending over, feeling like she had been punched in the stomach. She stood there for a moment, frozen, grief making her feel as though she had turned to stone.

But gradually, she came back to herself. She began to warm. Her mind protecting itself by moving those images to the deepest recesses of her brain. And bringing forward Alex.

She pictured the kiss. Relived the feeling of Alex's hands moving over her bare skin. So rough. So perfect, just like she had imagined. She wanted Alex. She couldn't pretend that wasn't what this was anymore. Why she was fixated on his mouth. Why she continually compared Asher to him.

It had all been a desperate attempt to cling to that crush. That safe, simple crush that didn't bring parts of her life crashing together with damaging, desperate impact.

She padded into the kitchen, her wet hair and dress leaving a trail of water droplets on the floor. She opened the fridge and took out a can of Coke. She popped the top and wandered into her bedroom, plopping down onto the bed. It was so strange that she had been in here only a few hours earlier wrestling with the idea of what to wear. It seemed like a different day. A different week. A different woman.

She lifted the Coke to her lips, tipped it back and caught sight of her reflection in the mirror. She lowered the can. It was gratifying, that she looked different. Considering she felt completely changed. And sure, some of that was the fact she closely resembled a drowned rat at the moment, but there was more to it than that.

Her makeup was all gone, washed away by the

rain. Her hair was hanging lank and stringy. The yellow dress was completely stuck to her body, and she could see her nipples through the thin fabric. It was amazing that she could feel embarrassed about that, all things considered. Considering she'd had her tongue in Alex's mouth only a few minutes ago.

Considering what he'd just told her about Jason.

She closed her eyes, a tear tracking down her cheek that she hadn't felt coming. What had Alex expected, telling her that? That she would be angry at him? That she would wish he was the one who was dead?

Clara set the Coke can down on the floor, curled her fingers around the edge of the mattress. She took a deep breath and leaned forward, lowering her head. She didn't know what she felt. She was so proud of the man her brother was, even though it was a sharp, painful kind of pride that stabbed her through the chest with every breath.

She felt sad. Angry. Lost. Jason had given up his life for his brother in arms. And he had left his sister behind. That hurt. It hurt, even if it shouldn't. It hurt even if it was selfish. But there was so much death in her life and it felt wrong that she should have to experience more of it.

At the same time, she knew if Jason hadn't acted as he did, it was possible neither of them would've survived.

And then, finally, the most shocking emotional ball hit full force and bloomed in her, spreading all through her midsection, making her feel weak, making her feel like all of her energy, all of her strength was draining away.

She lay down sideways on the bed, curling up into a ball.

Alex. She was so very, very grateful that Alex was alive. So warm, so vital. She couldn't imagine a life like that being snuffed out. And no, she hadn't been able to imagine Jason dead either. But Jason was dead. And Alex was here. And everything in her was so grateful for that fact.

Was that a betrayal? What did that make her? Because if she'd been asked hypothetically how she would feel in this situation, she would've guessed that she would wish Alex and Jason had traded places. And she knew that's what Alex had imagined she would want, as well.

She closed her eyes tight, more tears running down her face.

On the heels of that realization came a shiver of fear. What if she lost Alex? She had lost everyone else. What would keep her from losing him too?

For a moment that fear was a dark, oppressive thing that seemed to push down on her. That seemed to push her deep into the mattress, weighing her down, making it impossible to breathe. She felt dizzy, and she forced herself to draw in a long, slow breath, then let it out just as slowly.

Of all the things there were to worry about, losing Alex was not a rational concern. She knew that. But she had faced the worst so many times, it was impossible not to entertain the thought. And it was strange to think that Alex mattered as much as he did. But he had become a huge part of this point she was at in her life. A place she hadn't chosen to be. A place he hadn't chosen either.

She was just putting one foot in front of the other, hoping to get through, hoping to get to the next day. To the better day.

She rolled over onto her back, the cold air hitting her wet dress, making her shiver. She should get up. She should get in the shower. She should deal with herself, with reality. She didn't move. She just lay there, and she began to replay the kiss. Her first kiss.

His lips had been soft and firm, the stubble from his beard rough and wholly masculine. Just like the rest of him. All those things she had once assumed would be too much for her had been just right as it turned out.

But then, whatever she was going through, Alex himself seemed just right for it too.

Maybe it was because he got it. Maybe it was because, out of everybody, he probably understood her best.

And she knew, absolutely, that he had not told her about Jason to make her feel that way. No, he had told her about Jason to drive her away. But she didn't want him away. And if she could go back to the moment when he had walked away from her tonight she would.

She would go back to it, and this time, she wouldn't let him leave.

But beyond that… Well, she supposed she had some decisions to make.

It was a funny thing, because she had been putting off decisions for quite a few months now. Who would have thought a confession that brought her grief closer to the surface—and a kiss—would propel her closer to being functional.

Tomorrow. Tomorrow she would go and see Alex. And they would talk. Talk about Jason. Talk about where to go from here.

Tonight, she would take a shower and do her best not to catch a terrible cold.

Tonight, she would try to sleep without the memory of Alex's mouth, his hands, his everything, keeping her awake.

She had a feeling that of the two immediate objectives, she would fail at one of them. She sat up, pushed herself into a standing position and began to walk into the bathroom, peeling off her wet dress as she went.

And as she kicked the much debated dress onto the floor in a damp heap she had to wonder, if she had picked a different outfit, might she not have ended up hating her date and kissing the wrong man?

Her ultimate conclusion as she stepped into the shower was that she was very glad she had worn the yellow dress. No matter what happened next.

## CHAPTER ELEVEN

ALEX FIGURED IF he couldn't sleep he might as well drink.

He had a feeling that if he slept tonight, all he would have were visions of his friend's death. And if not that, then they would be visions of Clara's naked body. Right now, he couldn't quite figure out which would be worse.

If he was really lucky, both of those things would intertwine. It would be fitting, anyway. Considering that they were inextricably linked in many ways. He was in Clara's life because of Jason. Because of Jason's death. That was why she didn't have anybody. That was why she needed someone to *take care of her* for God's sake.

He stumbled into the kitchen, wandered over to the bar and began digging through the liquor supply to see if there was anything that looked like it might disrupt his brain enough that he could get some peace and quiet.

His body still ached. With desire for her. Desire he had no right to feel.

He was the worst kind of asshole.

But with any luck, soon he would be the worst kind of drunk asshole. Which wouldn't improve his status or the state of the world, but it would sure as hell make him feel better in the moment.

He poured himself a generous measure of Irish whiskey, and lifted the glass to his lips.

"Having a nightcap by yourself?" He turned and saw his brother Finn standing in the doorway, his arms crossed, his expression weighted with that kind of knowing, judgmental older-brother thing.

"No, I'm getting shit-faced by myself."

He knocked the glass back, welcoming the burn as it slid down his throat.

"Any particular reason?" Finn asked, walking deeper into the room and making his way over to where Alex was standing.

"Life?"

"Fair enough," Finn responded, taking hold of the bottle and pouring himself about half the amount that Alex had taken. "Though, you're not alone anymore."

He had a feeling his brother didn't just mean now, in the immediate moment. But Alex didn't want to acknowledge that.

"How is the work going around here? I know I've been kind of...absent lately."

"You've got your own stuff. Nobody blames you for that."

"Maybe you should," Alex said, not bothering to dull the edge in his voice. "You don't know the circumstances behind everything."

"No," Finn agreed. "I don't know much about your life, Alex. When you all first showed up, I thought Cain was a hard bastard to read. And he is, in some ways. But that's the thing. He's a hard bastard, and he isn't quiet about letting everybody know when he has a grievance. You and Liam, well, *you* seem easy. That's the funny thing about you. You seem happy. All the time. No matter what. And it's bull. I've come to that conclusion. Came to it quite a while ago. But I haven't yet figured out what the hell else is beneath it. You haven't shown me a damn thing. This is the first time I've seen you even close to breaking."

"Well, glad to share my moment of vulnerability. Does that make you feel like a big man? Like the kind of brother you've been dying to be?"

"Would it be a problem for you if I said yes? Would it bother you if I actually wanted to have a real relationship with the real you, and not just that ridiculous front that you try to pass off as reality?"

This was the second time in as many days that one of his brothers had tried to dig deeper with him. It was a funny thing because Alex thought he'd done a pretty good job of convincing everybody there was nothing deeper.

Half the time, he did a pretty damn good job of convincing himself.

Apparently, though, he wasn't as good at lying to his brothers as he had imagined.

"What is it you want to hear from me, Finn? That Liam and I had a hard life? We did. But we had Dad, so it seems kind of stupid to complain."

"Just because you had him doesn't mean you don't have issues because of him. I'm not under any illusion that my life would have been better if the old man had been around, Alex. I'm not envious of you. I'm not envious of Liam."

Alex shook his head. "Dad's a prick. If you were wondering."

"I wasn't. But it's always good to have assumptions confirmed."

"She was obsessed with the idea of keeping him," he said, thinking about his mother then, which he tried to do as little as possible. "She knew about all of you. Knew about women who had been left behind. She didn't want to be one of them. I'm pretty sure she poked a hole in some condoms to make me. To make sure that she could hold on to him after Liam was born, because she figured that maybe having another of his spawn would make him want to stay. I don't know why she thought two kids would do it when one had never been sufficient before. But the fact of the matter is he did stay for a while. We had him for quite a while, even though I'd say he wasn't much of a dad. It was more a performance art piece between the two of them. Dramatic fighting. A lot of cheating. I wouldn't be surprised if we had more siblings out there somewhere around the same age. Younger. Because Dad never was very good with birth control. He was never very good with control in general."

"Sounds like hell," Finn said.

He thought about the worst moment spent in that particular hell. Of the day when he'd been fourteen and nothing more than a punk-ass kid trying out getting in trouble to see what kind of attention he could get. Pushing too far. Far enough that he drove his father away. Far enough that his mother had finally openly turned on him.

Told him she wished he'd never been born.

And he wished he'd taken Liam's advice then. To just smile through it instead of messing it all up.

"It was," he said, his voice rough. "We didn't matter. We never did. Not to either of them. But the thing about that is you learn real quick not to depend on anybody. You learn real quick to depend on yourself. To make a life that is all about you. You have to make it count for yourself, or what's the point? I never tried to prove anything to either of them. Not to Mom. Not to Dad. Liam was the same. We went out and we made our own way. I don't regret it. I don't regret any of it. Yeah, I learned really early to just let it slide. Liam is not the same. I don't really know what goes on in his head, any more than you know what's going on in mine. Growing up with him didn't make it so that we confided in each other. Mainly, we just got in trouble together."

"You're closer to him. Whatever you might think."

"Maybe. But I don't know what he's been doing with his life. I don't know anything about what happened with Sabrina Leighton. I just know it has something to do with why he's here. I know that no matter how much he pretends he doesn't care about stuff, he does."

"And is it the same with you?"

"I care about some things. I care about doing the *right* thing. Which is what I'm trying to do with Clara."

He shouldn't have said that. He definitely shouldn't have said it the way that he had. Because using her name, not just calling her Jason's sister but referring to her so personally, was a tell, and he knew it.

"What exactly is doing the right thing by her?" Finn asked. Suspicious bastard.

But hell, they were drinking, and it was dark in the kitchen and no one else was there. So it seemed like as good a time as any to have some honesty. They had already started. Why not finish it? "Helping her dig out of the hole that she's in. Because grief makes it hard to function, and she hasn't been functioning that well. Her cell phone service was turned off."

"Wow."

"Yeah. Exactly. And her brother wrote me a letter. He left me a letter with his last will and testament, Finn. He asked me to make sure she was taken care of. I've never taken care of a damn thing in my life. Not even a pet."

He slammed his glass down on the bar, the violent motion somewhat satisfying. "I move a lot. I travel light. No connections. But Jason asked me… he asked."

"So you have to," Finn said, his tone grave.

Good. He understood. He got it. Alex picked his glass back up and took another sip. "I avoided doing it. I avoided doing it for a long time. And I had excuses. Because hell, I had to deal with things here. Grandpa was dead. I couldn't take her grief on board when I had all this Donnelly grief to work through. Plus, Jason was my friend. I felt that loss too."

"Right," Finn said, clearly not buying that the story ended there.

"I need to help her become self-sufficient. Not just financially, though I want that for her. But I need to help her move past this. The grief. The pain that she's in. And somehow, I need to not screw her."

Finn had the decency to at least pretend to look surprised by that statement. His older brother cleared his throat. "Right. So, that's a problem?"

"It's a damn *struggle*," Alex said, knocking back

the rest of his whiskey and pouring himself another. "She's a *virgin*."

This time, Finn choked. "Um. Okay."

"What kind of guy do you suppose ought to sleep with a virgin?"

Finn snorted. "Not you."

"*Not me.* Damn straight."

"But you want to."

"If I wasn't here getting drunk I would probably be driving over to her place right now. That's why I'm getting drunk. To keep myself from driving."

"Okay," Finn said again, maddeningly measured.

What the hell were older brothers for if not to freak out and punch you and act like all your inclinations were stupid and unreasonable?

Finn wasn't doing any of that.

"It's a damn mess," Alex continued. "I'm supposed to protect her. I'm supposed to take care of her."

Finn took a slow, measured sip of his whiskey. "Some people might argue that good sex is part of being well taken care of."

Alex frowned. "Is that a point you would argue if it was your younger sister in question?"

Finn put his hands up. "Oh, hell no."

"I didn't think so."

"But she's not my sister. And she sure as hell isn't *yours*."

"Jason was my best friend. Jason got himself killed saving me. I owe him my life. I can't give that to him. But you know, the least I can do is keep my dick in my pants."

Finn lifted a shoulder. "Sure. You could argue that. You could argue that all day long. But here's the thing.

Jason is dead. Clara is not." Finn tapped the side of his glass with his finger. "Does she want you?"

"She's a *virgin*," he said, emphasizing the word yet again. "And I'm not. I'm good at what I do. I could have her begging for it, but that doesn't make it right. It doesn't mean she actually knows what she's been asking for. Because, at the end of the day, sex is all I have to give her. We could have some fun. But that would be it."

"I'd think a woman in her position might want a little fun."

"What the hell, Finn? I did not hire you to play the part of shoulder devil. You're supposed to be older and more mature. And tell me to quit thinking with little Alex."

Finn pulled a face. "Don't you think that should be up to her? You think you're going to make all of her decisions? And you're going to make them based off what her dead brother would've wanted? That's not fair. She's a woman, and she's her own woman. You're not her keeper. I know you have this warped idea that you're here to take care of her, but you're not her father."

Alex blanched. "I *know that*. I'm not auditioning for the role. But I am trying to be the kind of protector that Jason expected me to be and not a damn sex pervert."

His brother laughed at him. *Laughed*, dammit. Then he lifted his glass and took another sip. "I guess that's admirable in some ways. But insulting. If she wants you, and you're throwing up all of these excuses because of what someone else wanted for her...

that's not respecting her. Not really. You can tell yourself whatever you want, but it's not."

"You know, I counted on you to tell me that I need to keep my zipper zipped. She's too young for me. More because of her lack of experience than her age. She's *never* been with a man. You think she should be with me?"

"Don't get me wrong, it's probably a terrible idea. But it's not about what I think. You really want to help her, you really want her to be self-sufficient, you want her to be able to move on with her life? Treat her like an adult. If she tells you no, then back your ass off. But if she wants you, treat her like a woman and not a child." Finn shrugged. "That's all I'm saying."

"And you're such an expert on this kind of thing?"

"I'm an expert on what happens when you spend too many years trying to protect a woman from yourself. You miss out on a lot when you assume you know what's best. Pro tip—you probably don't."

Fine for Finn to talk about that. When Alex and the rest of them had first shown up at the Laughing Irish, it had put Finn under a lot of stress, and his best friend, Lane, had been on hand to help him deal with his rage. But all the change, and the tension, had affected the relationship. Though ultimately it had been in a good way.

He appreciated Finn's intentions, kind of, but the relationship Finn had with Lane had nothing to do with what Alex was supposed to feel for Clara, or what was appropriate.

"Don't start using Lane as an example here," Alex said. "It's irrelevant. Whatever might happen between

Clara and me, it's not going to end in happily ever after."

Finn lifted a brow. "You sure about that?"

"I told you, I had to make my own way very early on. I had to figure out who I was, and what I wanted, and what I am is not a man who wants marriage and kids and all that. Not even close. I watched our parents fight it out. Let me tell you, they call it a nuclear family because when it blows up that fallout leaves damage that lasts for years."

"Whatever. I'm not going to tell you what to do. But if you were looking for somebody to reinforce your self-flagellation it isn't going to be me."

"Asshole." Alex drained his glass. "What good are you?"

"Better than you might think." Finn clapped him on the back. "Now, I'm going to bed. Because I have a woman in said bed, and I'm going to get laid."

*"Asshole,"* Alex repeated.

Finn grinned and walked out of the room.

Leaving Alex alone with the alcohol. Leaving Alex alone with all those justifications that Finn had just handed to him.

Alex didn't want to think. He wanted to drink. Unfortunately, he had the means to do just that. He had spent his whole life without Finn around, without most of his brothers. He was hardly going to change course now just because Finn had advised him to.

Nope. Not gonna happen.

He poured himself another drink.

## CHAPTER TWELVE

HANGOVERS WERE A BITCH. Alex sat up, pressing the heel of his hand against his eyeballs. He hadn't managed to get up in time for any of his jobs. He didn't have to look at the clock to know that. The sun was filtering through his window, too bright, too harsh, like an ice pick straight to the forehead.

He had come too far to fall apart now. But that's exactly what he was doing. Letting Clara down. Letting his brothers down. He should have been up early doing work at one of the two ranches and here he was, in bed.

He ignored the pounding in his head and swung his legs over the side of the mattress, standing up quickly, fighting the intense dizzy spell that swept over him as he did.

It had been a long damn time since he'd had that much drink. Well, it had been since Jason's funeral. And since then, he'd been too busy. Since then, he'd been focused.

That focus was long gone now.

His head continued to pound, so hard that it took him a moment to realize that there was an actual pounding coming from outside of his skull tube. It was the front door. He cursed, putting on a pair of pants, not bothering with a shirt, heading out of his bedroom and taking the stairs two at a time, then striding through the large common area of the house to the front door.

He was having a full-on Dracula moment. Sun was shining through the large floor-to-ceiling windows with unseasonable brightness, threatening to unman him completely. Apparently whiskey transformed him into a creature of the night.

"I'm coming," he growled in response to the persistent pounding.

He swung it open, and his gut tightened, his cock instantly going hard.

And just like that, all the whiskey and the ensuing hangover were for nothing. He might have forgotten for a few hours, but he remembered now.

Dammit, did he remember.

"What the hell are you doing here?" he asked, gazing down at Clara as he leaned against the door frame.

She was all big eyes and determination, her chin set at a stubborn angle, her lower lip sucked between her teeth. "I'm here to talk to you, jackass," she said.

"So talk," he said, folding his arms over his chest.

Gone was the gorgeous yellow dress from last night, replaced with a simple dark shirt and black pants—something of a work uniform he imagined. And it would have been great if the lack of pretty summer dress and exposed legs did something to dampen his desire for her.

It didn't.

He was reluctant to let her in. He was reluctant to let her too close.

But he was ready. Ready for her lecture. For her virginal outrage. She would yell at him for kissing her since she wasn't into him like that—for touching her at all, knowing what he did about Jason.

He braced himself. Braced himself to hear how much she wished he were the one that had died.

"How dare you?"

And here it was.

"I never claimed to be a nice guy, Clara. I just said I was doing the best I could to honor your brother's wishes."

"You…you get in my face, you do your very best to prove to me that I, in fact, don't have a damn clue what I want. I don't know what attraction is. That I don't know what it is to want somebody, and then you walk away from me? More than that, you drop a bombshell on me, and then walk away. And I don't even care if that's a tasteless analogy, all things considered."

He shook his head, incredulous, and then he regretted shaking his head. "That's what you're angry at me about? The fact that I walked away from you? You should be thanking me for that, Clara."

"Oh, should I? Thanks, Alex. It's super helpful when you let me know exactly how I should be feeling. Otherwise, how would I ever figure it out on my own?"

"Get as indignant as you want, but you're right, I am the person that demonstrated to you that you don't actually know what you want. You sure as hell don't want Asher, and we both know that."

He knew, he knew right down to his soul, that the moment he'd said those words he had consigned himself to getting his head torn off. He could see it in the evil gleam in her blue eyes, and when she walked right into the house, brushing past him, not waiting for an invitation, he could have sworn he smelled fire and brimstone.

"Okay. Let's talk. Let's talk about what we want. You want me, Alex. Me. I might be a virgin, and I might have just gotten my first kiss last night, but I know that. So tell me, from up there on your high horse, how does the view look?"

"What the hell are you talking about?"

"You know," she insisted. "You have so much to say about what I want, who I want and what real attraction is, and yet, you're hell-bent on denying ours even though you seem to want me to acknowledge it. That's bull, Alex. What's the point of it? To be right? To hurt me?"

"No," he said, the word coming out a bit more emphatically than he intended. It reverberated in his head, sent a shock of pain through his teeth and down his jaw. "No," he said again, this time a little more gently. "I walked away from you because I *don't* want to hurt you. And I sure as hell needed you to know the whole truth about Jason before I let you touch me."

"Okay. I guess I can appreciate that. Now I know." She looked up, her blue eyes suddenly going glassy. "What did you think I would say?"

So many things. He had expected her to come in here with recriminations on her lips, had expected her to demand he find the nearest graveyard and start digging a hole for himself while she found a demon to negotiate with.

"I don't know. But you needed to know," he lied.

"I don't think that's true. I think you figured the truth would do all of this for you. That you wouldn't have to stand in front of me and tell me you don't want me because I would tell you to go to hell."

It was so close to what he had actually been thinking that he wondered for a moment if she could read his mind. Then, he figured he probably just wasn't all that complex.

"Because you *should* tell me to go to hell," he said, the words strained. "Why haven't you?"

"Look around you. Oh, maybe not here. But go to the Campbell ranch and look around you, Alex. And you ask yourself who isn't there. Who's with me? Nobody. Not a damn person that I love. And you came into my life…and I have you. Jason gave you to me. You've been helping. You have. I don't wish you dead. And the worst thing about realizing that is that the moment I let myself think the words, I started to panic. Because I was afraid that wanting you here would be the same as signing your death certificate. Everyone I care about is dead. Caring about you sucks. But when you told me that, I realized that I did. I don't hate you. Don't ask me to."

He stood, frozen to the spot, and he wanted more than anything to cross the space between them and pull her into his arms. To offer her comfort if nothing else. To feel her soft cheek, to trace the line of her lips with the edge of his thumb. To offer her reassurance. To offer her a connection.

But he didn't. He couldn't. No matter what she said now, it didn't make any of this right.

"It would be better, you know," he said, his voice sounding like a stranger's. "It would be better if you wanted coffee boy."

"Well, no duh."

He laughed. "Nice to know you agree with me on that point."

"I do. I wanted to want him more than I have ever wanted anything before. Okay, that's a lie. I think I wanted an American Girl doll when I was six about as badly as I wanted to force myself to want to date Asher. To want him. But the thing is, I don't." She blinked rapidly, and he could tell that she was trying to hold back tears. "I've been trying to escape for the past six months. And he was about as…off the ranch as I could have gotten. But the fact of the matter is, I don't want off the ranch. And that's hard. It's hard to want a life that hurts. Everything in that house has some dark memory attached to it. But I can't leave it either. I love it. Entertaining the idea of being with Asher let me have a fantasy of a different kind of life. But unsurprisingly, much like coffee, I don't actually want it."

Even in his hangover-fogged brain, he suddenly made a connection between what Finn had said last night, and this moment. Clara was so much more than Jason's younger sister. She was more than a twenty-one-year-old virgin. She was more than any of those basic, reductive things he was trying to make her into so he could throw up walls and excuses and convince himself he was being an honorable man.

Clara was strong. She was brave. She wasn't innocent, that was for damn sure. She had lived through the kind of loss, the kind of pain that would make even the most hardened soldier curl up on the ground and cry like a child. She had gotten back up. She was standing. Standing right in front of him, challenging him, her blue eyes flashing with determination.

He had been selling her short. He hadn't really seen her. But he did now. Of course, he didn't know what the hell he was supposed to do with the revelation, but he saw her clearly now. For all the good it did him. For all the good it did them.

"Then what do you want?"

She let out a long, slow breath. "You. I want you."

CLARA FELT LIKE she had just run a marathon. Her lungs were burning, her heart threatening to pound its way straight through her chest. This was one of the hardest, scariest things she had ever done. Well, okay, it didn't exactly compare to attending the funerals of her family members. That was scarier. That hideous, final ceremony that stripped the last shreds of denial away.

But this... Coming all the way here to Alex's house—the house he shared with his brothers—standing in front of him and telling him that she wanted him...that was pretty damn scary too.

And he said nothing. He just stared at her with those unreadable green eyes, his expression hard as granite. He looked at her as though she hadn't just cut her chest open and let her pride fall out onto the floor in front of him, all vulnerable and just there for him to look at, poke at, judge. The move was his, and he wasn't making it.

At least if he said something insulting, something *horrible*, she could fight him. And fighting would feel better than this. Than standing here in this kind of hollow silence that seemed to echo in all of the tender places inside of her.

"You should go, Clara," he said finally, his voice rough.

That bit of roughness, the lack of smile—those were the only two indicators that this affected him at all.

Otherwise, he was like a mountain. Big, hard. Everything she wasn't. Right now she felt like a small, vulnerable creature desperately in search of armor. A burrow. Something to hide in, something to protect herself with. And she found herself without either.

"And if I don't want to go?"

Her pride was dead already. She might as well dance on its grave. A seductive little striptease to make sure she stayed buried.

"Then I will pick you up and carry you out of this house and put you in your truck myself," he said, his voice hard.

"Why? Because having me here tests you too much?" It took bravery to say that. More than she thought she possessed. She was surprised at herself. If nothing else came out of this, there was that.

"You don't want to find out."

Her phone buzzed, the timer she had set for herself going off. Dammit. "I have to go to work. I'm *not* obeying you." She took a step away from him, her voice trembling, her limbs trembling, her everything trembling. "We'll talk later."

"Not about this," he said. "I'll keep coming to your ranch, Clara, and I'll keep helping you with all of the things that I promised."

"You mean you'll keep coming to *your* ranch," Clara said. "*Your* ranch, that *you* own. It isn't mine. Not anymore."

"It will be. It doesn't matter what the legality—"

"It sure as hell does matter," she said, forgetting work. Forgetting everything but the anger pouring through her. "It matters. It's your ranch. You have everything. I don't have anything. I don't have any power in this. You have it all. And you don't even deserve it. You're a coward, Alex," she spat. "A coward who's hiding behind his dead best friend."

That comment was apparently a bridge too far. Because then Clara found herself being hauled off her feet, up against Alex's hard, uncompromising body. She half expected to find herself being carried out of the house, as promised. But that didn't happen.

Instead, he lowered his head, his eyes hard. "Hiding? You're accusing me of hiding?"

"If the denial fits," she said, digging in.

"Who exactly has been hiding, little girl? Because I'm not the one who was desperately trying to date somebody I didn't actually want to touch me. I'm not the one who spent months not paying her bills."

She struggled against him, her heart pounding, anger warring with enraging, growing arousal that she definitely shouldn't be feeling. "You're the one who spent months avoiding me," she said. "Months of waiting to do what Jason asked you to do. Then you kissed me. And then you ran away to your big brother's house. Why? You thought this was a fort that girls couldn't get into? You thought this would keep me away? I'm not afraid of you, Alex. I'm not afraid of your touch, I'm not afraid of your rejection. If you think I'm that fragile then you don't actually know me."

He reached out, caught her chin, held her face

steady. "And if you think nothing about me should scare you, then you don't know me very well," he said, his voice like gravel.

He did scare her. But not in the way he meant. He challenged her. Challenged everything she thought she knew about herself and what she wanted.

The truth of the matter was that she wanted him. And she was prepared to beg. Was prepared to make it impossible for him to say no, even if she didn't exactly know what that might entail.

She didn't need to know exactly. Not in practice. She was a woman. She was. Despite having spent a good portion of her life ignoring that fact. Denying that fact. Because throwing up a wall between herself and her desires seemed safe. And then she had attached them to a pretty safe target, all things considered.

But the moment Alex's lips had crashed down on hers last night, she had lost the ability to deny it. Had lost the desire to.

She was a woman. And all she needed to do was follow her instincts.

She dropped her hand between them, pressing her palm against the front of his jeans. She ran her palm along the seam of his zipper, feeling his hard length pulsing beneath her touch. He wanted her. There was no denying it. A man couldn't fake this, and as innocent as she was, she knew that.

He swore, crude and blunt. His voice like broken glass. His surrender more satisfying than she could have ever imagined.

He closed his eyes, his head falling back, and she couldn't stop herself from staring. At the strong column of his throat, the way his Adam's apple bobbed up and down as he swallowed. Looking for strength, she imagined. The strength to turn her away.

She had never felt anything like this before. Had never seen anything like it. A man at the end of his control. A man like him. A strong man. And suddenly she realized why that kind of too-much masculinity that Alex possessed was so appealing. It was because he was physically stronger than her. No question. He was a soldier, he was a man.

And right now, he was in the palm of her hand, and he was struggling against her.

The power she possessed as a woman was…it was intoxicating. So much greater than she had imagined.

"Clara," he ground out.

She stretched up on her toes, brushed her lips against that spot on his throat that had caught her attention only a moment before. She could feel his pulse throbbing beneath her mouth, and before she could fully process what she was doing she darted her tongue out and licked him. From his Adam's apple up to his chin, moving from smooth skin into morning stubble. His taste, that masculine texture, made it feel like an arrow had pierced her down low, between the legs, sending a pulse of aching desire through her body.

Yesterday, when she had gone on her date, she'd been a girl. Her understanding of the desire between men and women had been basic at best.

She knew the mechanics. But that wasn't the same as truly understanding.

One kiss from Alex, and she felt like a woman.

Sure, she was still a virgin, but she got it now. She really did.

Alex swept her up into his arms, holding her against him, and then he strode out of the entryway, carrying her up the stairs. Her heart slammed against her breastbone, and she began to question all of the conclusions she'd come to in the past few minutes.

That she understood. That she was ready.

His chest was bare, and being pressed up against all that skin made her feel… Well, it made her feel achy and needy, and it was just enough to overcome her anxiety.

Alex carried her down the hall, kicked open a door, one that clearly led to his bedroom, then kicked it shut behind them.

He crossed the room, setting her down at the center of a large bed, bringing himself down to hover over her, his lean hips settling between her thighs, his mouth coming down to settle over hers.

She brought her hand up to his cheek, scraping her fingertips along his beard, enjoying the feel of him, enjoying the contrast. Then she let her hand drift down to his bare chest, touched him the way she had when he'd kissed her last night.

This was different, though. It was different because there was intention coupled with the intensity. Because they were behind a closed door. Because they were in a bed.

Because she was on fire and there wasn't any rain to cool it.

His hand slid up beneath her shirt, his skin rough against hers. She loved that. Loved the contrast. Was quickly becoming addicted to it. It was like some kind of magic she hadn't known existed before this.

Strange. Because one of the first things you learned as a kid was the difference between boys and girls. But this was so much more.

It was hard and soft. Round and curved, blunt and angular. He was a mountain. And she was like the coastal mist that rolled in off the sea. Able to shift, to curve around his uncompromising lines, to overtake him utterly and completely as she did.

What she was learning now was the strength in the giving. In allowing herself to mold to him, and the effect that it had on his body.

She moved her hands down his back, gloried in the feeling of the musculature beneath her fingertips. Then she drew them back up, over his shoulders and down his chest, his abs, down to the waistband of his jeans. She stopped there. It had been one thing to grab hold of him downstairs when she had been trying to prove something. When she had been issuing a dare. It was all a little more intimidating now.

The bed, again. Making things feel more real. Making things feel more intense.

But then he cupped her breasts, still covered by the fabric of her bra, and she forgot everything. Forgot that she was afraid. Forgot that she was nervous at all.

Her nipples were sensitive, almost painfully so, and when he slid his thumbs over the tightened buds, she gasped, the bra padding not enough to keep her from feeling it all the way through.

He reached around behind her, unclasping the bra and grabbing it, along with a handful of her shirt, and dragging them up over her head. Then she was shirtless too. Her skin got hot, a slow flush that spread from her face on down.

She was…well, she was embarrassed. But not so much about being naked in front of him. It was about the fact that she didn't know how to be confident like that. Didn't know how to be sexual. And she wished that she did. She was just lying there. That was the embarrassing thing. That she had this gorgeous man on the bed with her, looming over her, and she had no freaking idea what to do with him.

Thankfully, he was not similarly affected.

Alex growled, bracketing her face in his hands, claiming her lips for an intense kiss. Then he wrenched his mouth away from hers, kissing her neck, her collarbone, making his way down to the curve of her breasts, down farther to her nipple. He drew one into his mouth and sucked it in deep.

Clara felt like a firecracker had been lit in her stomach, the heat, the crackles of tension creating a small explosion inside her.

She flexed her feet, tightening her leg muscles, trying to do something to counterbalance the tension that was drawing tight and low. That was creating little ripples at her core.

"Alex," she panted. "Alex."

"I know," he said, sliding his thumb over her damp nipple, where he had just had his mouth a moment ago. Then he turned his attention to her other breast, repeating the same action, robbing her of her breath. Of her ability to think.

He wrapped his large hands around her, just beneath her rib cage, his thumbs skimming the underside of her breasts, and then moving down her waist, down past her belly button, down to her hips. He moved his hands in, unbuttoning her pants, drawing the zipper down slowly.

She bit her lip, unconsciously flexing her hips, begging him for something. She wasn't even sure what. But her body seemed to know. Seemed almost entirely confident in what it required. He slipped his hand down beneath the waistband of her pants, of her panties, and she rolled her hips upward, forcing his hand into prime position between her thighs.

He groaned when his hand found her, when he pushed a finger down through her folds and it glided across the sensitized nerves there, sending a streak of white-hot lightning through her body.

"So wet," he growled, pushing his fingers back and forth. She was. She was shockingly, intensely wet, and she hadn't realized it until his fingers began to move. Until he had spoken those words. "You're killing me," he said. "Do you know that?"

She shook her head. She couldn't say anything.

He slipped one finger inside of her, the invasion unfamiliar, but blindingly satisfying. And as he worked his way in and out of her body he slipped his thumb over that place where she was aching for his touch, her whole body drawn tight, flexing her feet not doing anything now to provide a counterbalance to that tension.

Alex lowered his head, kissed her lips as his hand continued with its knowing movements. His hips were pressed up against her side, and he moved in time with the thrust of his finger. Short, sharp jerks that seemed reluctant in some way.

He gripped her chin with his free hand, turning her

face so that she was looking at him. His green eyes were sharp, intense, his lips pressed into a grim line. She couldn't look away from him. Part of her wanted to. Part of her wanted to close her eyes and blot out the reality of the moment. To not be quite so aware that she was lying in bed half-naked with a man who had his hand inside of her pants. To not be so acutely conscious of the fact that it was Alex.

That this was happening. That it wasn't a fantasy. That it was real. That it was happening to her right now. Something new and big and terrifying and more than she had ever had before.

But she didn't close her eyes. She didn't look away. She wasn't a coward.

And he was looking at her. Really looking at her. Because he wanted her. Her. This gorgeous, strong man, who had most certainly taken her up as a charge under sufferance, actually wanted her. And he saw her. That mattered. No matter what else happened after this, that mattered.

He flexed his wrist then, pushing a second finger in along with the first, and using the heel of his palm to grind up against where she was most sensitive.

She lost it then. She squeezed her eyes shut tight, bursts of light breaking behind them, her internal muscles pulsing around his fingers as she came hard. A gasp was torn from her throat, his name, the kind of moan that almost sounded like a bad parody of pleasure, but that she couldn't have controlled even if she wanted to.

Then Alex pulled away from her as though he had been burned, rolling over onto his back, his breathing hard.

"Alex?" She knew that wasn't it. She'd had an orgasm, yes. But that wasn't sex. And he still had… well, she hadn't even seen him. He hadn't seen her.

But there was something in the way he looked just then, in the lines on his face, the strain there, that told her everything she wanted to know without ever asking the question.

She asked anyway. "Alex, aren't you going to…?"

"No. You have to go to work," he said, his voice rough.

Yes, she did have to go to work. She was late. She was late because she had gone upstairs and had an orgasm with Alex Donnelly. "I'm already late," she said.

"You need to go, Clara."

She needed to go because he said she did. Just like the kiss had ended last night because he'd said so. Just like he'd carried her up the stairs and given her an orgasm because he'd felt like it.

He owned her ranch because Jason had left it to him. He was getting bison because he'd decided it was the best thing. The best thing for her.

And no one had asked what she'd wanted. No one had left a single decision about her own life in her hands.

But when the dust settled and Alex left, she was going to have to be in control of her own life. She couldn't be taken care of from here on out, and she didn't even want that. She was going to be a woman who stood on her own two feet, and she was going to start now.

Some decisions needed to be hers. This decision needed to be hers.

She took a step back from the side of the bed, and

then she shoved her jeans and her panties down her thighs, kicking them to the side.

Alex braced his palms on the mattress, pushing himself up, his expression hard. "Clara…"

"I'm late already," she reiterated. "I'm already going to have to come up with an excuse for why I wasn't there on time. I want this. More importantly, I choose this. And I haven't chosen anything in a long time.

"Look at me," she said, spreading her arms. "I'm a woman. I'm not a child. If you don't want me, then tell me so. Tell me to go to work, because the idea of having sex with me disgusts you. I don't want pity. But if you want me, and you're trying to protect me, you're trying to make this choice for me…don't. Because I've had it with that. I have had it with everyone else having more control over my life than I do. I want this. I want you. I haven't been ambiguous about that. So the question now is, what do you want?"

He sat up, holding his hand out, the expression on his face somewhere between regret and pain. "Come here."

# CHAPTER THIRTEEN

CLARA TOOK A tentative step forward, and then another. She reached out, taking hold of his hand, and allowing him to pull her down onto the bed, over him. She was completely naked, straddling him, offering him a full view of that nudity.

He reached up, grabbing hold of her hips, and she rocked herself forward, the rough seam on his denim abrading her sensitive skin. She shivered, but rocked against him again, relishing that lightning bolt of pleasure that shot through her.

"Tell me what you want," he said.

She planted her hands on his chest, scraped her nails across his muscles. "I told you already. Why don't you tell me?"

A ghost of that familiar smile touched his lips. "I want you."

"You can do better than that."

"I want you, Clara. I want inside you. I want to screw you until neither of us can see straight. And I shouldn't, God knows. But I want to."

She let her eyes flutter closed, let out a long, slow breath. "Good."

"Is that what you want?"

"Yes," she responded, slowly letting her fingertips drift over his abs, down to the waistband of his jeans.

She hesitated then, but only for a moment. Then she undid the button there, lowered the zipper until her own body proved to be a barrier to that. Then, she arched her hips upward and tugged the zipper down the rest of the way.

She moved down his body, still straddling him, but over his thighs now, and grabbed a hold of the jeans, and the waistband of his underwear, drawing them down slowly to reveal every inch of his masculinity.

He was bigger than she had imagined.

She swallowed hard, trying to combat the nerves that were swarming through her like honeybees.

It was an apt comparison, really. You had to risk some pain to get to the honey. That was what this would be like. She had already known that it would hurt. First times did, so she had heard. But it would be good. It had to be.

People didn't make absolute idiots out of themselves over sex because it was only okay. Just like they didn't gorge themselves on kale.

Alex was not kale. Alex was the cake of men.

She discarded his pants, and his underwear, throwing them somewhere onto the floor. And then, she took a moment to just look at him. To really revel in the decision she had made. To push this. To demand it.

She made really, really good decisions.

He was perfect. In absolutely every way. The epitome of masculinity. Those hard-cut muscles with a light dusting of hair over them a beautiful example of the difference between men and women. His shoulders were broad, his biceps and forearms heavily muscled. Even his thighs were muscular.

And then there was, well, *him*.

His cock.

Which was the dirtiest word she knew for that particular body part. One that had always made her blush. But kind of captured her imagination too.

And she decided now that she was going to go ahead and apply it. Since this was her fantasy. This was her moment.

"Wow. You're hot," she said, leaning forward, planting her hands on the mattress and crawling upward, dropping a kiss onto his lips, his hard length pressed against her softness.

He wrapped his arm around her waist, his hold firm, and then he turned them over, reversing their positions. "So are you," he responded, his eyes intense on hers. And then he kissed her, deep and dirty, like he was giving her a preview of what was going to happen next.

That kiss went on and on. There was no question mark at the end of this kiss. They both knew where it was leading. There was a certainty to the kiss, a desperate edge, but there was also something deep and confident that allowed them both to settle into it.

She shifted beneath him, widening her thighs, his hardness pressed against her slick flesh. He flexed his hips, sliding up through her folds as he continued to kiss her, his tongue moving expertly against hers, his teeth scraping her bottom lip before he took it deep again.

He timed the movements of the kiss with the flex of his hips, and drove up her arousal, making her feel so acutely turned on, it was almost painful. She felt hollowed out, empty. It was like hunger. Leaving her weak with wanting and desperate to be filled.

He broke the kiss, drew back slightly, rubbing his nose against hers, pressing their foreheads together. And then he smiled.

She whimpered, arching against him. She wanted. With all of herself. She had never felt anything like this before. She hadn't known this feeling existed.

And she knew that it was going to change her. That this was going to alter the way she saw things, the way she felt. But she didn't care. She wanted it. Was as hungry for that as she was for his body.

She wanted to be changed. She wanted to be different. She wanted Alex to be the one to make it happen.

It was perfect. In its own broken way. That he would be the one to do this. That he would be the man she wanted more than any other.

"Alex," she whispered, "please."

"Hang on," he said, leaning away from her and wrenching open the drawer to his nightstand. He reached inside, and then cursed. Then he pulled out a box of condoms—unopened, which did something indefinable to her emotions—and tore open the seal.

He took out a strip of them, tore one off and then threw everything else on the floor, quickly applying the protection.

"I'm going to try not to hurt you," he said, kissing her as he positioned the blunt head of his arousal at the entrance of her body.

He inched forward slightly, the head of him slipping in almost easily because she was so wet.

"It's okay if you do," she said, the words a broken whisper.

"Hell." He lowered his head, pressing his face

against the side of her neck as he thrust forward, just a little bit.

She flinched, a hard, pinching pain accompanying that movement. "Please." She just wanted him to do it. She wanted him inside of her. All the way. Even if it hurt. She didn't want this slow, mild pain—literally by inches. She wanted everything. Wanted to tumble headfirst into it. And if it hurt, that was fine. If it changed her, that was fine too.

It wasn't about every moment being full of pleasure. It was about need. Her need for him. Her need for this.

But she couldn't say all of that, not in this moment. And Alex seemed to understand that. Seemed to understand the wealth of information and that simple *please*.

On a growl he pressed himself the rest of the way inside. She gritted her teeth, grabbed hold of his shoulders, dug her fingernails into his skin. It hurt. But in her experience everything that changed you did. Good or bad.

She didn't know if in the end it would be good or bad. But she chose it. So at least there was that. It made this different from every other thing in her life that had changed her.

Alex moved his hand around to her lower back, down to cup her butt, lifting her slightly as he pushed in deeper. She let her head fall back, and she saw stars. "Are you okay?" he asked against her lips.

It still hurt. But it was what she wanted. Right now, it might well be everything she wanted. And *okay* didn't seem like the right word, but she couldn't think of anything monumental enough to capture the feeling.

"Okay," she said, trying to force a smile.

He kissed her, and she clung to him as he began to move inside of her. Deep. So deep. It felt like he was touching everything all at once. Parts of herself that had gone undiscovered until this. Until him.

Gradually, the pain went away. Gradually, that slide of his hard flesh inside of her started to feel more than okay. It started to feel more than good. It went way past physical. It reached the emptiness deep down inside, and it made her feel...

She opened her eyes, and they clashed with the forest green of his.

She wasn't alone. She was with Alex.

That thought brought on a wash of fire through her whole body, and she knew that he felt it too. Could see the response in him. His thrusts became less measured, less controlled, until it all just burned away. And there was no consideration for pain, no concern for inexperience. Which was good, because she didn't want them.

She wanted him. All of him. Everything.

She clung to him, meeting his every thrust with a roll of her hips, sliding her hands down his back, moving to grasp his butt. It was hard like the rest of him. After this she would need time to look at him. To look at all of him. Just to enjoy the work of art that was Alex Donnelly.

That would be great. But right now, she didn't need to look at him. She just needed to feel him. Everywhere. All of him.

"Alex." She gasped his name as her orgasm began

to build inside of her. It felt impossible. Too big. Too intense. Too much.

If her first release had been a thunderstorm, this one would be the whole landslide that came after. She had a feeling it would leave devastation in its wake. She wanted it anyway. Needed it.

He gripped her hips with both hands, holding her steady as he ground his body against hers, the hard, sustained contact sending her over the edge. She arched up against him, unable to hold back the cry of pleasure as her earth-shattering release overtook her.

It went on forever, her internal muscles pulsing around him, that sensation of being filled making it deeper somehow, more intense.

Then Alex went still above her, shuddering out his own release. It triggered aftershocks inside of her, little tremors of pleasure that made her shiver.

And then she came back to herself. And it was the strangest thing. Because it was broad daylight, and everything in the room looked exactly as it had before they'd had sex.

It didn't seem right. It didn't seem possible. That the entire place hadn't come down around them. That everything wasn't destroyed, altered in the way that she was.

It was a normal day, really. Except that she was naked in Alex's bed. Oh yeah, and she wasn't a virgin anymore. Stupidly, she felt a smile tug at the corners of her mouth.

"I was going to ask if you were okay. But you're smiling."

She looked up to find him studying her, lifted her shoulder. "Sorry. Was I not supposed to smile?"

"Better than frowning, I suppose."

He moved away from her, the loss of his weight and heat nearly making her gasp, then he turned his back and swung his legs over the side of the bed.

"I suppose," she said, sitting up and looking around, still feeling disoriented.

Not even a picture knocked on the floor. It didn't seem possible.

"I just need to go to the bathroom," he said.

She nodded. Then she got off the bed and started collecting her clothes. She was late to work. She was so late to work. She grabbed her pants off the floor and dug her phone out of the pocket. She had three missed calls.

"Dammit," she whispered.

"Cursing my name already?" She turned around and saw Alex standing in the doorway of the bathroom, stark naked. He was still beautiful. So beautiful he made her ache.

"Work," she said.

"Right," he responded, nodding slowly. "Are you in trouble?"

She wrinkled her nose. "Probably a little bit. I'll work it out. I just… I think I have to go."

He nodded once. "I'll come by tonight."

A little thrill of giddiness raced through her. "Okay."

She dressed quickly, then hesitated for a moment. Alex was still standing there, totally naked. And she wanted to kiss him, even if it wasn't cool. His eyes caught hers, and she saw the same need. She same heat. She took a deep breath, closing the space between them and claiming his mouth with her own.

Another good decision as far as she was concerned.

"See you tonight," she said in a rush, then turned and walked out of his room, taking the stairs two at a time.

She raced out the front door and to the truck, getting inside and jamming her key into the ignition. Then she dialed Grassroots.

She put the call on speakerphone as she maneuvered the car out of the driveway, her head and body still buzzing, an air of the surreal wrapping itself around her.

"Grassroots Winery, this is Sabrina."

"Hi," Clara said. "This is Clara. I'm on my way."

"Clara!" Sabrina hissed. "I thought that hipster guy killed you and made a beanie out of you. I haven't heard from you since you went on that date, and then you didn't show up to work."

Clara's stomach sank. "I'm sorry. I didn't mean to worry you. Nothing happened on the date. Really. And time just…got away from me today." It was a lie, and eventually she would tell Sabrina the truth. But she needed some time to process it herself.

"Well, get here as soon as you can. Lindy hasn't been down to the tasting room yet, so she doesn't know you're not here. And Olivia is on a later shift. Not that I think she would get you in any trouble on purpose, but you know how she is."

A rule follower to a fault. Yes, Clara was well aware of that. "Thank you. I'll probably be about a half hour."

"Okay. See you then."

She could be there quicker if she didn't make the

# YOUR PARTICIPATION IS REQUESTED!

Dear Reader,

Since you are a lover of our books – we would like to get to know you!

Inside you will find a short Reader's Survey. Sharing your answers with us will help our editorial staff understand who you are and what activities you enjoy.

To thank you for your participation, we would like to send you up to 4 books and 2 gifts – **ABSOLUTELY FREE!**

Enjoy your gifts with our appreciation,

*Pam Powers*

**SEE INSIDE
FOR READER'S
SURVEY**

# Get up to 4 Free Books!

**Suspense** ➤ ◄ **Romance**

We'll send you 2 Free Books from each series you choose plus 2 Free Gifts!

Try **Essential Suspense** featuring spine-tingling suspense and psychological thrillers with many written by today's best-selling authors.

Try **Essential Romance** featuring compelling romance stories with many written by today's best-selling authors.

## Or **TRY BOTH!**

# YOUR READER'S SURVEY
## "THANK YOU" FREE GIFTS INCLUDE:

▶ 2 lovely surprise gifts ▶ Up to 4 FREE books

**PLEASE FILL IN THE CIRCLES COMPLETELY TO RESPOND**

1) What type of fiction books do you enjoy reading? (Check all that apply)
   ○ Suspense/Thrillers ○ Action/Adventure ○ Modern-day Romances
   ○ Historical Romance ○ Humor ○ Paranormal Romance

2) What attracted you most to the last fiction book you purchased on impulse?
   ○ The Title ○ The Cover ○ The Author ○ The Story

3) What is usually the greatest influencer when you <u>plan</u> to buy a book?
   ○ Advertising ○ Referral ○ Book Review

4) How often do you access the internet?
   ○ Daily ○ Weekly ○ Monthly ○ Rarely or never

---

# YES! I have completed the Reader's Survey. Please send me
2 FREE books and 2 FREE gifts (gifts are worth about $10 retail)
from each series selected below. I understand that I am under no
obligation to purchase any books, as explained on the back of
this card.

Select the series you prefer (check one or both):

❏ **Essential Suspense** (191/391 MDL GMRQ)

❏ **Essential Romance** (194/394 MDL GMRQ)

❏ **Try Both** (191/391/194/394 MDL GLY6)

| | |
|---|---|
| FIRST NAME | LAST NAME |

ADDRESS

| | |
|---|---|
| APT.# | CITY |

| | |
|---|---|
| STATE/PROV. | ZIP/POSTAL CODE |

© 2017 HARLEQUIN ENTERPRISES LIMITED
® and ™ are trademarks owned and used by the trademark owner and/or its licensee. Printed in the U.S.A.

ROM-817-SCT17

◀ If offer card is missing write to: Reader Service, P.O. Box 1341, Buffalo, NY 14240-8531 or visit www.ReaderService.com ▶

**BUSINESS REPLY MAIL**
FIRST-CLASS MAIL    PERMIT NO. 717    BUFFALO, NY

POSTAGE WILL BE PAID BY ADDRESSEE

**READER SERVICE**
PO BOX 1341
BUFFALO NY 14240-8571

NO POSTAGE
NECESSARY
IF MAILED
IN THE
UNITED STATES

stop she was going to make next. But she didn't see much of a way around it. Well, she didn't have to go see Asher now. But she didn't feel right about letting it sit, considering what had just happened.

She drove down the highway in a haze, then turned sharply into Stim's parking lot.

She put the truck in Park and turned the engine off, then took a deep breath and shook her hands as she let it out.

It was almost impossible for her to process how she had gotten here. From her house that morning, to Alex's house, to Alex's bedroom. And then to here. But here she was.

She got out, suddenly very aware that parts of her were quite sore. She shoved her hands into her pockets and lowered her head as she walked into the coffee shop.

She was suddenly filled with a strange sense of déjà vu. Asher was standing there, his back to her, working on making a drink for a customer who was standing there waiting. She waited to feel something. Regret. Desire. That same awe that she had felt watching him make drinks just a couple of weeks ago.

There was nothing.

She was grappling with that when he turned around, white to-go cup in hand, and their eyes clashed. Then he smiled. Like he was actually happy to see her. She was a terrible person.

"I'll be right with you," he said. He turned his focus to the customer and handed the man his drink, made some quick small talk with him. Then returned to Clara.

Clara kept her eyes on the other customer, who was

putting a packet of raw sugar into his coffee cup. She was not going to start this conversation with an audience. So she waited. And Asher waited too. Awkward silence descended, and they both watched the poor man putting the sugar packets—way too slowly—into his coffee.

Finally, he walked out the door.

"Good to see you," Asher said. "You have something you want to talk about?"

"Is it that obvious?"

"The awkward silence kind of...gave it away."

"Right." She clasped her hands in front of her. "I can't go to Eugene with you."

He nodded once. "Okay. Is it because of that guy at The Grind?"

Clara closed her eyes. "No." She opened them again. "Yes. I mean...it's complicated. It is and it's not. But I can't... Something happened. With him."

Asher shrugged. "Okay. Well, if anything's ever... not happening with him, we should go out again."

She blinked. "Okay." Except she knew that she wouldn't want to go out with him, even when things weren't happening with Alex. Because one thing she had learned from her first sexual experience was how attraction felt. And it wasn't the same as whatever her crush on Asher had been.

"Don't be a stranger. Hey, before you go, do you want coffee?"

"I don't like coffee," she said.

He actually looked surprised by that. "You don't... But you order coffee from me all the time."

"Yeah. I liked you. Not coffee."

He looked a little dazed. "Damn. I guess I was

asleep at the wheel on that. But like I said, it's not a big deal. If things don't work out with him, seriously, come back and don't order coffee for me, just ask me out."

She shifted her weight from foot to foot. "I have to go to work now."

"Okay. See you around."

She turned and walked back out of Stim, more than a little bemused by what had just transpired. He really just…didn't care. Well, he did a little bit. Because he definitely seemed to like her. But he wasn't jealous. Wasn't possessive at all.

"What kind of new age, hippie crap was that?" she muttered as she got into her truck.

She didn't like it. She had gone on a date with Asher and Alex had just about morphed into a caveman. She liked that. Much better. She didn't want wishy-washy milquetoast feelings masquerading as respect. She wanted…she wanted to feel something. She wanted the man she was with to feel something. It didn't have to be love, it just had to be worth putting some effort into.

Something worth being changed for.

There was no doubt that being with Alex had changed something in her. Or maybe it wasn't being with him only. Maybe it was getting to the place where she had been brave enough to ask for what she wanted. To admit to herself what she wanted.

It was complicated. And it was big. And she had to go and let that sit in her chest while she did a shift in the tasting room.

As Clara drove down the winding road that led to Grassroots Winery she looked at the trees that lined the narrow roadway, being mindful of the fact that the twists and turns could be deadly if she took them for granted. She sighed. She'd been twisted and turned by life quite enough, thanks.

Though, now she felt a bit twisted and turned in a good way.

The corner of her lip turned up into a smile and she drove on in silent amusement at her own double entendre.

Maybe she was too immature for sex. Or maybe she was exactly the right kind of person to be having it. Because at least she was enjoying it.

Enjoying the fact that she was no longer a virgin.

She hadn't thought much about it. Mostly because she hadn't defined herself by it. No one in town did. She was defined by her losses. She was the sad girl who had lost both parents. And recently, the sister of a deceased war hero. Loss was what defined her. Not something she'd held on to.

She blinked back unexpected tears as she pulled into the lot at the winery. Then she looked in the mirror in the truck's sun visor and grimaced. Great. She hadn't really thought to check her hair and makeup.

She looked... Well, she looked slightly wrecked. She had gone in to talk to Asher like that.

She cringed in horror. Clearly, she was not as smooth as she imagined. He had asked if something had happened with Alex and she had confirmed it, all while looking like something had definitely *just happened* with Alex. And the worst part was, it wouldn't even be gross assumptions on his part. It was the absolute truth.

She groaned, smoothing her hair into place and

wiping at the mascara smudges beneath her eyes. Then she took some gloss out of her purse and slipped it over her lips. They looked pink and full on their own, but she preferred that everybody thought it was from makeup. And not from getting seriously kissed recently.

She collected her things and walked quickly across the parking lot, then across the green lawn that led to the tasting room. Normally the rusting setting brought about a certain amount of peace. For a few reasons. It was beautiful, first of all. But also, it wasn't her responsibility. It was a lovely place that somebody else took care of. That she was just able to go to and find a certain amount of respite. Even if it was a work shift.

But she felt no peace today. None at all. She felt... well, a little bit giddy. And like she was wearing her recent conquest on her sleeve like a Girl Scout badge.

Achievements in knot tying, making a campfire and losing her virginity.

She rolled her eyes at herself as she walked into the tasting room and shuffled straight into the back to dump her things. When she came out from the kitchen area, she nearly ran into Sabrina, who was standing there with her arms crossed.

"Okay, spill. What really happened?" Sabrina looked avidly interested in Clara, and Clara felt transparent.

"I lost track of time," Clara said, looking behind Sabrina and hoping to see a dining room full of people. Because that at least would give her an excuse to be busy and not talk. Sadly, it was early yet and the place was empty.

She hurriedly began searching for bar towels to

fold. Towels were always necessary. And they'd keep her hands busy and give her something to look at that was *not* Sabrina.

"You don't lose track of time, Clara. So tell me. Are you sleeping with him?" Sabrina asked, clearly on tenterhooks for interesting gossip. For once, Clara had some.

But it was a loaded question. A seriously loaded question. And one that Clara could choose to sidestep. Or at least, one that she could use to her advantage, because Sabrina meant Asher. She did not mean Alex.

"I can honestly tell you that I am not sleeping with Asher," she said, grabbing a damp towel and beginning to wipe down the nearest countertop with extreme officiousness.

"Are you sleeping with *somebody*?"

Apparently she was transparent as hell.

"Are *you*?" she countered.

"No," Sabrina returned easily. "Not even a little bit. Not even close. And anyway, this isn't about me. Did you miss your work shift because you are sleeping with someone?"

"Yes," Clara mumbled.

"Clara! I cannot believe you weren't going to tell me. If I'm going to cover for you—and I have been covering for you today—then I need to know the circumstances of what's going on."

"I'm sorry. I was going to tell you. Eventually. I don't have anyone else to tell. You're…you're the best friend I have, and I know we haven't even hung out outside of work, so that says sad things about my personal life, but it's true. It's hard when everything you are is bound up in the sad things that have happened to you. And people either want to only talk about that, or they don't want to talk about it at all. And sometimes they even avoid you because they don't want to talk about it. But you don't do that. I know it's because you've unfortunately been through the same stuff. But regardless, it makes me feel close to you, and I appreciate that."

Sabrina looked surprised. And pleased. But she pushed down what looked like the start of a smile. "Not close enough to me to tell me that you're sleeping with someone," Sabrina grumbled.

"Because I had never done it before," Clara all but exploded. "I didn't feel ready to talk about it. I don't feel ready to be here facing people. It just happened. And…it's stupid. I never really thought much about it. I mean, about being old to have not done it with somebody before. But I guess I kind of was. And now I'm kind of dealing with all the implications of it after it's already happened. And now it's weird. It's weird, because here I am at work and already telling you I was a virgin a couple of hours ago and I'm not anymore."

Sabrina blinked, and her mouth opened, then shut again. "Well. That's not what I expected."

"You didn't know you'd made friends with somebody who was so cool, did you?"

Sabrina pulled a face. "Are you okay?"

"Yes. I'm good. I mean, I'm a little bit crazy, but I'm good."

"You're not weird," Sabrina said. "Or crazy. There's nothing wrong with waiting for the right person."

Clara laughed. "I don't know if he's the right person. I just know that it happened. And that I wanted it to. I mean, I kind of pushed him into it. Not that he wasn't excited about it. You know."

Sabrina looked slightly uncomfortable now. "Right."

"But it's not like I'm in love with him. And it's not like it's going to be forever. It's just that it was time."

"Clara," Sabrina said. "It…you didn't sleep with Asher, did you." It wasn't a question.

"No."

"So it was…"

"Yes," Clara said in a rush.

She trailed off into silence, and she noticed that Sabrina's cheeks were getting increasingly pink. Then she lifted her head, her eyes full of a strange expression she couldn't quite read.

Clara shifted uncomfortably. "Yes," she repeated.

Sabrina let out a long, slow breath. Then she bit her lip, looking like she was debating what she was going to say next.

"Sabrina," Clara said gently, "I just overshared to a massive degree. And I never do that. I have never done it with anyone. Because I've never liked anyone enough to do it. So whatever you're going to say, I'm not going to be upset. And I'm not going to judge you. I know you want to say something, so just say it."

"How good was he?"

That was not the question Clara had expected. *What were you thinking?* Or *Did you know that I used to get it on with him too?* was more what she was expecting given her extreme reluctance.

"How *was he*? He was…well, I mean it was great.

It was great, though I don't have anything to compare him to."

"But amazing, right?"

"Yes."

Sabrina closed her eyes, a wistful expression on her face, and Clara had to wonder if she was thinking of Liam. It was clear to Clara that even though it was ancient history, Sabrina wasn't over Liam. And there was no mentioning Alex without her thinking of Liam.

"That's good to know," Sabrina said. "I mean, nice to know at least one of the Donnelly brothers lives up to the hype."

Clara couldn't tell if that was a burn directed at Liam or not.

"He's not Liam," Clara said.

"I know," Sabrina responded. "I do. But it's impossible not to wonder about similarities."

"I guess." She supposed it was impossible if you were still hung up on your ex. But since Clara didn't have one...

"This isn't about me," Sabrina said. "I'm sorry. I'm being weird about the fact that he's Liam's brother, and I know that. But Liam being back in town is making me a little bit crazy."

"Do you still love him?" Clara asked.

Sabrina laughed. "No. I don't love him. I don't think I ever did. I mean, how much can you love somebody when you're seventeen and ridiculous? You don't know how the world works. You don't know what you actually need from life. From a man. He wasn't a man either. He was a boy. Older than me, sure, but still a boy. So I don't love him." She blinked rapidly. "I might hate him. But I don't love him."

There was so much bitterness in what Sabrina said. And it made Clara feel…well, she didn't know quite what it made her feel. A little bit nervous, truth be told. Because she knew that Sabrina had not set out to be hurt by Liam. She knew she hadn't set out to fall in love with him, in whatever way a seventeen-year-old could fall in love.

*But she was a teenager. And you're not.*

Still, one thing that Clara didn't need was another wound that was never going to fully heal. She didn't want Alex to be a wound.

She wrinkled her nose. He wouldn't be. That wasn't what this was about. It wasn't about Alex. It was about her. She knew that he was only going to be here for a short amount of time. She knew that he was only here to help get the ranch established. To get the bison brought in.

And that was good. It really was. Because she had taken some control in that. And she had finally tapped into a part of herself that she'd been ignoring for a long time. It was healing. Or it was part of it. Part of making herself more than a creature of grief tossed around by life's waves. Against all those damn rocks.

And when Alex left, she would be a fully, sexually awakened woman. With bison. That was the dream. Well, maybe not so much the bison. But it was *a* dream.

"I'm sorry he hurt you. But I'm going to be fine," Clara said, more to herself than to Sabrina.

"Girl, I hope so. But if in the end it hurts… At least he was good, right?"

Clara closed her eyes. "I think no matter what happens this will be worth it."

Sabrina's sigh was definitely wistful. "With all the pain Liam left behind, I wish I had more of those memories."

And that, more than anything, confirmed to Clara that what she was doing was fine enough. Necessary enough.

"Well, I pledge to make memories with Alex's naked body."

"Hell yeah." And then Sabrina lifted her hand and Clara just stared at it. "High five. No high five for sex? Okay."

Clara laughed. "Wait. I will give a high five for sex."

Her friend lifted her hand and they engaged in the world's saddest, most immature high five.

It was a very strange day. Clara had propositioned a man, lost her virginity, broken up with another man and taken a work friendship into real friendship territory. All in all, she was going to count it a win. And in this sad run of losses, she would gladly take it.

# CHAPTER FOURTEEN

ALEX FELT LIKE a damn teenage boy. Except never once as a teenage boy had he smuggled condoms in a paper bag that also contained soup and homemade bread. But that's exactly what he was doing now.

Standing on Clara's porch with a brown paper bag of deceit, ready to do for a second, third and fourth time what he should never have done even once.

But, oh well. Hell was hell, he supposed, unless you bought into the levels of it. And anyway, he was probably already headed to the lecherous pervert level, so he supposed he might as well go all in.

Right before he could knock, the door swung open and Clara answered it, looking bright eyed and disheveled, her feet bare. She was dressed in a pair of sweats and what looked like a thermal top that clung to her slight curves. She was beautiful. So beautiful he could hardly breathe.

"Hi," she said, sounding breathless.

"Hi. I brought... I brought soup."

"I don't like soup," she said.

"We had stew together last week."

"Stew is different than soup," she insisted. "I don't like soup. Stew is good. But I'm not—" she cleared her throat "—hungry anyway."

She stood there, looking at him, her expression laden with very unsubtle meaning.

"Not hungry, huh?"

"No. Not for… Well, come in."

Relief spread through him. No, Clara wasn't subtle, but he realized then that he had been a little nervous that her assertion she didn't want food might have been her way of trying to send him away. Apparently not.

He walked inside. The little space was cozy, warmed by a fire lit in the woodstove off the living room. He could hear it popping and crackling against the wrought iron, a strange, homey sound that reminded him of a safe, comforting childhood he'd sure as hell never had.

Before he could say anything, Clara took the paper bag out of his hand and looked inside. Her eyebrows shot up. "Are those condoms? Or very oddly shaped, rubber saltines?"

"I brought soup and safe sex," he said. "I'm recently informed you don't like soup, but I am hoping that you're interested in the sex."

She sagged with relief, her petite shoulders dropping, a smile lifting the corners of her mouth. "I am extremely interested in the sex." She set the bag down, and then turned to him, stretching up on her toes and grabbing hold of his face before kissing him.

He just stood there, his hands resting at his sides as he let her take the lead. She was so… She was sweet, and there was something both innocent and incredibly dirty about the kiss. Something to do with the fact that she didn't know what she was doing combined with the fact that she was clearly very enthusiastic about it. Desperate for it, even. Desperate for him.

He had spent a good portion of the day being angry at himself. Regretting what had happened up in his bedroom. Regretting that he had taken her virginity when they hadn't had any time. That he had done it in the morning, with the edges of his hangover still crowding around them. Regretted that he had proven he wasn't worthy of the kind of trust that Jason had placed in him. And then at some point, midafternoon, he had just quit caring. Because really, there was no point in having regret about it.

He had already known he wasn't the man worthy of that kind of trust. Because he already knew what he was worth. It had touched him. Deep. To know that somebody had trusted him like that. To know that his friend had seen him as the kind of person who would step up and take care of Clara. And the fact of the matter was, he had. But Clara wasn't a child. She was a woman. And the interaction he was having with her now was separate from Jason. Separate from his intentions, and from his wishes.

The only real regret Alex had at this point was that his friend wasn't alive to punch him in the face. That would make things feel equal. It would make things feel fair.

If Jason was here, something might have still happened with Clara. Or maybe it wouldn't have. Because maybe she wouldn't be in the space that she needed this. And maybe he wouldn't be either. Maybe she would be off dating a nice hipster guy that took her out to restaurants she hated and then had safe, nonthreatening sex with her in his tiny house. Which probably wouldn't even rock when they had sex, because he would surely be gentle enough with her not to cause that kind of commotion.

But Jason was dead. And that meant she needed something else. Maybe right now that meant she needed him.

God knew for whatever reason, he needed her.

And so he let her kiss him. And he enjoyed it. But there came a moment when letting her take the lead was no longer a question. Because it was no longer possible.

He gripped her hips, drew her up against him, let her feel how hard he was. How much he wanted her.

He wasn't going to resist this time. He wasn't even going to pretend. He wasn't serving a higher purpose, right now. He was serving the purpose of his own need, and since it seemed to serve hers, as well, he was going to go with it.

His own mother didn't much care whether he lived or died, so there wasn't a whole hell of a lot of point in pretending he was anything more than he was. Anything more than a man who had once been a boy nobody much wanted.

But Clara wanted him. At least physically. And he saw no reason at all not to take her up on that.

He kissed her deeper than she kissed him. Dirtier. And he showed her that there were some benefits to skill.

She tasted like surprise. Expectation. Innocence. And that shouldn't turn him on. But it did. It damn well did. Same as that soft thermal top she was wearing and those unassuming sweats. Clothes that told him she absolutely hadn't taken for granted she'd be having sex tonight. And that was hot too.

He lifted her up into his arms and headed into the living room, holding both her and the condoms. There was a small, braided rug on the floor that didn't provide much in the way of cushion for them. But, in the interest of efficiency, he grabbed a red blanket off the couch and threw it down over the rug, providing them with a little bit more.

He deposited her onto the makeshift bed, then straightened.

"Take your shirt off," she said, her words surprisingly bold.

He smiled. "Are you making demands now?"

"We had to go too fast earlier today," she said. "And now, I want the chance to really look at you. More than I did before."

He whipped his shirt up over his head, not seeing any point in arguing, since their objectives seemed to more or less match up. He got on his knees in front of her as she leaned back on her forearms, halfway propped up, her eyes roaming over his body shamelessly. He leaned over her, planting his palms on the blanket on either side of her, bringing his face down close to hers. "So, honey," he asked, leaning in and kissing the side of her neck. "How was your day?"

She gasped. "That's not fair. I can't think when you do that."

"Good," he responded. "I don't want you to think. If you think too much, you'll probably end up sending me home."

"No chance," she gasped as he nibbled his way down to her collarbone.

"Really? Why is that?" He needed to hear it for some reason. Needed to hear exactly what she was getting out of this. Maybe because—no matter what he told himself—he actually needed something to add to the pile of justifications he was stacking up in his brain. The justifications that made having sex with Clara okay.

"Because I want to do this here," she said, lifting her hands and sliding them down his chest. "Here in this house. I've had so many things happen here. So many bad things. My whole life is in these walls, Alex. And so much of it is bad. So much of it is pain. I want some good things. Some things that feel good. You feel good. And I know this isn't going to last. I know you're just here to look out for me. I know that this is all for Jason."

"Stop right there. This—" he waved his hand between them "—this is not for Jason. This is for me, Clara. And I can dress it up in my own head, and I can tell myself it's for you. I can tell myself it's because you begged, because you're asking me to help make pretty memories here in your living room. But the fact of the matter is, I'm doing this because I want you. And I need you to know that. Don't dress it up. Don't pretend that I'm some kind of nice guy doing you a favor. Don't let me pretend that either. I'm a horny jackass, and I just want inside you. Beginning and end of it. Okay?"

Her eyes darkened, her breath coming faster. And he wondered for a moment if she was going to shove him off her. He would deserve it, certainly, after that little speech. But he had to clear the air between them.

He couldn't let this strange, cozy, romanticized situation cloud the reality.

"That's the best thing you could have said," she responded, her voice breaking. "Because that's... I don't think I've ever been irresistible to anybody. No, I know I haven't been. Because everyone has done a great job of resisting me up until now. Up until you. That's what I want. I don't want pity, Alex. I don't want to be somebody's project. I don't want to be your dead friend's sister. I just want to be me. For just a little bit. And that's always been impossible here. Because as much as my tragic history is contained here in this house, it's contained here in this town too. It's what everybody thinks when they see me. I'm glad you see a desirable woman. I think in the end it's going to help me see it too."

Whether she was the one who closed the distance and started kissing him, or he did, he wasn't sure. But it didn't matter anyway. Because then, he was kissing her. Long, deep and intense, pouring all of the emotion he felt into it. He didn't know what the hell the emotion was. Some kind of pounding desperation that he had never quite experienced before.

This was wrong, and he didn't care. It was the definition of entanglements, and he didn't care. Alex had never had a girlfriend in his life. He didn't do the emotional stuff. And Clara was never going to be his girlfriend, that much he knew. But this wasn't some quick hookup between deployments. Wasn't some one-night stand with a woman he met at a bar off base. This was Clara. And he couldn't disassociate that from the moment. He didn't even want to.

She was ten years younger than him, and so much

less experienced, but with all she'd been through, the losses and struggles, he felt like she might understand him better than anyone else in his life.

He shouldn't care about that. When had he ever pondered whether or not he was understood? Never. And he shouldn't start now. Hell, this was far too much thinking during a kiss anyway.

So he shoved it all aside. All of it. Except for her delicate scent. Skin, soap and little else. Except for the way her delicate fingertips brushed against his skin. Except for the soft, sweet little noises she made when he parted her lips with his tongue and tasted her deep.

He pushed his hands up underneath that soft, completely unsexy shirt and pushed it up over her head. He removed her bra too, left her bare before him. The sweet, slight curves and enticement he wasn't going to try to resist.

"Indulge me," he said, knowing that he was pushing things, and not really caring. He was past the point of good taste, past the point of salvation. Might as well revel in it. "You had never kissed a man before me."

She bit her lip, shook her head.

"That means no man has ever touched you like this." He lifted his hand, slid his thumb over one tight, pale pink nipple, the answering tightness in his own body almost more than he could stand.

"No," she said, the answer choked.

"No man has ever done this either." He lowered his head, pressing a kiss to her soft stomach then moving down lower, to the tender skin just beneath her bellybutton.

"No," she gasped. "Alex?"

He forced his fingers beneath the waistband of her sweats, dragging them down her thighs and off her body, and then he just kind of hung out down there. Looking up at her bare, pale legs, at the extremely innocent pair of cotton panties that was stealing his view of that most feminine part of her.

He reached upward, pressing two fingers over her cloth-covered center. "Are these little foxes? Oh, and they have little hearts next to them." He pressed more firmly against her, and she gasped. He stroked her, reveling in the way her hips shifted restlessly against his touch. "Very cute."

"Do you really…" she panted "…want to have a conversation about my panties right now?"

"I might." He curled his fingers beneath that cotton border that lay at the crease of her thigh. "It's a pretty interesting subject."

"I don't understand why we're talking."

"I have a lot to say."

"How?"

"I just thought you needed to know how damn pretty you are," he said, leaning forward and pressing a kiss to the inside of her knee. "So." He punctuated that word with a kiss to that sensitive skin on her thigh. "Damn." Another kiss, this time higher. "Pretty." And that brought him right to those fox panties.

She was watching him, a mixture of horror and fascination in those blue eyes. She wasn't going to let him forget she was inexperienced. No chance of that.

It gave him ample time to look at himself. At his conscience. At his choices. But he found he still didn't care. If anything, it only got him hotter.

Slowly, slow enough that she had the chance to really understand what was about to happen, he swept the panties to the side. And he cursed.

"What?" she asked, sounding genuinely concerned.

"Just so pretty," he managed to force out through his tightened throat.

He shifted his hand, sliding his thumb along all that pale beauty. She gasped again, and he took his exploration deeper, parting her folds and slowly stroking her up and down, until she was making small, whimpering sounds.

"As much as I like the underwear," he said, curling his fingers around the fabric, "it has to go now."

He stripped it off her body, discarding it, then turned his focus back to her. Instinctively, she lifted her hips upward, and he was more than happy to respond to that invitation.

He lowered his head, tasting her, the need that had been consuming him since he'd had her earlier today only intensifying as he got the first hint of her flavor on his tongue.

He wanted to pleasure her, he really did. But that was just going to have to be a side effect to satisfying the beast that was roaring inside of him, demanding that he devour her.

For himself. For his own desire.

His own needs.

He gripped her hips, pulled her toward him and licked her, long and slow. She let out a sharp, short squeak, lifting her hand and threading it through his hair, pulling it hard.

He didn't know if she was trying to make him stop, or if it was just a response, but either way, he kept on going. Her hands came to grab hold of his shoulders, fingernails digging deep into his flesh as he continued to pleasure her.

He brought his hand up, pressing two fingers deep inside of her as he circled her clit with the tip of his tongue, before soothing it with one long, slow lap.

Her hips were pulsing against his mouth in time with his movements, demanding more, signaling how close she was.

Alex cared about that. Somewhere, dimly in the back of his mind. But mostly, he was just obsessed with having more of her. Now that he had embraced the idea of having Clara, he was insatiable. Drowning in this obsession, in this need that verged on pain.

He curved his hands around, palming her ass, lifting her more firmly against his mouth. And she screamed. Her release tearing through her, her entire body shuddering in his hands.

Just because she was satisfied, didn't mean he was. He kept on licking her, tasting her, until she was begging him to stop, but he pushed, just one more, and he felt her explode again. Then he raised himself from between her thighs, gathered her into his arms and held her until she began to piece back together.

"Alex," she said, her voice thick, like she was drugged.

He kissed her. Let her taste her own desire on his lips. He drew back, hurriedly shucking off his jeans and underwear before grabbing the box of condoms. He took out a square, tore the packet open and protected himself quickly before moving back to her.

"I don't think I can," she said, her voice sounding shaky, weak. "I mean, I don't think I can come again."

"I think we should test that theory," he said.

He hooked her leg over his hip and thrust inside of her, the passage easy this time because she was so wet with the evidence of her previous releases.

"Oh," she gasped, holding on to his shoulders. "It feels so good this time."

"Because you're more than ready for me now." He nuzzled her neck, kissed her, blazed the trail up to her mouth, before capturing it. "You want this," he said against her lips. "Tell me how much."

"I want this."

"You want me," he said, the words unexpected, even to him. "Tell me that. Tell me you want me."

"I want you, Alex."

He didn't even have to ask for his name. She had already known enough to give it. That he needed to hear it. That he needed to be sure that she wanted him. That she didn't just want a Band-Aid for grief. That she wasn't just taking him instead of Asher because he had somehow become the more convenient lay.

"Alex," she said again, when he withdrew and thrust back home. "Alex," she repeated as he began to establish a steady rhythm designed to drive them both crazy.

She was so hot, so tight, squeezing him just right. He thought his head was going to explode. He was pretty sure all of him might explode. He wanted to make it last. This time, it mattered for her.

Because he was the only man to ever be inside of her. And he wanted to make sure that he was the man she remembered. Forever. For always.

He pumped into her, his pelvis grinding against her clit with each thrust, and she lifted her hips to meet him each time. He had never been with a woman who seemed quite so in awe of what it meant to be with him. Who seemed so enthralled with having him buried inside of her.

He supposed that was the perk of being with a virgin. Sex itself was exciting. Was a novelty. But he wanted it to be more than that for her. He wanted it to be the best damn sex she would ever have. The sex that all future sex was compared to.

He wanted to ruin her for other men. Which was a damn fine thing, since he knew this couldn't last, and that was not what he should want.

Didn't matter. Apparently, part of him, possibly the part buried inside of Clara, was all caveman. And right now, there was no point in fighting it.

He withdrew slowly, then flexed his hips forward, pressing back in just a bit before pulling out again. He repeated the motion a few times, until she was sweating, until she was whimpering. Until she was begging.

She lifted her head, grabbing hold of his face. Then she looked up at him with those blue eyes, sparkling with need, with tears. Damn, that hit him square in the chest like shrapnel. He could hardly breathe. And she kissed him. Not a deep kiss. Just her lips against his.

It was sweet. It was simple.

It pushed him right over the edge.

He slammed back inside of her, all thoughts of teasing her, of impressing her with his skill, completely lost in the ragged race to the finish. He was desperate now. Desperate for release. He needed her. Needed this. And he was going to damn well take it.

When it overtook him, he was lost. He lowered his

head, pressed it against her collarbone, a low growl escaping his lips as he thrust into her one last time.

Her own sound of pleasure, a high, kittenish noise, mingled with the feral sound of his. And that feeling of her release, her internal muscles pulsing around him, sent an aftershock rocking through him.

He lay on top of her, breathing hard, sweat beading on his forehead. The only sounds in the room their breath and the crackle of the wood stove.

"How was that?" he asked, rough and ragged.

A smile spread, slow and sweet over her face. "Like a spoonful of honey."

# CHAPTER FIFTEEN

CLARA COULDN'T REMEMBER the last time she'd felt this
happy. But it was a strange kind of happy. One that
was weighted with a heaviness that wasn't oppressive so much as simply apparent.

She was lying on the floor, still on the blanket she
and Alex had made love on, and he had gone to the
bathroom to handle condom practicalities.

She rolled over onto her stomach and looked at the
paper bag that was only a few inches from her. He
had brought soup, but she wondered if he had anything else in there.

She hadn't bothered to look much past the condoms.

In fairness to her, condoms were fairly distracting.
Or at least, the implication of condoms.

She reached out and grabbed the bag, lifting the
soup container. There was a loaf of bread, wrapped
in plastic wrap.

She took it out and examined it. White bread,
which she *did* like.

She got to her feet, holding the loaf of bread in her
hand, taking a moment to be mindful of all the interesting twinges and aches in her body. She was a hard
worker, and prior to taking on the amount of ranch
work she did, she had been involved in dance. So

muscle aches were nothing new. But these were new muscle aches. Different. Part of this strange, wondrous thing that had happened to her today.

She didn't bother getting dressed to walk into the kitchen. She sought out a jar of honey, a couple of spoons and the butter dish.

Then she took those things back to the blanket. She tore off a hunk of bread and spread a bit of butter on it, then drizzled on some honey.

That was when Alex returned.

He looked at her and smiled, that easy grin of his. He was still naked too. And she just stared as she took her first bite of bread. She groaned, though she had a feeling it had more to do with watching the shift and bunch of his muscles as he made his way across the living room and sat down on the blanket beside her, and not so much to do with the butter and honey. Even if it was good.

It wasn't hot-ass-naked-Alex good. But then, nothing was.

"Did you work up an appetite?" he asked.

"My appetite is always on the verge of being worked up," she responded, popping the rest of the bread into her mouth and chewing thoughtfully. "Though I'm sure we burned some calories."

"Naturally."

It was strange, sitting on the floor with him like this, completely naked. Talking to him just like they had done last week. Eating bread and honey. Strange that she could be comfortable with him like this. It should be awkward. But it wasn't.

"So what's the plan, Clara?" he asked, breaking off his own piece of bread and dipping it in the honey.

"For world domination? For the rest of my life? Or for the rest of the evening? Because those are different answers."

"For us," he said. "For the rest of this."

She looked down, and for the first time she felt a bit self-conscious. A bit like he was seeing too much. "I'm not counting on you staying here forever, if that's what you mean," she said, forcing herself to look at him. If she could let the man inside of her body, she could certainly have an honest conversation with him. "I understand the terms of the will. Nobody in my life has ever stayed with me, and that's not me trying to make you feel sorry for me, that's just the truth. I've learned not to count on anyone to be there always. And to never depend so much on somebody that I couldn't survive without them. Because inevitably, I've had to survive without the people I love."

She cleared her throat, then continued. "I like you, Alex. I do. And this is really fun. But the will said a year, or until this place is operational. I figured we would work out a way for you to get your investment back, and then I would go back to running it alone."

Alex frowned. "You know, Jason didn't want to leave you, Clara. He didn't. I don't think he planned on sacrificing himself. I think it's just who he was. It was in him. I know it mystifies you that he went back to the military after your dad died."

Clara rubbed her arms with her hands. Trying to warm herself. She was suddenly, inexplicably cold. "I want to understand."

"You're angry at him, and I don't blame you for that. But he wasn't leaving you. I know he saw it as standing in the gap for you. For the whole country.

He believed in what we were fighting for, Clara. More than almost anyone I knew. He was more than just a good soldier following orders. He felt the work in his soul. And he thought nothing of dying for those he saw as his brothers in arms. For me. He just did it." Alex's Adam's apple bobbed up and down, and she wondered if he was feeling the same kind of tightness in his chest that she felt in hers. "He didn't hesitate. He didn't pause to think. He just…reacted. And if he hadn't, we'd probably both be dead." He cleared his throat. "And he was afraid that if something like that happened, you'd feel like you'd been left alone. That you would have a difficult time with things. Because he'd seen you lose people before. He loved you, Clara. If you believe in anything in this world, let it be that."

Clara pressed her hands against her eyes and sat still for a moment, pushing back against the pain. Pushing back against the tears. "I don't doubt that. Yes, I wish that he would have stayed here with me. I wish he hadn't gone back. I'm proud of him. I am. I just feel like I've lost enough, and sometimes I still can't believe that I had to lose him too."

"Of course."

"I'm as used to loss as a person can be," she said. "I don't like it, but it's part of me. And I want there to be more parts to me. This thing between us…it feels like a good way to explore those other parts. To find them. I know you're worried about this changing me. Changing something. But I want it to, Alex. I need to change."

"So that's what you want? Sex while I'm here?"

She nodded. "Yes."

"I can do that."

"You're a giver, Alex."

"I sure as hell am," he said, shooting her that grin that made her stomach do all kind of acrobatics.

How was it she was sitting on her living room floor naked with this man? Any man really. But this man in particular. He was so...

He made her hurt. Looking at him hurt. But not in a bad way. Not in the ways that grief and loss and all those things that had come before him had. Looking at him was like looking out at the ocean, looking up at the mountains. Knowing there was so much beauty in the world, and she would never see it all.

That was looking at Alex. Knowing there was so much more to him, but it would never be for her to discover. And she had something burning in her. Something she wanted to give. To go deep with someone. To find a way to understand and be understood. To find a way to be naked with someone in more ways than skin.

Because she was so damn lonely. Being with Alex was like pressing cold hands in front of the woodstove. She wasn't warm yet, but she ached. The numbness was gone. The haze. It was all sharp and clear and painful now. Evidence of how far she had to go before she could feel normal again.

Before she could be totally thawed out.

She settled against him, pressed her head to his chest and her hand just over his heart. He wrapped his arms around her and laid them both back down on the rug, tugging the blanket over them.

It was strange to be naked like this in her house with a man. Looking at the totally familiar surroundings, listening to the mundane sounds she always heard on cold nights. The pop of the fire in the wood-stove, the logs settling and shifting as they burned. The clock in the kitchen ticking away.

But she could hear Alex's heartbeat too.

And she wasn't alone.

"I was at ballet class when my mother died," she said, her voice sounding strange and muted.

Alex didn't say anything, the slight tightening of his arms around her body the only piece of evidence he'd heard what she said. They lay there in the dark, their breathing mixing together. There was something comforting about the darkness right now. Almost as if it covered them like an extra blanket. Insulating them—or at least, her. Making what she was about to say possible.

"Jason had to come and get me," she continued, the memory as fresh now as it had ever been. "He was home in between tours at the time, and he'd been doing all he could to help take care of everything. To take care of me. I was doing something at the barre, and then I looked out the windows that let the parents see into the rehearsal room from the waiting area and saw him standing there. He looked so…resigned. He didn't look sad. And that was what scared me the most. Because at that point, Jason almost always looked sad. This was different." She blinked hard, trying to keep the tears from falling. But then, it was dark, so she supposed tears were okay. "We were in the middle of practicing for a recital. I never went back after that."

Her mother had loved to watch Clara dance. She hadn't really found it in her to do it after that. Because it had made her think of her mother. Because it had reminded her far too much of that moment when she had looked up from her practice and seen her older brother standing there waiting to impart the worst news imaginable.

They had known it was coming. But knowing the storm was coming didn't prepare you for the devastation. It just foretold it.

"How old were you?"

"Twelve," she responded. "And I had to... I had to do everything alone."

"I'm sorry," Alex said, reaching down and stroking her hair, the affectionate gesture so much more than she'd had for a long time.

"I had to do all the...the growing-up stuff alone. My first bra. My first period. I didn't have anyone I could talk to about it. I've never... I've never really had anyone to talk to. Which is probably why I'm talking to you about my period."

"I've been inside you, Clara. Talking about a period is hardly more intimate than that."

Her face heated and she snuggled against his chest, the hair there rough against her cheek. "I guess not." She swallowed hard. "But I've never... Thank you."

She had been alone for so long, and this closeness brought the isolation into sharp relief. Her father had spent the years after their mother's death working himself to the bone from dawn till dusk. Jason had gone back to the military.

It was only four years later their father had died of a heart attack. Almost as if the weight of his loss had ultimately become too much and destroyed his body completely, crushing it beneath the weight of all that sorrow. Jason had stayed home from the military after that. But when Clara turned eighteen he'd reen-listed. And there had simply been no time to find out who she was apart from grief. Apart from losing the people she loved. She was trying to do it now. Trying.

Telling him the story of the day her mother died was a starting point. She'd never talked about it. Jason had been with her, he'd lived it with her, and so had her father. But they were both gone now. She was the only one left who had experienced the grief of that day and she wanted to say it all out loud so he could picture it too. So she had someone to share it with, even if it was a terrible thing to share.

It made her feel close to Alex. And she wanted that. At least right now, she wanted to know what that was like.

"It doesn't seem fair," Alex said after a long pause.

"Not at all."

"No. I mean… It doesn't seem fair that you had to lose your mother and father when they cared for you. When they had a life they were happy with, maybe. Were they happy with their lives?"

"It's hard for me to remember a time before my mother was sick. But my father loved her. And he changed once she was gone. He never recovered from it, and I think he died of a broken heart more than a heart attack." In so many ways, she'd lost him when she'd lost her mother. Like his life had been buried deep with her. "I think they were happy with their lives. Before."

"My mother was never happy." Alex's words, the fact that he was sharing with her, made her stomach tighten. "The only thing she cared about was my father, and I don't know that I would call it love.

I remember seeing some Bible verse on the wall at a friend's house when I was a kid. Something about love being patient and kind. And I knew, sure as hell, that whatever my parents had wasn't love. There wasn't any love in my house."

"I'm sorry, Alex," she said, her chest tightening with sympathy.

"Don't be sorry for me. I'm sorry for you. I'm sorry for your parents. Because they actually did care. And they didn't get to have each other long enough. My parents had each other for way too damn long. And then when my father finally did leave—because that's just what he does—my mother could never accept it." His hold on her went even tighter, his muscles tense, and she had a feeling there was even more to this than he was saying. But he didn't continue. And she wasn't going to push.

Because she didn't want to do anything that might compromise this moment. This time spent with him lying on the floor. Just being together. This time feeling like she knew somebody. And like he knew her.

"Why did you join the military?" she asked. Mostly because she wanted to understand him. But also, part of her wanted to understand Jason. She had a feeling Alex was the closest she would ever get.

"I wanted to feel like I mattered," he said. "Maybe that's stupid. And I guess now that I'm thirty-one and not eighteen, I see it differently. I'm not sure I carried that motivation with me through every tour. I'm not sure that's what sticks with me now. But in the beginning that was why. I wanted to do something that counted. To be something more than a poor kid with a mom who was mostly drugged out of her mind and an older brother who had left home and never looked back."

"What about your dad?"

"Oh, I try my best not to think of him at all. I don't blame him for anything. I don't give him credit for anything. Because my mom gives him plenty. And I think that's way too much thought for one asshole to have directed at him. He had four sons that he abandoned. He had a wife that he was never faithful to, that he never bothered to stick around for. The only thing he gave any of us was his name. He doesn't deserve deeper consideration than that. I refuse to give it to him."

She nodded, but didn't say anything. Then she snuggled further into his hold, finding an immense amount of comfort in the steady beat of his heart.

It represented everything this house had been without for far too long. Life. Someone to share it with.

And right now, whatever the flipside of this was, whatever the ultimate consequence for this moment of happiness, she was going to take it.

She'd had too much of the alternative. Didn't she deserve this?

As Alex's calloused fingertips trailed up and down the line of her back, flirting perilously close to brushing against her ass, and then going past flirting, she decided that she did.

So she kissed him. And after that, they didn't talk at all.

## CHAPTER SIXTEEN

HE WAS DOING the walk of shame. There was no way to dress it up. Returning to the house in the wee hours of the morning before the sun was even up. But, judging by the light in the kitchen, at least one, and probably all of his brothers were absolutely up. Not that it should come as a surprise to him. The ranching business kept early hours. And running a dairy meant those early hours were even earlier.

He figured since he had been absent so often recently he had to get his ass back this morning. Or maybe he was just tempting a lecture. Maybe he thought he deserved one.

He had spent the night with Clara. On her living room floor. And now his entire body ached. In a couple of different ways. It ached because he was over thirty and he was just too old for that nonsense. It ached because he'd wanted nothing more than to have her again this morning, rather than leaving her there, sleeping peacefully in front of the waning woodstove fire.

But he had left her. And he felt like he deserved some kind of additional medal of valor.

Of course, all of the actions from the night before basically nullified that.

He had taken her virginity only yesterday morning, and by 2:00 a.m. he'd had her at least five times. There had been absolutely no concession given to the fact that she was inexperienced and might be sore, not that she'd been anything less than enthusiastic even once. No. Still, he hadn't even thought of that. Not until he had woken two hours after the last time and begun the drive back to the Laughing Irish.

Now the full reality of the situation was beginning to settle over him. And he had a feeling his brothers would be more than happy to drive it home. They would not be kind.

Not even Finn, who had been in favor of this. He couldn't be. Alex had played the part of horny jackass. What the hell were older brothers for if not to try and keep you on some kind of straight and narrow?

Though, he imagined that might require his brothers to know the way to the straight and narrow. And frankly, he wasn't sure any of them did.

He walked up the steps and into the house, into the kitchen, where the three of them paused in their coffee drinking and turned to look at him.

"Good morning," he said, his voice sounding like gravel. "Where the ever-loving hell is the coffee?"

"Drank it all," Cain said, lifting his mug to his lips. "Didn't expect you."

"Sorry," Liam added, not looking anything of the kind.

"What the hell am I supposed to do?" Alex asked.

"Make your own damn coffee, princess," Finn responded, taking a long, slow sip of his own and taunting Alex with the vision of someone else getting caffeinated.

"Too damn early," Alex muttered, walking over to the coffeemaker.

"Well, I guess you should be a little more responsible with your time management," Liam said, his voice maddeningly calm. As far as Alex knew, Liam Donnelly didn't know the meaning of the word *responsible*. His older brother was a hellion, and had been from the time they were adolescents. Getting a lecture on respectability from him was just hilarious.

"Got your full eight hours, did you?" Alex asked.

"Maybe even ten," Liam responded, his lips quirking upward into a smile.

He had probably slept in a bed too. Though, he certainly had not had sex five times yesterday. But Alex couldn't even feel smug about that. And, had he hooked up with just any woman, he would have been. He would have rubbed it in his brothers' faces.

But this was Clara. And he couldn't do that. He felt…well, he didn't regret it. But he did feel guilty. And that was a damn complex emotion. Particularly for a man who disliked complex emotion, or emotion of any sort. He preferred for all of his feelings to come from two places. His stomach and his dick. Anything more than that was unnecessary.

And yet, here he was, scowling around the kitchen, looking for the coffee.

"So where were you?" Cain asked.

"You *have* a teenage daughter, Cain. It isn't me."

"Oh, I know. But if you're going to engage in a grand performance, coming home when you know all of us are going to be in the kitchen, then I'm going to assume you want to be called to the carpet. Or the stone floor, as it were."

Dammit. He wasn't even wrong.

"I was out," he said, reverting to sullen teenager then and there, and basically making a mockery of what he'd just said to Cain.

"Obviously. Probably had sex. And it must be sex you're ashamed of."

Finn shot him a knowing look. "You did it, then?"

"Please. That's what the kids call it, Finn," Liam said. "If Alex was out fucking, I expect him to say it like a man."

"Watch your mouth," Alex said, shooting his brother his most deadly glare.

Liam's eyebrows shot up. "Oh. Well, I didn't realize you had a *special* lady."

"You don't know what you're talking about," Alex said, "and you need to watch your mouth."

Cain assessed Alex for a moment, and then his jaw went slack. "No, Alex," he said. "You didn't... Not with that *girl*."

"She's a woman," Alex shot back.

"A woman who is barely five years older than my daughter," Cain said.

"And if I had a daughter, that might be a problem," Alex said. "But I don't. And I'm a hell of a lot younger than you, old man."

"Still," Cain said. "You're supposed to be taking care of her, not banging her."

"Are you going to help me out here?" He directed that question at Finn. "You're the one who advised that I go for it."

"Right. And did you actually take my advice? Are you telling me that you legitimately thought through the entire thing and acted based on what I said?"

No. Obviously he couldn't say that, since there had been very little in the way of thought from the moment he had kissed Clara yesterday morning to him standing here in Finn's kitchen today.

"She's a grown woman," he said to Cain. "And she made it perfectly clear that she wanted it. I respect her."

"Neat trick," Cain said. "Turning it into being about respect."

"That was Finn's fault too," he said, feeling defensive.

Finn shrugged. "Since when do you listen to me?"

"Bunch of assholes." He didn't normally get angry. Didn't normally let much of anything ruffle him. But his body was still on fire from a night with Clara, and his conscience was burning too. His brothers were cutting far too close to his own concerns, and he just didn't need it. Not when he felt bad enough, and was running on almost no sleep.

He stood in the center of the kitchen, not really sure where anything was.

"Did you need help making the coffee?" Cain asked.

"That would be good," he said, deciding to take his brother's sarcasm as a serious offer as he moved over to the kitchen table and sitting down. "I didn't sleep."

"Yeah. And you're kind of grumpy for a man who didn't sleep for the reasons you didn't sleep," Liam pointed out.

"And you don't think I know it's messed up? You're right. I came in here so you three would yell at me."

"That's very interesting, Alex," Liam said. "What in your childhood made you feel the need to do that?"

"Screw you."

"You seem like you have a lot of anger," Liam replied, unfazed.

"You seem like you have a lot of jackass."

"Why don't you bring her over for dinner?" Finn asked mildly. "I bet Lane would like to meet her."

"It's not that kind of thing," Alex said. "And before you get in my face, she knows that."

"I meant," Finn continued, "because Lane would like to talk to her about carrying her honey in her store. She really liked the sample you brought back. And she's always looking for new products for the mercantile. And, not only that, but for her subscription box too. She said something about how honey would ship well? I don't know. But I trust her expertise on the subject. She could really help kick-start that part of Clara's business."

"It is too damn early in the morning, Finn," Alex said. "I need coffee. I can't think."

"Well, you don't have to. Why don't you have her over?"

"And have you all sitting around leering at us?"

"Come on," Cain said. "We're not going to do that. Lane and Alison might. I can make no guarantees there."

"Do *not* tell Violet."

"Why would I tell my teenage daughter who her uncle is sleeping with? I question why *I* know who you're sleeping with."

"I don't put much past you, considering you're catching up on all that big-brother garbage."

Cain smiled. "It's true, I am. Being raised an only child, knowing that my younger brothers were out there, not benefiting from any kind of torment from me to help build their character, well, things like that are probably the reason you're taking advantage of this nice young lady."

"Screw. You."

"No time for that," Cain said, picking up his cowboy hat from the table. "Have to go milk cows."

"You're legitimately the worst."

"No," Cain said, "that's not fair. I'm *illegitimately* the worst. You and Liam are the only legitimate ones."

"Could you not spread that around?" Liam said. "It will damage my cred."

"Sorry you don't get to be a bastard," Cain said cheerfully. "But you do make up for it by being a bastard."

"True."

Alex wasn't sure how he felt about the change in his relationship with Clara. Wasn't sure how he felt about his brothers knowing about it. Or being here and working the ranch with them at all. He wasn't sure quite what he had wanted. To be told to stop, maybe. So that he could see just how strongly he felt about it. So that he could spend some time justifying what he was doing out loud.

But heckling aside, they were just…accepting. Of him. Of what he was doing. It was weird. It was weird to be in this kind of situation. Weird to have this kind of closeness.

To have these roots, which were starting to grow so deep.

He even felt closer to Liam, closer than they'd been growing up. You would think they'd have a strong brotherly bond already. And they did. It wasn't that they didn't. But there were strange gaps in that relationship that Alex couldn't quite figure out. Strange pockets of resentment that he felt Liam had toward him. Or maybe it wasn't resentment. Maybe it was just the fact that Liam didn't know how to forge connections with people any better than Alex did.

At the end of the day, they might have grown up in the environment that most closely resembled a regular old sitcom family. But it wasn't. They had been raised in the twisted, toxic version of *Leave It to Beaver* that had damaged both of their perceptions of family. And he didn't have to have a heart-to-heart with Liam to know that.

And Clara had been left with nothing. And he had crashed into her life, and maybe even given her something. Right now she felt like he had.

But he wondered how long she'd feel that way.

Though, the damage was done. He'd had sex with her—there was no going back and he didn't actually want to.

Which meant he had to double down on what he was here to do. Take care of her, take care of the ranch. Leave her better off than when he came.

*And then what, asshole? You're going to run into her all over town? Act like nothing happened?*

He looked around the room at his brothers. At this family they were making.

He'd never been good at roots. Never been good at permanent.

Because in his experience that only ended one way.

Maybe he should listen to that. Maybe there was a reason for it.

"All right, you worthless sons of bitches," Cain

said, standing up. "Are we cowboys, or are we cowboys?"

"Ranchers," Liam said.

"Dairy farmers," Finn added.

"I'm a cowboy," Cain responded. "Now let's get to work."

Alex watched as his brothers walked outside. Cain was right. They were cowboys. But Alex was also a soldier. And he had a mission. After he took care of business around the Laughing Irish, he was going to get to work in a serious way on Clara's ranch. It had been left in his control, and dammit, he had to take control.

CLARA WAS THOROUGHLY distracted at work the next day. But she didn't know how anyone was supposed to concentrate when memories of a very naked, very sexy Alex kept flashing through their mind. Memories of the things they had done. Of everything she had let him do, begged him to do. She was like a stranger to herself.

"Are you okay?" Sabrina asked.

Clara made some kind of dreamy sound and she was sure her smile was along similar lines.

Sabrina's eyes narrowed. "You could be less smug."

"Less smug about what?" Olivia crossed the room, popping into the conversation at just the wrong moment. Clara and Sabrina just exchanged a glance, and Olivia immediately looked crestfallen. Clara wasn't used to being the one on the inside. Was used to being the one that felt like she was standing on the perimeter of the friendship or on the outer edges of a joke.

The way that she and Sabrina were interacting was clearly making Olivia feel that way.

And Clara didn't like that at all.

"A guy," Clara said, stumbling over her words. "A guy that I…like."

Olivia brightened, clearly pleased to be brought into the loop. "Oh! That's nice."

"I guess so. I didn't really… I didn't expect for things to happen with him. But he's…"

"He's sexy," Sabrina finished.

"Yes," Clara said, shooting her an evil glare. "He is sexy."

"Do you love him?" Olivia asked, clearly interested now.

"No," Clara said, her answer rushed.

Olivia didn't seem to know how to respond to that. "But why would you date someone you didn't want to marry?"

"That's *how* you fall in love with somebody," Sabrina said, her tone sage.

"Well, obviously. But I just meant…where do you see it going?"

"Nowhere," Clara answered honestly.

"That's what I don't get. Just dating to date. And just…sleeping with someone to sleep with them."

"Because he's hot," Sabrina said, speaking very slowly. "Did you not hear that part?"

"I did," Olivia offered. "I guess that kind of thing just seems…dangerous to me. You could get hurt."

Clara's face felt warm, and her throat felt like it had been rubbed with a particularly spicy pepper. Because she didn't want to get hurt. She felt like she knew exactly what was happening with her and Alex, but Olivia looked so concerned, voicing Clara's own deep fears, and it made it feel too possible. That she might forget it was temporary. That he wasn't staying.

"Well I don't just... I know that... I'm not expecting anything from him," she stammered out.

"Okay," Olivia said, clearly skeptical. "I couldn't stand something that open-ended."

Sabrina gave Olivia a sideways glance. "Aren't all relationships open-ended to a degree? I mean, you really never know what will happen."

Olivia looked slightly stricken by that. "Not Bennett and me. I mean, we're going to get married. And he's a good man. When he makes that commitment he'll keep it. And that's what I want. I want everything in my future to be secure and set. Well, and I want a little farmhouse. And a golden retriever."

"That's very specific. I guess I just wanted a guy to love me," Sabrina said. And it forced Clara to wonder about Liam again.

"I just want to not be alone for a while," Clara said. "I've been alone. In that house. For so long. And Alex...being with him makes me feel not so alone."

Olivia looked subdued by that. "I'm sorry," she said. "I didn't mean to sound judgmental. I just... worry. I have a sister who really went off the rails and I feel like having a plan for my life... I just want to make choices and stick with them. So I know where I'm going." She cleared her throat. "But I want to be supportive. I'm not used to having friends. But I want to. And I realize some of it is my fault. If you've felt alone all this time, Clara, and I never noticed, I never did anything about it... I'm sorry."

"Me too," Sabrina said.

"You don't have to apologize. If there's one thing I know about basically being the specter of death, it's that people don't really know how to interact with you. I know it's not personal."

"I don't see you as the specter of death," Olivia said, looking incredulous. "I'm just kind of a self-ish bitch. Completely wrapped up in my own stuff. It's easy for me to get obsessive about my life. And about everything with… Well, wanting an engagement ring."

"You're in love," Clara said, "I think love makes people obsessive."

"Yeah," Olivia said, chewing on her lip. "I suppose it does."

"I'm not even in love," Sabrina said. "I've just been dealing with all the changes happening with Damien and Lindy's divorce. It's hard to accept that your big brother is a gigantic asshole."

Clara cringed. "I guess it is." She took a deep breath, wanting—needing—to mention Jason all of a sudden. "My brother is a hero," she said softly. "Alex told me that. Jason died saving him. He saw his friend in danger and he stepped in front of a bullet for him."

And for the first time, grief wasn't what led with that thought. When she made that declaration, she just felt proud.

"That's amazing," Olivia said softly.

"It is. And I wish… I wish he were here. But there are a lot of people who are here because of him. And that's kind of, well, it's kind of big. Certainly bigger than anything I've ever done."

"My brother has never sacrificed anything," Sabrina said, her tone bitter. "In fact, to serve his own needs, he basically detonated a bomb in the middle of our lives."

"I am sorry about that. But Lindy seems like she's doing an amazing job keeping the winery afloat."

"If she wasn't, she would never let any of us know," Sabrina said. "She was my sister-in-law for ten years. I know her pretty well. But I also know how hard it is to know her. She wants to put on a smile, keep her hair and makeup in perfect order and tell you everything is fine. She doesn't like help. She doesn't like to *need* help."

Clara frowned. "I don't suppose any of us like to need help. We've all been going through things and not talking about it."

"True enough," Sabrina responded.

"I think I could get used to talking about it," Clara confessed.

It was a relief to know she had friends she could talk to. Not just about Jason, but about Alex. And that they would be here when it was over. That when he was gone she wouldn't be alone again.

She would need that. Regardless of how well she controlled her feelings, she would miss him when he wasn't over at the ranch all the time.

She wasn't in love. She didn't want to be. She didn't want forever. She just wanted to follow this thing as far as it would go. Wanted to see how it would change her. How it would remake her.

The door to the tasting room swung open and Dane, Lindy's brother, a bull rider who was between competitions and coming back to the winery regularly to support his sister, walked in carrying a tray of cheese and a bottle of wine. "I have some things for you to test out, ladies," he said, heading across the room and setting the tray and wine in front of them.

"What is this?" Sabrina asked.

"Cheese from the Laughing Irish. Lindy is interested in partnering more with them and seeing what we can do with pairings. I don't know what any of that means. I'm just repeating what she said."

"Sounds like a good experiment to me," Olivia said, all but falling on the tray of cheese. Sabrina followed suit, though with less enthusiasm.

Clara had a feeling Sabrina was secretly afraid consuming anything from the Donnellys would result in her immediate death.

Clara wrinkled her nose. "I don't really like cheese. I mean, I do like cheese. But not weird cheese."

Dane's eyebrows shot up. "Okay. Wine then?"

"Eh."

"How did she get a job here?" Dane asked. It was a good question, honestly.

"Back off, Dane," Sabrina said. "She's our friend."

And it was those words that kept Clara warm the rest of the day.

## CHAPTER SEVENTEEN

THAT WARM AND FUZZY feeling turned into something else entirely when Clara walked back through the door of her little farmhouse. She was tired. The winery was slammed today with a couple of bachelorette parties and a large tour group of elderly women who had, frankly, been a lot more wound-up than the bachelorette crew.

But when she walked into the house, something was different. It was brighter. It took her a moment to realize that all of the lightbulbs had been replaced with a different kind. The light was no longer a soft yellow, but just a shade whiter. And had she not been so overly familiar with her surroundings she might not have realized that, but she had lived in this house her entire life, and to her, the difference was marked.

The house also smelled good, which meant that Alex had brought food from his future sister-in-law. She wandered into the kitchen and pulled the lid off the Crock-Pot, seeing macaroni and cheese inside. Well, she did approve of that.

The house was remarkably clean, and she noticed the bills that had been sitting on the counter were gone. A strange kind of panic clutched her. She had intended to handle those soon. She really had. She didn't need Alex to take care of all this for her. She frowned, and then began to walk back toward the front door. Just then, Alex made his way up the steps and into the house. And when he walked over the threshold, the floorboard didn't squeak.

"What happened to my floorboard?"

"What?" He looked like she'd smacked him in the face. She supposed he expected her to sound grateful. She didn't feel grateful.

"It squeaks when somebody who weighs over two hundred pounds steps on it. Why didn't it squeak?" she asked, her voice steadily getting higher and higher.

"I didn't realize that was your home security system, Clara. It didn't squeak because I fixed it."

"I didn't ask you to fix it," she said, panic clawing at her now. "I didn't ask you to do anything with my bills either."

"I had a house cleaning service come in today while you were gone. They filed the bills. Though I took care of the ones that would let me pay. Some of them I needed your information for. But I got your phone turned back on, so you're welcome for that too."

"Alex! This is my life, you can't just come in and overhaul everything."

"Actually," he said, moving deeper into the room, filling the space with his broad chest and shoulders. "I can. This is my house, Clara. This is my ranch. Your brother entrusted it to me. He entrusted you to me. And I have to make sure that everything is taken care of. It was all fine and good to come in and plan a few things, build a new fence and order some bison. But I'm trying to get things in order for you."

"It's too much," she said.

"It's a lot, I know. This whole thing. And I'm trying to make it less work for you."

"No, what you're doing is too much," she said.

"Clara, you're being unreasonable." He paused, sighing and then pushed his hand through his dark hair. "My brother thought you should come over for dinner to talk to Lane about the honey thing. But I'm happy to have that conversation with her. There's no reason for you to have more on your plate. She really liked it. And she does want to carry it in the store."

"Alex, if I have the opportunity to meet with Lane to talk about my product, don't you think I should do it?"

"Clara, I'm more than capable of doing it. Anyway, for now I'm technically in charge of the honey."

"You can take it and shove it up your ass, Alex. This is my ranch. You're not staying here. You're not staying with me. I have to know how to handle this stuff. You can't just do it all for me. I don't care how good your intentions are. Though, right now I have a feeling this has more to do with you than with me."

"This has everything to do with you," he said as he crossed the space on his way to the Crock-Pot. "Should I dish you some dinner?"

"No! Because I am not a child. I can dish my own damn macaroni and cheese, asshole." Clara stomped over to the Crock-Pot and jerked a bowl out of the cabinet above it. Then she slammed it down on the counter and wrenched the spoon from Alex's hand. She began to angrily ladle a portion into the bowl.

"I am an adult woman, thank you very much."

"Despite the fact that your diet basically consists

of items from a children's menu at a low-grade restaurant chain, I'm well aware that you're a woman, Clara."

"Yes," she said, "of course you are. At least when you want to screw me. But then you get this attack of… I don't know, *misguided chivalry* and suddenly you're treating me like a child again."

"You're the one who said that you had nothing and no one for the past few years. I'm trying to be someone."

"And I…" Her throat closed up, and she didn't know how to respond to that. Because, yes, just last night she had been thinking about how wonderful it was to have somebody. Just last night she had wanted to forge that bond even deeper between them so she could have something more than that scooped out, hollow loneliness that sometimes seemed to be what she was made of.

But this felt like too much, and it felt more than a little bit frightening. Because she could get used to this. To him. To his big body filling up this small space. To him changing lightbulbs and fixing squeaky boards that her father and brother had never gotten around to repairing.

But she had to remember that he was making this house her home. Under no circumstances was it ever going to be *their* home. And that was fine; she didn't even want that. She was only just starting to consider figuring out a life that transcended the aching loneliness and grief she had lived with for so long. The last thing she needed was to become dependent on somebody. Particularly a man.

Particularly him.

"Just talk to me before you do things," she said, feeling the anger drain out of her as she took her bowl and went to sit down at the small kitchen table. "And I want to go to dinner at your house."

It hit her then, with a kind of raw shame, that it was very likely he didn't want her to come to dinner because he didn't want her to be too enmeshed in his life. Like it was all fine for him to come over here and inveigle himself into the very fabric of her existence, but she couldn't come sit at the dinner table at his brother's house without it being a drama.

"If you really want to," he said. "But my brothers know I'm sleeping with you."

She choked on a hot noodle, melted cheese scalding the back of her throat. "Oh." She cleared her throat. "So what?"

"They'll probably tell Lane and Alison. And that means they're going to know too. And while you and I both know what this is, they're not going to. By which I mean they're undoubtedly going to grill you."

It was childish to be angry that he had talked to his brothers about their relationship. That he had told them that it was nothing more than the physical. Because hadn't she just had a conversation with Olivia and Sabrina about that very thing? Yes. She had. Really, she did not have a leg to stand on.

Except she felt like she did.

She felt indignant. The idea of him sitting there with his brothers and laughing and elbowing each other over what had happened last night, when it had been truly transformative and intimate to her, made her feel exposed. Made her feel young and stupid and small.

"It's not like I walked in and announced it," he added, not sounding defensive but…protective. It warmed her, even though she tried to fight it.

She looked up at him, at his concerned, serious green eyes that made her want to punch him in the face. "But I came home at about four-thirty this morning, and they aren't idiots."

"Well. Okay," she responded, still feeling a little bit hard done by.

"That was just a warning. I can't promise they're not going to make a lot of comments and try to encourage us to open up a wedding registry."

Clara laughed, because there was really nothing else to do. The idea of Alex marrying her was far too absurd. The idea of her wanting to get married was even more absurd.

"That funny?"

"You know it is," she said, getting up from her chair and walking over to the fridge. She opened it and dug around until she found a can of Coke in the back. She really needed to go to the store. She popped the top on it and took a long drink.

"You still want to come to dinner?"

"I damn well do want to come to dinner," she said fiercely.

"All right." He took a deep breath. "How about tomorrow? The bison are coming in a few days. It would probably be best to get this taken care of before then."

"I'm going to have to learn all about the bison too," she said, tapping the Coke can.

"You don't. We can hire somebody."

"Alex, I need to know what's happening on my

own ranch. Because it's going to be my ranch, and my ranch alone, when you leave. At least, the day-to-day of it. I need to be able to take care of it. If somebody can't come into work, I'm going to be the one the responsibility falls to. If the bison are going to be a massive part of what makes this a moneymaking operation then that control needs to be in my hands. You're not helping me by handing me something I don't know how to take charge of."

Silence settled between them, and she knew she was right, because if she wasn't, Alex would've clapped back with a comment immediately. But she had forced him to think. He was probably mad, but he couldn't disagree.

"All right. I promise you we're going to go over everything you need to know to make sure you can take part in the bison stuff."

"Good. I think I could be very accomplished at bisoning if I was just given a chance."

"I don't think that's a verb."

"It is," she insisted, taking another sip of Coke. "It's a new verb. One that I made up for just this occasion."

"Great. Well, I will make sure you're well versed in bisoning."

She nodded. "That's what I want."

"I do live to give you what you want."

Tension wound tight around them. And she realized then that he hadn't made a move to touch her. Hadn't made a move to kiss her. She wondered what was happening with that. If it was just because she had yelled at him the moment he walked in the door over squeaky board issues, or if he was deliberately holding back. She didn't want to ask. She didn't want to make the first move.

"I have more work to do outside," he said.

"That's fine," she said, sitting back down in front of her dinner.

"I might just head home tonight."

She swallowed hard, her throat feeling scratchy, and she wondered if it was from the earlier macaroni and cheese burn or because it just hurt so damn much in her chest that the pain was starting to climb upward.

"You work tomorrow?" he asked.

"Yes."

"Do you want to meet here and I'll drive you over to dinner?"

"That would be good."

"All right. I guess I'll see you then."

"Okay," she said.

He turned to go, and panic welled up inside of her. She launched herself at him, wrapping her arms around his shoulders and pressing her face against his back, right in between his shoulder blades. "Thank you," she said, her voice muffled.

He didn't move, and for a moment she just held him like that, until her hands—of their own volition—slid down his chest, just ever so slightly.

He turned his head, looking at her out of the corner of his eye. "You're welcome," he said, his voice rough.

She leaned forward, and that was all it took to get him to arch back slightly and claim her mouth. She held on to him tightly, turning her head and meeting his lips as best she could. It didn't allow for the deepest kiss, but there was something about the desperation inherent in the angle that she quite liked.

She could feel his heart raging beneath her palm, and really, her own heart was beating fast, as well. She wanted more. Instantly. The moment they started kissing, she wanted everything.

"I should go," he said, the words sounding labored.

"Sure," she responded.

Except, there was no *sure* about it. She didn't understand why he had to leave. She didn't understand why he couldn't just spend the night.

She wasn't going to beg him to either.

"I have to be up early," he said.

As excuses went, it was lame. They both knew that Alex was a soldier, and that he was tougher than a little bit of sleep deprivation. Still, she wasn't going to press.

"See you at dinner," she replied, brushing her fingertips against his chest, over his heart, before letting him go.

And when he was gone, and she sat back down with her mac and cheese, she didn't cry. Much.

## CHAPTER EIGHTEEN

CLARA SEEMED SUBDUED if oddly determined when Alex came to pick her up for dinner the next day. He had a feeling that leaving her alone last night hadn't sat well with her, but just assuming he was going to spend the night every night, establishing a situation where he did, didn't sit well with him.

What was between them couldn't last. Plus, he had to pay attention to what was happening at the Laughing Irish. He couldn't spend too many nights away, couldn't go wandering up to the house past time to start work whenever he felt like it.

At least, that all made for a convenient excuse. And he could pretend it had nothing whatsoever to do with the tightening in his chest that occurred every time he looked at Clara.

It was happening now. Even though she was being determinedly silent while giving off icy waves in the passenger seat of his truck.

"How did you sleep last night?" she asked, breaking the silence, her tone arch.

Okay. At least she wasn't going to make him wonder what this was about. It was about exactly what he suspected it was about.

"Not good. And alone."

She looked over at him, blinking rapidly. "Oh?"

"Did you expect me to lie? I haven't lied to you yet. I'm not going to start now."

"Well, you weren't exactly honest with me last night. You acted like... You acted like you didn't even want me."

He was grateful for the fact that he was driving. Because if he wasn't, he would have grabbed her and pulled her toward him. Hauled her up onto his lap and showed her just how much he did want her.

"I didn't want to make assumptions," he said.

She snorted. A completely inelegant sound. "There was no assuming involved in this. You knew I wanted you. I kissed you before you left. And if I hadn't, you wouldn't have touched me at all."

"Clara," he said, doing his best to stay calm. "I was being a gentleman."

"No you weren't," she said. "You were being scared."

Then he did pull the truck over. "Excuse me?"

"You heard me," she said.

A car drove by on the two-lane road, but no one came after that. They were in a small turnout with deep, muddy ruts carved into it, the woods on one side, the vacant road on the other.

"I'm wondering why exactly you think a twenty-one-year-old almost virgin would scare me?"

She shrugged. "I suppose that's exactly why I scare you."

The problem was, she was right. Not so much because of her age or her lack of experience, but all of the things that combined to make Clara *Clara*. She was an unknown entity. One he didn't know how to manage. He could tell himself he knew exactly how it was going to go. That he had a plan. But she was about as predictable as an Oregon weather forecast.

Sunny unexpectedly, then the storm clouds rolled in. And sometimes, a torrential downpour seemed almost certain, and then it didn't come.

The trouble with her wasn't her inexperience, it was the fact that she made him feel like he was the inexperienced one.

The fact that she made him feel like he had no idea what the hell he was doing.

"We are pretty tangled up, honey," he said finally. "Our livelihoods. Our bodies. Our past. Our pain." He gritted his teeth. "I don't want to be a part of adding to that tangle, Clara. And I want to make sure I respect the boundaries we've established."

"But I didn't ask you to," she said, her voice sounding dry. "You're treating me like I'm more fragile than I am. And that's just…that's exactly what I'm tired of. When you leave—and I know you're going to, Alex, I know you are—I want to feel stronger. I want to feel like I know how to do this. This man-woman thing. I want to feel like I have more to me than sadness and a ranch that doesn't work. I want the ranch to be working and I want to know how to work it. And I want to be known for more than just grief. I want to be more than grief. I feel like this is a part of that."

"So that's what you think? You're just going to orgasm your way to a better life?"

"Well, I've tried crying my way to a better life, denying my way to a better life and hermiting my way to a better life. Even if this doesn't work, it seems like the more fun option."

"I guess it's as good as anything."

She reached across the space between them, her fingertips touching his. "Better."

Looking at her made his chest ache. She was so pretty. So hopeful in this moment. He wished he had the ability to have that much faith in anything. In sex, in someone else.

He pulled his hand away from hers and put the truck in Drive, pulling back out onto the empty highway.

They spent the rest of the ride in relative silence, and Clara rolled the truck window down partway, letting the chilly air filter into the cab. He turned to look at her, the sight of her upturned face aiming toward the air, her eyes closed, her blond hair whipping back behind her, doing something strange to the inside of him.

He turned his focus back to the road, and he kept it there for the rest of the drive.

Finally they pulled up to the Laughing Irish ranch, the grand, custom log home looking almost ostentatious for some reason. Maybe because he had been spending so much time at Clara's more modest spread.

They both got out and headed toward the front door, and when he glanced at Clara he noticed her cheeks were turning pink.

"What?" he asked.

"I haven't been here since we…well, that was the first time I came here. And it was the last time I came here."

He tried not to laugh. He was unsuccessful. "That is an interesting double entendre."

She wrinkled her nose and punched him with a closed fist, right in the shoulder. "Don't."

"Then don't make it so easy."

"You're the worst, Alex."

He didn't know what came over him then, but he didn't bother to stop it. He reached out, wrapping his arm around her waist, then walked them both backward until the post at the bottom of the porch stairs prevented any further movement.

He leaned in, pressing his nose against hers. "But you like it."

"Hi, Alex."

Alex whipped around and saw Lane standing in the doorway. He released his hold on Clara slowly. Clara was bright red now.

"Hi, Lane," he said. "Do you know Clara?"

"We've met," Lane said. "But I wouldn't say we know each other. Nice to see you again."

Clara nodded, looking like her face was about to catch on fire.

The look Lane was giving him turned hard. "Why don't you come in for dinner?"

He pressed his hand to Clara's lower back, and the two of them made their way up the porch. But on their way inside, Lane waylaid him with a firm hand to the center of his chest. Clara walked into the house, and Lane resolutely slammed the door shut, leaving Clara inside and trapping him outside with his cranky-looking future sister-in-law.

"What are you doing, Alex?"

"I'm about to eat dinner at my house, Lane. Is there something strange about that?"

"You want to eat the dinner that I made. Which means you have to answer my questions. Otherwise, I'll throw you out to the barn with the cows."

"Under whose authority?"

"My own, jackass. I don't need to hide behind your older brother."

"I hate to break it to you, but I've faced down scarier opponents than you."

"Blah blah, soldier man," she said, her tone dry. "Answer my question."

"I did."

"I want to know what you think you're doing with her," Lane said.

"I think I'm having fun," he returned, feeling irritated that he was being put in a position where he had to justify himself.

"And you think that she's the kind of woman you should have fun with?" Her brown eyes were glittering with something dangerous, and he had a feeling that if he didn't give the right answer she was going to cut him in a vulnerable place.

"What the hell kind of fun has she ever had?" Now he just felt angry. Because sure, he didn't have marriage and family and kids to give Clara, but she didn't want them anyway. She had stated explicitly what she expected to get out of this. And it wasn't like he hadn't considered her feelings. He had. He wasn't a damn monster. "She's had a lifetime of crap. Beginning and end of story. If I can give her something else, I'm going to do that. And I don't need a lecture from you, no matter how well-meaning."

"You're my little brother, Alex."

"We're the same age, Lane," he said.

"Whatever," she responded, waving a hand. "You're Finn's younger brother. Consequently, it feels like you're my little brother. And if a good lecture is what you need, then a good lecture is what I'm going to give you."

He didn't know what to do with this. With this increase of people up in his business. He had spent most of a damn lifetime with nobody caring what he did. With a mother who considered him incidental—a failed experiment—and a father who had abandoned him outright.

His older brother had been way too busy dealing with his own stuff, and Alex understood that. But he had never had people—so many people—so interested in what he was doing.

He traveled light, and he moved a lot. This wasn't anything like his normal existence.

"Don't worry about it," he said. "It's not something I haven't beaten myself up over already. Anyway, it was your fiancé who suggested I go for it."

She blinked rapidly. "Finn?"

The fact that his brothers obviously hadn't gone and told on him immediately, but actually kept his confidence, warmed him. Slightly.

"He figured if she wanted it I should respect her choices."

She made a strange sound in the back of her throat. "Of course he did. Just know that I'm watching you, Donnelly. I'm watching you closely."

"Noted," he said, putting his hand on the doorknob and starting to walk into the house. Then Lane grabbed him and tugged him in for a hug.

"I want you to be happy, Alex," she said. Then she pushed him away, patting him on the shoulder. Alex was too stunned to respond.

Not just by her show of affection, but by this idea that he should be happy.

It had never really been a goal of his. Had never really been on the horizon.

"Thanks," he said, his throat unusually tight.

"You're welcome," she said, her voice soft. "I'll let you eat dinner."

"Thanks again," he said.

"I'm very magnanimous."

Then they both walked into the house, and the smell of the good food that Lane was cooking put some of what had just happened out of his mind.

Clara had been dragged off to a corner and was making conversation with Cain's fiancée, Alison.

Cain's daughter, Violet, was perched on a stool at the kitchen island, drinking a Coke and tapping her foot.

"Hi, Uncle Alex," she said.

"Hey, kid," he responded, because he knew it would make her mad.

She didn't even gratify him with a scowl. "I didn't know you were babysitting today," she said, her expression bland.

He narrowed his eyes. "Brat."

"Cradle robber."

"Hey, when you're forty and you come to Christmas dinner with a boy toy I'm going to owe you for that," he said.

She frowned. "Is that what you imagine my future looking like?"

"Absolutely. Wealthy, eccentric woman with some muscle-bound puppy trailing behind you."

"*What* future are you planning for my daughter?"

His brother's voice broke into his and Violet's conversation.

"Don't interrupt him, Dad," Violet said. "It was just getting interesting. Now, this boy toy—which is a lame term, by the way, I prefer masculine devotee—do I have him on a leash?"

"And we're done," Cain said.

"*Dad*," Alex said, affecting a mocking tone. "You're so lame."

"The lamest," Cain agreed.

They served up dinner and, thankfully, it was something he knew Clara would like. Just basic spaghetti, with nothing overly shocking in the sauce. He wondered if Lane had remembered him telling her that Clara was opposed to onions.

The strangest thing about the entire experience was that it didn't feel all that strange. It felt all right to have Clara here. She didn't feel out of place, and beyond the first few encounters with Lane and with Violet, there was really nothing else out of the ordinary.

And as everybody made conversation around him, Alex did his best not to think too deeply about the fact that it didn't just feel okay, something about it felt right.

CLARA FELT A little overwhelmed by the presence of the entire Donnelly clan. But fortunately they were also so talkative that the spotlight never seemed to be on her. Finn and Cain bantered easily with their fiancées. Liam, the brother Alex was closest to in age, sat there looking around the room, watchful. He was tattooed from his wrists up to where his bare skin was covered by his short-sleeved shirt. She had a feeling the tattoos extended underneath too.

Alex, for his part, seemed almost like a different person when he was with his family. He was always quick to smile, and quick to make a joke, but it was magnified now. As if he was keeping things almost determinedly light. Nobody seemed to be acting as though it were out of the ordinary, though, so she assumed that it was simply what he did. How he interacted with them.

"So how much honey do you think you can sell in my store in a month?"

Clara blinked and turned to look at Lane. "Oh. Right." The honey. That was why she was here. Not for a meet and greet with his family, like they were a real couple or anything like that. She was here for business. That was why she had fought for this dinner.

"On average, I can get about sixty full mason jars of honey. And once I expand, I can do even more."

"That's great. I have some honey in the store, but from nobody as close as right here in Copper Ridge. And my focus is definitely to get things as local as possible. If working with you will allow you to expand, that would be great, because I have a lot of monthly boxes that go out beyond what we could carry in the store."

Lane started to talk about the particulars of her subscription box service, and how she included sample sizes of local products. And Clara started to feel buzzed. If this worked out, there was a possibility she wouldn't end up having to work farmers' markets, which was all the better as far as she was concerned, since not having to be present when her products were being sold would enable her to get more done.

"Well, if we're only doing sample-size jars in the box I'm betting I can provide you with enough to go out even now."

Lane brightened. "That would be perfect."

"And you know, once the bison get to the ranch, we can do fresh meat in the store, if you're up for it. And if you want, I can look into making jerky. That would ship."

Lane tapped her chin. "I'm very intrigued by that."

Clara felt pleased that she had thought of the jerky idea on her own. "Obviously, I would have to wait and see how well all of that turns out, but we can start with the honey for now, and then when I have other products, I'll be happy to bring by some samples."

"Here's the question," Lane said, addressing the entire table. "I've heard that Clara here is quite picky." She looked at Alex. "So, are you actually going to eat the bison?"

Clara wrinkled her nose. "I'm not sure why I would do that."

Lane laughed. "It's good. And it's lean. Anyway, I think you have to sample your own product, don't you?"

"I might have to leave that to Alex," she said.

"Well," he responded, a strange smile frozen on his face. "I suppose I can sample it for you."

"Before you…quit working at the ranch?" Clara asked.

She didn't love the needy little sound in her voice.

"Yeah," he responded, a muscle jumping in his jaw. "Before the control goes to you."

She wasn't entirely sure she bought that explanation. She thought that maybe, just maybe, the first thing he had said was more accurate. It was just a strange response if he hadn't meant anything more than when he quit working at the ranch in the capacity that he was. Because it wasn't like he wouldn't be around to try a bite of bison burger or something.

The Laughing Irish was close enough to her place for him to come by sometimes.

*Yes, idiot, but he'll be done sleeping with you then.*

Yes, he would be, and in theory, she was okay with that. In theory, it was all good. In practice, it hurt a little bit in the region of her heart.

Dinner wrapped up, and at least on the score of making a deal with Lane, Clara felt good. When it came to Alex, she wasn't sure.

"Can you give me a tour of the place?" she asked him, keeping her voice low as she approached after the family dispersed.

"All right. But you've seen most of the house."

She wasn't going to correct him by reminding him that, basically, the last time she'd been here she'd seen the living area, then had been carried straight up the stairs and directly into his room. Mostly because she knew if she brought that up, she was going to start having flashbacks to the afternoon when he'd taken her virginity, and the last thing she needed was for her whole face to turn bright red.

"Well," he said, "we can start here in the dining room. This is the dining room."

"Awesome," she said. "You're really good at this. If you ever get out of ranching, you could be a tour guide."

"Sure," he replied, leading the way out of the dining area and back into the kitchen. "I mean, I have traversed deserts. I suppose I could lead groups of tourists."

"No doubt."

He led her from the kitchen into the living room, with its floor-to-ceiling windows that overlooked the majestic mountain view. There was a large, river rock fireplace that Clara imagined was extremely cozy in the winter. She also imagined the downside to living in a place that was populated by so many people was the fact that you could not use the fireplace for what she was imagining it might be fun to use that fireplace for.

That was just evidence Alex had corrupted her in some way. Because it made her feel like she was right back in front of the woodstove at her own house, with Alex's hands skimming over her naked curves. There had been a time when all she would have thought of when she'd seen a fireplace was how nice it would be to have a cup of hot cocoa in front of it.

But no. Now the only thing she could think of was how much fun it would be to have Alex ravish her in front of it.

"Living room," he said. "Perfect for family game night or, in our case, family arguments."

"Do you have a lot of family arguments?"

He lifted a shoulder. "*I* don't have them."

Given what she had witnessed at dinner, she wasn't that surprised. Alex seemed to argue with her with relative ease, but for some reason, he seemed to take the stance of being more easygoing and laid-back in the presence of his family.

He showed her a few more rooms, and then the two of them headed up the stairs. "Of course, I can't possibly breach anyone's privacy by giving you a tour of the bedrooms. But I can show you mine."

She wondered then if that had been her entire motivation behind asking for a tour. Not because she wanted him to take her into his bedroom so that they could…well, maybe she wanted that a little bit. But she realized she also wanted to see his bedroom when she was in a frame of mind to actually look at it. Because the first time she had been in there, she hadn't exactly taken in her surroundings. Well, nothing beyond the bed, anyway.

Alex pushed open the door to his room and left it open. Possibly as a sign that he wasn't going to jump her. Not that she would mind if that was his intention. But she had a feeling he was still in this weird space where he thought keeping his hands off her was something she wanted or needed in some way.

She looked around the room and was surprised by how little it contained. Oh, it was full of furniture. There was a dresser made of roughhewn wood and a bed that matched. The bed itself was a kind of lodge-style with a plaid blanket spread out on it and matching pillows. It was neat. Tidy. And she imagined that had something to do with Alex's military background.

There were pictures on the wall. Of the scenery surrounding Copper Ridge, of deer and bear. It was a generic collection of things you might find in a bedroom—any bedroom—in a log cabin in the Oregon mountains.

But it had nothing to do with Alex. Absolutely nothing at all.

And it occurred to her then that even though he had moved into this house, he didn't really live in it. And she had to wonder if he was even himself when he was around his brothers. All of it felt like something temporary. And it made her heart clench tight, made a fist of fear clamp hard around her throat.

"This room doesn't look like you."

"Excuse me?" he asked.

"This room. It doesn't look like you. It looks like some interior designer came in and made their best approximation of what a woodsy environment might look like if it were turned into a bedroom. But it doesn't look like you."

"What would my bedroom look like, in your imagination, Clara?" He crossed his arms over his broad chest, lifting one eyebrow.

"It would look like *you*," she said, feeling insistent, and frustrated that she wasn't able to nail down an apt, easy description. But then, there was no apt, easy description for Alex. Alex was more complicated than that. Alex was…well, he was essentially Alex. And there were so many layers of him to try to get through that it was incredibly difficult to distill him into just one sentence. Particularly if you were trying to use interior design to do it.

"So it would have my face printed on a bedspread?"

"No," she said, feeling irritated. "It would just have something of yours in it. And none of this is yours, right?"

"I didn't bring anything to Copper Ridge with me beyond one bag of clothes. The room was already furnished. Why would I bother to move any furniture out of the place I was living on base?"

"I don't know," she said, starting to pace. "But that isn't the point. You've been here for months and you haven't actually moved in. And your brothers... You're so weird with them. I mean, you're just very..."

"What, Clara? You're going to offer a critique on my bedroom and my personality? Do you really feel qualified to do that?"

"I've seen you naked, big man," she said. "So I feel pretty damn qualified to give commentary."

"A lot of women have seen me naked, Clara," he said, his voice somehow rough and gentle at the same time.

The words sent a twinge of pain through her chest, but she didn't allow them to get to her. Because that was what he wanted. He wanted to undermine this feeling that she knew who he was, that she might know what was happening here. But she was determined to not be undermined.

"Are you planning on staying here, Alex?" She hadn't planned on being so direct, but if it worked, it worked.

His lips twitched. "I've never stayed in one place for very long. I like to keep my options open."

"But your options aren't open, are they? You're planning on leaving. Once you're done with my ranch, you're planning on leaving."

He let out a long, slow breath, pushed his hand back through his long dark hair. "I don't know. That's the best answer I can give you. I'm not used to this," he said, waving his hand around. "This whole family house bullshit. This family togetherness thing.

Liam left home when I was sixteen, and I never really saw him much after that. I joined the military; he actually went to college. That was the thing that surprised everybody the most, you know. Not just that Liam had the drive to get through college, but the fact that he had apparently done well enough all through high school to get himself a scholarship. At least that's what I figure must have happened since there's no way he could have gotten the kind of money he would've needed to go. But trust me, as much of a screw-up as that guy acted like when we were teenagers, it didn't make much sense."

"Ah. So you both do it," she said.

"We both do what?"

"You both pretend to be something you aren't. Liam pretends not to try. And, let's face it, he must try really hard. Because scholarships don't accidentally fall into your lap and neither do the grade-point averages that earn them. But I watched him there at dinner, and you're right, he doesn't look like the kind of guy who spent his time hitting the books. And then there's you. You act like everything's a joke to you, Alex, and I wonder if anything is. I wonder if that smile is backed up by anything at all, or if it only goes as deep as your face."

His smile—the one that was almost permanently fixed on his face, twisted slightly, his upper lip curling into what nearly looked like a snarl. "Doesn't matter, does it? What do I have to complain about, anyway?"

"What do you mean? Why wouldn't you have a right to complain?"

"Because I'm not dead, Clara. I'm alive. I'm stand-

ing here in front of you. I can go on to have a pretty
damn amazing future, don't you think? I certainly
can't walk around feeling like I'm not supposed to be
here. That makes a mockery of it, doesn't it?"

Pain bled through those words, and they reached
down inside of her and made it difficult for her to
breathe. Made her gasp with the intensity of his emotion. He felt guilty. But it was something more than
that.

"Tell me," she said quietly, sitting down on the
edge of the bed. "Tell me about that day."

His expression turned harsh, his eyes looking almost wild. "You don't want to hear about that."

"Maybe I don't. But I might need to. It's important."

"No, I think it's important that you're spared the
details of your brother's death. I'm connected to it. I
know that. But you don't need that on you."

"Alex I… I care about you. I really care about you.
I don't want you to have to carry this alone. You're
helping me. With my ranch, with feeling like I'm
stuck in neutral, not going anywhere in my life. And
I want… I want to be there for you too."

"If I wanted to talk about it, I could talk about it
with anyone else. I could talk about it with one of my
brothers. I certainly don't need to dump it on you."

"You haven't talked to them," she said, her tone
soft. "And I don't think you will. So tell me. Please."

She wasn't sure she was ready to hear about it.
Wasn't sure she could stand to hear the story of the
day. She knew Alex wasn't going to give her details that would disturb her too much, she knew he
wasn't going to traumatize her. But she also felt like

he needed to be able to recount it. He was owed that. Because he was alive, and in his own words, he was standing. Except she had a feeling he was just barely standing.

He was on the verge of breaking apart, and he would insist on smiling the whole entire way. Until it was too late for her or his brothers or anyone to do anything to save him.

"This is exactly what Lane was worried about," he said, the words broken. "That I was going to hurt you."

"Maybe before it's all over, we'll hurt each other. And it will be equal. How about that?"

"Well, you can make it a goal, if you want."

She shook her head, sitting down next to him on the bed, sliding her fingertips down his forearm and lacing her fingers through his. "Tell me, Alex. I can't stand this. Knowing that the same thing that hurts me is hurting you. I know that Jason died. And his death hurts. But I'm not the only one with grief. And you… Well, you feel guilty on top of it."

He didn't bother to deny that.

"It was just routine stuff," he said, looking straight ahead, his eyes fixed on the wall in front of them. "We were on patrol and we got ambushed. There was someone hiding behind… I guess it was a rise. A hill. And suddenly the sand was exploding around us as bullets hit everywhere. And all these things go through your mind, like do you run away? Run toward it? Go low or go high? It was hard to tell where it was coming from, what was coming next. And then Jason just…stepped in front of me. Like it was the easiest thing to do. Like it was the only choice to make."

His Adam's apple bobbed up and down, the words getting rougher. Alex closed his eyes. "He shielded me. Then he went down and I... I ended that bastard on the hill, Clara. I found him and I killed him. But it was too late. Too damn late."

"What happened?" she asked, looking down, a sick feeling in the pit of her stomach. "After."

"I really wished he wasn't dead," Alex said, tightening his hold on Clara's hand. "I never had much use for religion, but I know that Jason did. He talked about God and hope like it was something easy. And I tell you, I've never bargained with God before. But I did in that moment. Because I couldn't imagine that Jason was the one who'd be taken. He had you. He had this place to go back to. I just..."

"Did he tell you he figured he'd be fishing in heaven if something happened to him?" she asked quietly, thinking back on the earlier conversation the two of them had had.

Alex laughed, the sound rough. "Yeah. He did. He'd say, 'Well, at least we know if this goes to hell, I'll be upstairs fishing with the big man.'"

"That sounds like him," Clara said, her throat almost unbearably tight now. She did her best to keep tears from falling, but she wasn't completely successful.

"I see it when I close my eyes," Alex said. "I see him. Not how he looked when he was alive."

Her stomach clenched tight. She wanted so badly to carry all of this for Alex, but she wasn't sure she could bear it. Jason had been her brother. The idea that he had been through all of that, that his body had suffered so much trauma was almost too much for her to think about.

But Alex had seen it. And he couldn't stop seeing it. It hurt her to know that. Went somewhere deeper than hurt.

It was so strange, because when Alex had first come around, she'd been so wrapped up in her pain. So wrapped up in her anger at the fact that Alex had been put in a position where he owned her. Or at least, owned her livelihood.

He had been the enemy in the beginning. And then after that, she had seen him as strong. As the soldier. As the one who was taking care of her, taking care of everything, of her life.

He had been the rock in her mind, at first to throw herself against, then to test herself on. The rock by which she had determined she would become stronger.

But she hadn't considered there might be a weakness in him too.

He was stoic, and when he wasn't being stoic, he was smiling. But now she felt like it was all a game. Like it was all for show. She wanted to break the rock down and find the man underneath. She wondered if he would ever allow it. If it was even possible.

"Alex," she said, rubbing her fingertips over his knuckles. "I'm glad you're here with me."

He looked at her, and there was something pleading in those green eyes. Something that she couldn't quite figure out. He wanted something from her, and it wasn't what she was giving. Dammit, she didn't know what to give him. She wanted to. She wanted to give him something, to take care of him in some way, in the ways that he had taken care of her. But she didn't know how. She just didn't care anymore that she was making the first move. Because it didn't matter. Right now, pride didn't matter. All that mattered was Alex. All that mattered was making sure he felt some of what she did. This big expanding thing in her chest that made it nearly impossible to breathe.

That made it feel like this, like the two of them together, was the most important thing.

Like maybe bison and the future didn't matter so much.

Like maybe nothing mattered outside of this house, outside of this room.

She got up quickly, stumbled toward the door and slammed it shut, clicking the lock.

"Clara?"

"Don't," she said, returning to the bed. "I just want… I just want to make you feel better."

She reached out, gripping the hem of his T-shirt and jerking it over his head.

He was so beautiful, her Alex. But she didn't just look at him now and see a gorgeous man. Instead, she saw a warrior. A wounded one. Maybe he didn't have scars on his body. Maybe he hadn't been physically injured. But he had the kind of pain, the kind of injury, that might develop an infection. That might fester inside of him, grow, spread, until it eventually killed him.

She put her hands on his chest, feeling all that heat, all that life beneath her palms, and she kissed him.

Alex sat there, frozen, and simply let her kiss him.

Simply let her take the lead. He tasted like desire, grief and need. And most of all like Alex. Her Alex.

Heart thundering in her chest, she broke the kiss, feeling dizzy. Feeling determined. Then she got on her knees in front of him, planting her hands on his muscular, denim-covered thighs. She looked up at him, their eyes clashing. That same expression was there on his face, pain and pleading.

But still, he didn't say anything.

"I want—" she fumbled with his belt "—I want you to understand."

He didn't ask what it was she wanted him to understand, and she didn't volunteer more information. Because the funny thing was, she wasn't fully sure what it was she wanted him to understand. Maybe it was less about understanding and more about a feeling. That she wanted to take this emotion growing in the center of her chest and plant it inside of him. This certainty he was meant to be here. This feeling that he mattered. She wondered if he would ever believe it. If he would ever understand. Like she did. Deep down inside her soul. She felt it with a certainty that surpassed anything else. That surpassed the surety that the mountains would still stand tomorrow.

She was so sure, and she knew he was anything but.

But if she could, she would open herself up and let him see it. She would carve it all out of her chest and give it to him.

She didn't know what else to do but this. Didn't know what else to do but lower his zipper and pull his jeans and underwear partway down his thighs.

He was beautiful. There was no other word for it.

She would never have thought she'd call that part of a man beautiful. But he was. Thick and perfect. Like he was made for her. She'd had him inside of her. And now she wanted to taste him.

She leaned forward, testing his length with the flat of her tongue. He was so hot, so perfect.

He reached out, grabbing hold of her hair. "Clara," he said, his tone a warning.

"Alex," she said, keeping her own voice soft. "I need you to understand. I need you to understand how much I...how much I want you. How much I want this. How good I want you to feel." But she wasn't sure it mattered. Because there was a kind of reckless confidence rioting through her. A certainty that desire would be enough here.

She wrapped her fingers around the thick, hard base of him and took the tip tentatively between her lips, sucking on him, running her tongue around the head until he groaned.

She knew he wanted her to stop. But she also knew he wanted her to keep going. So she did.

They were here. That was the thing. They had both lost so many people, both lost so much. She wasn't sure where either of them would be standing in five years' time, just that they would hopefully be standing. They were the ones who were left. The ones who were still here. And she wanted to do everything she could to revel in that knowledge.

They were alive. They were *alive*, and they didn't need to exist in endless pain. They could have pleasure. They deserved it. They could be happy, couldn't they?

Right now, she felt like she could at least.

Except this was so much like pain, and she couldn't explain why. Why she felt hollow between her thighs and needy and achy, desperate for him, even while she wanted to do nothing more than pour this pleasure on to him.

He jerked his hips upward, driving himself deeper into her mouth, and she adjusted the angle so she could take him. He was beyond himself, and she knew it. And that made her feel like she was being pleasured herself. But there was something satisfying in the denial of it. In this moment of focusing on him alone.

"Clara," he said, his voice a protest now. "Clara, *don't*."

But she didn't stop. She didn't. And she knew it would end this way, without her finding her own satisfaction, but she didn't really care. Because this *was* her satisfaction. Right now, this was all she needed.

She tightened her grip on the base of his shaft as she continued to work him with her mouth, his hips moving reflexively as she did. She sucked him in as deep as she could, swirled her tongue around his shaft.

"Clara," he said again, tightening his hold on her hair, his body shaking beneath her. And then he shuddered out his release, and she worked every last bit from him, held him until the last tremor stopped moving through him.

She felt like she'd been storm tossed. Like his orgasm was echoing inside of her. She rested her head on his thigh, her breath coming in short, sharp bursts.

His fingers tangled in her hair, and she waited for him to apologize. Waited for him to say it was a mistake. That he shouldn't have done it. She didn't want him to say any of that.

And he didn't. For once, he didn't. He didn't go all overprotective soldier and act like she was a helpless victim who needed rescuing from his lustful intentions.

No. He just sat there, breathing hard, his breath matching hers.

He stroked her hair, and it pulled slightly because he was all tangled up, but she didn't mind. It felt good. It felt good to be with him like this. To live in this moment. To live.

"Clara," he started, and she winced. Afraid the apology was coming now. "Damn."

She laughed, which was possibly a ridiculous thing to do after you had just given a man a blow job. But she couldn't help it.

"Is something funny? Because I have to tell you, with your face down there still, it's a little bit insulting."

That made her giggle. "I'm not laughing at your... at you. I'm laughing because I'm happy."

"That made you happy?"

She looked up at him, smiling. "That made me happy."

He reached down, sliding his thumb over her cheekbone, his green eyes serious. "I like making you happy."

"Yeah," she returned. "I like it too."

"You didn't have to listen to that story," he said.

"I wanted to. You're sleeping with me. And if you can't tell me about all of that...well, then you can't tell anyone, can you?"

He took a deep breath, his chest pitching sharply. "That was the plan."

"To not tell anyone?"

"There's nothing to tell. At most, I'm a coward who watched his best friend die."

She hauled herself upward, moved so she was sitting next to him. "You're not a coward. What happened happened. And it happened like it did. I don't regret it. That's a hard thing for me to…it's hard. It makes me feel like a traitor, but wishing it had gone differently wouldn't change it anyway and then you wouldn't be here."

"Would that be such a bad thing?"

"Yes," she said, her voice a whisper. "Yes, Alex, it would be."

"You lost enough already with your parents. Then him too. And I can't help but feel regret."

"But you can't," she said. "You shouldn't. You're here. We have to live, Alex. We're here, and we're alive. Jason isn't. And he can't be, no matter how much we wish it were different. So we have to do the living."

"Sweetheart," he said, his voice ragged. "I'm not sure I know how to do that."

"Well, you can learn, right? I'm learning things too."

"Yeah, you're learning pretty damn quick."

Pleasure spread through her. And since ignoring her pride had worked so well only a few moments ago, she thought she might as well go for broke. "Will you spend the night with me tonight?"

For a moment, she thought he might tell her no.

Thought that he might give her some lame-ass excuse about boundaries.

He nodded slowly. "Yeah."

She squinted. "Is it just because I gave you a blow job?"

He snorted, standing and tugging his jeans up over his lean hips. "Maybe. Although, I probably would have anyway, but it has to be said that I'm in a pretty good mood now." He smiled, and this time, the lines around his mouth looked deeper. "I mean, a good mood, all things considered."

Yeah, *good* was an awfully simplistic way to describe the mood, the moment, but she also felt that he knew that. That there was more to this moment than simply *good*.

It felt like a release, like a relief, so there was that at least.

"Now we have to go downstairs and face everybody. And you know they're going to know something happened," she said.

"Hey, you're the one who attacked me."

"I did not attack you."

"Funny—" he treated her to a lopsided grin "—I feel pretty damn attacked."

"Come on, Alex. You're a soldier. You should be able to withstand anything."

"Not anything," he said, moving his thumb up and down her face, sliding it around the edge of her lower lip. "Not anything."

## CHAPTER NINETEEN

IT WAS BISON DAY. It was nice, and it was clear, and Alex had woken up in Clara's arms. So all in all, he had a feeling it was going to be a pretty decent day.

He had warned his brothers that he wouldn't be down at the ranch that day, that he had obligations at Clara's that had to be fulfilled. They, of course, had winked and nudged each other and put the word *obligations* in air quotes because they were jackasses.

But Alex didn't care. Something had changed between him and Clara since their talk at the house. Since he had spilled his guts about everything that had happened with Jason. Since he had told her the whole story.

He had never wanted her to have any of those images in her mind. And no, he hadn't been graphic, though sadly, his memories were. But just giving her that many details made him feel like a prick.

She said she could take it. Told him she could handle it. That she wanted to. And he'd wanted to treat her like she could. Like she was that strong. Because hadn't she asked him to do that about a hundred times already?

So he had.

They hadn't spoken of Jason since then. Though, he had spent the last three nights at her place, eating dinner, having sex. And during the days, he'd been getting up early to go to the Laughing Irish and handle his obligations there, before returning to work at her place.

But today and tomorrow would be entirely devoted to the bison. Clara had the day off from Grassroots, and she was standing by to help oversee the project.

When he walked onto the porch he took a deep breath, exhaling slowly and watching as the air caught hold of it, making it bloom into a cloud that floated away on the breeze. It was the kind of air that bit you right in the throat, that early-morning sharpness that he'd come to love over the years.

He'd hated it at first, sure. Because early mornings always meant not enough sleep and too much hard work. As a teenager at the Laughing Irish he'd just wanted to crawl straight back into bed.

Not now though. Funny how things changed.

Suddenly Clara came bounding down the path from where the beehives were. Her cheeks were cherry red, and she had a big smile on her face. She was wearing a knit hat and a sweater that conformed to her petite curves.

There was something strange about this. Something domestic. And he didn't even hate it. In fact, part of him wanted to linger in it. Just stand there and enjoy this moment, standing on the porch, Clara running up to greet him, looking at him like he was every inch the returning hero he knew he wasn't.

*Maybe she needs you.*

He shoved that thought aside.

"Where have you been?"

"Checking the bees," she said, sounding chipper.

"I need to get a coffeemaker over here," he said.

"Oh, really?"

"If I'm going to stay the night and go straight to work in the morning, I need me some damn coffee."

"You're too dependent on that stuff," she said, sniffing.

"Says the girl who is powered by sugar."

Her forehead wrinkled. "You're super judgey, Alex."

"Somehow, I think you'll survive," he returned.

"Somehow," she said, "with hot chocolate and bison." She did a small hop. "The bison are coming!"

"Look at you," he said, amused by her enthusiasm. "The Paul Revere of bison."

She grinned. "That does beg the question, are the bison coming by land or by sea?"

"I don't believe they are seagoing bison."

"But you aren't certain."

"I am fairly certain, actually."

The two of them walked toward the barn, and Clara was almost bouncing next to him. He reached out and grabbed hold of her hand, squeezing it a couple of times. She looked up at him and smiled. That feeling of rightness overtook him, that same one that he'd had on the porch only a few moments ago.

Someday this would be Clara's. Clara's on her own. And then probably Clara's with another man. And she would be happy. So he should be too.

He checked his phone and saw that he had a text from about twenty minutes ago, the driver of the delivery truck letting them know he would be there soon. That meant they would pull in at any moment.

"I've got the heavy equipment all fixed, and we

can use that to move the bison between pastures," he said as they moved into the barn.

"I'm looking forward to that," she said.

"Good. And then over the next couple of months we should work on hiring a crew. Bison are pretty low-maintenance all told, but you're going to need some help."

"That's good. I do like a low-maintenance ruminant."

"And seagoing ruminants, apparently."

She shrugged. "I like what I like."

"Yeah. You also like me, though. So your taste is suspect, on that we can agree."

"True," she said brightly. "True."

That made his chest feel like it was splintering. Folding in on itself. Cutting him deep. Not because she'd meant to hurt him, not even because she had. Just because some part of him—some part long forgotten—felt like it was waking up, battling against defenses inside of him. "You're right about food, though."

She nodded. "I am definitely right about food. Other people force themselves to eat things that aren't very good. They do it because it's trendy, or they do it because somebody on the internet told them it was good for them. I eat what I like. Because as a man once said to me, the concept of 'good for you' is pretty complicated, Alex."

"He sounds like he was a very smart man."

She waved a hand. "Eh. He's okay."

"I bet he's handsome too."

She shot him an evil glare. "His ego is out of control."

"I imagine it's because women throw themselves at him all the time. At least, strange blonde ones with an affinity for bison and bees."

She ignored him. "Life is too upsetting to try to force yourself to eat kale on top of everything else."

He laughed. "Well, I agree with that. Although, I don't mind kale."

"That's it," she said, slapping her thigh and pointing dramatically away from them. "Get out."

"Wait a second, you went to a farm-to-table dinner with that jackass—"

"Asher," she supplied.

"Isn't that what I said? You went to that dinner with him, where I'm pretty sure you ate kale—"

"I hid it in the planter. And anyway, I don't have to eat kale to get you to like me."

"Oh, really?"

She flashed him a bright smile. "No. Because you already like me. Also, I give blow jobs."

"Can't argue with that."

"You're easy, Donnelly. Face it."

"That I am," he said, forcing a smile.

If only that were true. If only he were easy. As easy as he pretended to be. The funny thing was, he knew that Clara saw through the easy stuff he put on display. But, for whatever reason, right now he didn't challenge her.

When the large livestock truck pulled in, carrying the small herd of bison in the back of it, he and Clara climbed into the front and directed the deliveryman toward the field where the bison would live.

Then they released the gate on the back of the truck. It took the large, lumbering animals a few moments to figure out what was going on, but then, once the first one made his move out of the vehicle, the rest of them followed.

The truck driver helped Alex and Clara guide the animals into the field, and once they were in, Alex closed the gate behind them.

"I assume you know what to do with them from here?" the driver asked.

"We've got it covered," Alex replied.

After the driver left, Alex and Clara just stood at the fence and watched the animals graze. Something washed over him then, a sense of satisfaction. This was the first thing he had really taken control of on his own.

He had wanted to make a difference in the world, and so he had joined the army and become a soldier. That was about bravery. It was about the willingness to obey orders, even when the orders were hard. The willingness to serve a greater cause, and sacrifice yourself if necessary.

This, this was different. This was about building something with his own hands, making decisions. About having to live through the failure, which was not something he had planned on doing in the military.

It hit him then, square in the gut. That was part of what bothered him so much about everything that had happened with Jason. It felt like a failure. A failure on his part. And what he had expected to do with failure in the military was die for it.

He hadn't been prepared to live with it.

"They're kind of beautiful," Clara said, stepping up on the bottom slat of the fence and leaning over the top of it. "I mean, in that way a giant, walking rug can be beautiful."

"They are," he said.

But it wasn't just them. It was the whole place. The sprawling, green fields surrounded by trees, sharp, pine-covered mountains rising up and cutting into the horizon.

This was a place worth building a life in.

At least, for a man who was worthy of that life.

CLARA AND ALEX stayed outside, working in the garden and with the bees, and watching the bison graze until the sun sank behind the mountains, and blue twilight began to bleed over the landscape.

Then they walked back to the barn and spread a blanket out on the ground, a lantern hanging on a peg on the wall, illuminating the space with a pool of yellow light.

Alex took a cool chest out of the bed of his truck and brought it in, producing sandwiches—exactly the kind that Clara liked—and Coke.

They sat there with the barn doors wide open, looking out at the landscape beyond. The mountains looked like spilled ink, blotting out the stars, and the moon shone bright and clear.

"This was a good day, Alex," she said. "And I've had enough truly awful days to know that when you have a good day you have to hang on to it for as long as you can."

"I'll drink to that," he said, tipping his can of soda back.

"I think I can count how many good days I've had."

"Tell me about your good days, Clara," he said, leaning back, resting on his forearms.

She took a deep breath and forced herself to smile, because otherwise she might cry. "My fifth birthday."

"That's a good age. For most people, I imagine."

"I remember it being pretty good. I got a pony," she said, shaking her head, flipping her hair out of her face and laughing. "I'm not kidding."

"Was that your first horse?"

"Yes. And I loved her. There was also a pink cake with those little round sprinkles that make the frosting kind of crunchy."

"Definitely a good day."

"The first time I saw Jason in his uniform," she said, swallowing hard, trying to keep tears from falling. "I was so proud of him I thought I was going to explode. We all went out to dinner. We went to Beaches, which we never did, because it was so expensive. Mom didn't eat, but I didn't really think anything of it." She blinked. "Maybe it wasn't such a good day."

"Did you feel happy then?"

"Yes."

"Then it sounds like it was good."

"When I got my first ballet shoes," she said, "I never wanted to take them off. I shuffled around the hall in them, doing really wild leaps, because I was only six, and I didn't know how to do any actual ballet positions yet." She laughed. "I wore them outside to the barn to help Dad feed the horses."

"Did you love to dance?"

That was another thing that felt weighted. Heavy. Why were all her good memories twisted now? Gray.

Faded with time. The pony she'd had to give up after her mother had died because there'd been no way her father could handle the extra animal. One that wasn't contributing in any way. And Clara didn't have much time to ride anyway, since she had to help around the house with chores.

Jason in his uniform. Joining the military.

She wondered if he'd died in that uniform.

Her mother not eating, because she had been ill, even though no one had known it yet.

The ballet shoes.

The one thing she had ever loved to do off the ranch, that had been the first thing to go after her mother had died.

Too expensive, unnecessary, not enough time.

The idea of going back to the dance studio, where she had first found out about her mother's death, had felt like an impossibility anyway.

"Yes," she said, the word strangled. "I did love to dance."

It had been stolen, twisted, along with so many other things.

"You were practicing for a performance the day you found out about your mother?"

She nodded. "Yes. And I never went back after that."

"You never got to perform it."

She shook her head. "No. I couldn't face the idea of ever going back. Anyway, there was so much to do around the ranch. We all tried to go on while Mom was sick. We all tried to pretend that we were going to get back to normal. So that whole time we didn't interrupt what we were doing. But then...after she died… Well, Jason had to help take care of me, I had to take care of things in the house and around the ranch. My dad seemed to have four times the work he used to have, but I think he was just burying his grief."

"And you quit doing everything you loved."

She drew her knees up to her chest, misery expanding in her breast. She nodded silently. "Yes."

"Dance for me, Clara."

She looked up at him, at those sincere green eyes. "I don't remember how."

"I think you do. I bet you remember the dance you were practicing, the one you never got to perform. Show me. I'm here. And I want to see it."

Clara's heart was thundering hard, and honestly, she wanted to. She wanted so badly, in this moment, at the end of this very perfect day, to recapture something she had never thought she could have again. That feeling she'd had when she'd danced. That simple, sweet happiness that had been lost on that day all those years ago. It wouldn't be good. She knew that. She was out of practice, and she had long ago let those muscles get soft.

But the feeling. She just wanted the feeling.

She stood up from the blanket, moved into a vacant spot in the barn, the floor covered with dirt and hay. "You can't laugh at me," she said, giving Alex a warning look.

He was leaning back, just out of the pool of light, and his expression was shadowed. "I would never laugh at you."

She believed him.

She took a deep breath, and maneuvered herself into first position. Then, she began to dance.

ALEX COULDN'T BREATHE. Clara, wearing blue jeans and a T-shirt, dancing to classical music in her head, her movements graceful, slow and precise, was the most stunning thing he'd ever seen.

And it wounded him. What she'd said about her good days.

It killed him. He knew life wasn't fair. Hell, he'd always known it. Sometimes you were just born into a hard life and there was nothing you could do about it. Nothing but smile through it, not let it get to you. He'd done that as much as he could in his own life.

But with her...with her it struck him as being wrong. Unfair. She should have more good days. So many she'd lose count.

More than that, he wanted to give them to her. That conviction burned deep inside him and it felt perilously close to hope.

But hope hurt. And he didn't want it.

She was nervous, he could tell, and sometimes she stumbled. But she kept on going. Her eyes closed, her face tilted toward the light. And he could see when she began to forget she had an audience. When she shook off her nerves, her concerns about him watching her, her fears over getting a step wrong.

He could see when she just started feeling it. And the strange part was that he could feel it too. It was a helluva thing. He had never imagined that Clara— who loved macaroni and cheese and had just hopped around him like an excited puppy waiting for the bison to arrive, who kissed with enthusiasm, if no real skill—could be graceful too.

Could take his breath away.

A slow smile spread over her face, and she swept her arms in an elegant movement as she turned, then did a small hop, landing almost soundlessly.

She did another turn, and then transitioned into a leap that looked effortless, as easy as if she had never stopped practicing. She looked weightless. As though with each movement she had shed some of the baggage she carried around on her shoulders.

And for just a moment, he was right there with her. For just a moment, he felt like he could breathe. Like he was lighter inside too.

Then she turned, pausing, her hands on the hem of her T-shirt, her expression indecisive. For only a moment. Then she pulled her top over her head. She shed her layers with each move. It was erotic, it was sexy, but it also felt different than any kind of striptease he might have seen before.

Maybe because it wasn't a tease.

It was just Clara. Honest, open and uncovered. Bare to him.

The lantern light cast a glow over her pale skin, her nipples tight in the cool night air. She kept on going till she was completely naked. Until she was dancing with nothing to hide at all.

She glided forward, and dropped down to the floor, moving toward him, her blue eyes glittering. "That's not part of the original routine," she whispered.

"I didn't figure," he said, hardly able to speak around the lump in his throat.

She crawled forward, her hands on either side of

him, her breasts brushing his chest. "Alex," she said, still whispering.

"What?"

"Thank you. Thank you for asking me to dance."

He groaned, wrapping his arms around her waist and pulling her against him. She was so soft. So damn soft. And naked. And it was like he'd never touched a naked woman in his life. Maybe he hadn't. He couldn't remember. Because this was Clara, and there was no one like her. No experience he could compare her to.

"Did it make you happy?" he asked, his mouth pressed against hers.

He tasted a tear as it slid over her top lip. "Happy. Sad. Everything. It's hard for a moment to be only happy when so many moments in my life are connected to sadness in some way. But I think it makes this feeling deeper than. Fuller. Sometimes it feels like too much." She lifted her hand and dragged her fingertips over his cheek. "But it's better than that fog. It's better than hiding."

He caught her wrist and turned her palm so he could kiss it. "Is this better than hiding?"

"So much better."

He didn't ask her if this was happy. Because he knew the answer already. Deeper. Fuller. Too much.

So he just kissed her. Kissed her until they were both drowning in it. Kissed her until neither of them could breathe.

"This is a much better memory," she said, kissing the corner of his mouth.

"What?"

"A better memory. For the last thing that happened

after a dance. Being with you. Being held by you. Being kissed by you. This is better."

He slid his thumbs across her face, wiped away her tears. She'd cried way too many times in her life. Had experienced way too much hurt. If he could take it all away from her he would, and give her more happy moments. More bright spots, he would. If he could trade with her, he would, but he didn't have any more good memories to give.

But she looked at him like this was a bright spot. He was part of one of her happy days.

He didn't deserve that. He didn't deserve her. But if there was one thing he'd learned over the past few years, it was that justice didn't exist in the world, and some men paid prices they shouldn't, and others got rewards they could never hope to earn.

That was Clara. For him. For now.

And he wasn't strong enough to do anything but let himself get washed away by the tide.

## *CHAPTER TWENTY*

CLARA WASN'T A very good cook, but she was more
than capable of opening cans of SpaghettiOs. So
maybe it wasn't the most glorious spread. Bowls
of SpaghettiOs and cans of Coke poured into wine
glasses—which she had never used before, but were
still in the cupboard from years ago.

She had put a flower in the center of the table too.
And maybe that was stupid. Or lame. But she had
never really had a boyfriend before, so she didn't
know exactly what she was supposed to do when she
wanted to do something special for him. Well, except
for what she had done the other day.

Just thinking about the past few days with Alex
made her feel like she was breaking apart inside. But
it wasn't in that bad, hopeless way that grief had broken her apart so many times before. It was different.
Deep and rich. And wonderful even when it hurt.
She wanted to hold on to it forever. Knowing that she
couldn't was part of what made her feel like she was
being pulled apart in the first place.

She frowned and wiped her hands on her jeans.
She wasn't supposed to want this to go on forever.
She wasn't supposed to feel like she wanted this thing
with Alex to last. This was all about carving out the
life that she wanted to move forward with. Not about

putting herself in another impossible position where loss was inevitable and pain was certain.

It was funny to think that only a few weeks ago she had been planning some kind of strange, elusive future with Asher that she knew she would actually hate. But she had been so convinced that she had to be a different person in order to be happy. That in order to find some sense of normalcy she had to become a person that was entirely separate from the one who had lost her mother, her father and her brother.

That to be with someone she would have to push those losses down deep, hide the fact that she preferred sugary drinks to coffee. Hide the fact that she had the palate of a five-year-old and no interest in changing it. That she would have to be someone else, something else, to be interesting to a man. To be interesting to herself.

She didn't feel that way now. Somehow, being with Alex like this made her feel more centered, more who she was. Made her feel more at peace with certain parts of herself. She didn't feel she could say she was at peace with what she'd lost. She wasn't sure that was possible. But she definitely wasn't sitting around feeling stagnant. Definitely wasn't feeling consumed by that pain anymore.

There was a middle ground, she was learning. She didn't have to forget about the life she had lived up to this point, that had brought her here. Didn't have to let go of everything that made her Clara in order to be happy.

But all of that was supposed to be a revelation moving her to a point where she could stand on her own feet, not one that made her feel like she wanted to cling to Alex forever.

She was twenty-one. She should date other men. She should sleep with other men.

She didn't want to.

Part of her feared that, much like her resolute dislike of kale and her certainty that she would never like coffee as much as she liked cocoa, there was no man out there who would appeal to her the way that Alex did. And it wouldn't take sampling to prove it.

She had a feeling she was even more picky about men than she was about food.

Only one would do.

She frowned even more deeply and looked at the front door, hoping that Alex would come in soon.

He had been taking care of her. Bringing her food, helping her organize her bills, bringing the bison to the ranch, arranging for that contract with Lane so that she could sell the honey in her store.

She wanted it to feel more equal.

The front door swung open, and in he walked, bringing with him the smell of hay and sunshine and hard work. It seemed like he had brought the air in with him too. Like she could breathe fully for the first time all day.

"Hi, stranger," she said, resting her hand on the back of the kitchen chair and treating him to a smile.

"Hi," he said, surveying the table. "You cooked?"

"I microwaved."

"I'll take it." He bent down and kissed her, and it left her feeling dizzy.

He sat down at the table and then picked up the

wineglass, taking a drink. He frowned, his brows locking together. "What is this?"

"It's Coke."

"I did not expect soda in the wineglass."

"Did you really think I found a nice red to pair with the canned pasta?"

"I guess I wasn't thinking."

Her lips twitched. "It's a little bit of a Clara dinner." She sat down and picked up her own glass.

"I think I can handle it."

"Do you?" There was a needy note winding its way through the words, and she kind of hated it. Hated the fact that the question was kind of a leading, layered one. Even if she hadn't meant it to be. How long could he handle it? Did he actually like it? Could he handle it for a long time? Could he handle it enough to make this a place where he stayed?

She wouldn't say the rest of that. But she felt it. It burned hot inside of her breast, and she did her best to just take a sip of soda and look nonchalant.

"You know," he said after he took a bite of the SpaghettiOs. "This isn't that bad."

"It's amazing," she said. "Only snobbery prevents you from admitting it entirely."

"I'm not sure about that."

"I'm telling you," she continued, "people eat things they don't like because of what they're told is better."

"And I'm telling you that most people genuinely think homemade pasta is better, but we don't need to argue about it."

He smiled, and it felt real.

She would remember that smile. When she remembered her good days.

But it made her wonder. It made her wonder why his smiles so often weren't real. Why he seemed to play the part of the funny brother in front of his family. Why he was so married to a facade he didn't need.

She had seen more to him. She had seen him angry. She had seen him grieving. And she still liked him.

"I'm going to ask you something," she said.

"Should I be scared? Because that sounds a lot like a warning."

She lifted a shoulder. "I don't know. I guess that depends. Do my questions scare you?"

He smiled again, but this time it looked more forced. "You're pretty scary, Clara Campbell."

"Well, I'll be gentle. Alex, why do you feel like you have to be happy all the time?"

His smile slipped. "Have I acted happy all the time around you?"

"No. But I get the feeling that's what you do with everybody else. For some reason. And I don't know why. I think you've shown me a lot more than you show other people."

When she said that, he drew back slightly as though she had slapped him. "It's just social graces, Clara. People in general understand that. Given the amount of time you've spent dealing with all the crap life has handed you, maybe you don't realize that. But people don't want your baggage. So you push it down."

"Even with your brothers?"

"I don't know those bastards. I live with them now. I'm getting to know them."

"Are you?"

His jaw went tight, the lines by his mouth deepening. "I don't recall giving you permission to have open access to me, honey. We're sleeping together. That's it."

"That's it? Like sleeping together is nothing? Like it's so small?"

"I've slept with a lot of people."

"So what? That wasn't this. None of it was."

She knew that. She knew it with all of herself. Because how could anything else be what they had? If he'd had it before, then he'd have it still, she was sure of that. No, this was something unique. It was something singular. She didn't need to have had a lot of sex to know that. There was no way it was this easy to find somebody you could laugh with and cry with, grieve with and then have amazing sex with after. She could never have danced for anybody else. Not the way she had for him yesterday. She couldn't even admit to Asher that she didn't like coffee until she didn't care anymore what he thought. How could she have done any of those other things?

"I don't care how many women you've slept with. You told me about Jason. And you haven't told any other women about that, have you?"

"Just because you have sex with somebody doesn't mean you share things."

"No," she said. "Not with them. But with *me*."

"I haven't been with anyone since Jason died."

She blinked. "No one?"

"No."

"But you've been here and…and I'm sure a lot of women would…"

"Well, I didn't want to."

Hope and defiance filled her in equal measure.

"Until me. You didn't want anyone until me. And you're trying to compare me to other women, to other sex. You can't. We're not like anyone else, and I know that. I don't have to have had another lover to know it."

He was looking at her, looking at her like he was confused and dumbfounded by everything she was saying. It was so clear to her. So clear this was a singular thing. And he was the one who was supposed to have experience.

"What?" she asked.

"I don't think I've ever met anybody less afraid than you," he said.

"You were in the army. I'm pretty sure you've met a lot of brave people."

"Not very many people would come at me like this, Clara. And even fewer would show so much of themselves with no guarantee of getting anything back."

She was confused, and she was frustrated. She didn't understand why he was acting like she was breaching some kind of social contract by pushing for personal information. Maybe to Alex, being naked with someone wasn't personal. She might not understand that, but she could take on board that he felt that way. But even so, wasn't their relationship something else? He'd watched her brother die, a man they'd both cared for. He was sharing her grief with her. And that seemed like the most naked you could be with someone. Shouldn't they share their feelings?

Alex looked defeated. As if he couldn't quite come up with a response to a near-virgin's verbal manifesto on why their sex was surely different than any he'd had before. But it was. She knew it. She *felt* it.

"Clara," he said, his voice weary. "That's not how this kind of thing works."

"Why are you acting like there's a rulebook for this?"

"Because there always has been in the past."

"You just sleep with women and don't tell them anything? You sleep with them, and you never get to know them? You see them naked, and you touch their breasts and their…and you never…you never get to know them any better than that?"

"Yes. That's how it's always worked. You don't have to know a woman to screw her."

Clara frowned, her head starting to throb. "What's the point of that?"

He looked at her, his expression bland. Forced. "It feels good."

"Sure. But doesn't it feel lonely?"

He stood up, clearly irritated with her now. "It's not about feelings. It's about getting off."

"But what we have is about more than that. You can't pretend that it isn't. We do more. We feel more."

"Don't get ideas about this," he said, looking tired all of a sudden. "Don't start thinking this is going to be forever."

"I don't," she said, standing up and planting her hands flat on the table. "There's such a thing as middle ground, you know? I'm pretty sure I'm capable of wanting more than just your body and not expecting that I get your entire soul. But you more than anyone understand me. I mean, I think you could. And I think that I could understand you. I don't need you to just be big muscles and a male member. I don't need you to just be the guy that's here running my ranch. You can be you."

"Nobody wants that, trust me."

"Bull. I want it. Stop pretending you know what I want. Stop pretending you know what I can handle. And most definitely don't protect yourself by pretending you're protecting me. I am a grown-ass woman," she said. "And I might drink hot chocolate and eat pasta out of a can, but I know my own mind. And I know what I can handle. I did not make it this far in life, standing tall, by being weak. Do you think that your problems are going to crush me? I am much harder to break than that. If I was that easy to break, I would be smashed already."

She was breathing hard after that, feeling drained and elated. "You can tell me things, that's my point. We should be able to talk. I think we can do that without your being afraid I'm going to ask you to marry me. I just want... I want things, and I don't really understand them. But I feel a lot. Some of the best things I've ever felt. And it's because of you. I just want to keep doing that and having that. But I need... I need more of last night."

Alex sighed heavily, and he picked up his jacket from the back of the chair. "Thanks for dinner. I'll see you tomorrow."

"Where are you going?"

"Home."

"Aren't you going to stay and sleep with me?"

He looked astounded. She couldn't figure out why. "Why do you want me to stay and sleep with you? I just *offended* you. We just had a fight."

Silence settled between them and she could see

that he was serious. That he really thought he had to leave because she was upset.

"That doesn't mean I don't want to have sex with you. Alex, I want to be with you. Just because we had a fight doesn't mean I want you to leave."

"That doesn't make any sense to me."

"Why not? Because when you're with women, it's all about good feelings and only good feelings, is that it?"

"That's all anybody wants, Clara. Nobody wants to deal with bad moods and getting yelled at and putting up with with my crap. Why would they?"

"Why wouldn't they?"

"Nobody wants to deal with other people's problems. They all have their own."

"Don't you think the sex is better after you share something that matters?"

He looked completely dumbfounded by that question. "I don't understand."

"After I danced for you last night. Wasn't the sex better?"

"Sex is good. In general. That's why people make asses out of themselves over it. Why they make bad choices in order to have more of it," he said. "You don't need to know someone for it to feel good."

"It's better when you care. It's better when you understand what somebody's offering you." She looked down. "At least, it was for me. After I told you all that, after you told me everything about that day with Jason, it was better for me. Because it just feels like more."

ALEX WAS AT a complete loss. He had no idea how this woman he'd written off early on as being little more than a girl had rendered him speechless and completely unable to think. She was reckless with her words. She said bold things that could only come from someone who was very brave. Or someone who had never had her heart broken.

She came at him, again and again. And it didn't matter how much of a dick he was. It didn't matter that he kept telling her he had slept with other women, using that to hurt her. She still came back at him. She still believed the sex they shared, the physical connection, the emotional connection was special. And the worst part was, he couldn't even convincingly disabuse her of the idea. Because it *was* special. There was nothing and no one else like her, and there never had been.

Hot chocolate, honey bees, hatred of vegetables and all.

As much as he wanted to, he couldn't pretend otherwise. But she should let him. For their mutual sanity, she should let him.

And here she was, calling out something that not even his brothers ever had. Even though he had a feeling they knew. He had a feeling they all knew well that his smile covered up a whole lot of ugly hurt. But they had too much of their own to go digging through his.

It was what he counted on.

But Clara wouldn't be placated.

"Clara, I don't think this is a conversation you want to have," he said, aware of the condescension in his tone and wanting to punch his own face for it.

"Yes, I want to have this conversation. Because I have spent my life not having important conversations. I have spent my life losing people before we could talk about things. If you don't have the conversations right now, then you never know if you're going to have them.

"I was supposed to have a whole life to talk to my mother about boys and sex. I was supposed to have a life receiving wisdom from my father and trying to figure out who I wanted to be. He was supposed to see me graduate and encourage me to go forward and be an adult. I was supposed to have more time with Jason. For me to understand who he was, as a man, as a full human, instead of just the way I looked up to him as a little girl. I'm never going to have those chances. I'm never going to have that conversation. You act like I should be afraid of this." She faced him dead on, those blue eyes completely serious, full of fire. "But I'm not afraid of the conversations we *can* have. I'm afraid of all the ones we might not have because of time. Because of that bitch called fate that sneaks in and steals everything I've ever loved. I've lost too much to be afraid of this."

"The kind of stuff you're talking about is the sort of relationship that I'm never going to want."

"Why, Alex? It doesn't make any sense. Is it your mother?"

"You want me to stand here and talk about how my mother didn't hug me? How pathetic is that? No, my mother didn't hug me. But I'm a grown-ass man. I've been through the military. I've seen more. I watched my best friend die. Do you honestly think that has any bearing on who I am? That it's bigger than bombs going off around me? I don't see how the hell it could be."

"Because all of the stuff," she said, gesturing wildly, "all of the stuff that we go through builds our lives whether we want it to or not. It's the foundation. Believe me, I know all about that. I know all about resenting those things that came before, resenting what they turned me into, and trying to change it. What do you think Asher was about? He was a fantasy. A fantasy of everything I might have been if I had gotten to be a normal person my age. But I wasn't. And I'm not. There's no use crying over it, but I can't deny it either. You can't pretend that just because you've been through difficult things since then, what happened with your mother didn't damage you in some way."

"Because I don't want to get married, I'm damaged?"

She let out an exasperated sigh. "Probably. Most people want that. They want to spend their lives with somebody."

"Do you?"

He felt like an ass redirecting the question like that, but he didn't know what to do with this direct, full-on line of questioning either. He crossed his arms and waited, watched as the color mounted higher in her cheeks.

"I've never gotten to make a choice," she said, her tone gravelly. "I had to give everything up to do chores the ranch. And I suppose, to a degree, I'm still doing chores on the ranch. But I'm taking steps toward more. At least, I like to think I am. I wouldn't say definitively one way or the other if I want to get married." She looked away from him, licked her lips. And he gritted his teeth against the certainty that she did want to get married. And that it might even be to him.

But that was because she was inexperienced. It was because she was young. It was because she was conflating this thing between them with emotional feelings, since the physical ones were so damned good.

She was lonely. She hadn't had anyone able to pay her this much attention in years. Her mother had died. Then her father had been consumed by grief before he was gone too. And Jason had been absent.

Alex had created this space where she *needed* him, and he had done it for his own ego. He could admit that to himself, at least. But it was sure as hell doing a number on her.

"I already told you. My mother had me so she could make my father stay. He didn't stay. End of story."

Clara blinked, and then she looked up at him, luminous blue eyes narrowing slightly. "How old were you when your father left?"

"It doesn't matter. Everybody else's life centered around that bastard, and I don't pay him one more thought than I need to."

"Liar," she said.

The word hit him square in the chest like a brick, making it impossible for him to breathe.

"What is this? You think you know all of my inner workings? You think you know more about me than I do? My father was a useless asshole. All he ever did was travel the country knocking women up, as if he didn't have a concept of basic biology. He would make a show out of staying with them for a while, just long enough that they would hope, and then he would leave. He's not worth thinking about, it's not worth missing him or wishing he had stayed."

"Except you do. You did."

Anger rushed through him like a tide and he walked toward her, pressed his hands on the table on either side of her, closing her in. "You don't know what the hell you're talking about."

"The problem is that I do. And it is so hard to watch this, Alex. It's so hard to watch you try to pretend that nothing hurts when I think deep down inside you're like me. You're broken not because of war, not because of Jason. I'm not saying those things didn't hurt you, but they didn't make you. You're broken up because of all these things that happened to you when you were a kid, but unlike me, you can't even admit it."

"I wasn't happy when my father left," he said, pushing off the table and away from her, pushing his hand through his hair. "Are you satisfied?"

"No, I'm not satisfied. I'm not happy that you're hurt. I'm not happy about any of this. But I want for you to be able to share with me."

"None of it matters."

She whirled around, her tiny fist striking him square in the chest. "It does matter. Stop acting like *you* don't matter, Alex. Stop acting like your pain isn't important. Like you weren't worth Jason's sacrifice." She took a deep, heavy breath, burying her face in her hands. "Stop acting like you think you should have been the one to die."

She looked up at him, her eyes meeting his. "I don't know what I would do without you. I need you, Alex. And that isn't a small thing. In a very short amount of time I've come to need you. And I don't need you to smile. I don't need you to pretend that everything is fine. I don't need for you to be this strong, rock facade while everything underneath it is falling apart. I need you to be real. I need you to be human. Because God knows I haven't had enough humans in my life. I haven't let myself need somebody…" She swallowed hard. "I haven't let myself need somebody." She took a deep, shattering breath. "Not for a long time."

"You picked a pretty damn sorry savior."

Clara sputtered. "You picked me, asshole. You came storming into my life like a hurricane. You were strong and capable and wonderful. You made me want to lean against you. You made me think it was possible. So don't go acting like I somehow messed up. It was just you. You came in and became something that I couldn't live without. If you aren't worth anything then how would that even be possible? Your pain matters. All of you does. Not just your smile. Not just this everything-is-all-right stuff that you throw around."

He took a step toward her and reached out, cupping her cheek. He felt ashamed when he realized that her skin was wet. That she was crying because of him. Because of this. "It's our foundation, right? Like you said. I think I might be built on something cracked. Something broken. My parents left me. My father did physically. My mother did emotionally. My life has always worked out best when I moved around a lot. When I didn't depend on any one place or any one person. It's how I survived. I'm not sure I know how to be any different."

"Are you going to leave? You're going to leave your brothers, aren't you? You're going to leave me."

"Clara…"

"You can talk all about how you haven't decided, but I think we both know you have."

"I wanted to make sure you were taken care of. That's all."

"What about you? Who's going to take care of you?"

"Nobody needs to. I've been taking care of myself for a long damn time."

"Well, it's the same with me. But it was sure nice to have you here. It was sure nice to have you take care of me. Just because I didn't need it, doesn't mean I don't appreciate it."

"I'm a selfish bastard, Clara," he said, stroking her cheeks with his thumbs. "Because I enjoy your needing me far too much. And I shouldn't. Because I know I have to leave, so I shouldn't want you to need me at all. But no one ever has. You want to take care of me? I don't want that. I don't dream about that. But let me tell you…having you need me…" He could hardly speak after that, could hardly form the next words past the lump in his throat. He didn't know why he was telling her this, except she had said she wanted his honesty, and for some reason he wanted to give it. In this small space of time when they were together, he wanted to have this. Wanted to do this. There had never been a single damn person in his life that he had told everything to.

Liam had been a good enough older brother, but he had been distant. His parents…he was nothing but a nuisance to them. Conversations in the army didn't center around lame-ass childhood trauma. It was more about whether or not you thought you were going to get your ass blown to hell by an IED. How badly you wanted to get some R&R so you could go to McDonald's to get a burger and maybe later find a woman to screw.

There had never been anyone else he could talk to.

And there had certainly never been anyone who had needed him.

"My mother needed me for one thing," he said, his voice rough. "To make it so my dad felt obligated to stay. And then do you know why he left? He left because of my 'teenage bullshit.' His words. I wasn't an easy kid, but then I really wasn't the easiest teenager. Liam always told me I had to keep smiling no matter what, but you know, it got too hard."

"Well maybe that was easy for Liam to say. Maybe they didn't treat him like they treated you."

"No," Alex said. "I don't think it was easy for him. But it mattered to him because I think it kept things in the household more sane. Because it…it kept my dad there."

"Alex…"

"When I was fourteen, I went off the rails. I started getting into fights. Cutting school. Basically anything that got me into enough trouble that my dad had to come down to the school and deal with me. Look at me. Finally one day my dad told me that he couldn't stand being around me anymore. Liam had been all right. That's what he said. But me… He couldn't stand me. Couldn't stand anything about me. He said he was done with this parenting stuff. He said it was a good thing I was the only other kid he had. And that there was a reason I was the last one. As if any of the others had been planned. But that's what he said. It's what he said when he left, and it's what he told my mother. So me, her last ditch effort to keep her husband with her—I was a total failure. I had the exact opposite effect, so no, no one has ever needed me. And the ones who did… I let them down. So I shouldn't enjoy this. I shouldn't enjoy your needing me at all. But I do. God help me, I do."

Clara made a choked sound and closed the distance between them, kissing him, hard and fierce, no skill inherent in the movements. It was all need. The kind of need that reached into those dark, hollow places inside of him and made him feel like— for just a moment—he might find some light. Might find some relief. The kind of need that he craved like it was water or air.

And he should push her away. He should be a man and stand on his own feet rather than depend on a woman. Depend on *this* woman, who sure as hell didn't need a big old soldier leaning against her until she fell apart the rest of the way.

But for now, he wanted to. For now, he wanted her to need him, as desperately as he wanted to allow himself to need her. And whatever the hell came after tonight, whatever the hell came after this moment, didn't matter so much. At least, he was going to pretend that it didn't.

Because her kiss was a salvation he couldn't hope to earn, and he was a temptation that never should have been put in front of her. But somehow, it all worked. Somehow, right now, she seemed to fill all the empty places inside of him, and he was doing it for her, so how wrong could it be?

Pretty damn wrong, probably. But he couldn't make himself stop either way.

She would always taste like rain to him. His lips had first touched hers when the storm had rolled in and the air was heavy with the promise of thunder. That would always be Clara. New and fresh, far too sweet and innocent for him.

He lifted her up off the ground, held her against his body and walked them both down the short hallway into her bedroom. It was wrong. This was. Maybe. Having her again when he knew she wanted more than he could give in the long run. But he wasn't strong enough to make another decision. No way in hell.

The only thing he was strong enough to do was push her back onto the bed, settle himself between her thighs and kiss her deep and hard. To strip her clothes from her body and revel in every inch of her naked skin.

Her breasts, so pale and smooth, those irresistible pink tips making his mouth water. He kissed her there, where he needed to kiss her, lapped at her with the flat of his tongue. Her body arched beneath him, and he felt an answering shudder race through his. He had never felt so desperate for a woman in his life. And he knew—he knew—that she was right. That this felt deeper, felt bigger because of all they had shared. That it was more because she knew who he was. Really knew. Because he had seen her strength, her incredible brilliance in the face of hardship. Because he had seen what she had given up. He had watched her dance.

He had been her first lover, and the fact that that was the case in large part because of the grief that she had suffered was not lost on him.

Because maybe she was right about that too. If life had gone her way, perhaps she would have thrown herself into dance. Maybe she would have developed a taste for kale and she would have dated men like Asher. Would have had sex in high school, maybe after the prom. Because her life would have looked a lot more normal. If she wasn't tied to the ranch. If she wasn't still here just doing the chores, as he feared she might be.

He had come here to give her something. To take care of her until she was ready to run the ranch herself. And then he was going to leave. She was right. That had been his plan. From the very beginning, somewhere in the back of his mind, he had always known that he wouldn't stay here in Copper Ridge. Not at the Laughing Irish. Maybe he'd bury himself in physical labor in the middle of the woods in Alaska. Who the hell knew?

But part of him had always known that he would leave before he was asked to go. That he would remove himself from these people, from this family, without waiting for it to run its course.

But she needed him. He knew that too. Knew it in the pit of his gut. And he could be there for her. She had said that he was worth it, and he wasn't entirely sure he would ever agree. But what he did know, sure as hell, was that she needed him in a way he hadn't initially realized.

But that was for tomorrow. Tonight he was simply going to indulge himself. Tonight he was going to let himself have her in the way that he needed.

He stripped his clothes off so he could hold her against him, skin to skin, and then he moved down her body, blazing a trail of kisses and licks right down the center, past her belly button, to that tender skin just beneath, and then he feasted between her thighs. Tasting her, delving deep until she screamed. Until her pleasure coated his tongue, and he felt like he might drown in it. In her.

He got some protection and applied it quickly, pressing his cock against her entrance, sinking into her slowly, reveling in her tightness. In her heat.

And when he was seated entirely inside of her, he made eye contact with her, and he felt it all the way down to his soul.

This wasn't just sex. It wasn't sex like he'd had it before. She could see him. And he knew her. He had thought she was basically a child when he had first come here. Had acted as though being young and in-experienced meant she didn't know as much as he did. But he was wrong. He was the one who didn't know.

Didn't know what the hell he was doing here. With her. *In* her.

Pleasure washed through him, but it was more than that. It had teeth. It grabbed him by the throat and clamped down tight. Made it impossible for him to breathe. Made it so that he could barely think. All he could do was feel. Her soft skin, that tight clasp of her body around his. The need that was building inside of him turning into something that surpassed need and moved right into necessity. If he didn't have her, if he couldn't stay here, he might actually die.

He was a man who had stared death down. Had it come close enough that he could taste it. Like metal and terror. But this was different. It was a kind of sweet ache that started in his chest and wrapped its icy fingers around his rib cage, tugged like it was pulling it apart.

And when he came, just as she did, her fingernails digging into his shoulders, her internal muscles squeezing him tight, it wasn't just an orgasm. Not even close. It had as little to do with pleasure as getting shot did. No, this was a baptism. Baptism and holy fire that he knew was going to leave him altered. Leave him scarred.

And maybe it would save him. Maybe she could.

But something had to change. He had to change.

And as he lay there in the bed with her afterward, holding her against his chest, he knew exactly what it had to be.

He wasn't the one who had to leave. It was her.

## CHAPTER TWENTY-ONE

When Clara awoke the next morning, her nose was itchy. Her eyes fluttered open and the pale morning light made her squint. And then she realized why her nose was itchy. Her head was resting on Alex's broad body, her hand tangled in his chest hair. And apparently, that same chest hair was tickling her nose.

Her heart swelled, so big she thought it might break through her own chest. She knew she wasn't supposed to want this forever. But something about this moment felt like it could easily last that long and she wouldn't mind. Just being here with him. In this still time before her feet had to hit the ground. Before she had to head to Grassroots, before he had to head to the Laughing Irish. When it was just him. Just her. In this house.

She snuggled deeper against him. He was what she would remember here. Now this was what she would remember. And it wouldn't take away those other memories. No, nothing would. Just as she had told him yesterday, that was her foundation. But this wasn't insignificant. It was part of her now. Part of who she was becoming. And she was definitely in the process of becoming.

Becoming the woman she wanted to be. The woman she was choosing to be. Though, right now she thought she could happily stay this woman, lying up against Alex's chest forever. Too bad that wasn't a very high-paying gig. She could be his human body pillow. She let her hand drift down to his abs, those hard, ridged muscles that sent a little thrill through her every time she saw them. Every time she touched them. Then she let her hand slide down farther and found him hard, ready as he always was in the morning. So maybe she didn't want a job solely as his body pillow.

She wondered if Alex had the budget for a high-class courtesan.

"You awake?" His voice was husky from disuse and that sent a little thrill through her, as well.

She loved this.

She had a feeling she was perilously close to loving him.

"Yes," she said, her voice scratchy too.

"How did you sleep?"

"Pretty good." She brushed her fingertips over his arousal. "Though, I thought about you all night. I dreamed about this."

"Did you?"

"Yes. Alex, being with you... Alex, I..."

He jackknifed upward in bed, his feet planting hard on the floor. Then he stood up, pacing across the length of the room. She knew that he was upset. Still, she allowed herself to watch the fine muscles in his back that tapered down to his waist, to his tight ass. An ass she wanted very much to dig her fingernails into.

"Stop," he said.

"What?"

But she knew what. She had been about to say something emotional, something that was stupid. And she knew it. And apparently so did he.

"Clara, I did a lot of thinking last night."

"Did you? Then I think maybe I did something wrong. I know I'm new at this sex stuff, Alex, but I'm pretty sure that men aren't supposed to be able to think during all that."

He didn't smile. He looked grim. "I didn't sleep last night."

"I'm sorry."

"No, I needed to think. I needed to figure this out. Jason's will said that I should stay until the ranch was established, and I've been thinking in those terms. Of getting you on your feet, and then leaving. But that was wrong."

Her heart crawled up into her throat, her entire body tense, on high alert. "Was it?"

"I'm not the one who needs to leave."

Clara felt like she'd been slapped in the face. "What do you mean by that?"

"You were right. I figured I would be the one to leave. And in the back of my mind, I was thinking I would probably leave Copper Ridge. That eventually my brothers wouldn't want me around. But look, that's all past stuff I should have quit thinking about a long time ago. Stuff that I carried over from my dad's leaving. The idea that somebody might not want to deal with me? It doesn't come from nowhere, but I can't shirk my responsibilities just because of that crap. Like I said, I'm a soldier. I've been through worse. I've seen way worse. There is no reason to walk away from a sure thing because I'm trying to preemptively keep myself from having those tough conversations."

A corner of his mouth lifted up into a smile. "Anyway, like you said, it's not the conversations you have to be afraid of. It's the ones you never get to have. So I figure I need to stick around and have those. I've done a lot of leaving my whole life. Ever since I grew up, I decided to make it something I controlled. So I was the one who moved on. And you... Clara, you're the one who's done the staying. You gave up everything for this place. For this ranch. You never got to choose if it was what you wanted. It fell into your lap. And I was about to throw it right back on you too. But as long as I'm here, as long as I'm the one getting it started... You need to go. You need to go away for a while, and when you're finished, you can come back and you can decide what you want to do with the ranch."

"I don't..." She felt dizzy. Breathless. There was just enough truth in what he was saying that it was difficult to roundly deny any of it. But at the same time, everything in her violently denied it. She didn't want to leave. This place was her safety. All of her life, all of her experiences were bound up in it. And he wasn't just talking about her leaving the ranch. He was talking about her leaving him.

"Alex," she said, her words coming out scratchy. "I don't want to leave."

"You don't know that. And you've never had the chance. You need to take it. I don't know why it took this long for that to become clear to me. Maybe because, like I said, I'm just used to being the one who moves on. But Clara, you gave up everything for this place. And you shouldn't have to give up any more."

"What do you think I'm going to do, Alex? Do you think I'm going to go join a ballet company? Because that ship has kind of sailed."

"That's just it," he said. "You can do whatever you want. Whatever you need to."

She took a deep breath and squared her shoulders. "What if I want to stay here? What if I decide I want to be here with you?"

"Why would you want to do that?" he asked, the words ragged.

There was only one reason, really. Only one thing that could make her this crazy, this willing to risk her pride, her feelings, *herself.*

She wasn't almost in love with him. She was just plain in love. It was scary. Because she knew what it meant to love someone and lose them.

But Alex was worth it. Worth everything.

"Obviously it would be because I love you," she said, tilting her chin up, giving him her best defiant expression.

Something in Alex's eyes caught fire, then just as quickly, it went flat and cold.

"You also love pasta from a can," he said.

"Yes," she said, "I do. And I'm not really sure what that has to do with anything."

"You love pasta from a can because you had to make your own meals for half of your life. But if you went to New York, hell, if you went to Italy, you would try something else. You would try real pasta, and you would realize that there was something better out there. I'm not saying you don't think you love it. I'm not even saying you don't love it. I'm just saying you would probably be less impressed with it if you had the real deal."

"What the hell makes you not the real deal?" she asked, feeling increasingly frustrated. "Alex, I was a virgin, not an idiot. And anyway, I have been out on a date with Asher. It's not like I've never dated anybody else."

"Yes, you went on *a* date with him, and it went badly. And you and I have chemistry. There is no denying that. But you were interested in him. And you thought that you could make something happen with him. Now you think that about me. And that's normal. It's what normal people do. They date somebody for a while, they think maybe there's a future, and then they find out there isn't. But you don't just try it with one person."

"Maybe I just love canned pasta," she said. "Maybe I always will."

"I don't think that's the case. And anyway, the one thing I know you can't do is spend your life wondering. This place fell in your lap after tragedy. And you stayed here out of your sense of duty. And that's impressive. You're a good daughter. And a good sister. But you don't owe your entire life to this ranch. If your father were alive, would you be here?"

She didn't have to think about it to know the answer. "No."

"You don't have to be here now. And that doesn't mean you will never want to be. But don't you think you owe yourself the chance to find out?"

"What does that mean for us?"

He shook his head decisively. "There isn't an us. It was only ever for a limited time."

"Alex, I don't even know where I would go. I don't want to go anywhere else. I don't want anyone else." Panic clawed at her. Tore at her throat. "You can't force me to leave."

"We're done either way," he said.

His face was like iron, a muscle jumping in his jaw.

"We can't be done. You're still naked. I'm naked. We're here together and we are naked." She meant it in more than just a physical way. She meant it in every way.

Her throat felt sore, raw. From all the unshed tears of the past decade. Because if she had cried all the tears that her sadness demanded, she would have dried up completely into a husk. Would never have done anything else.

"I don't want to be done," she said. "Shouldn't I get a say?"

"That's my point! You need to have a say. And if you're here with me, I'm just another weight tying you down. I am not going to be another de facto decision that is forced upon you by your circumstances. And this ranch doesn't have to be one either. It took me all this time to realize this is probably what your brother wanted. To make sure that if you didn't want this place, you didn't have to have it."

"Well, what about you? What about what you want?"

"I want to give you what you deserve," he said, sounding ragged. "And who gives a damn about me?"

"I do. I give all the damns. I give every damn."

"Clara," he said slowly, and she knew she would

be angry about what he said next. She just knew it. "I care about you. More than I ever have for anyone. So you have to let me do this."

"When you say you care for me, is it because of Jason? Is it because I'm his sister?"

"No. It's because you're *you*. Because I know you. Because I know everything that you gave up to keep this place going. Because I know what all of this cost you. And you told me that when all of this was over you wanted to be able to find out who you were apart from your grief. And that's a fine goal. But you can have more than that. You can find out who you would have been if none of it had ever happened. You'll have the money from the military soon. It's more than enough to live on. You can go wherever you want. And until then, you can take a loan from me."

He was offering her freedom. But she felt like he was tying a weight around her chest. One that was forcing her head down below the water. It didn't feel like freedom.

But there was a part of her, just big enough, that wondered if he was right. That wondered if she had to go and experience life. Or how would she ever know? It was the same part of her that had obsessed over Asher. The part that wanted to know what life might be like if only things had gone differently.

And here was Alex, handing it to her.

Her Alex. Who smiled so easily and hid such deep pain. Who had a wall up in front of him, even while he stood there naked.

And she knew then that no matter what, he would never trust her if she didn't do this. That he would never believe she had chosen him.

And he would never ask her to choose him either.

"Alex," she said, his name broken on her lips. "I love you. And you are not a can of SpaghettiOs."

"I don't know what that means."

"I don't have to go try somebody else to know that."

"I can't be the person that you need. And you'll see that. You will. You'll get away from this place, away from me. And the whole world is going to open up."

"Alex…"

"I care for you," he said, cutting her off. "But I don't love you."

His words went straight through her heart. "Not even a little?"

"Part of me wishes like hell that I could. But it's best that I don't."

She wanted to shout at him. Wanted to scream that he was a liar. But he was standing there saying it was over, and it felt way too much like death for her to keep the tears from falling. This abrupt, awful end that she hadn't seen coming. That had hit after such a beautiful night together.

Yes, exactly like death. It didn't make sense. And it couldn't be stopped. So she just stood there, her fingertips going numb, a rock lodged in her throat that made an ache spread from there all the way down through her chest.

But she couldn't argue with death. She could argue with Alex. And she damn sure would.

"Are you tired of putting up with me?" she asked. Remembering what he had said about his father, completely not above using it against him now. "Is that what this is?"

He whirled around, his green eyes fierce. "I am trying to do the right thing. I can keep you here, and I could have sex with you every night, hold you, make a profit off the bison, wake up the next morning and do it again. But I am trying to be something other than a failure. To be something other than a disappointment. Your brother threw himself in front of a hail of bullets to keep me alive and I owe him so much more than this."

"So is that what this is? This is you sacrificing?"

"No," he said, his tone harsh. "I want to do one thing right. Let me do it. Let me do this one thing."

Tears made her throat feel thick and tight, emotion compressing her chest like a band. She couldn't breathe, she couldn't think, and worst of all, she couldn't argue.

"Could you not be noble, Alex?" she asked, her throat crackly. "Could you fight for the *wrong* thing instead?"

He stood so straight and tall then, and she could almost see a uniform on him, even though he was standing there naked. But there he was, the soldier. Fighting this war that was tearing him up inside. And she was almost certain it wasn't really about letting her go. Wasn't really about letting her experience all of these things. It was the side effect, she believed that. But there was something else to it, as well, yet she couldn't figure it out. Couldn't think around the pain that was blooming inside of her.

Couldn't fight with conviction because she was afraid that he was right.

"Don't ask me to do that," he said.

"Fight for *me*."

"I am," he responded, his voice hard.

"Can't you just be selfish? Can you say that you're keeping me? That you aren't going to let me go?" For a moment, the idea of that kind of security, of the kind of safety she could find in Alex's arms, held tight against that muscular wall of a chest for the rest of her life seemed like the most beautiful, certain future she could imagine.

Seemed like the only thing she could ever want.

He shook his head. "I'm not looking to use another person as my Band-Aid, Clara. That's the one thing I won't do. I will not make another person's life all about me."

And it was on the tip of her tongue to tell him that he was. That this *was* about him, whether he couched it in self-sacrifice or not. But she stood there, watching the years stretch before them in her mind's eye, and she saw them as two people trapped forever in this house. Two people forced together by fate or God or whatever it might have been.

And she knew he would always question it. Because he questioned it now.

"So you just want me to go. Anywhere."

"I want you to have the choice." He sighed heavily. "It's important."

She nodded, her lips numb, her entire face starting to feel numb. Her fingertips were cold, and she imagined that she might not be able to feel them next. And that it would be a blessing.

"I guess I should pack," she said, more out of a desire to be shocking than an actual desire to pack up her things. She had a job, and she didn't have the money yet. And regardless of what Alex said, she wasn't taking a loan from him to finance their breakup.

"You don't have to leave the house right away. You don't have to pack up," he said. "I'm not going to live here. I'll continue to take care of the place while you're gone. I can hire people, like we discussed."

"What about my bees?" she asked.

The stupid bees. She tried to think back to a time—not that long ago—when her fondest dream had been to live in this tiny house forever with Asher and her bees. And now she couldn't even imagine why she had wanted Asher. And even though she liked her bees, she couldn't really figure out why they mattered either.

Her whole chest was a slash of pain, and it was hard to remember liking anything at all.

"I'll make sure your bees are taken care of. The ranch is my responsibility for now, and that means all of it."

"Well, I'd better make plans, anyway," she said, her words stiff. "I don't even like wine. So I'll probably quit the winery."

"Right."

"Maybe I'll drive down the coast. I've never been to California. I've never been to Disneyland."

"Disneyland is a happy place, I hear," he said, the words flat.

She wasn't going to be happy anywhere. Not for a long time. She knew that. But, she wasn't going to say it. What little pride she had, she was going to go ahead and preserve.

"Alex…" She swallowed hard. "You changed me."

He reached out and touched her chin, sliding his

thumb over her bottom lip. "I hope to God that's a good thing, Clara."

"Me too."

He dropped his hand then, and went into the bathroom. She could hear him dressing, and she decided she couldn't be there when he came back out. She ran to the closet and pulled on a pair of underwear and bra, then grabbed a dress, tugging it over her head and running into the main part of the house before flinging herself outside.

She ran down the front steps, moving blindly through the property. Heading toward the bees, she realized belatedly when she caught sight of the hives. They didn't bother her without her protective gear on. At least, not when she wasn't messing with the hives. She sat down on the ground, not caring if she got mud on the dress, and drew her knees up to her chest. The bees buzzed lazily around her, drunk on honey, and completely unconcerned with her presence.

Apparently, she didn't much matter to anybody. Apparently, she was so easy to leave. So easy to let go of.

A sob caught in her throat.

*Jason.*

It was so hard not to be angry with him. Even when she was proud. Because he had left her too. Dammit all, he had left her just like everybody else. That loss, that abandonment, was so sharp right now it was like a knife lodged into her throat.

She choked on a laugh. "At least Alex is changing it up. At least he's sending me away."

She tried to imagine this future he was talking about. This one where she went out and decided what she wanted to do. Had a road trip, decided if she was going to go to college for something. Visit a city and decide that maybe that suited her more than country living.

But everything just seemed dark. It seemed dark and it seemed blank. She couldn't imagine herself away from here. Couldn't find her way forward.

Which, she supposed, was as good a reason as any to need to be somewhere else. To need to see somewhere else.

Because she didn't know. Because she'd never experienced another place. Because she didn't want to be like her father and grow old on this ranch with a broken heart.

And that was what it came down to. He had sent her away. He had said they wouldn't be together, even if she stayed. So in the end, she would be just like her father. Doing the chores, aching for somebody who was no longer here to hold her.

No. That she wouldn't do. She wouldn't. She *couldn't*. She wouldn't exist in this house with yet another ghost.

That was what Alex would become to her. A ghost. She had been a fool to think that she could touch him just for a little while and not miss it when it was over.

He thought she should go have experiences. Eat homemade pasta just because other people said it was good. Sleep with other men just because people thought it was the thing to do.

She didn't need those things. And somewhere down in her soul she knew that.

But right now, she figured she had to go out and

have them. Because the alternative was dying of a broken heart.

And there had been too much damn death in her life for her to sit around and accept her own.

Clara rose to her feet and looked out across the property. At the well-worn path that she'd forged over the past year of tending to the bees. The path that forked one way going to the barn, the barn where she had danced for Alex and then made love with him. To the house, the house she had been born in. The house her father had died in. The house where she had received the news that her brother was gone.

The house where Alex had held her by the woodstove, his heart thundering against her cheek. That house that had seen so many losses and so many gains.

What would it be like to walk on ground she hadn't worn grooves into? To wake up and not know where she was?

She was going to find out. She was determined she was going to find out.

# CHAPTER TWENTY-TWO

ON HER DRIVE to work the next morning, Clara was feeling bleak. The money had been in her bank account this morning.

A whole lot of money.

Money because her brother was dead. Money that meant she wasn't tied to this place if she didn't want to be.

She hadn't seen Alex since he'd told her to leave yesterday, and she was intent on avoiding him until she actually did leave. She wasn't going to line up anything permanent, at least not for the time being. But she was going to take some time off from Grassroots so she could take a drive down the coast and possibly get as far as San Francisco. She wasn't sure about going any farther than that. She wasn't sure if she wanted to chance driving in that kind of traffic. This was the problem. She had been so stationary for so long, she wasn't entirely sure how to break out of it.

On a whim, she pulled into Stim on her way to the winery. She took a deep breath, her heart pounding hard as she got out of the car and walked into the coffee shop. She hadn't seen Asher at all since her grand announcement that she just wasn't that into him, and it felt strange to go seeking him out now.

But something was pushing her to talk to him. Even if she didn't know what.

"Clara," Asher said, smiling when he saw her, "it's been a while."

"Yeah," she said, wrapping her knuckles on the counter.

"Your usual?"

"No." She shook her head. "I hated my usual. Hot chocolate. And can you like…add something sweet to it?"

He looked appalled, but to his credit didn't lecture her about the evils of refined sugar. "If you'd like that, I can definitely do it."

"I would."

She stood there for a moment, rocking forward on the balls of her feet as silence stretched between them.

Finally, he spoke.

"So how are things?"

"Okay. I got my heart broken. Not a big deal. And I'm kind of planning to go on a road trip. So. That's cool. Not the broken heart. The road trip."

"Damn," he said. "That is a lot of things."

"Yeah. I just need to get time off work. And I think I'm going to go to San Francisco."

"That sounds like fun."

"Yeah. I don't know. Maybe it will be. I haven't been. I mean, I've never even been to California. So that could be fun."

"I've driven down a bunch of times." He kept his concentration on stirring the drink in front of him. "So if you want company, I could maybe go down with you."

"I…" She couldn't quite figure out the offer. If

he wanted to go down with her so he could keep her company, or if he wanted—expected—that they would sleep together. Though, it would kill two birds with one stone, she supposed. That other experience Alex seemed to think she needed before she knew her own mind and desires.

The very idea of it made an involuntary shudder go up her spine. She was not ready to sleep with another man. She didn't know how ready she would ever feel, but she was most definitely not ready to sleep with another man two seconds after Alex broke up with her.

"I was kind of in love with him," she said.

The words caught in her throat as it tightened. And she realized they were a lie. Because she wasn't *kind of* in love with him. She was totally in love with him. And there was no amount of life experience needed for her to know that beyond a shadow of a doubt.

"That's rough," he said. He pushed the drink in her direction. "But it doesn't have to be anything serious for us to have a little fun together."

He looked at her, all handsome and bearded, his dark eyes the same color as the hot chocolate he'd just made for her, and just as warm. But she didn't feel enticed or seduced or anything.

It didn't have to be serious for him. But it did for her. She realized it then. It absolutely had to be something serious for her to sleep with somebody. She was pretty sure she had known she was serious about Alex from the moment his lips had first touched hers. That there was something different about him. About the way he made her feel, the way he made everything around her feel. Like it was alive and exciting when for so long it had all been gray.

"Thank you. So much. That's very nice of you to offer your…services. But it just doesn't work for me." She took a sip of her hot chocolate and frowned. It was hideously bitter.

"Sorry to hear that," Asher said, no anger in his voice at all. Honestly, his lack of intensity about it all undermined any of the flattery inherent in his hitting on her. "Is your drink good?"

"Great," she said. Then she frowned even more deeply. "No. It's not great. It's disgusting, actually. I just can't do this dark-chocolate heresy. I basically want a melted candy bar. And, I know that's not sophisticated or healthy for me, or any of that. But I just don't care."

Asher laughed. "Okay. I have no idea why I like you so much. Because you are completely different than me. But I really wish that you liked me too. Because I think we could have fun together."

"You want to sleep with me," she said, for some reason not feeling even a little embarrassed to make that assumption.

"Yeah," he said. "Is that a big deal?"

"It is to me. I think that's the problem. I don't like coffee. I think sex is a big deal. I need sugar in my hot chocolate. I'm just not the same kind of person. Ironically, I fell in love with somebody who really isn't the same kind of person either. But that's the difference. I love him. I love him, and he doesn't love me back. I have to go lick those wounds by myself. With hot chocolate that doesn't make me want to gag." She set the cup back down on the counter. "No offense."

He laughed again. "I don't really take your culinary word as law. Also no offense."

"That's…that's fair enough."

"See you around, Clara."

"Maybe," she said. "Maybe not. I might end up moving to California. Maybe it will suit me." But she knew it wouldn't. Just like bittersweet cocoa never would.

She turned and walked out of the coffee shop feeling somehow both deflated and buoyant. She had gone and stated her opinions, and she had confessed the fact that she'd been dumped out loud.

She got into her car and jammed the key into the ignition.

Then she sighed. She was just going to have to do it at work now too. But she had friends there now. Unlike when she had lost Jason, she had some people to talk to.

She supposed that should feel like a bigger consolation than it did. But really, not much felt consoling at the moment.

She continued on to Grassroots feeling more than a little bit tragic, and by the time she got there, she was in a pretty full-scale funk.

But Sabrina smiled when she walked into the room, and she really hadn't anticipated how much it would mean to have somebody that was happy to see her when she felt so damn low.

"Oh no," Sabrina said, the smile sliding off her face almost as quickly as it had appeared. "You look like you've had a trauma."

A tear slid down her cheek. "I have."

"Damn Donnellys," Sabrina said, slamming her hands down on the table. Thank God the tasting room was still empty, and there were no customers. "I knew it. They're assholes. Absolute assholes. They can't help it. They think they're God's gift to women, and honestly, who can blame them? But…"

"I don't know what Liam did to hurt you." Clara cut Sabrina off mid-tirade. Alex had hurt her, yes. But he had reasons, and they were even good. She was sad, and angry, but she couldn't just burn his whole character to the ground because she was wounded. "But it's complicated. Alex and I. He said some things…he's not wrong."

"Let me guess," Sabrina said, "he said you were young. And that you didn't know what you wanted."

Her words were so close to the truth it was almost shocking.

"I…well, yes. But it's not completely untrue. I mean, I am young. And I haven't really experienced life. He says I need to do that. And maybe I'll…travel. Go to school. Who knows? He's not wrong about my inexperience."

"But don't you find that so painfully patronizing?"

"He wasn't patronizing. He's afraid."

Sabrina looked struck by that. "Afraid?"

"Yes. He's been through a lot. I don't know what all you know about their childhood, but it was really hard. And life has been hard for him since. And I just think he doesn't know how to take a good thing. But who am I to talk? I don't know how to handle good things either. I don't know what I want. I mean, so much of my life has been decided for me. And until I really make a decision, how will I know?"

"Does the idea of all these possibilities make you feel excited? Or does it make you feel like you've died inside a little bit?"

Now Clara felt *totally* deflated and she could tell by the look on Sabrina's face that it showed.

"I thought so," Sabrina said. "I think new possibilities are supposed to feel exciting. I think when a grown man is running scared, and he tells you it's for your own good but it feels more like you got stabbed through the heart…it's not for you. So, yes, I think you're right. I think he is probably afraid. But he's trying to make you think he's also being benevolent. Pretty sure he's just being a coward."

The tasting room door opened and in walked Lindy—the owner of Grassroots Winery, Sabrina's former sister-in-law and their boss. She was a striking blonde, very well put together, every inch the competent business owner, but without that polished, hardened look that you might expect from somebody who ran a more corporate office. No, she looked exactly like a vineyard owner should. Her hair falling in soft waves, her style a kind of elegant, easy chic.

She was willowy, and at first glance she might be easy to write off as fragile. Until you saw the glint of steel in her eyes.

"I was looking for you," she said, directing that comment at Sabrina.

"Is that good or bad?"

"I hope it's good. Because I have a new opportunity that I want to talk to you about."

"Actually, I was hoping to have a talk with you too," Clara said to Lindy.

"What's up, Clara? Is everything okay? Everything going all right since…?"

"As well as it can be, thanks," she responded. "But I wanted to talk to you about taking an extended amount of time off. The payment from the military came in today and…"

"Of course," Lindy said. "Take as much time as you need. I could never tell whether you needed the work to keep busy or whether you needed a break… Anyway, whatever you need…and you know that the job is always here for you."

"Thank you," she said.

"Now," Lindy said, turning her focus to Sabrina. "I just got off the phone with the Donnellys. We're going to be working on a partnership with the Laughing Irish."

The color leached from Sabrina's face. Clara felt her heart crumple for the other woman, even though it shocked her that her heart was able to crumple more than it already had.

"Of course," Sabrina said, her voice sounding strange, almost automated. "Whatever you need me to do."

Lindy looked back at Clara. "Can you hold down the fort for a bit?"

Clara nodded. "No one will be in for at least another half hour, I imagine."

"Thanks." She put her hand on Sabrina's shoulder. "Let's talk in my office."

That left Clara to her own devices. Left her to ruminate on everything Sabrina had said. That Alex was mostly protecting himself under the guise of protecting her. She didn't disagree. But it still didn't make any of it untruthful.

It still didn't change her plans.

She had fully intended to become a more self-sufficient woman in part through this relationship with him. And she wasn't going to waver on that now. No matter how much it might hurt.

It was a strange thing to realize, that while she had experienced some of the worst pain that life can throw at a person, her heart had never truly been broken before.

It was broken now.

And it made it hard to breathe.

But she was going to move on. To keep on moving. The alternative was unthinkable.

# CHAPTER TWENTY-THREE

ALEX FELT LIKE the biggest ass in all of creation. More than that, he was pretty sure he was dying. At least, he imagined this was what dying must feel like. Waking up this morning without Clara in his arms had been awful. But the crazy thing was, it wasn't unusual. He had spent thirty-one years waking up without Clara, and only a few days waking up with her. There was no damn reason that doing so should feel so normal. So right. He'd never had the expectation of someone in his life being permanent before. Why he should think it now was beyond him.

He hadn't been wrong when he told her she needed to go out and experience life. He hadn't been. He couldn't just be another thing that happened to her. He refused. He was the collateral damage in too many people's lives already. His father's. His mother's. His own damn best friend's.

He bit back that familiar pain, that familiar resentment, and put his mind back to the work at hand. He was trying to patch up some damn barbed wire, and he kept putting the fencing through his finger. But then, there was something good about that. About the punishment of sending that hard steel straight through his flesh. He deserved it. That was the thing. Because he hadn't been enough for anyone. Ever. Not his mother, not his father, not his friend, and not his brothers.

And in the end, he sure as hell hadn't been enough for Clara. Clara, who deserved a damn sight better than a man who was little more than a failed experiment as a son, as a soldier and as a lover.

"Hell!" he shouted as the barbed wire went through his finger again, not so much because it hurt, but because sometimes that word just needed to be shouted.

"What's going on over here? Doesn't sound family friendly, that's for sure."

Alex looked up and saw Liam coming his way. Ironic that it would be Liam who found him like this. Especially considering it was Liam who had been on his mind so much lately, as he rehashed the past. As he tried to dissect what the hell had gone wrong in his life to bring him to this point.

"It's called hard work, asshole," he said. "But I doubt you would know much of anything about that."

"I know enough. Why are you out here working by yourself and cursing up a blue streak?"

"Since when do you care if I work by myself?"

Liam released a sigh and bent down, picking up a pair of fence cutters as he did. "Are you going to tell me what's going on?"

"No."

"Don't be an idiot, Alex. Tell me what the hell is happening."

"Why should I? It's not like you and I were ever that close. The both of us ending up here kind of forced a relationship…"

"There was no forced relationship. You're my younger brother. You always have been. We have a relationship. By birth. Through blood. No forcing required."

"We are blood related. I'll give you that."

"Look. You're in a mood. You look like you would tangle with a pissed-off bull if you were given half a chance right about now, so I'm going to go easy on you. I'm going to go ahead and let you have all this unfair pity party crap you keep spouting. For a second."

"You don't think it's fair?"

"We've been here for a while now, and you haven't said a damn thing to me about not feeling like we're close. Hell, we hit the bars more times in the last couple of months than we ever did in the past few years. You were my wing man."

"You were mine."

Liam laughed. "Doesn't matter since neither of us got laid, right?"

Alex's lips twitched. "Guess not."

"Anyway, you could have punched me when I got here. Or any time in the past four months. And now you're up in my face?"

"Because I'm trying to figure out where the hell my life went wrong. What is wrong with me, Liam? What the hell is wrong with me that a few fistfights at school were so god-awful that our father left?"

Liam just stood there staring at him, so he continued. "I was getting in trouble at school. Beating up other kids. Dad said he didn't have time for my crap. He said he'd already raised one kid, and he didn't need to do another one. He was done with my teenage bullshit."

"That's what Dad said to you?"

"Yes. And when he left, he made sure that Mom knew it. That Mom knew that her great hope for keeping the two of them together had failed. That I had failed."

"That's absolute bull," Liam told him. "It was never fair for Mom to put that on you. Another kid has never kept a couple together—if anything they only drive them apart. That's just common sense. Kids don't make life less stressful. They screw it up more. That is what kids do. That had nothing to do with you."

"It had everything to do with me, Liam. Everything. And at that point, even you were hardly ever around. And the minute you could leave, you left. And you never came back at all."

Liam's eyebrows locked together, his expression hard. "Are you mad at me for that?"

"I'm mad at everybody. I'm mad at everybody who had a hand in that ridiculous mess we called a house growing up."

"They're not my favorite people either," Liam said. "Believe me when I tell you that you don't know everything that went on in that house."

"Liam…"

"No. You listen. You didn't see all of it. I'm glad. Because I damn well wanted to make sure that you kept smiling, Alex. Remember that."

"I do," he said. He gritted his teeth. "It was the last thing you said to me before you left. Keep smiling."

"Yeah," Liam said. "Well, I meant it."

"It wasn't enough to make Mom forgive me," Alex said. "After Dad left. There was no amount of good behavior that could redeem me at that point. So I figured I'd have to go redeem myself away from everything else. Become a soldier. That didn't seem to work either. It sure as hell didn't fix anything in me. If anything I ended up more broken."

Silence settled between them and then Liam spoke again. "Does she love you?"

"Yeah. She does. I mean, she thinks I'm a coward and that I'm a liar. That I'm just protecting myself. That I can't deal with things." He paused, his throat working up and down. "I don't know how to deal with things," he said, dropping the wire cutters and punching his own fist. "I wanted to keep it together for you. I wanted to fix things after I screwed it up so bad with Dad. I wanted to make my life count, Liam. I tried to find something. I went into the military. My best friend died for me. *Me.* I'm nothing more than a hollowed-out husk of a person. Fake smile and all. And he died for me. It wasn't supposed to happen like that."

"Why not?" Liam asked, folding his arms over his broad chest.

"You would feel comfortable if a man sacrificed his life for you? Jumped in front of a gunman to save you?"

"Hell no. But I'm asking you why you don't. Because here's the thing—nobody took a bullet for me. But somebody did it for you. He's not here. You are. Why can't you accept that?"

"Because it's not fair."

"Life isn't fair, Alex, or were you absent on the day they handed the lesson out in the school of hard knocks? Because I was there. I was pretty sure you were too."

"It should've been me. Bottom line. Nobody cares whether I live or die, and I'm not being self-pitying when I say that. It's the truth."

"I care," Liam said, his voice rough. "I care, Alex. Our house was a living hell, and the only reason I stayed there as long as I did was because of you. You think our mother hated *you*? I was the reason she was tied to Dad in the first place. I was the reason she had to have you so that she could try to keep the man. Even though I don't think she wanted him all that much. She *despised* me. She would have left me for dead if given the chance, and believe me, she tried."

Alex didn't know what to say. He and his brother weren't the kind that shared a whole hell of a lot. And this was news to him. He had always assumed their mother had a better relationship with Liam. Not that he believed she had a warm fuzzy relationship with either of them, just that maybe she hadn't made him feel as much like he was the world's biggest inconvenience.

"I don't know what to say."

"You're worth it, you dumb asshole. You've been worth it. Every step of the way. Everything I shielded you from, everything he protected you from in the military..."

"I didn't ask for it," Alex said. "I didn't want it. I didn't—"

"Why is it the worst thing to you? Why is it the worst thing in the world to admit that you're worth something?"

Alex felt like he was standing on the edge of a cliff. On the edge of something he couldn't see the bottom of. Maybe it was the open, empty cavern of his soul. This dark, hollow black space that he felt nobody would ever want to jump into. That nobody would ever want to deal with. Hell, he didn't like dealing with it. Why would anybody else?

"If I was worth dying for…then why the hell couldn't Dad come down to the school one more time and talk to the principal? Why was what I did so damn bad that he left? Why was there no amount of good behavior, no amount of bad behavior, to get them to see me as anything more than an inconvenience?"

Alex shook his head, drew a breath and continued. "That man that knew me for just a few years jumped in front of a bullet to save me. *Me*. He gave his life for me. My own parents don't remember my birthday. And maybe it's better that way. I don't want to hope there's anybody who might love me, because dammit, I don't want to need it. It's easier. It's easier to shut down and smile. Even if the smile is fake. You can pretend it's real. And it is the easiest damn thing, Liam. To give nothing. To let nobody get close. But she…"

He cut himself off, realizing he was perilously close to crying all over his brother about their parents, about a woman. They just didn't have that kind of relationship. He didn't have that kind of relationship with anybody.

"I was going to leave," Alex said finally.

"What?"

"Here. I was going to leave here. There's a reason I only brought one bag of stuff. There's a reason I barely unpacked any of it. I was going to leave. That was my plan all along, whether I fully acknowledged it in my mind or not doesn't matter. I was always ready to pick up and go, no matter what. When it got too hard. When it got too real. I didn't want to *want* this. I didn't want to want this relationship with you, this relationship with Finn and Cain that we were never able to have growing up. Because I'm so tired, so desperately tired of hoping for something that I can't have."

"What if you could have it?"

"That is exactly the thing I can't think about. It's exactly the thing I can't let myself want."

"Why not?"

"Because I will be damned if I end up on my knees in the street again watching somebody I care about drive away while I cry like a little bitch." He took a deep breath. "I made myself matter. I made myself a soldier. So that my life would be about serving the country, so that it wouldn't be about fixing Mom's pain anymore. That's what I was to her. I was this thing that she created to fix her pain, and I couldn't even do that. In the end, I made it worse."

"I bet she said that to you too."

"Oh yeah, she said it to me. She said it to me more than once. I was the worst thing that ever happened to her."

"That makes me feel bad. She always said I was the worst thing that ever happened to her. So you're the favorite even when it comes to being the least favorite." Liam shook his head. "Unbelievable."

He tried to laugh at his brother's joke. He couldn't. Couldn't force that smile he'd spent half his life faking. "I can't do this anymore."

Liam shrugged. "Then don't. You've been not

doing it for a long damn time, right? You fill the void with army stuff. Random women. Moving from place to place."

"What?" It was the last thing he'd expected to hear from his brother.

"Why try?" Liam continued. "The whole not trying thing, the whole fake smile thing, it's served you well. I ought to know because I do a pretty similar thing."

Alex frowned. "Yeah."

"Of course, if it was still working so well, and if you were perfectly happy with it, you wouldn't be out here stabbing your hands with a barbed wire fence."

"I didn't stab myself on purpose."

"You kind of did."

Liam made him sound stupid. Self-destructive. Alex had to wonder if he had a point.

"It doesn't matter. You were right. It is better. What I've been doing this whole time works. There is no reason to ruin it now."

"No reason at all. No beautiful, blonde reason."

Alex gritted his teeth. "She's too young. She's only ever been with me. She doesn't have any experience with other men. She doesn't know anything beyond this town, her ranch and her grief. More than enough reason for me to encourage her to go and see more."

"That's bull and you know it. Someone who's experienced the losses she has is more mature than she should have to be. The life you live has more to do with your age than years."

Alex knew Liam was right about that, and still, something in him resisted. "It wouldn't be fair of me to throw my stuff on her."

"But you want to," Liam said. "You want to, or you wouldn't be out here acting like a miserable son of a bitch."

"What the hell do you know about women?"

Liam swung his arms wide, then brought them back together, punching his palm with his fist. "Absolutely nothing."

But the nothing was weighted. Alex was about to press further, but Liam continued. "Look, I'm not one to talk about being emotionally well-adjusted, since, well, I'm not. Pretty obvious, all things considered. But it seems to me that you're trying to protect yourself from getting hurt, when you're actually already hurt."

Alex cleared his throat, flexing his fingers. "It's just a little barbed wire."

"You know what I mean. She loves you?" he asked a second time.

"So she says."

"You don't want to hope that it's true, because the fact of the matter is that you love her already. But you're afraid. You're afraid because you already know what it's like to love somebody and have them walk away. You know what it's like to love somebody and have nothing but poison come out of their mouth. But you also know what it's like to have somebody care enough to throw their body in the path of bullets for you, Alex. And I don't think he did that so that you could live a half life for the rest of the years he bought you."

"I doubt he extended my years so I could screw around with his sister either."

"Maybe not. But I bet he wanted her to be happy."

"That's why I sent her away," Alex said. "That's why I told her to go. I said that I would take care of the ranch, and she could go do what she needed to do. Because that's the thing, even if I thought I was worth all her affection, even if I could hope to have it, she deserves to have some choices in life. And if I went at her, telling her that I loved her, well, right now she would say that she loved me too. Because she is twenty-one, because she was a virgin. Because I took advantage of her inexperience, of her innocence. She would stay with me, and she would regret it."

"Are you sure that's not all of Mom's baggage talking right now?"

"Who the hell knows? There's too much of this to sort through. But, baggage or not, I think she deserves a choice. A choice that isn't forced by me, by any declarations."

Liam looked around them, at the still, quiet setting. "All right. But she's not here. So you tell me… Do you love her?"

"I don't want to," Alex said, his voice sounding like gravel.

"But you do."

"It's impossible. And it's only going to end in a hell of a lot of pain."

"Yeah, well, life is painful all around. It hurts. It hurts to want something. But it hurts even more to want something and find out there's nothing in it. That it wasn't worth it. To pour yourself into something that brings no satisfaction in the end. And yeah, I'm speaking from experience."

"What experience?"

Liam laughed. "Do you know how much money I

made on investments? A lot. Like, I don't need to be here. I could be on an island somewhere financing my life from my Swiss bank account. I spent years on that. And then I stood there in a big office that I hated, looking at a city I liked even less, asking what the hell my life was and what the hell I'd been doing with it. And then I got the call about this place."

"You never... I didn't know. How did I not know that about you?" Alex asked.

"Because we're messed up."

That did make Alex laugh. "Yeah. Yeah, I guess so."

"I didn't blame you, you know," Liam said finally.

"For?" Alex asked, something tightening in his chest.

"Dad. And I never told you to smile so you'd be easier for other people to deal with. It was so life would feel easier to you."

Alex studied his brother, and he felt that gulf between them, wider than usual. All of the stuff that happened when they were kids that they didn't talk about. The years they hadn't talked because Liam had left home and he hadn't shared much about where he'd gone, and Alex had been in the military.

Alex had made himself a family there. A brotherhood.

He had brothers here and he'd been planning on leaving. Because he was afraid of what they'd have to deal with if they ever talked to each other, him and Liam. If they ever really talked. And he was afraid of what it would cost to bond with his brothers. To try again with family when with his parents, all the trying in the world hadn't done any good.

Liam let out a long, slow breath. "This thing with Clara…yeah, if you lose her, it's going to hurt like hell. And you and I both know, better than almost anybody, that hope of any kind isn't cheap. But here you are, and you've got somebody who loves you. And if you just took that step. Well, if you just took that step, maybe somebody would love you back. And maybe it would work. And maybe it won't. But if you don't try, you're never going to find out." Liam cleared his throat. "If you run scared, Alex, then running scared is all you'll ever have. Even when you're standing in a fancy corner office. Trust me on that."

Alex tried to breathe, but his chest felt like it was caved in. "I love her," he said. The words felt strange, foreign on his lips. But they weren't wrong.

He'd tried hard to reduce Clara. To think of her as too young, too vulnerable. But she wasn't. She was strong. She'd weathered loss, and she still had so much hope in her. She was resilient in ways he could never hope to be. She looked at him and understood more about what he was feeling in a given moment than even he did. She saw through his BS. She called him on it.

She was the kind of woman that could make him a better man. Already had.

And he'd blown it all to hell.

"I do love her," he repeated. "But I sent her away."

"Good job," Liam said drily. "You wrote the ending you're afraid of for yourself. So that you didn't have to live in fear of it. Didn't you?"

And with clarity, Alex saw himself, down on bloodied, scraped knees in the middle of the road, crying after his father, who had ridden away on his

motorcycle and who Alex knew wasn't coming back.
His teenage face hot with anger, shame and tears.
Yeah, he had sent her away. And Liam was right. He
had done it so he could confirm everything he already believed. So he could keep himself from getting hurt again. From having it happen when he least
expected it.

But he didn't quite know what to do about it either. Because as much as he wanted to go get her,
as much as he wanted to call her back…what if she
needed that time away?

He could never keep her there, he would never trap
her. And that was the other thing. He would never use
her to sap his wounds, the way his mother had used
him. Absolutely not.

"Maybe someday…"

"That's a lie. A lie you're telling me and yourself,"
Liam said. "You either take the chance now or you
won't take it."

Alex just stood there, curling his fingers into fists.
And it took him a while to realize he was holding on
to a bundle of barbed wire, and it was digging into his
palm. He swore and dropped it to the ground, blood
seeping out of the wounds in his hand. But it didn't
have anything on the pain in his heart. He felt like he
had barbed wire wrapped around that. Made it impossible to think. Impossible to breathe.

"I want her to have what's best," he said, looking
down at his bloodstained hand. "That's all."

Liam's mouth firmed into a grim line. "Suit yourself then." He bent down, picking up the coil of barbed
wire that Alex had just dropped.

"What are you doing?"

"I'm going to help you fix this fence, and then we're going to go get a drink. Because you're right. I did leave you alone back then. I was too caught up in my own pain to see that I had left you and yours. But I'm not going to do it again. You're my younger brother, Alex, and I fucking love you. So we're going to go get a beer and commiserate about your girl problems."

"I don't know if I want to do that."

"Too bad. I didn't ask. I told you."

"Having an older brother is overrated."

"It sure as hell is. But lucky for me, having a younger brother isn't."

# CHAPTER TWENTY-FOUR

CLARA WAS MISERABLE, and the motel smelled like brine. Eternal dampness, possibly mold and some kind of hideous soup she did not want to eat from the restaurant next door. As it turned out, she didn't want to eat anything in the entire place, and had ended up having a packet of oyster crackers because apparently it was too much to ask for a place to have a nonseafood option.

The bed was hard, and the covers were damp, and she hated her life in general right at this moment.

After a day's drive down the coast, she had stopped in Crescent City, California, for the night and had grabbed one of the few places with a vacancy, which had turned out to be a mistake. There were a lot of adorable little places to stay, but this wasn't one of them.

She stood up and walked across the purple carpet, opening the motel room door and walking out into the parking lot. She wrapped her arms around herself and stared out across the street at the ocean. It was mostly dark, the low-hanging clouds feeling a whole lot like doom pressing around her.

She took a deep breath. At least, out here, the air was fresh.

She walked across the lot, and to the first crosswalk, dashing across the two-lane road and over to a rocky point that overlooked the ocean. The sun was a vague, yellow-gray spot, making its way down into the sea slowly.

She was in a different state. In a different place. But her heart was back home.

That realization hit her like a shock to the system. Her heart was in Copper Ridge. And it was her home.

There were so many things to sort through, it was a lot like trying to look through the mist and make the vague, murky shape of the mountains clear. So many things. The way she felt about Alex, the pieces of resentment that she felt about her life. Her grief. And underneath all of that, that certainty about who she was.

Losing Jason had made her want to be somebody else. Because Clara Campbell clearly had a target on her back, so why would she want to be her? Clara Campbell had been shaped by all of these unfair, hideous events.

And so she had wondered… What her real life was supposed to look like. Who she might have been if she had been raised by two happy parents who were still alive. If her brother had lived.

That, in her mind, had been real.

But with a clarity that defied the fog around her, she realized that the Clara who was untouched by loss and tragedy was the fantasy.

This was her real life. These challenges, the struggles, had created her, the real flesh and blood woman that she was. She had been realizing this over the past couple of weeks, that her grief was part of her, not a separate entity that could be lifted away. Because the people she had loved were part of her. Even though they were gone. They had made her who she was, and losing them had shaped her, as it should. Because that was love. It was real, it was deep, it was affecting. And it changed the course of your life. Changed the choices you made.

Love had made Jason leave the military the first time so he could stay with her. And love had also sent him back out to fight for his country. Love had been the thing that made her give up her horse, that made her give up dance, so that she could be with her father and help him on the ranch. Even though he had been distant, even though he had been hurt, it had allowed her to spend that time they had left close to him.

She couldn't resent those times, because the years she had with him had been far too abbreviated. She couldn't resent the sacrifices she had made. And who they had made her into.

She had loved to dance back then. And maybe, if she had stayed with it, she would love it now.

But she had given her heart over to the ranch. To making it work. To keeping that legacy alive for her family.

She didn't resent it. How could she? She wanted to stay there. She wanted to go back there. And yes, someday, maybe she would travel. Maybe she would see the world. But that house that was part of all the defining moments in her life would always be her home. It would always be her touchstone. As Copper Ridge always would be too.

This was who she was. Yes, she was only twenty-one years old, but at this point in her life she had already experienced the kind of loss most people didn't experience until a whole lifetime had passed. She'd had to truly sit down and grapple with the fact that the number of years a person got wasn't guaranteed. And given that, she had already thought about the kinds of things she might regret.

Standing there now, she thought about that again.

If she died tomorrow, she wouldn't regret not spending time in a college classroom, not having a different job. She wouldn't regret that she hadn't seen the Eiffel Tower or the southernmost part of the California coastline.

But she would regret not spending another night in Alex's arms. She would regret not being able to tell him that she loved him every day.

It wasn't the *things*. It wasn't the sights, the smells, the tastes. It was the people. That was what life came down to.

It all came back to love. No matter how painful it would be, no matter how much the loss might hurt, it was the biggest, most beautiful, most valuable thing the world had to offer. And it wasn't worth trading for anything.

Clara took a deep breath of that California air. And she didn't feel any different. Didn't want anything different. Didn't feel like she wanted anything other than what she'd wanted before.

Mostly because the air might be different, but she was the same. And her heart was still in Copper Ridge. Her heart was with Alex, and wherever he might go.

She thought about all the things he had told her. About the pain he had experienced when his father had left. When his father had abandoned him because Alex was just too much trouble.

About how he had watched his father leave, and how he had never returned.

Such a strange thing, watching Alex try to save her. Especially when she had a feeling that she needed to save him. That she needed to go back to him. Because nobody else ever had.

All the other times in her life when she had lost somebody, there had been nothing she could do. Because death was final. And she had thought that his breaking up with her felt a whole lot like that. Sudden, shocking, a blow she could never recover from. But with death, there was no recourse. There was no bargaining, there was no arguing.

And Alex wasn't dead. She could argue with him. She could fight.

She could fight *for* him. And she was going to.

Because she didn't need to see the world to know she had found her home. She didn't need to see the world to know she had found her heart.

Alex Donnelly was her heart, Alex Donnelly was her home.

She was done being powerless. She was done letting life decide her fate. She sure as hell wasn't going to let one stubborn-ass soldier decide it either.

She took one last look at the ocean and then turned and headed back toward her motel room. She wasn't going to sleep here tonight. No, she was turning around and driving herself back home.

Because Alex wasn't a bill she was going to leave unpaid, he wasn't a chore that she was going to mindlessly keep doing. He was important. And she wasn't going to shut down now.

Clara Campbell had spent her life feeling like it would be better if she could be somebody else. But for once, she was glad to be herself.

Because she loved Alex Donnelly, and while she had a lot of things in her past that she might wish weren't hers, if she could be with Alex, she'd have a future she'd be more than happy to call her own.

THE PROBLEM WITH BISON was that they were low-maintenance. So when he wanted to go work out his frustration, wanted to find some hard labor to punish his body with, it was hard to find.

Clara was gone. He didn't know where. Because she hadn't told him. Which was why he found himself at that hipster coffee shop, about to interrogate Mr. Man Bun.

Alex walked in and he could tell the other man was surprised to see him.

"Hi," Asher said, recovering quickly. "Can I help you?"

"Where's Clara?"

Asher raised his eyebrows. "You think I know where she is?"

"I think you might." Well, he hoped he might. He knew Clara wasn't into Asher, but he could see her coming here in a fit of rage at Alex, that was for sure.

And if Asher didn't know anything, he would drive further inland to Grassroots and interrogate everyone who knew her there.

Asher crossed his arms over his chest. "What would you do if I told you she was at my place?"

Oh good. Just what he needed. For toothpick hipster douchebag to want a fight.

"You don't want to have a fight with me," Alex said. "Your vegan diet puts you at a disadvantage. And if it somehow doesn't, then you can sure as hell believe that my military training does."

Asher laughed. "She's not at my place. And I'm not a vegan."

"Well, you get points for being unpredictable, I'll give you that. Do you know where she is or not?"

"That depends. If she didn't tell you, then I assume she doesn't want you to know where she is. She told me that you broke her heart."

"I did. Because I'm an asshole, and I would like to remedy that."

"Well, you have that going for you at least. She went to California. That's what she told me she was going to do." Asher offered him a smug-looking smile. "I did offer to go with her. She declined."

Alex frowned. "Good thing."

Asher shrugged. "If you don't want her then you can't get mad because another man does."

"I do want her, that's the thing. I was just too much of a coward to accept it."

Asher shrugged. "People make such a big deal out of this stuff."

"The fact that it's all casual to you proves that you don't know anything about love yet. Trust me. Some woman is going to mess you up someday too."

"I doubt it."

"You just tempted fate, man," Alex said. "And I'll look forward to watching that bite your ass."

Alex turned around and walked out of the coffeehouse, back into the parking lot. She was in California. She was already gone. He got back into his truck and started to drive toward her place. She wasn't there. There was no reason for him to go there. And the bison really didn't need him today. He still wanted to do something. Still wanted to feel…something. Closer to her, maybe. Even if he didn't deserve that kind of assurance.

His entire chest felt like it was made of shattered glass, and every time he breathed, it hurt. Every time his heart beat, it hurt.

This was the cost of hope. Of hoping that someday he could have her. That someday, she could forgive him. That they could both be in a place where they could be together.

But he did hope. He hoped he could fix it. That it wasn't too late.

He started to turn into her driveway at the same time as a little white car that looked an awful lot like Clara's.

She whipped in front of him, and then stopped the car. Which was when he realized that it was Clara. He stopped his truck behind hers, and got out. And she got out at the same time, her face flushed, her eyes a little bit puffy, dark circles underneath them.

"What the hell are you doing here? That skinny-jeans hipster told me you were in California."

"I was." She sounded out of breath. "I drove eight hours to get back here. I drove all night. I haven't slept."

"Clara Campbell," he said, "that is just dangerous."

"Don't scold me, you jackass, it's your fault."

"It's my fault? I didn't make you drive back overnight."

"Yes, you did. Because you made me go away in the first place." Her eyes filled with tears. "Don't send me away again, Alex, please. I love you. And there are few things in this world that are certain, and even fewer that are great. But me loving you…that's definitely one of them."

Every wall inside him crumbled, all his defenses. Hell, he nearly crumbled. Instead, he closed the distance between them and wrapped his arms around her, held her tightly against him, resting his chin on her head. He didn't say anything, didn't move. Because he was afraid to break this moment.

Finally, he spoke. "You came back for me."

"Of course I did."

"No one ever has before," he said, his throat dangerously tight, hard pressure building behind his eyes. "I drove you away, and you came back."

"You say it like it's surprising. Like it's a difficult, or incredible thing, but Alex, coming back for you was the easiest decision I've ever made."

"Aren't you going to see the world?" He cleared his throat. "See what else is out there?"

"There's a lot out there. More than I could ever see in a lifetime. I know that. But I also know that there's nothing out there that I need as badly as I need you. I told you, it's not the conversations that scare me, it's the ones I don't get to have. It's not all of the sights that I don't see, it's the missed hours spent with the people I love. With the man I love."

"Clara, I am so sorry. I'm so sorry I sent you away. I'm sorry that I was such a coward, that I tried to tell you what you should want, what you should feel. I'm sorry I've been such an arrogant bastard from the moment I came into your life." He traced a line beneath her lower lip with his thumb, her warmth, her softness, sinking down into his soul. "But I had to do something to try to control the situation, to keep you at a distance. It's what I always do. My parents did hurt me. And it's the hardest thing in the world for me to admit that. For me to admit that it damaged me when my father left. That every time I even thought about getting close to somebody, all I could picture was them leaving me and never coming back. But I pushed you and you... Here you are. You can't know how much it means to me. That it was everything I needed. Everything in the whole world."

"I was afraid you might be right," Clara said. "And I had to cross that state line to be certain that you weren't. Because you are right about one thing, Alex. I haven't experienced a lot of things. And I had that feeling the ranch, this life, was something forced upon me, something I didn't choose. And even though it hurt me when you sent me away, I do think that it had to be done. Because I had to stand there on the coastline in another state to know what choice I wanted to make.

"I want this. This life is mine. And no, I would never have chosen the tragedies that marked me. But they happened. They made me. They created me. I can't pretend that it's some stranger's life. That it's something I could shake my way out of if I only found the right person, or the right way to vacation from my own existence. If I can have you, then I'm happy to be me." A tear slid down her cheek. "I'm happy to be here where I am. I don't want to be anyone else. Not if the woman I am can be the woman that you need."

"I love you so much," he said, tightening his hold on her. "Clara, I love you with all that I am. You're stronger in who you are than anyone I've ever known. You make me want to be stronger too. You call me out when I need it, and give me grace when I need that too. All this time I kept saying you needed to get out there and learn about life, like I had something figured out that you didn't. But you…you're smarter than me. Wiser where it counts." He met her gaze, his heart pounding like he'd just run half a mile in an eighty-pound rucksack. "I want to be worthy of the sacrifice that Jason made. I want to be worthy of your love."

She took a step back, brushing her hand over his cheek, and he was aware that his face was wet.

"You are," she said, her voice laced with conviction. "You already are. It's your parents that didn't deserve you, Alex. It was never you that was the problem. Ever."

"Life has a lot to answer for," he said, trying to force a laugh.

"It does. We've been through more than anybody should have to go through. But then, we have each other now. So I guess we have a lot to be thankful for too."

For the first time in as long as he could remember, Alex smiled and there was nothing forced about it. It was real. And it came from somewhere deep inside of him that Clara had woken up.

From a place of hope.

"It's the funniest thing," he said, "because I accused you so many times of not knowing who you were or what you wanted, but you've always known. In fact, you know more about who you are than most people twice your age. You know what you like, and you don't apologize for it."

She laughed. "That's not exactly true. I tried to be different. I tried to want different things. You were the person I was myself for. And it was the easiest thing. You make me happy to be me. And it's the first time I can remember ever feeling that way."

"You make being me feel like enough," Alex said, grabbing hold of her hand and pressing it against his heart so she could feel it raging. "And I can honestly tell you it's the first time I've ever felt that way."

"You're my SpaghettiOs and hot chocolate, Alex. Perfect for me."

"That's all I ever want to be."

## *EPILOGUE*

HE WAS PERFECT in every way.

Clara Campbell didn't even try to hide the look of longing, the look of love, that was currently etched onto her face.

She crossed to Alex, all hot and sexy in his black hat, white T-shirt, jeans and cowboy boots, and looped her arm through his.

She thought it was nice of Lane to include her as a bridesmaid in her wedding to Finn, especially considering Clara was a new friend of hers. But, as Lane had told her, she was family, and that meant she was included in the wedding.

At least, she would be family soon enough.

Clara touched the engagement ring on her left hand absently as she and Alex walked down the aisle. In just a few months, they would do it again, as husband and wife. Alex had been so cute and uncertain when he'd proposed. Adamant that if she felt it was too soon, she didn't have to say yes. That he could wait for marriage.

But Clara didn't want to wait. She finally had what she'd always wanted, and she wasn't going to wait to jump headlong into her happy ending. Or more aptly, her happy beginning.

Alison and Cain came down the aisle next, Cain looking down at his fiancée with no small amount of pride. Their wedding would be next, and then Alex and Clara's.

Only Liam, who walked down the aisle next with Lane's friend Rebecca West, was still alone.

Right before the bride came the flower girl. Who was sixteen and wearing a long, black dress, and was very clearly trying to look like she wasn't ecstatic as she dropped flower petals. But not even the determinedly grumpy Violet could actually look grumpy at a wedding. At least, not a wedding where the bride and groom were so clearly madly in love.

Last came the bride, who, in spite of the casual dress on everyone else and the rustic outdoor location on the Laughing Irish Ranch, was dressed like a princess, because it was what she'd always dreamed of.

Her strapless dress billowed out whenever she took a step, her long dark hair falling in soft curls around her shoulders, her eyes bright.

Clara had watched so many dreams die. Watching these new dreams come true around her, living in her own dream, with the man she loved, was more incredible than she could have dared imagine.

The wedding itself was beautiful, and there was hardly a dry eye in the place when Lane and Finn made their vows.

Afterward, Alex and Clara danced together on the makeshift, dirt dance floor, with lights strung overhead and free-standing heaters offering warmth in the cool evening.

"You know, Alex," she said, resting her head on his

chest, "I always felt like my life was shattered into a whole bunch of pieces. And I had no idea how any of it was supposed to fit together. Until now. Until you. For the first time, everything fits. And I don't even have to pretend I like kale."

Alex laughed and picked her up, spinning her in a circle. "No. No, you definitely don't."

He set her back down and she kissed him, breathless. "Thank you," she said. "Thank you for being here for me."

"Thank you for coming back for me," he said, lifting her fingers to his lips and kissing them.

She closed her eyes, love washing over her. Joy washing over her.

Then Alex leaned in, his breath hot against her neck and she shivered. "You know, I went and got honey earlier today."

"You?" she asked, jerking back and looking at him in surprise. "You braved the bees?"

"I did. And I'm warning you, I have some creative ideas in mind for how I might use that honey."

"Oh, really?"

"Yes. I thought I might enjoy licking it off your skin."

She blushed and looked around to make sure no one could hear them. "Indeed."

"Not exactly what you had in mind when you pictured your quiet beekeeping life, is it?"

"No. No it wasn't." Because no, she didn't just have bees. She had bees and bison and love, and it was more than she'd ever thought possible. "But then... I don't think there was any way I could have predicted you, Alex Donnelly."

"I like to keep things interesting."

She laughed. "One thing is certain. It's going to be a wild ride, cowboy."

\* \* \* \* \*

*Finn, Cain and Alex Donnelly might*
*have found their happily-ever-afters,*
*but Liam Donnelly and Sabrina Leighton*
*still have unfinished business between them.*
*Look for their unforgettable novel,*
*CHRISTMASTIME COWBOY,*
*from Maisey Yates*
*and HQN Books!*

*Read on for a sneak peek...*

# CHAPTER ONE

Liam Donnelly was nobody's favorite.

Though being a favorite in their household growing up would never have meant much, Liam was confident that as much as both of his parents disdained
their younger son, Alex, they hated Liam more.

As much as his brothers loved him—or whatever
you wanted to call their brand of affection—Liam
knew he wasn't the one they'd carry out if there was
a house fire. That was fine too.

It wasn't self-pity. It was just a fact.

But while he wasn't anyone's particular favorite,
he knew he was at least one person's least favorite.

Sabrina Leighton hated him with every ounce of
her beautiful, petite being. Not that he blamed her.
But, considering they were having a business meeting today, he did hope that she could keep some of
the hatred bottled up.

Liam got out of his truck and put his cowboy hat
on, surveying his surroundings. The Grassroots
winery spread was beautiful, with a large, pictur-
esque home overlooking the grounds. Trees and forest surrounded the facility on three sides, creating
a secluded feeling. Like the winery was part of another world. In front of the first renovated barn was a
sprawling lawn and a path that led down to the river.

There was a seating area there and Liam knew that during the warmer months it was a nice place to hang out. Right now, it was too damned cold, and the damp air that blew up from the rushing water sent a chill straight through him.

He shoved his hands in his pockets and kept on walking. There were three rustic barns on the property that they used for weddings and dinners, and one that had been fully remodeled into a dining and tasting room.

He had seen the new additions online. He hadn't actually been to Grassroots in the past thirteen years. That was part of the deal. The deal that had been struck back when Jamison Leighton was still owner of the place.

Back when Liam had been nothing more than a good-for-nothing, low-class troublemaker with a couple of misdemeanors to his credit.

Times changed.

Liam might still be all of those things at heart, but he was also a successful businessman. And Jamison Leighton no longer owned Grassroots Winery.

Some things, however, hadn't changed. The presence of Sabrina Leighton being one of them.

It had been thirteen years. But he couldn't pretend that he thought everything was all right and forgiven. Not considering the way she had reacted when she had seen him at Ace's bar over the past few months. Small towns.

Like everybody was at the same party and could only avoid each other for so long.

If it wasn't at the bar, they would most certainly

end up at a four-way stop at the same time, or in the same aisle at the grocery store.

But today's meeting would not be accidental. Today's meeting was planned. He wondered if something would get thrown at him. It certainly wouldn't be the first time.

He walked across the gravel lot and into the dining room. It was empty, since the facility had yet to open for the day. A rustic barn with a wooden chandelier hanging in the center. There was a bar with stools positioned at the front, and tables set up around the room. Back when he had worked here there had been one basic tasting room, and nowhere for anyone to sit. Most of the wine had been sent out to retail stores for sale, rather than making the winery itself some kind of destination.

He wondered when all of that had changed. He imagined it had something to do with Lindy, the new owner and ex-wife of Jamison Leighton's son, Damien. As far as Liam knew, and he knew enough—considering he didn't get involved with business ventures without figuring out what he was getting into—Damien had drafted the world's dumbest prenuptial agreement.

Though why Sabrina was still working at the winery when her sister-in-law had current ownership, and her brother had been deposed, and her parents were—from what he had read in public records—apoplectic about the loss of their family legacy, he didn't know. But he assumed he would find out. About the same time he found out whether or not something was going to get thrown at his head.

The door from the back opened, and he gritted his

teeth. Because, no matter how prepared he felt philosophically to see Sabrina, he knew that there would be impact. There always was. A damned funny thing. That one woman could live in the back of his mind the way she had for so long. That no matter how many years or how many women he put between them, she still burned bright and hot in his memory.

That no matter how well he had prepared himself to run into her—because he knew how small towns worked—the impact was like a brick to the side of his head every single time.

And no matter that this meeting was carefully orchestrated and planned, he knew it was going to be the same.

And it was.

She appeared a moment after the door opened, looking severe. Overly so. Her blond hair was pulled back into a high ponytail, and she was wearing a black sheath dress that went down past her knee, but conformed to curves that were more generous than they'd been thirteen years ago.

In a good way.

"Hello, Liam," she said, her tone impersonal. Had she not used his first name, it might have been easy to pretend that she didn't know who he was.

"Sabrina."

"Lindy told me you wanted to talk about a potential joint venture. And since that falls under my jurisdiction as manager of the tasting room, she thought we might want to work together."

Now she was smiling.

The smile was so brittle it looked like it might crack her face.

"Yes, I'm familiar with the details. Particularly since this venture was my idea." He let a small silence hang there for a beat before continuing. "I'm looking at an empty building on the end of Main Street. It would be more than just a tasting room. It would be a small café with some retail space."

"How would it differ from Lane Donnelly's store? She already carries specialty foods."

"Well, we would focus on Grassroots wine and cheese from the Laughing Irish ranch. Also, I would happily purchase products from Lane's store to give the menu a local focus. It would be nothing big. Just a small lunch place with wine. Very limited selection. Very specialty. But I feel like in a tourist location that's what you want."

"Right," she said, her smile remaining completely immobile.

He took that moment to examine her more closely. The changes in her face over the years. She was more beautiful now than she had been at seventeen. Her slightly round, soft face had refined in the ensuing years, her cheekbones now more prominent, the angle of her chin sharper.

Her eyebrows looked different too. When she'd been a teenager they'd been thinner, rounder. Now they were a bit stronger, more angular.

"Great," he returned. "I guess we can go down and have a look at everything sometime this week. Gage West is the owner of the property, and he hasn't listed it yet. Handily, my sister-in-law is good friends with his wife. Both of my sisters-in-law, actually. So I got the inside track on that."

Her expression turned bland. "How impressive."

She sounded absolutely unimpressed. "It wasn't intended to be impressive. Just useful."

She sighed slowly. "Did you have a day in mind to go view the property? Because I really am very busy."

"Are you?"

"Yes," she responded, that smile spreading over her face again. "This is a very demanding job, plus, I do have a life."

She stopped short of saying exactly what that life entailed.

"Too busy to do this, which is part of your actual job?" he asked.

On the surface she looked calm, but he could sense a dark energy beneath that spoke of a need to savage him. "I had my schedule sorted out for the next couple of weeks. This is coming together more quickly than expected."

"I'll work something out with Gage and give Lindy a call, how about that?"

"You don't have to call Lindy. I'll give you my phone number. You can call or text me directly."

She leaned over to the counter and took a card from the rustic surface, extending her hand toward him. He reached out and took the card, their fingertips brushing as they made the handoff.

And he felt it. Straight down to his groin, where he had always felt things for her, even though it was impossible. Even though he was all wrong for her. And even though they were now doing a business deal together and she looked like she would cheerfully chew through his flesh if given half the chance.

She might be smiling. But he didn't trust that

smile. He was still waiting. Waiting for her to shout recriminations at him now that they were alone.

But she didn't. Instead, she gave him that card, and then began to look...bored.

"Did you need anything else?" she asked, still determinedly cheerful.

"Not really. Though I have some spreadsheet information that you might want to look over. Ideas for the layout, the menu. It is getting a little ahead of ourselves, in case we end up not liking the venue."

"Like you said, you do your research."

Her friendliness was beginning to slip. And he waited. For something else. For something to get thrown at him. It didn't happen.

"That I do. Take these," he said, handing her the folder that he was holding onto. He made sure their fingers didn't touch this time. "And we'll talk next week."

Then he turned and walked away from her, and he resisted the strong impulse to turn back and get one more glance at her. It wasn't the first time he had resisted Sabrina Leighton's appeal.

He had a feeling it wouldn't be the last.

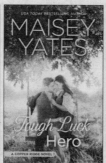

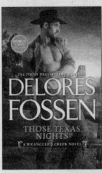 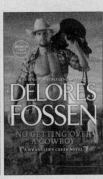 

**New York Times bestselling author**

# JODI THOMAS

**Two families long divided by an ancient feud.
Can a powerful love finally unite them?**

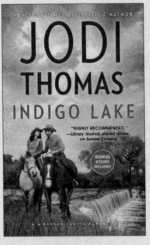

Blade Hamilton is the last of his line. He's never even heard of Crossroads, Texas, until he inherits land there. Riding in on his vintage Harley-Davidson, Blade finds a weathered ranch house, an empty prairie and a dark river that cuts a decisive path between the Hamiltons' land and that of their estranged neighbors.

When Dakota helps a stranger on the roadside, she isn't prepared for the charisma of the man on the motorbike—or for the last name he bears: Hamilton, of her family's sworn enemies, representing all she's been raised to loathe. The problem is, it looks like Blade is in town to stay, and there's something about his wolf-gray eyes she just can't ignore.

Lauren Brigman feels adrift. Unhappy in work and unlucky in love, she knows she ought to be striving for more, but she's never truly at peace unless she's at home in Crossroads. If the wider world can't satisfy her, is home truly where her heart is?

**Order your copy today!**

**HQN™**

PHJT936R

# Get 2 Free Books,
## Plus 2 Free Gifts –
just for trying the *Reader Service!*

STRS17R